Praise for *The Canterbury Papers*

"Brims with authentic historical detail . . . suspenseful."

– *Minneapolis StarTribune*

"A beautifully plotted and fascinating story. Rarely does a historical novel have this much pace and intrigue. I thoroughly enjoyed it!"

– Robert Alexander, *New York Times* bestselling author of *The Kitchen Boy*

Praise for *The Rebel Princess*

"A fast-paced historical mystery with plenty of suspense and intrigue . . . Healey does a fantastic job."

– *Historical Novels Review*

King's Bishop

CALUMET
EDITIONS
Minneapolis

Second Edition December 2022

10 9 8 7 6 5 4 3 2

ISBN: 978-1-959770-46-6

Cover and book design by Gary Lindberg
Cover photo by Judith Koll Healey

To Terry —
Thanks for all the
great help in life
& money! Happy
reading! Best
Judy

King's Bishop

Judith Koll Healey

Judith Koll Healey

CALUMET
EDITIONS
Minneapolis

Also by Judith Koll Healey

The Canterbury Papers (published in German as *Die Gesandte der Löwin*)

The Rebel Princess (published in German as *Das Königsking*)

Frederick Weyerhaeuser and the Opening of the American West

The Fire Thief (poems)

For John Berryman
Poet, Scholar and Friend

"Ah, but we die to each other daily.
What we know of other people
Is only our memory of the moments
During which we knew them. And they have changed since then.
. . . We must also remember
That at every meeting, we are meeting a stranger."

—T. S. Eliot, *The Cocktail Party*

The Kiss of Peace
"This is a sign of peace. Let peace be made in your conscience when your lips draw near to your brother, do not let your heart withdraw from his."

—Sermon of St. Augustine # 227

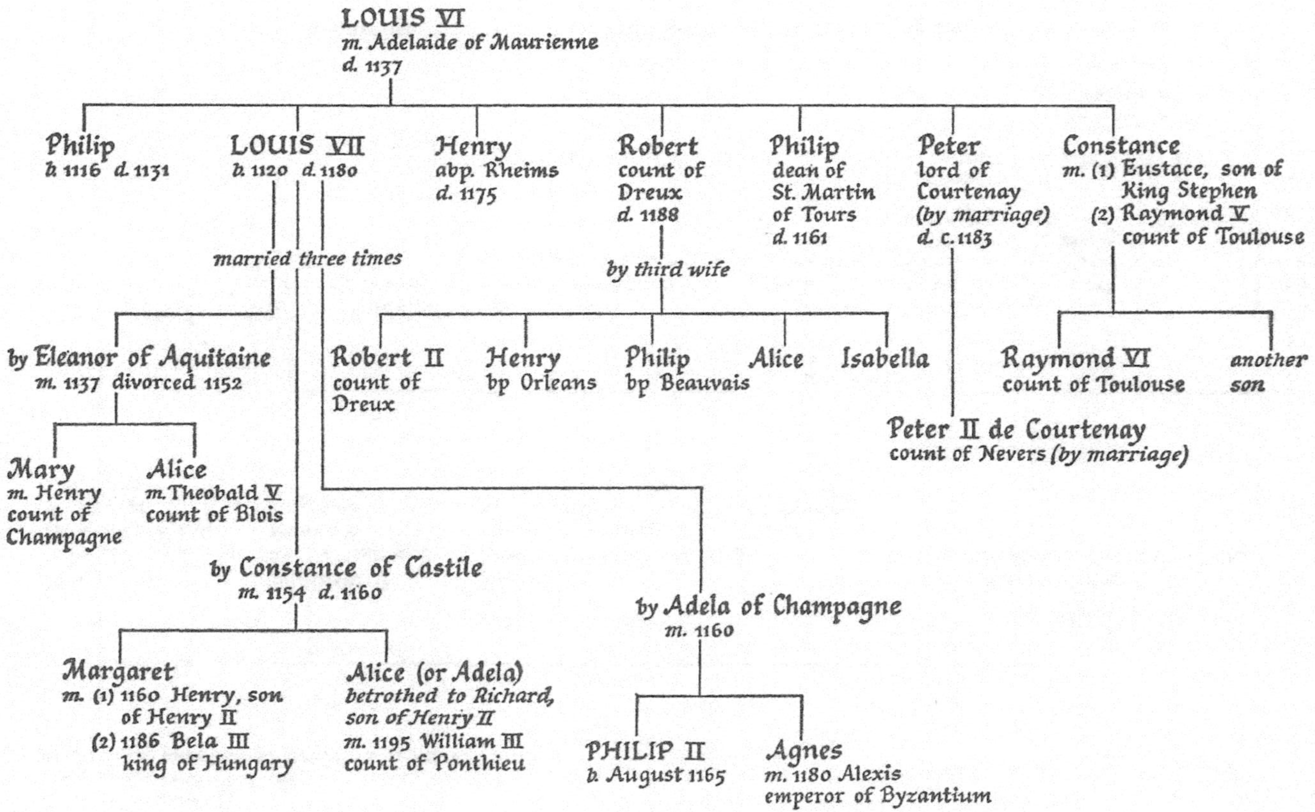

The family of King Louis VII

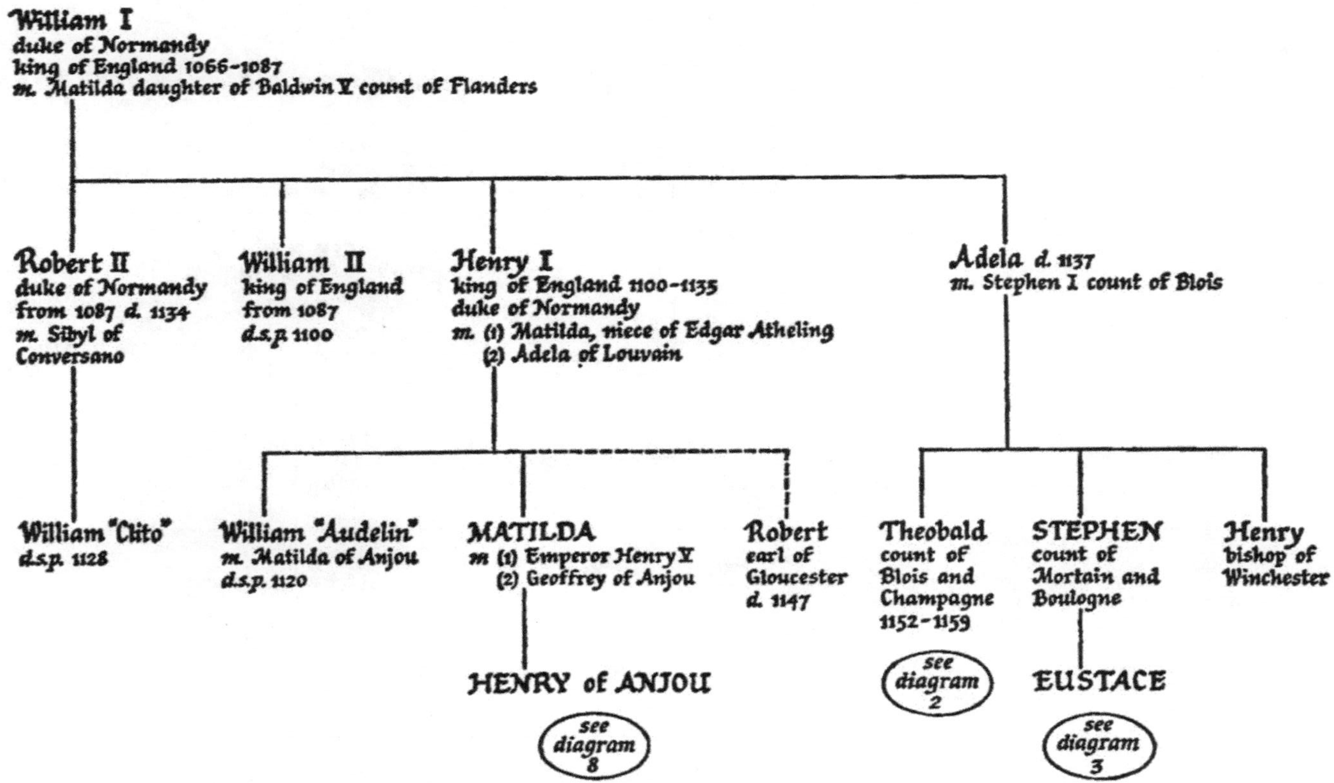
William I
duke of Normandy
king of England 1066-1087
m. Matilda daughter of Baldwin V count of Flanders
Robert II
duke of Normandy
from 1087 d. 1134
m. Sibyl of
Conversano
William II
king of England
from 1087
d.s.p. 1100
Henry I
king of England 1100-1135
duke of Normandy
m. (1) Matilda, niece of Edgar Atheling
(2) Adela of Louvain
Adela d. 1137
m. Stephen I count of Blois
William "Clito"
d.s.p. 1128
William "Audelin"
m. Matilda of Anjou
d.s.p. 1120
MATILDA
m (1) Emperor Henry V
(2) Geoffrey of Anjou
Robert
earl of
Gloucester
d. 1147
Theobald
count of
Blois and
Champagne
1152-1159
STEPHEN
count of
Mortain and
Boulogne
Henry
bishop of
Winchester
HENRY of ANJOU
see diagram 8
see diagram 2
EUSTACE
see diagram 3

Contenders for the duchy of Normandy and the kingdom of England

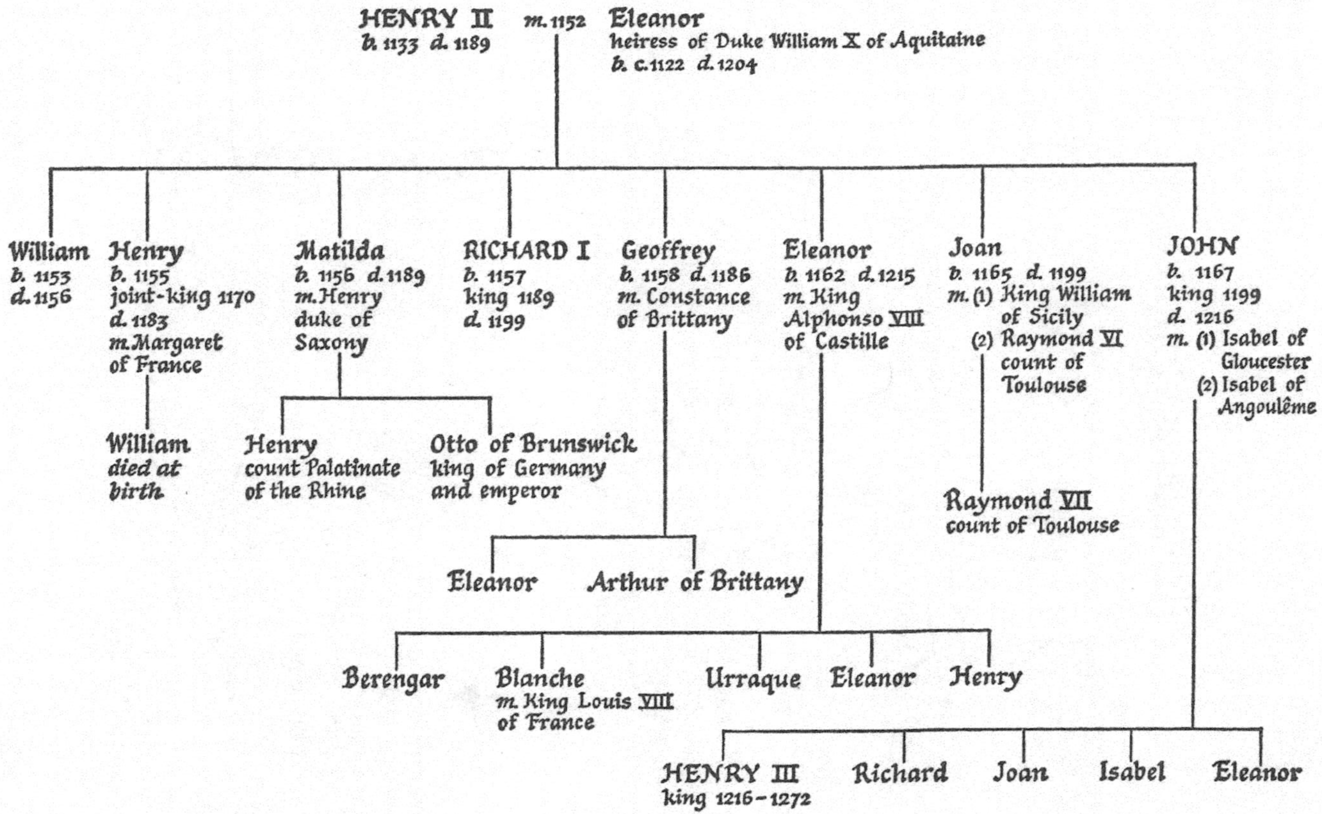

8. The children and grandchildren of Henry II and Eleanor

Plantagenet Dominions c. 1170

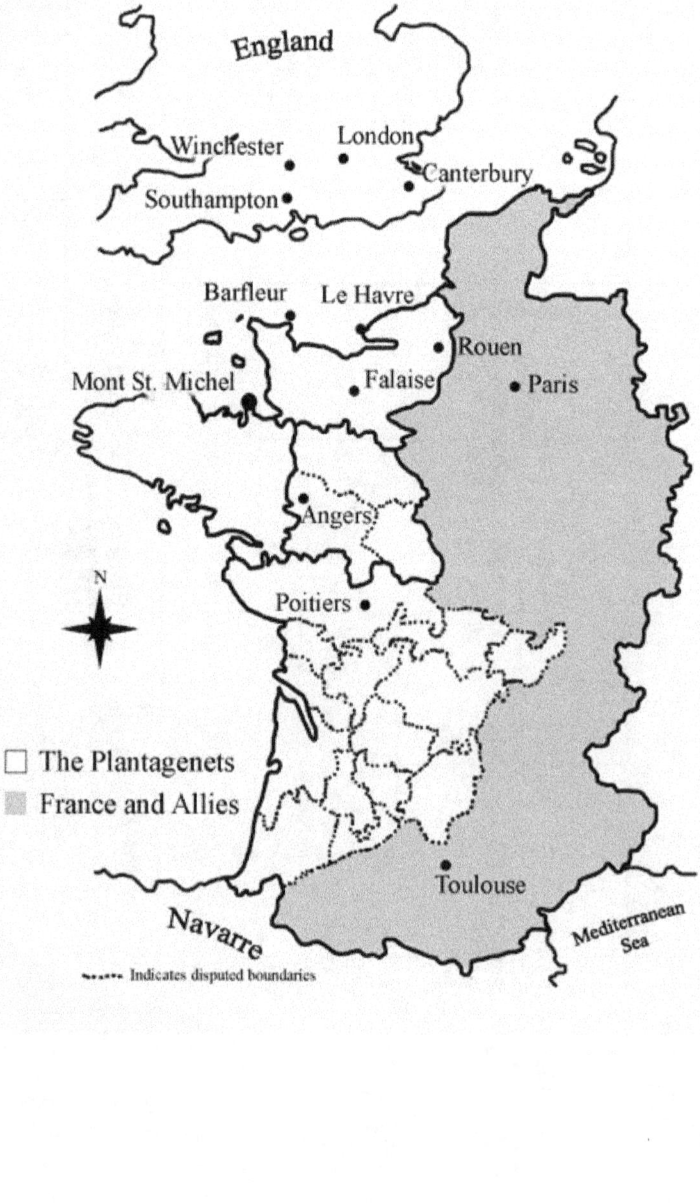

Dramatis Personae

The Plantagenet Family

Henry II	King of England, Duke of Normandy
Eleanor of Aquitaine	Queen of England, Duchess of the Aquitaine
Geoffrey of Anjou	Father of Henry II
Empress Matilda	Wife of Geoffrey, mother of Henry Former wife of Emp. Henry V of Germany Daughter of King Henry I of England
Henry, Richard, Geoffrey, John	Princes, Sons of Eleanor and Henry
Matilda, Eleanor and Joan	Daughters of Eleanor and Henry
Geoffrey the Bastard	Illegitimate son of Henry II, later Chancellor of England
Geoffrey and Robert of Anjou	Brothers of Henry II

The Capet Family

Louis VII	King of France, former husband of Eleanor of Aquitaine
Constance of Castile	Second wife of Louis
Adela	Third wife of Louis and sister to the family of Blois
Marguerite	Daughter of Louis and Constance, fiancée of young Prince Henry
Alaïs	Youngest daughter to Louis and Constance, betrothed to Richard
Constance of France	Sister to Louis and married to the Count of Toulouse

The House of Blois

Stephen	Cousin to Empress Matilda and King of England 1135–54
Henry of Blois	Brother to Stephen, later Bishop of Winchester
Henry, Theobold, Adela	Nephews and niece to King Stephen Married into the house of Louis VII

The Church

Thomas Becket	Chancellor of England later Archbishop of Canterbury
Alexander III	Pope and Bishop of Rome
Thibault of Normandy	Archbishop of Canterbury
Roger Pont l'Eveque	Bishop of York
Gilbert Foliot	Bishop of London
Henry of Blois	Bishop of Winchester and brother to King Stephen
Robert of Torigny	Abbot of Mont St. Michel and Chronicler
Arnulf	Bishop of Liseuex
Rotrou	Bishop of Rouen

The Counsellors and Advisors to King Henry

Richard de Lucy

Richard du Hommet

Robert, Earl of Leicester

William FitzStephen

Prologue: Henry in his Toils

5 January 1171
Argentan Castle

"Not my fault, not my fault." He heard the voice murmuring from far, far away, and it was only after a moment's foggy reflection that it occurred to the king that it might be his own.

"Keep moving, rouse the household," Henry muttered, his strong sword arm flinging wide on the lumpy straw as he strove to punch his way upward out of his drugged sleep. "Must ride at first light."

A spasm of unrest gripped him again as he struggled to open his eyes. Danger all around. The dark-cloaked figures stalking his sleep hovered still. At this moment, when he was finally vulnerable, all the shadows of his past gathered upon him. Order horses ready. Move at dawn. Out race them.

Gradually, Henry forced his eyes to open and focus. The heavy oak beams of the ceiling met his gaze, and he blinked several times to be sure of what he saw. His clothes stuck to him from the sweat of his sleep and yielded an old, dank smell. He began to sense himself again and to calm somewhat.

Try to recall what happened. How did I come here? Something bad, something terrible. Why does my head hurt so?

Wait. Some fragment just out of reach. Something about Thomas. Bat away the cobwebs. What? What was the voice saying? Thomas hurt. No, dead. Tom is dead.

Henry grasped the bedpost and hauled himself to a sitting position. Thomas! Thomas killed, violently murdered! And Henry heard again those rash words he himself had uttered not a week earlier in front of all his court. Not only was the dearest companion of his youth gone, but he had a growing sense—with that absolute supernatural clarity that was his gift, even in his present state—that he, Henry, Count of Anjou, Duke of Normandy, and King of England, he and no one else, would carry the cross for that violent act. He had as good as ordered it with his rash words. He knew in his soul he was to blame.

Thomas, my Tom, friend of my youth, my chancellor, my archbishop, what woeful path have we gone down together that we come to this end? What firestorm have we two created? And now you have left me—alone—to deal with all the jackals.

Henry flopped back on the bed, his strong, square body splayed out in defeat, despair flooding his heart. He closed his eyes, but the scenes came anyway, unbidden. The first time he had seen Thomas at Westminster, pushed forward by Thibault as the best and brightest of his protégés. Tall, dark, a sweet face and intelligence shining out of his sky-blue eyes. Unafraid and open, older than Henry yet younger, taller than Henry yet weaker. Memories crowding in.

Oh, God in heaven, Thomas.

Galloping in the New Forest, racing to a draw, both overcome with laughter at the end, scarce able to sit on their exhausted horses. And the surprised look on Tom's face, in his fancy chancellor's residence, when I cantered into the dining hall on my horse and vaulted over the end of the table, demanding to be fed. Thomas, demurring when offered Canterbury, fingering his finery and shaking his head with that strange, ironic smile. Then later: the pinched face at Clarendon, the set jaw at Northampton when he came in carrying his own episcopal cross—like the weapon it was—the stricken look on Thomas' face when he, Henry, denied him the kiss of peace and sent him back to England in the company of John of Oxford, his sworn foe. "Betrayed," his look had said, "How could you, even now when you offer me peace?"

Henry turned his face to the wall and wept. But there was no peace, even in tears. That other face that shaped his life forced its way before him. Eleanor.

What was it she said years ago when I decided to name Thomas Chancellor of all England? One of those fancy arguments she had learned in Paris when she was Louis's young bride? That fellow Abelard. Some kind of dialectic. If a shield was white on the outside and black on the inside, what color was the shield? She had said: "Beware of Thomas." But not why to beware. Did she see what I could not? Was the inside of the shield black? And is that why she has left me. . . That I could not see what she saw?

Yes, now that it was over and the consequences had to be faced, he, Henry, could reflect. How could he have been so wrong about a friend? Or maybe, the king thought, rolling on his side with difficulty and swinging his bowed horseman's legs over the edge of the high bed, he had not been wrong. Perhaps he had been paying attention to the wrong side of the shield. Not this, but that. Not what you say, but what you do.

And then a memory descended on Henry, and his spirit calmed a little. An old fable told to him by Greta, the nursemaid his mother, Empress Matilda, had brought to Anjou from Germany when she married his father, Count Geoffrey. Greta, who taught small boys their lessons with stories.

There was a hunter—he could still hear the husky, low voice as clearly as if she were in his chamber at this moment—there was a hunter walking through a forest, shooting rabbits and small game. Two rabbits watched from behind a tree. "Look," said one little rabbit to the other, "the man. He's crying as he shoots his arrows into us." The other little rabbit turned to him, "Don't watch his eyes," he said, with a wise edge to his small voice, "Don't watch his eyes at all. Watch his hands."

Part One: The Beginnings
1151–1154

September 1151, Fathers and Sons
Somewhere in western Normandy, close to the Anjou march

Count Geoffrey's lean face assumed a coquettish look, at odds with his leathered skin and blunt features. "You fancy the queen, then." His words carried no hint of a question. His son Henry could scarce see his father's face across the table, so dim was the light in the tavern. The fire gave warmth against the early autumn night air but not much light. The younger man, the one with the square face and the freckles not now visible, felt a surge of blood to his face. He was grateful for the dusk.

The older man, tall, sandy-haired, the heir of Fulk, the mad count of Anjou, deftly speared a piece of eel and carried it to his mouth. As he chewed, he regarded his son. The look was appraising and not entirely friendly, the brows knit and thin lips slightly pursed. A silence ensued.

The son bore a strong resemblance to the father in his coloring, slightly reddish hair still tousled from the fast ride of the afternoon and his cheeks warming with the wine his father poured liberally for both. But there the resemblance ended, for young Henry's face was broader than his father's, and more open. Where Count Geoffrey's visage was lined with the experience and plotting of his thirty-eight years, his son's was the picture of candor. The eyes were different, also. The dark eyes of the elder were habitually narrowed with calculation, while Henry's open, intelligent grey eyes were his most arresting feature. As he raised his solemn gaze from the pigeon he was tearing apart, he appeared so like his mother that the Count paused. Henry looked at his father for one long moment without speaking.

"So, what do you say, lad?" Geoffrey genially prodded his son. At eighteen years, Henry was no lad. He had gone twice to England to fight for his mother's right to the English crown, the first time when he was only sixteen. His father knew that, but the interchange with his heir was usually a game with him. Count Geoffrey sensed that somehow, he must rein in his son's sense of himself, that if he did not, the son would supersede the father.

"What is it you are asking, Sire?" Henry finally responded. He knew there would be no peace, that the count meant to engage him on this issue of the queen of France. "I thought of the two of us you were the one more smitten with the charms of King Louis's wife."

The pair had stopped for the night beside the Loire River, well north of Angers. Their visit to the court in Paris had been a great success. Young Henry and Count Geoffrey had done homage to Louis, King of France, as feudal obligation demanded. Geoffrey had renewed his vows for Anjou, and Henry was presented as vassal for Normandy, which his father had won for him.

Only one aspect of the entire experience was marred for young Henry. Count Geoffrey had shown too much attention to the charms of the queen of France for his son's comfort. The count's wife, the empress Mathilda, King Henry's daughter and rightful heir to the throne of England, sat in Angers castle awaiting news of the conflict in England. She had barely escaped from Oxford castle with her life, as she fled alone on horseback, in disguise. Yet here was her husband, openly fawning over the French queen at court while his wife's cousin, Stephen the usurper, still held most of the English barons to his cause. Henry was, not for the first time, mildly disgusted with his father.

"Bah, all show." The count's eyes glistened in the candlelight. "Although she is still a tasty piece, despite her age."

"She's scarce thirty, Father." Henry continued to empty his trencher of the spiced stew that rested in it. "Not terribly old."

"But too old for you?" the count persisted.

Now Henry saw which way the count was steering the conversation. He was in earnest, and he meant to have his son's response.

"Here, have some of these lampreys. They are the finest I have ever tasted." Geoffrey could still ooze charm when he chose. His son had seen the young bon vivant emerge in his father often enough.

"No, not for me, Sire." Henry shook his head. "I don't trust them. You don't know how long they have been out of the water." His memory of illness from bad eels dated from his first foray into England on behalf of his mother's cause several years earlier. He never forgot the experience. With gratitude, he ladled more good Norman beef stew onto his trencher.

"Bah," the count said again. "No courage."

Henry was undisturbed by this challenge. He had plenty of courage, and they both knew it. His father liked to use words as others used a poignard, teasing, testing, thrust and parry. It was a game with him.

"Why are you asking me about the queen?"

"Because I want you to take her to wife." The count speared another of the eels.

Henry choked on his beef, then made as if his response had been to a piece of gristle which he spat onto the floor. He blotted his lips with his sleeve.

"Father, you must have noticed," he said dryly after a long quaff of wine. "She has a husband, and he happens to be the king of France." Henry shook his head, summoning a smile though he felt no cheer. "I think you ask a fool's question."

"Ah, but there I have you." The count's visage lit up with a smile so broad, his son could not remember another like it on that dour countenance. "All the days you spent in those useless tournaments in Paris, trying to impress the French nobles, I spent gathering information from the knights lolling about in the Great Hall and at the tables spread for our delight. Queen Eleanor and King Louis will soon receive word from Rome that their request for a marriage annulment is granted. The queen will revert to her title of Duchess of Poitiers and will return to her lands in the south, and here. . . " Geoffrey had his two-pronged fork in his hand, and he stabbed it in the air in his son's direction "…is the best part."

"I'm certain," Henry said, with no attempt to keep irony from his voice. "You are about to tell me King Louis will give her back her lands in the Aquitaine."

"Exactly right, my boy." The count's mouth dropped. He stared at his grinning prodigy. "How did you know?"

"Because, Father, while you were gathering the court gossips in your corner, I also gathered information from the knights on the field before and after our games. Everyone knows the king and queen will separate. And that he is going to let her keep her dowry lands as the price of his freedom. He needs an heir, and she has not provided him with one."

"I'll wager she took a fancy to you." Count Geoffrey, suddenly tuning in to his son's interest, now had a smirk and narrowed eyes. "You're not telling me everything, are you?"

"It's quite possible she noticed me in the lists," Henry said, but he was thinking instead of his one solo meeting with the queen, unexpectedly, in the halls of the Conciergerie. She was hurrying through with only a maidservant for company. He was coming in alone from the tournaments, sweating, pulling at his coat of mail. She had stopped him with her extended arm as he rounded a corner too fast, almost but not quite colliding with her.

"You are Henry of Anjou," she had said. "I saw you perform on the field today."

"Yes, my Lady," Henry bowed.

"Well done, you, on the field," she smiled, leaving her hand for just a moment longer against his chest. Then, remarkably, she added, "I have heard of your exploits in England as well. We will meet again."

His father knew none of that, but Henry remembered every second of the encounter. As it happened, the two did not meet again, except in public, but something mysterious had transpired, had passed between them like a breath in that brief encounter. Count Geoffrey had no idea of the depth of personal interest Henry now had in the queen's annulment. Although the young duke of Normandy had no plan, he had a sense of impending fortune. But he was not about to inform the count of any of these thoughts. Perhaps later, as events unfolded. But this was not for his father to manage, as he habitually controlled everything. This project would be Henry's own.

"So, you see what is so important here, lad." Geoffrey was pouring again from the wine beaker, filling his own goblet and slopping some on the table in the process. "It's land, Henry. Land and power. Court that woman as soon as she is free. If you don't do it, your brother Geoffrey will."

"I'll ponder that advice, Father," Henry said, rising. "But for now, I'm off to bed. We ride out early, as you have said."

"Yes, yes. I suppose you'll be after that fetching maid who brought us our plates," the count muttered. "I'll stay here a while longer."

"Until the morrow, then, in the stables at first light," Henry said, with a gesture that was half wave and half salute. He smiled to himself, but the count did not notice.

The young duke of Normandy had no need of the inn's serving girl this long evening. He had a book in his leather travel sac and a candle in his room and that was enough. He had things to think over. When the count was sober in the morning, they could talk further. Or perhaps he would keep his own counsel and wait for news from the Paris Court. Somehow, he knew his fate was bound up in the visit they had just made to the French royal demesne. But it was not clear yet how that was so.

* * *

Some hours later, Henry was rudely awakened by the wrinkled face of the hosteler close to his own, the man shaking his shoulder. A single candle illuminated his anxious face.

"Henry of Anjou, Sire, wake up."

Henry sat upright, his hand reaching for his sword.

"No, My Lord, no need for that," the old man said hastily. "It's your father. He is very ill and calling for you."

"Ill? I just left him at supper a few hours back." Henry blinked away his sleep.

"I know. The malaise has come upon him suddenly." The old man was babbling. "I'm certain he was ill when he arrived at the inn, only he did not show it." Witless with fright, the hosteler appeared certain he would be blamed for this turn of events.

"Those damn eels!" Henry followed the old man out, pulling his tunic over his head as he went, leaving his sword behind. When he arrived at his father's chamber, he nearly tripped on a garment on the floor that looked familiar. He recognized the brown shift the plump, young maid had been wearing. She was nowhere to be seen.

Henry looked down on the long, narrow face, glistening with sweat in the moonlight.

"Father," he began, but the count raised his hand for silence. Then he struggled to speak himself.

"Son," he said, a word he rarely used with Henry. His next words were labored but clear. "Keep. . .the land. . .we have." He took a deep breath, then doubled over with pain and a projectile of half-digested lampreys came forth. Henry backed away for a moment, then returned to the bedside.

"Wait!" The count lay back and swallowed twice.

Henry remained silent, watching his father's mouth. Soon, another effort.

"Marry… the… queen." A long pause. "Have many . . . sons." Count Geoffrey of Anjou fell back against his pillow of straw. He spoke no more.

The count lingered for two long days in stomach agonies and a pool of sweat. Finally, on the night of the second day, he died. Henry had sat by his bed for all the hours of those long days and nights, but the count did not speak again.

At daybreak on the third day, Henry mounted his horse and began the journey home to Empress Matilda to tell her of her husband's demise. He did not relish the task.

May 1152
Poitiers, Poitou Provence, the Aquitaine

The day was alive as only spring can come alive in the southern counties. The sun smiled on the earth, the birds chattered, the younger sons of the farmers turned the soil, releasing a rich, vibrant scent. Young Henry of Anjou slowed his cantering horse as he approached the bridge of the river Garonne on his way into Poitiers. He began whistling as if he owned the world. And why not? Soon he very nearly would. His thoughts wandered as he slowed, allowing his companions to catch up. He half turned his horse and saw his young aide, Richard de Lucy, coming alongside the group at a trot. Then Henry slipped back into his musings.

The bargain has been struck, arrangements settled, down to the details. Oh, it was true, there were awkward moments there in Paris, negotiating under the very noses of Louis and Abbe Suger and the others. But the mettle of Queen Eleanor is no longer in doubt! God's teeth, she is amazing. Cool as you please in the court and clear as you please when she met with me ensuite. Count Geoffrey would have been proud. The queen was all woman, too. When I saw again that cool beauty, that slender body, that determined face, I knew she would bear me sons. It is her destiny. Despite Louis's disappointment in having none. With me, it will be different.

The ceremony of her annulment was an odd event, all the king's advisors looking grave and the Queen herself, beautiful in a scarlet gown with pearls twined in her beautiful, full dark-auburn hair, scarce covered with the light silk scarf wound in the back, a nod to modesty and convention. Eleanor is known for neither, but what a performance that day! She signed the papers put in front of her with a flourish of the quill and a little, sad smile, as if she were loath to be set aside by King Louis, as if she wanted to remain in Paris, when all the world knew she had finished with Louis long ago.

Ahh, but she knew not only what she was leaving, but what she was going toward. And of that prize, Louis and his advisors had not one whisper. The queen needed a protector, and she found it in the house of Anjou, my house! All her lands in the Aquitaine that Louis was giving back to her would now be combined with my lands—Anjou, Normandy and Brittany. And one day soon, I'll take the English crown from Stephen and complete my realm. After all, England is my mother's rightful patrimony from her father, old King Henry.

Eleanor is a decade older than I and still a beauty, even so. Strong looking, yet elegant. Tall, but fine-boned. And those green eyes, they sparkle while they take your measure and flash fire a moment later when she thinks you might cross her. It will be a pleasure to tame her. She will give me sons, I have no doubt.

Together we will form such a formidable alliance that even the King of France will not dare challenge us!

Henry grinned as he thought of Louis. How outraged the king of France would be when he found out that Eleanor had married him, a mere duke of Normandy and count of Anjou. And to top it off, married in such a truly indecently brief period following her annulment. Hah! Scarce two months had passed. Louis would be furious. Henry could almost envision him casting his eyes heavenward when he got the news, even while he was gritting his teeth to keep from blasphemy in his anger. Louis would never allow himself to lose his royal temper. The king of France would probably hasten to the chapel for prayer when he was told of Henry's coup to calm his baser instincts, his urge to kill his young, renegade noble.

Henry actually liked Louis, although the king's pious pronouncements were often like to drive him mad. Louis should have been a monk, not a king. Poor Louis. Well, he, Henry, had snatched Louis's wife out from under him, and he could afford to be sympathetic to the man's position. It's true, under the feudal laws, Henry should have sought permission from Louis for any marriage. But the king would never be inclined to give agreement to this union, which would create lands twice the size of France right at his own back door. So why bother to ask and signal the plan? Easier to ask for royal forgiveness later.

With all of this good fortune, why would he not be whistling? The handsome young Richard de Lucy rode up beside him. "You are of good cheer today, My Lord." His grin, pasted across his boyish, tanned face, was lopsided as usual. "Would you like some more good news?"

"One never has enough glad tidings, my friend. What would you?" Henry turned to de Lucy with a questioning look. He was always cheered by his close friend's optimism. Just five years younger, the Duke of Normandy had come to depend on the loyalty of this graceful, dark-haired aide, and on his keen and quick mind.

"A courier just caught us up and gave us news that will please you. You have a son! Born two months ago in Normandy. It was that woman, Yekani. You must remember that adventure last year."

"Indeed, I do!" Henry laughed with delight. "Ah, that is good news, Richard. My first son, and I shall have many more, God willing. Send the boy's mother a pound of silver from the English cache and my very good wishes. Tell her I'll come for my son someday. Wait." Henry pulled up his horse, and his companion, who was turning to ride away, stopped. "Send also the message: I want the boy named Geoffrey, after my father."

"Yes, Your Grace," Richard said, smiling. He had been a particular admirer of Count Geoffrey and was pleased to see him remembered in this, the first son of his scion. He had no doubt Henry would keep his word and that the new son would one day ride beside the Duke of Normandy, no matter the circumstances of his birth.

"This is a good omen, My Lord. It promises well for your marriage."

"You may say so, Richard. Although one must be careful not to be too hopeful for the future. One never knows what time will bring you." Henry's smile faded a little, thinking of his father's sudden death.

"But My Lord," de Lucy rejoined, "what could go wrong now?"

"I think nothing, my friend." Suddenly a surge of confidence overtook the younger man. "I confess to you that this is the first day of my certainty that England will soon be mine. I will build an empire. Nothing can stop me now." They had reached the ducal castle of Poitiers as they spoke. The bridge had been lowered at their approach. Henry waited for his small band of knights to collect in one group before starting across. Then he looked up.

On the battlements stood a lone figure, a tall, slender figure in a flowing robe of striking blue with a girdle of pure gold thread that caught the sun. Her veil fluttered in the wind as she looked down on them and slowly waved a welcome. Henry looked up to his fortune and his future. And he was well pleased.

* * *

She received him in the Great Hall. She was seated on the dais when he strode in. She had no one with her, nor did he, at her request. They faced each other down the long, empty stone space, lit only by the torches on the wall.

"Madame," Henry was stripping his riding gloves from his hands as he greeted her, walking toward her. He paused before mounting the dais, for no reason that he could name at that moment. Perhaps he sensed an air of *noli me tangere* about her slender figure that reached even him, with his habits of bluff action. He made a bow of courtesy and waited, his brows raised and his eyes narrowing.

What did she have in mind, asking me to leave my entourage outside the hall? What is her plan?

"Duke Henry," she replied, with the slightest inclination of her head. "Welcome." Then she said no more.

There was quiet in the great hall. Henry, for whom silence and stasis were foreign, could stand it for only the space of one long minute.

"Madame," he said again, striding forward without invitation. "If I am truly welcomed, may we not be closer?" In a leap he was on the dais, and upon her, although her steel look and slight withdrawal stopped him from touching her.

"*Bien sûr*, My Lord." She rose from her chair, the throne of the dukes of Aquitaine, and took a step back. But he saw that it was not out of fear. Her profile in the light of the slanting sun coming through the cuttings in the stone wall revealed her fine facial bones, high cheekbones, remarkable green eyes drilling into his. *Mais, premier, j'ai des questions pour vous.*"

"*Vous*? You speak to me formally? But we will soon be man and wife!"

"That may be, but we are not yet."

"But you have signed the agreement. In Paris. It was witnessed!" Henry felt his famous temper rising.

"Gently, My Lord Duke, gently if you please." The queen—why could he not stop thinking of her in that way? —moved swiftly yet with grace to a sideboard and poured two beakers of rich, red wine. One she offered to him, holding it out without moving, so, again, he had to come to her. He took it, puzzled.

What game does this queen play?

She raised her glass to him, and he had no choice but to follow suit.

This time Henry had enough sense to wait before he spoke again. Some instinct held him in check. The queen sipped the wine and then nodded to him as if to say it was safe for him to drink. He smiled—it hadn't occurred to him until that moment that the wine might not be safe.

Finally, he also drank, as if sealing some kind of pact. He was a soldier in the making and a stranger to courtly interactions, and he had no idea what was going on. Then the queen smiled, a smile so open and charming he wanted to seize her, to cut through the game and take his proper due as her husband then and there. But still, uncharacteristically, he paused.

"My Lord Duke, first allow me to say that I am in great sorrow about the death of the count, your father. I want you to know the depth of my sorrow on your behalf. I could not adequately express this when we met in Paris, for it was never the right moment, and we were never alone."

Henry stood still, mesmerized by her competency in the world of manners and by such an elegant statement. He had much to learn, indeed. But the queen was not finished with his lesson.

"A sudden and precipitate ending to a noble and active life. I know you must feel his loss acutely."

Henry nodded, wordless for the moment. How does one respond? His mother, Empress Matilda, would never have made such a genteel remark, and certainly not about his father, Count Geoffrey. Matilda, the only woman Henry had known well up to now, was no model for the courtly virtues, having been sent at a young age to the harsh court of Germany for early marriage to the emperor. The experience had only sharpened her wit and firmed her sense of entitlement without offering her any patina of *noblesse oblige*. This woman, about to become his wife, was certainly cut from a different cloth.

"Thank you, Duchess. "He bowed deeply. "Your kindness overwhelms." *Where did those words come from?* The gravity of the young duke's response seemed to touch her. She inclined her head in response. Then, there was another sudden change in her mood.

"Now, to our business. I asked you here to speak to you alone, without our advisors." She set her goblet on the table behind her without looking, apparently feeling that one taste of the wine should be enough to reassure her fiancé of her good intentions. "We shall meet later with them, but I wished to talk with you in private first to ascertain certain things about your intentions."

Henry looked as startled as he felt. *Am I expected to attend my betrothed with a bevy of counsellors, like Louis with Abbe Suger in tow?*

And why is she telling me how we will meet? I'll be the one to decide how we conduct our business. How does she think this marriage will go? Anyway, she herself chooses? She has the wrong man for that!

He did not understand her, and his rising temper was in danger of overcoming his manners.

"Madame," he said, scarce able to modulate his voice. "I have no need to bring advisors with me to greet the woman who has agreed to wed me. And I do not understand the purpose behind your words, so speak plainly if you please. What is it you want to discuss? Are you about to break our betrothal agreement, made in Paris in front of at least four witnesses? If so, say so now, and I shall call in the law clerks to record it."

"Softly, Sir Duke." Eleanor gestured to the two imposing chairs set toward the back of the dais where her father, the Duke of Aquitaine, and his duchess sat when holding court. "Let us sit and further discuss our agreement. I have no intention of breaking our betrothal at this time, but I want to clarify some items we did not officially discuss in Paris. Due, at the time, to the stress of having to do all in secret until the annulment of my marriage with the king was finally announced."

She moved to sit, and he could do no other than to follow. To remain standing in her seated presence placed her on a higher plane than he, and after all, she was no more than a duchess, his equal now that she was no longer queen. He had to keep reminding himself that she was no longer queen.

"I asked you for a private conversation to obtain your views on certain matters." She turned slightly in her chair to face him, and he did likewise. He was again startled by the clear, green eyes staring at him with neither fear nor affection nor any other emotion. Just gazing with an unsettling directness.

"Such as?" He was not enjoying this; talking was not his forte. Oh, give him even a small band of loyal men and a good, strong fight any day. But not to be ensnared in this verbal game of *jeu de palme*! "Madame, be clear. What is it you want from me?"

"With the marriage that will take place tomorrow, we join our lands. You get the Aquitaine and suzerainty over counties as far as Toulouse.

You already have Anjou and Normandy, which means that, together, we surround Louis on the west, the north and the south."

"Yes, that much is clear to anyone," he snapped, before he could stop himself.

"You also have the best claim to the throne of England, which will make you more than a duke and count . . ."

"And make you a queen again," Henry said, a light dawning dimly in the back of his mind.

"I fully intend to be queen again, but I also do not mean ever to give up my own lands. When my father arranged my marriage with Louis's father shortly before they both died, part of the agreement was that I would keep my ancestral lands myself."

"So that's why Louis's advisors allowed you to take them back at the time of the divorce." Henry was beginning to see how things worked. He had spent no time prior to this conversation on this question, but he saw now that he should have wondered. "What is it you want from me regarding this? The same agreement?"

"No, I want more from you," Eleanor said coolly. "I know that you will be king of England someday. The news of the pope's backing of your mother's claim spread over all Europe."

"That was several years ago when Archbishop Thibault of Canterbury sent that young clerk Thomas Becket to Rome to argue for the rightful claim of my mother. That's when Stephen threatened to have Eustace crowned king along with him, and Thibault took our side." Henry grew thoughtful for a moment. "Thibault, as Archbishop of Canterbury, was the only man who could crown the king. And he refused to crown Stephen. He persuaded the pope to wait also." He paused, scanning her face with his open gaze. "You always knew I'd be king. So, you've been planning to align with the house of Anjou for three years? And here I thought it was my father's—I mean my own—idea." He grinned with sudden good nature.

Eleanor smiled enigmatically, a look Henry had observed on his cat once when it was presented with a bowl of cream. "You see, I knew Becket in Paris years ago when I was a young bride. And if he were acting on behalf of the house of Anjou, I had great confidence that your family would triumph. Becket is no fool."

Henry absorbed this news, frowning, then looked up to meet her green-eyed gaze.

"Madame, you said a moment ago that you wanted something more from me than the merger of our lands and titles. What is it that you seek?"

"I want to govern by your side."

"Do you now?" Henry turned even further toward her, astonishment written all over his open, young face. "In what way, Madame, do you think that arrangement would work? There can be only one king. And I intend that it should be me. I am the one who will win the throne that belonged rightfully to my mother before the English barons deserted her cause for that ninny Stephen."

"I'm not interested in English politics, Duke Henry. Of course, you have the best claim to the throne. And you have already fought well for it, so I hear. But I do not intend to be a decorative wife, a docile bearer of children. My will is as strong as any man, my education in Greek and Latin—and rhetoric—as good as any cleric's and better than most. I am as fit to rule as those who are currently on the thrones of our neighbors. I want to sit beside you and be a part of the decisions you make." She put her hands on the arms of her chair and her lovely face hardened with her passion. "And in return, I give you vast lands, and I will give you sons to succeed you."

Henry's mind reeled. This was a complication he had not foreseen when he proposed this marriage. Everyone knew Louis, king of France, was setting aside his queen because she had born him only daughters. Count Geoffrey had wanted him to marry Eleanor for her land. Neither of them had thought about whether the duchess had aspirations of her own. Were women supposed to think like this?

"How do I know you will give me sons?" He shot back. He heard the hostility in his voice, more than he had intended.

"I was made to bear sons." She said matter-of-factly, ignoring his belligerence. "Although I am older than you by a decade, I have many good childbearing years ahead of me. Our first two children will be sons, and they will be amazing."

Henry looked at her for a long moment. His eyes dropped to her hands, white with pressure on the arms of her ducal chair. He looked again at her beautiful, oval face set against the future with nothing but willpower that matched his own.

Nothing has prepared me for this. I must go with the force of the river. With her force. For now.

"Yes, all right," he said, finally. "You shall have your bargain. I will include you in my councils of government." He paused. "But women have no place in councils of war. There, you will not be welcome. And anyway, some of that may have an impact on the father of your daughters, King Louis. So, you will be well out of those discussions."

"We shall see," she said maddeningly, opening yet another door he thought to close.

"Ah, there is one more point." She smiled, a brilliant expression coming over her face. Henry was reminded of nothing so much as a beautiful cat. "Louis will marry again. He is desperate for sons. But if he has more daughters, and the stars are well aligned, I intend our sons should marry with the daughters of the king of France."

Henry stared at her, thunderstruck. *Who is this woman?* They had not yet consummated their marriage; indeed, she was only two months free from Louis, and she was already plotting the future of his realm. His realm! With Louis's daughters, which did not yet exist. And his own sons, who were even more in question, given her childbearing performance up to now. He shook his head to clear the dust from his thoughts. This was all too complicated for him, who wanted nothing more than the crown of England to cap his continental holdings. Who would think about marriage when neither crown nor children were yet his?

"My Lord Duke?" She raised one delicate eyebrow and then smiled again, sunshine spreading across her lovely face. "Do not look so surprised. My father, Duke William, taught me to think of how the events of life might go, to shape them with plans. You think that you and your father chose me for your wife and queen, but I have equally chosen you. And together, we will prosper."

She raised one delicate hand as if in question, and Henry was suddenly seized with a longing to possess that hand, that lovely smile, that head, which carried so many complicated and weighty plans, so foreign to his soldier's training.

He extended his hand, the traditional sign of knights, to show they had no sword and meant peace. Eleanor did not look surprised as she placed her own, smaller-boned hand in his horseman's grip. Nor did her face change as he unwittingly crushed it in his own larger paw. When he released it, he knew he had made the bargain of his life.

"Madame," he said, "let's gather the bishop of this good town and solemnize our vows this very afternoon. There is no point in waiting any longer now that we have agreed on our future together."

When they rose, Henry gave her a long look but did not take her in his arms. That could wait. The important business was finished.

September 1152
Limoges, Aquitaine

"My love, you are beautiful." Henry was exhausted. He turned on his side and pulled away slightly to better study her fine-boned face and tousled hair, beautiful even now after the sweaty, bed-soaked efforts of the past hour. A shadow crossed her features as she shook her head, and he instantly regretted his remark. But why?

The Duke of Normandy and the Duchess of Aquitaine had retired to her royal pavilion for a conference after entertaining the representatives of the townspeople for the mid-day dinner. The pavilion flaps were down, indicating to the rest of the camp a need for privacy between the rulers as they had instructed their servants at the beginning of their *chevauchée* through Eleanor's lands. Both Eleanor and Henry were serious about their intentions to conceive the first heir to their united titles sooner rather than later. The tent was redolent of their efforts, their faces shiny with exertion.

Why does such a remark not please her. I thought all women wanted to be told they were special. She is truly more beautiful than most, but perhaps she thinks such a remark a cliché, said by every man after fucking his woman. Is it too common? Why are women so difficult?

Minutes had passed in silence as Henry was lost in his own thoughts. But then he noticed that Eleanor still frowned.

"Why does such a remark not please you?" Henry finally asked.

"I do not want to be admired for my face. Beauty will fade. I want to be admired because I am a ruler, because I have my father's kingdom and now, joined to you, lands even more vast." She spoke with the tone of a Caesar. "You see how my subjects have welcomed us."

"Indeed, they are most demonstrative. I have enjoyed watching them pay homage to you. And, from side remarks, they seem very happy to have thrown off their overlord, the king of France." Henry laughed.

She turned on her side once more to face him. "I think they are impressed that you have not taken over, that you have been content to have their homage paid first to me, their duchess. Louis was forever placing himself in front of me when we toured my villages. You do not do that."

"Well, why should I? You are the ruler they have known." Henry sat up, feeling more confident now that the conversation had turned to matters of state. And anyway, the time for lovemaking had likely passed. "I have no need to march in and usurp your place in the hearts of your people. If there is ever a firm hand needed, I will be there with my men to enforce our rulings. But these are, and always will be, your own ancestral lands."

He threw on a tunic and marched to the tent flap, pulling it up and attaching it. This would be a sign to his closest companions that he was available for orders, if needed. A soldier first, he was always in search of fresh air; loved sleeping out in the open. And always in the back of his mind was the moment when next his men would need him.

"Henry, for the love of the sweet Savior, close that flap." Eleanor, not ever to be considered a prude, pulled the sheets closer to her body. "I'm still in a state of undress."

"Oh, sorry, my Love." Henry let the heavy flap fall with a thud, then lit several candles on the table from the one burning. "But hasten, if you will. The afternoon sun is setting, and we still must preside over dinner with our own people before dark. Remember, in autumn and even in gentle hills, the sun sets earlier."

Eleanor extended her legs over the edge of the rumpled bed and stood, pulling on her linen shift with one graceful motion. "Perhaps the best idea would be for you to remove yourself to your own tent and receive your captains' reports." She spoke with some humor. "I shall make ready for our last official meal of the day."

Eleanor was intrigued with this young husband. She was still getting to know him, assessing him and did not find him wanting in most respects. Now she watched him with interest as he, all unawares, was unrolling the two parchments that had been delivered just before she had decided to distract him an hour earlier.

Stocky of build, not handsome but strong looking, she rather liked his sandy-red hair, his roughness of manner, his blunt nose, even his freckles. And when, as he sometimes did, he turned the gaze of those wide, penetrating grey eyes on her, even she, Eleanor, duchess and once and future queen, occasionally blinked.

As these thoughts occurred to her, she donned a robe of shot grey silk that had been carelessly tossed on the camp stool an hour before. Then she pulled back her long, luxurious auburn hair and quickly wrapped a scarf around it.

Her actions were not too soon, for suddenly, the bell outside tinkled, and the flap was raised before Henry could bark an order. Richard de Lucy, Henry's lieutenant in charge of the small company of men that rode with the couple through the Aquitaine, entered the tent. Richard de Lucy was possessed of rare good sense in a fighting man and a polish that Eleanor secretly hoped could rub off on her new husband. He had a polish more reflective of the courts of France than most of the Normans who had gathered around her husband possessed, and these same manners caused him to blush when he saw the queen in her informal dress.

"What, ho?" Henry asked sharply. De Lucy would not have breached the closed tent unless it were important.

"Your Grace," he bowed first to Eleanor, then turned to Henry. "I would not willingly disturb you, but I saw the flap raised a moment ago, and Sire, you are needed."

"What's the problem?" Henry was crisp, suddenly the military man, capable of handling any situation. Eleanor observed him, fascinated with the quick change in his demeanor.

"The abbot of the local monastery, Sire. He has refused to send the customary victuals for our evening dinner. And we have used all of our current foodstuffs at mid-day to feed the townspeople."

"The abbot refuses. It is his obligation to feed the duchess when she makes her visit. Does he not know his duty?" His volume rose with each sentence. He threw a metal goblet against the tent pole. Eleanor was certain the entire camp was now listening. She had never seen anger rising so quickly in Henry in the few months they had been man and wife, and she watched with a sort of horrified interest.

"God's teeth! Did we not send to him?" He barked. "Was he reminded of his honor?"

"Of course, Your Grace." De Lucy was ever the courtier, even when addressing his military chief, who was in a fit of anger. "His reply was that he had no obligation to feed us. The strictures on feudal law are that the abbot must feed us if we are visiting the town under his protection. Not to mention the laws of Benedictine hospitality. But he claims he does not have an obligation to send us food because we pitched our camp *outside* the town walls. We always do that to avoid dislodging the townspeople. We have done so at every village we have visited on this progress. No one has refused us our due before this." He paused. "We await your instructions."

What happened next was astonishing to the young duchess, who watched with rapt attention. Her husband's rage seemed to grow, rather than abate, with the request for action. Roaring with rage, the king threw himself on the bed so recently host to their avid passion and proceeded to tear at the covering until he had revealed the straw beneath. He grasped handfuls of straw, rolled onto the floor and began to chew on the straw, shouting unintelligible acclamations, mostly involving parts of the body of God. A strange foam appeared around his mouth. His normally ruddy face was so red his wife feared, for a moment, he would expire. The scene went on for two or three minutes.

He lay still for a moment breathing heavily, then rolled neatly onto his side and was on his feet, brushing off the straw from his clothes and spitting out a bit of it from his mouth.

He moved to the table at the side of the pavilion and poured himself some watered wine, which he swilled around in his mouth and then spat out. Eleanor could see, through the still open tent flap, a ring of faces gathered outside, listening, trying to get a glimpse of the storied Angevin temper in action. She just shook her head in wonder and perched on the edge of the camp stool to await the next developments.

"Well, then, if the abbot is upset that we have pitched our tents outside the walls, we'll just take the walls down." Henry announced this in a firm but somewhat hoarse tone of voice. "De Lucy, take half our force and begin to dismantle the south wall of the village. I've inspected the walls, and they are loosely set. One side of the walls down will be sufficient. They need a lesson in hospitality."

"And tell du Hommet to take the other one hundred men and go into the fields around the town to gather wheat and small animals. Tell the cooks to prepare whatever they bring back. And let's have all this done before we must sit down to dinner in the dark. The sun will not last more than two hours." Henry threw back his head and swallowed the last of his wine. All vestige of his tantrum had disappeared, leaving Eleanor to wonder if he could summon such a performance at will or if he needed a spur to do so.

When de Lucy had gone, Eleanor rose and walked to stand deliberately in front of Henry. "What was all that about?" she asked.

"The Angevin counts were famous for their tempers," Henry shrugged, having recovered himself somewhat. His breath was only now returning to normal rhythms. He poured a goblet of wine and held it out to her. She saw his arm shaking slightly. "When I was a child, I saw my grandfather, Count Fulk, throw a fit of anger one time, and it was most effective on those around him. Everyone immediately began to placate him, execute his wishes. No one wanted to see another one of those demonstrations."

"But did you, in yourself, just now, feel that much emotion?" Eleanor was unsure of her own feelings about her young husband's temper.

He looked at her over the rim of his own goblet. "At first, no. But I allow myself to gather anger within. And soon, it needs expression. Then it takes me over. By then, I could not stop if I tried." He grinned. "It's rather like making love."

Eleanor shook her head. That was quite a performance.

For a moment, they looked at each other. Then she spoke again, this time in a different voice, the voice of the duchess. "My Lord Duke, do you think it wise to tear down the village walls? Did you mean what you said in the grip of your wrath?"

"Yes, I meant it." Henry slammed his goblet down on the table. "I care not if it is wise. It is what I must do. Else the entire country will know within a fortnight that they may treat their over-lords in any fashion that suits them. Such an action may assist the abbot in the future to make the right decisions." Henry paced the length of the pavilion, then turned. "Hah! Calling upon the letter of the law to avoid his obligations to his countess. Who does he think he is? The villagers will not soon forget this incident." Surely she would agree with his plan.

Eleanor took a long sip of wine, then raised her gaze to meet her husband's and nodded. Neither spoke. He turned and left the tent. She began to dress and gathered her thoughts.

3 January 1153
Barfleur, Norman Coast

Henry lay in his soldier's bed on the second floor of the inn that had provided quarters for him and his ten closest officers. The rest of the small band, no more than 140 of the best Norman and Angevin knights he could assemble, were scattered in homes throughout the village. Barfleur was a port village, and the seamen and their families were happy to have the extra income from travelers waiting for happier weather. Henry much preferred the quiet of the inn, where he could think and plan.

The rain drumming on the wooden roof lulled him into a momentary reverie.

Blow, west wind, blow
So the small rain down can rain.
Christ, that I were in my bed
And my love in my arms again.

That old refrain from the English soldiers, learned when I first went to fight Stephen. After Matilda escaped from Oxford, dressed as a page and riding alone on a horse. God's beard, what a woman my mother is. Almost frightening. But after that winter, she said it is my turn; the crown is mine to take. And well, I did then, for the first run. Only a lad, sixteen summers, but still, I landed and fought through two battles. Then the mercenaries revolted, wanting their pay. And my mother said I should never have gone when I didn't have the means with me. And even Uncle Robert of Gloucester turned away, saying it was an ill-planned expedition and I should dig myself out of my own hole. But then I had the brilliant idea of asking Stephen. If he wanted me to go home, he could pay my soldiers. And so he did, along with the order to return to Anjou.

Which I complied with. For a time. But it was when he sent the money that I knew I had him. He did not have the killer inside him. He could have finished me off then and there, but he didn't. My mother would have done. And so can I. Finish them off.

But I also know how to play a waiting game. What was Matilda's favorite image: oh yes, the falcon. "Dangle the prize before their eyes but be sure to withdraw it before they taste it. Then you will keep them eager and find them devoted when you need them."

There lived a wife at Usher's Well
And a wealthy wife was she;
She had three stout and stalwart sons
And sent them o'r the sea.

Just as Matilda sent us over the sea with her good advice. Or rather, she sent me. Well, Geoff will come along now that I've sorted him out over Normandy and Anjou. And young Robert never made any trouble, a sweet lad. Yes, my brothers will support me now. So close to power I am. And they know it.

So, come to it, will Eleanor. There is another woman who could kill if the stakes were high enough. Christ, that my love were in my arms! The fair Eleanor. I think she might be the equal of Matilda in valor. Wonder how the two women will get along at Rouen when Eleanor goes there to birth our child. That was the last news she gave me when we parted. "Oh, by the way, I am already quick with your son," she said, as I mounted my horse, as if it were news of no matter at all. God's full breath, what a woman! "Fare you well." And she slapped the horse's rump herself to send me on my way before I could say anything, turning to look back at her in amazement and seeing that cat-smile. I nearly forced my horse around right then to go back to her, but I knew that would have spoiled her amazing moment!

Henry suddenly threw his legs over the side of his cot and stood up. He had made his decision. Enough of rain patter on the roof. Action was what he needed.

"De Lucy! Du Hommet! Now, come." And his captains came running from the inn's fireside dice games, happy to be on the move again. "Rouse the men. This damn rain is never going to stop. We've been cooped up here for a fortnight. I'll have no more of it. We board ship at noon today. We are for England, storm or no storm. If God wants us to arrive, we will. If God wants us to triumph and recover the crown, then by God's name, we shall. Round up the men! We have fifteen hundred archers waiting for us on the coast of England. This time we shall give Stephen a true run for his crown." Suddenly the inn, so quiet for days, was alive with activity. Torches were lit, fires in the kitchen begun, and a great smell of food and rustle of gear filled the air. Henry rubbed his hands together with glee in front of the fire as he waited for his men to gather. This was more like it! Action was his tonic.

August 1153
The Norman Ducal Court at Rouen

The two women sat together in the empress' small chamber, deeply ensconced in large chairs piled with cushions. It was mid-August, but there was a chill in the old castle, where the cold stones held a remembrance of winter through the short season of summer. The empress Mathilda even had a woolen shawl around her shoulders, a fact not lost on her son's wife, who marked well everything about her rival for Henry's attention. Servants had laid a fire, and the women were grateful for it, for the northern winds had racked the castle walls the night before, and the rain had left everything damp, foretelling the end of summer.

Mathilda, once empress of Germany and now countess dowager of Angers, kept her court in Rouen, the center of Normandy. That northern province bestowed by Count Geoffrey on her eldest son, Henry, shortly before the count's unfortunate demise, had become her refuge when Henry married. The countess was here to avoid living at Angers with her new *belle-fille*, the duchess Eleanor. But now that same duchess, who had usurped her seat at Angers by virtue of marrying Henry, had come to disturb her peace here at Rouen. They were natural rivals, being both women of mettle and only a decade apart in age.

The older woman picked at the needlepoint work on her lap. The younger woman, large with child, appeared absorbed by the parchment book in her hands, only occasionally glancing at her companion with some amusement. In the week that she had been with Henry's mother, she had sharply noted her many habits. Matilda hated needlework, had called it "fools' work," but nevertheless engaged in it because she was more content with something to occupy her hands. A book never lasted long in her lap. That restlessness was the same as Henry's, Eleanor thought. But he always had the outlet of action, denied now to the aging Matilda. No wonder she had a disposition like a sour apple.

Eleanor smiled at the memory of her own active life, riding off with her women alongside Louis when he took up the cross and headed for the Holy Land. No matter that people called her "Amazon," she had chosen to take it as a compliment. Even now, after years had passed, she knew she could relive all that given the chance. But Henry's mother lived with the knowledge that she could not, for she now was too old. Eleanor felt a creeping tinge of sympathy for the old dragon.

Even though they were nearly the same height, the older woman appeared taller, perhaps because she was so thin. Her face was lined with the concerns of several kingdoms. Perhaps her face had shown worry ever since she was sent as a little girl to live at the German court, destined to marry an emperor in a strange land awash in a foreign tongue. Matilda had later struggled for the crown of England bequeathed to her by her father, King Henry, the first of that name. Indeed, in her long campaign against her cousin Stephen she had shown the tenacity of a rabid hound. But the strains of this fight were showing now, and her figure, despite her iron will, was bending around the shoulders with age. Her mastiffs, two of them, noble and intelligent dogs, were stretched at her feet. But they, too, seemed tired, with eyelids that insisted on drooping despite the dogs' best efforts to look alert.

Eleanor looked at her book, one she treasured. The troubadour Bernard de Ventadour had made a gift of it when he left Angers for England at Henry's summons. Why, oh why, had she agreed to come to Rouen to birth her first child? At least at Angers she had the poets and *trouveres* around her. Here, everything was so austere.

Oh, yes, now she remembered, she thought wryly. She had agreed to come to Rouen before she met her hostess-to-be, Henry's mother. What a difficult woman she had revealed herself to be. How imperious her attitude with servants, with secretaries, with her own son's new wife. But it was too late now for her to make the journey back to her own castle. She, Eleanor, duchess of Aquitaine in her own right and now duchess of Normandy also, had no choice. She would have to live out her confinement here until after the birth.

Eleanor sighed audibly. Matilda turned her attention away from the fire.

"Do we not please the Duchess of Normandy with our hospitality?" she snapped, as if reading Eleanor's mind. "If not, you are free to go elsewhere."

"Madame," Eleanor, lifting her head from the book, met her *belle-mere*'s gaze. She took some pleasure in refusing to use the royal title Mathilda demanded from others. "You and I no doubt would both be happier if I were back in my own court at Angers. You know how reluctant I was to leave, particularly when I discovered that none of my *trouveres* were to be allowed here." She spoke in pleasant tones to take some of the sting from the remark. "But My Lord Duke Henry insisted that I be here for the birth of our son."

"Are you so certain the child you carry will be a boy?" The eyes in the pinched face narrowed.

"Absolutely certain, Madame." Eleanor gave a knowing half-smile. "It is My Lord's wish that I be here, safe with you, when the babe is birthed. This way, he persuaded me, I would have support during my confinement and," she glanced sideways at the little bed that had been set up in her mother-in-law's chamber for the occasional baby showing, "you would have the pleasure of being the first to see your grandson."

After a slight pause, Eleanor could not resist one more comment. "I try," she added, casting a look in the older woman's direction, "to accommodate my husband's serious requests, as you no doubt did with Count Geoffrey."

The unmistakable flicker of a sideways glance signaled Eleanor that the empress was not pleased with the remark. Perhaps she had heard the rumors of Eleanor's alleged romance with Count Geoffrey. That was gossip created to widen the gap between Eleanor and Louis, but Matilda could not know that. Count Geoffrey had been a simple dalliance and only that. And it was over when Eleanor saw Henry.

Mathilda was readying a rejoinder when Eleanor held up a finger, looking toward the doors of the chamber. The faint noise was growing unmistakably louder. It was no doubt the sound of boots and spurs, accompanied by loud voices and some laughter echoing down the stone hallway, coming in their direction. The hounds leapt to their feet, growling.

Both women rose, Eleanor with some difficulty as her child made her heavy. Henry strode into the room with his constant companions: de Lucy, as usual, beside him and Richard du Hommet, Robert of Leicester and young William FitzStephen bringing up the rear, all chattering like magpies. Henry, appearing so unexpectedly, startled Eleanor out of her usual calm. Her first thought was foreboding. Had something happened, something so grave he must need bring the news himself?

Without hesitation, Henry went directly to his mother, now standing also, and embraced her, greeting her—if not with affection—with respect. Eleanor's reaction was immediate. She sat down again in her chair so that when Henry turned his attention to her only a moment later, he was forced to lean over and offer her a half-embrace, awkwardly. She turned stiffly aside, making his approach no easier. Even Henry, never the most subtle of men, could sense a chill in the air.

"How fare you, my duchess?" He asked formally, at a loss as to what else he should say in the face of her action.

Eleanor replied coolly, "Well enough, My Lord, as you see. We are not far off from the birth of your son."

Henry laughed, his bluff, hearty, chopping laugh. "You say it is a son. I cannot but admire your certainty, Madame."

Eleanor, relenting, turned to him and gave him her hand, accompanied by a baleful look. Henry, in a flash of light, realized his earlier error and whispered in an undertone as he leaned down again to kiss her cheek, "Forgive me, my Love, but my mother is the elder."

"We did not expect you, my son," Mathilda interjected to recapture her son's attention. "What brings you here? What news from England?" Her tones were urgent, as if she were alone with her son, that he alone mattered in this instant.

"Mother, the most amazing developments. That's why I had to come and tell you myself." He threw off his cloak, cut short in the Angevin fashion, and clapped his hands for servants. Maurice, the head steward, bustled into the room, breathing hard.

"Wine for my men, and food. We have ridden hard and are weary," Henry ordered in the grand manner befitting the lord who has returned to his own castle. "Set the table in the great hall. There is not room here for all of us to dine."

"What is the news?" Mathilda's eager look held within it all the hopes she had nurtured for years that the crown of England bestowed on her by her father, King Henry, then stolen by Stephen, would finally return to her family.

"Stephen's son Eustace is dead! He was at Faversham, laying waste to the land around the abbey there with his routiers over some imagined insult. Suddenly he caught a fever and died the next day. A fortnight past, this was. Now Stephen of Blois has no heir to the throne he usurped from you. When he heard the news of his son's death, he apparently saw it as an act of God against him. He sent to parley with me. He has given his word that he will make me his rightful heir now. We can finally end this vicious war."

Matilda fell back slightly at these words, her hands reaching for the safety of the chair. In one step, Henry was beside her, supporting her. He caught both his mother's elbows with his strong, block-like hands. "My Lady mother, this is the end of all your efforts to claim the throne the barons stole from you because you were a woman. England has come back to our family!"

"Oh, my son!" Matilda's reserve fell away. She dropped her head on Henry's shoulder and began to weep. "At long last, at long last!"

Eleanor, still seated, watched them, various emotions flickering over her face. So, Henry had been right all along. She would be queen once again, this time with her own power. And her sons would rule England and most of the continent. The marriage had been well worth it.

Pushing her weight from her chair by her arms, Eleanor rose unsteadily. Seeing this over Matilda's shoulder, Henry passed his mother, still unsteady, to the hearty arm of Richard de Lucy and turned to his wife.

He raised her fully, and the embrace into which she was folded was powerful. She drifted against him; they were briefly one, then suddenly, she pulled back with a quick intake of breath.

"Madame, what is it?" he asked, frowning. Was she still put out that he had greeted Mathilda first? But no, something else.

"I believe *le bebe arrive*. Call the servants. I need . . ." She pulled further away and doubled over with a gasp, water flowing from her and soaking her skirts. Henry wasted no time, grabbing a goblet of wine from the surprised Earl of Leicester.

"Here, my love. Swallow this." He held the cup to her lips, and she drank. "Now, you must lie down for the safety of the babe." He lifted her and laid her gently on Matilda's bed. The empress, sidelined for once, was torn between her joy at the impending birth that would ensure the succession of her kingdom and her annoyance that her *belle-fille* had chosen this moment to seize the stage. Ah, well, such is the price of victory, she thought.

Hours later, Henry lay alone in the ducal chambers, his mother insisting that Eleanor rest in her own chambers for the night. The birth had been fast, simple and uncomplicated, *grâce a dieu*. Hah! Louis's two daughters by Eleanor had warmed her up for childbirth. And Matilda clucked like a hen over the new child as if there had never been such a boy. All resentment at her son's wife had disappeared, swallowed up in this joyful event.

How did she know it would be a son? She must be a sorceress. That would account for those bewitching green eyes. Of course, I need not have worried; she's given birth before. But never a son of mine. He was so little, so red and wrinkled. And mother, so cold always, yet when she saw that baby emerge, her face shone with satisfaction. She was thinking the same thought that I had as if we were one: Just as always when I was a child. I know what she was thinking tonight. There, in that child, is the line of Henry, king of England. He will be its hope. Only she was thinking of her father, Henry, king of England, for her aging face is turned toward the past. And I am thinking of Henry, Second of that name, king of England. Me. Myself. My face is turned toward the future, and I see that it is bright indeed.

19 December 1154
London, On the Road to Westminster

"Henry, for the sweet Saviour's sake, could you please slow down?" Eleanor was an excellent horsewoman, but even she was having difficulty keeping up as the retinue flew through the snowy landscape. The barge had brought them only so far from Bermondsey, the temporary royal demesne southwest of Westminster, and now they must finish the journey to the great abbey overland. "I know you are eager, but it will be no help at all if we arrive at our coronation ceremonies in four pieces. You're going to kill us all on this damnable ice!"

"Madame," Henry turned to look at her, slackening his pace only marginally. "I thought you were as eager as I to move this day to its conclusion."

"Yes, but I want to live through it." Eleanor was breathing hard, a satisfaction to her husband who rarely saw her labor through anything—except birth, he thought to himself suddenly. And with that, he did slow somewhat to accommodate his queen.

"All is in readiness for us at the abbey?" She asked this, not for the first time. "You and Thibault have seen to it?"

"My queen," he said with amusement, "You think me a rough soldier, I know, but in a matter such as this, I have left nothing to chance. Abbe Thibault has all in readiness for us. My staff has been at his disposal for this occasion since news came that Eustace died."

"Indeed. You were certain when you heard Eustace was dead that Stephen would give you the crown upon his death, even before Stephen sent his message to you that he wanted to talk." Eleanor cast a glance at her husband, now keeping to her side.

"I have always been certain the crown would be mine. It was just a question of when."

Eleanor smiled. "And blessings on the soul of the great William who saw with foresight that a major part of his conquest of this bleak land depended on owning the church. *C'est grâce* à *lui que nous avons les* éveques *du Normandie.*"

"Well said, my dear. Every major bishop in England a Norman by birth and faithful to my efforts. Roger Pont l'Eveque at York, Gilbert Foliot now here in London, . . ."

"And Thibault, the most powerful of all at Canterbury," Eleanor finished for him as the great towers of the Westminster came into sight.

"And only too happy to crown the rightful king, the direct grandson of the first Henry," he added with satisfaction.

Suddenly, in a markedly different tone, "Eleanor." Something in his voice caused her to glance sideways sharply. "You have been crowned before. I have spent every effort to make this, your second crowning, as magnificent as the event in Paris all those years ago when you married Louis. You have given me two sons. I am grateful for that. You deserve to be queen. And when I have to go back across the channel, as I will next year, you will be regent in my absence, as we agreed. We place our trust in you."

It was the first time she heard him use the royal "we," the usage of kings. From today onward, he would be one with England.

"My Lord," Eleanor said, nodding, as she accepted this tribute from her rough youth, now a powerful ruler in his own right. "As you wish."

"No, Madame," came the gallant reply, "always, as *you* wish. And now, let us make haste, for we still have the robing ceremonies, and the procession, and the crowning. Indeed, I will be grateful to reach Bermondsey again before the sun rises tomorrow." Henry spurred his horse, and the queen matched him as they led their followers forward at a brisk pace.

And true to his word, no effort, nor silver, had been spared to make this coronation regal and gorgeous. Eleanor remained surprised throughout the event by the complexities of the rituals here in England. In France, all was tied to the church, but here the barons and earls played a great part, so the state was prominent apart from the church. Still, she noted, it could not have been done without the archbishop.

They entered by the north door and went in haste to the foyer behind the great altar, between the north and south ambulatories, where the robing ceremonies were to take place. Although they stood almost across the generous space, with their retinues gathered about them, they were facing one another, and Eleanor had a clear view of her spouse as they worked. She could see, could almost feel, Henry's impatience with the layers of royal wool, velvet and ermine that he was obliged to don and his frustration with the ceremony surrounding this action. Each of the major barons and churchmen had assigned roles, and each must undertake his task in order. At one point, Henry seized the buckle from the earl of Chester and fastened it himself, the earl retiring abashed.

Henry looked up at that moment and caught Eleanor's gaze upon him. He suddenly smiled the young man's grin that always amused her. He could read her thoughts, even here, in the most public place of all their realm. That epiphany warmed her heart. Yes, he had been the right decision for her; there was no doubt in her mind now.

Finally, all was ready, and the long winding procession of robed choirs, priests, bishops and barons began the march. Eleanor and Henry were nearly the last to leave the robing chambers with their attendants and right glad of the opportunity to do so. The sun, shining through the stained-glass windows when they had begun, was now growing weak with the advancing winter dusk. Eleanor thought to herself: Perhaps Henry had not been far wrong when he voiced the hope they would be back at Bermondsey before dawn.

Eleanor was too disciplined, too schooled in the ways of monarchy, to appear awed by Westminster Abbey Church as she passed down the side aisle to process up the middle. Built by Edward the Confessor, the saint-king, a century before, it had been intended to make the church a permanent part of the life of the English people.

To those same people, she presented a picture of all that they loved about France and its domains, all its beauty and elegance. Straight and tall she glided, her heavy, jeweled cape held up by her ladies, the wives of the Norman barons. The people fell silent as she passed, subdued by the pageant and its significance for them. The war had ended. They had a king.

She was well satisfied that this was a ceremony the people would remember. Hundreds of torches lined the walls, and thousands of candles blinked on chandeliers above. The crowd outside the abbey had been in tumult when the royal party had ridden up with their small retinue. Now, those lucky enough to be inside by invitation, the barons and their spouses, all the major churchmen and the wealthiest of the burghers stood, packed like lemmings up the nave, to see the new king and his beautiful wife, now twice a queen.

At the same stately pace, the queen and then the king arrived at the quire in the middle of the church, the place named for the eight-page music manuscripts the monks chanted from in their daily office. Now, briefly, as they passed through this walled area, they were hidden from the crowd. In moments the royal couple re-emerged, arriving at the glorious light and color of the main altar. Thibault, archbishop of Canterbury, stood smiling on the steps, waiting for them.

Meanwhile, Henry had other things on his mind.

Ah, well, yes, Eleanor's right again, dammit. I did agree to all of this folderol. Thibault convinced me we must put on a show for the people. There must be no doubt in their minds. The years of indecision on the English crown are over. It belongs to me and to no other. Even Stephen finally agreed before he died. He swore to it.

Eustace. Should have been named "useless" in the English tongue. Was there ever such a simpleton. Even at the last, showing anger to the town of Bury St. Edmonds after they refused him lodging. Ravaging their land. The peasants said he deserved to die. It might have been the bad fish or it might have been the peasants. Tyrants deserve what they get.

I will be a different kind of king. My model is not Stephen, who let the country fall to rack and ruin, all to hold on to a crown that belonged to my mother by right. I will bring us back to the time of my grandfather, the good King Henry. I will restore the rights he once gave the land and all of his laws. We will have order and justice here.

The procession wound down the aisle. They passed through the choirs in the middle of the abbey church, clouds of the new plainsong rising on either side as psalm and antiphon rose on either side of the aisle and were nearly to the high altar. There, Archbishop Thibault waited in his own richly trimmed robes to bestow on Henry the crown he had fought for half his young life.

The archbishop droned on, as he must do. Henry stood in front of the high altar. He was anointed with oil. He received the scepter. Then the archbishop approached to place the crown of the kings of England upon him. The archbishop, the head of the church, crowning the king, the head of state. It was the perfect melding of church and state.

But the glorious conclusion of the coronation ceremony, the placing of the crown on the head of Henry of Anjou, startled him. Amid the great cheers of the people flooding around him, Henry made his way to the throne, the great chair in front of the high altar. He sat and faced his people, smiling broadly in triumph.

Still, he felt surprised, which he tried to disguise. What was this? Only that he found the jeweled crown of Edward the Confessor astonishingly heavy.

20 December 1154
Bermondsey Castle, London

"My Lord," Eleanor was hustling through the halls of the drafty castle at Bermondsey when she saw her husband coming from the opposite direction, head bent close with two of his constant advisors. Robert of Leicester and Richard de Lucy were also his justiciars, responsible for governing under Eleanor when Henry was away. De Lucy, with his handsome, cheery face and famous wit, she liked well indeed, but Robert of Leicester was a different matter. He was older and weighty in both body and manner, a bit on the arrogant side, and no friend to women who wanted power, although he was known to be fond of them in other ways. But she had to admit, with his dark hair shot through with grey and proud Roman nose, he was still a handsome man. And Henry found him useful. When Robert brought his castles in the Midlands to Henry during his last round of fighting against Stephen, it was a turning point. Henry was loyal, and Leicester was here to stay. She sighed and signaled to the king her desire to speak to him by putting out her arm.

Henry was so engrossed in conversation with his companions he nearly walked past the queen, and it was Leicester who called attention to her majesty. He stopped abruptly, causing de Lucy to jostle his new sovereign. The knight apologized with alacrity.

"Madame," Henry bent over her extended hand in courtesy.

"My Lord King," Eleanor smiled. "I have been searching for you. We must attend our guests. They are pouring in through the doors like spilled milk. The master of ceremonies has sent for us. We must hasten to the great hall now."

"Madame, Archbishop Thibault has asked for a short, private meeting. He takes precedence on my time over the waiting crowd. I shall join you immediately after I hear his brief."

"Ah, the archbishop." Eleanor paused. "If it is a matter of state, I should join you, no doubt." Eleanor was not shy about the business of government, especially since she was to be regent in Henry's absence. And she was keen enough to know what was so urgent that the archbishop of Canterbury, that same Thibault who had only yesterday crowned them king and queen of England, must delay the formal opening of their Christmastide festivities.

"Always, as you wish, My Lady." Henry nodded and took her elbow, holding on to the sleek green velvet sleeve firmly. "Come this way then. I have no desire to keep the archbishop waiting."

They turned into one of the smaller chambers, led by Robert of Leicester, who had brought the message to the king. Outside the room, Eleanor noticed two men seated on benches. One, a dark-haired man with an intense frown, looked up. Then he smiled, a bright, open gesture. He looked vaguely familiar, but she had seen so many faces in the past two days that this one had no context. And what, she fretted, could the archbishop want that could not wait until the morrow?

Thibault, archbishop of Canterbury, stood ramrod straight and stately in front of the blazing fire, hands clasped behind his back, staring into the flames as if to find wisdom there. Or perhaps he was watching the cinders pop onto the hearth in a comfortable rhythm and thinking of nothing at all. Archbishop Theobald, as the Saxons called the Norman bishop Thibault, was tall, even with the bending of age. He was a formidable-looking man still. His broad shoulders belied his body, thinning beneath his fine vestments. He held himself with regal grace, long practiced. His face was narrow like a fox and marked with lines, but he still had a full head of grey hair that swept off his forehead and added to his gravitas. And his eyes, she had seen in the light of the abbey when she knelt before him for her crown, were as shrewd as ever she had known. This man had held on to the seat of Canterbury for nearly twenty years through all the politics of the English civil war and the changes of the barons. He had managed to avoid crowning Stephen while keeping his post even while Stephen held the power of the throne. He was nobody's fool.

"Ah, My Lord King," the archbishop turned at the sound of voices. He was prepared for them. "Thank you for coming." He moved forward and made a modest obeisance to the man he had just crowned. Henry immediately took both his elbows, as expected, and raised him up.

"Let's dispense with formalities, Thibault," Henry said. Eleanor, who was learning that her husband did very little without purpose behind it, marked the greeting informal and Norman. Certainly, a message there of kinship.

Henry's party crowded into the room behind the queen. Her attendants had dropped behind as she had joined the king but with de Lucy, Leicester and several others who had gathered, the small chamber was filling rapidly.

Thibault, as she was now to think of him, made another bow to his queen, lower than it needed to be, which was returned by a courteous nod. He turned back to the king, who was already restlessly pacing in front of the fire. This, also, Eleanor had learned. Henry never stood still unless it was required of him publicly. Amazing that he knelt long enough to receive the crown, she thought, and that nearly brought a smile to her face.

The archbishop had fallen neatly into step with the king while the rest of the company stood still with respect.

"Your Grace," the archbishop said casually, his strong preaching voice softened for Henry's ear. "I wonder if I could have a word alone? My message is quite private."

Henry stopped, looked keenly at the archbishop, and then turned. "I would confer with His Eminence alone for a moment."

The group of men shuffled through the door opened by the guards as if reluctant to leave a scene that might make for good gossip in the dining hall later. Eleanor stood quietly.

Henry seemed to notice her suddenly and added, "Of course, the queen may stay if she wishes. I value her advice in all things."

Eleanor did wish. In fact, she would not miss this conference for all the world. What was the old fox going to tell the young fox? She moved to the table beside the warm hearth and poured a goblet of wine, more to occupy herself than from any need.

The attendants outside closed the door. Eleanor perched herself on one of the scribe's stools available near the table and waited with interest.

"All right, Thibault. What is so important that the queen and I must keep our Christmas court waiting while we hear it?" Henry passed by the table, picked up a stone paperweight and fiddled with it as if his large hands had their own impatience, which he could not quite control.

"My Lord King, you know how long I have been at Canterbury." An easy introduction, Eleanor thought. He will remind him of his loyalty next.

"Yes, yes. I am aware. Nigh upon twenty years, I believe."

"Nearly so. And I have seen much that passes for politics and warfare in that time, as you know." The archbishop seemed in no hurry, or was he just building a foundation for something important?

"Thibault, what is it?" Henry slammed the inkpot down impatiently.

"I mean no criticism in what I am about to say about the reign of your mother's cousin, Stephen."

"I hope not," Henry replied, his tone tinged with irony.

"You know also how strong Canterbury has been for the Norman cause in the recent troubles. There are three of us from the abbey of Bec who have held this office in the past one hundred years."

"Yes, yes, I am aware of that. Bec in Normandy has been a marvelous abbey to produce Lanfranc, Anselm and yourself. Anselm, what a scholar."

Henry paused for a moment. "To be brave enough to give counter-arguments to your own philosophy in your writings and then attempt to dispute them. . .that takes courage." Eleanor found herself impressed despite her inclination to be cynical. Either Henry had actually studied Anselm, or he was persuasive enough to convince this churchman that he had, which amounted to the same thing. Perhaps this young husband was more than just a horseman and strong sword arm.

"But what has this to do with today?" Suddenly the king was back in the present, impatient, his moods as slippery as his fingers were searching.

"When Stephen became king, he had some serious faults."

"One of them was underestimating my mother and her rightful claim to the throne of this land." The tone was abrupt. Henry did not want a recap of the twenty years' war for the crown of England now that he had won it.

"Yes, but there were others. He surrounded himself with men who were only acting in their self-interest."

"The barons, Waleran and the Beaumonts, for example," Henry stated. "I'm aware of what went on at that time."

"What you may not have been apprised of," Thibault said, now picking his way carefully with words as the king had stopped pacing and faced him, hands on hips, a bad sign, "is two events that were to prove his undoing."

"Go on," Henry said. "I remain interested in your opinion on history if we can use it to apply lessons for the future."

"The first was my own appointment in 1135 to Canterbury."

"Why was that a mistake?" Henry seemed suddenly on the verge of being amused.

"The seat should have gone to Henry of Blois, Stephen's brother. But Waleran and the Beaumonts were looking out for Bec as it lies in his lands in France, so he persuaded Stephen to name me."

"That put you in a difficult spot, did it not?"

"Not really. I always tread carefully with my brother bishops. But the decision upset Henry of Blois. And it encouraged grumbling among the barons as they jockeyed for position with the king." Now it was Thibault's turn to fiddle with something, taking the poker to the fire as he avoided Henry's keen gaze.

"And Henry of Blois now has the seat at Winchester, which brings him a handsome income, so he must be satisfied."

"Yes, but what happened next is what was really important. The Beaumont brothers over-reached in their desire for control. They set up a fracas to discredit Roger of Salisbury, he who had been your grandfather's chancellor. The king was obliged to ask for his office, for his men disturbed the 'king's peace.' The result was that the chancellery . . .with all its benefits . . . was given over to the barons for distribution to their favorites." Thibault finally looked up as he spoke these words.

Henry and Thibault now faced each other, almost as equals. The archbishop was taller by almost half a head, and the king was obliged to tilt his head somewhat to issue his challenge. Despite that, the king's stance, his voice, his very eyes, maintained his regal superiority. Eleanor watched, fascinated.

"Sire, Roger of Salisbury was the man who made your grandfather's kingdom run. You have often spoken of returning this kingdom to the methods of King Henry, the first of that name. You are right to do so. But I tell you, when the king was absent, he had no more competent vice-regent than Roger of Salisbury and his chancery clerks. Roger was respected, and his destruction and that of his nephews and son, who was replaced as chancellor, was a keen blow to the management of this realm."

"And you want me to know this why?" Henry now seemed remarkably patient; his eyes narrowed as he followed the archbishop's words carefully.

"Because you will form your government right after these Christmas revels have finished. Because I want to be sure your reign will last. Because you need competent men, not political 'new aristocrats' who can scarce write their own name, to run your government for you."

Henry's hearty laugh broke the spell that had fallen over the room, encompassing even Eleanor, still as a squirrel caught watching from a tree. A broad smile spread over Thibault's face as well.

"I take it you have such a man at the ready for me?" he said when he could speak, wiping moisture from his eyes. "That was as neat an introduction as I could have made myself. How could I possibly argue with both history and competence?"

"Yes, Sire, I thought as much," Thibault murmured. "But all true."

"Well, call him in then. I take it he is one of the two men sitting patiently outside the room, waiting." Eleanor was again taken by surprise. Henry missed nothing. More like herself than she had thought.

"Indeed, your majesty." Thibault went to the door but paused with his hand on it. "This man is no stranger to your cause. He was my envoy to Rome when I petitioned Pope Eugenius to prevent the crowning of Stephen's son Eustace. He is learned, but most of all, he is the most competent clerk I have ever met. His father lived near our abbey at Bec in France, and we knew each other when he was young. That's why I agreed to take him into Canterbury a few years ago."

Henry began pacing again. "Yes, yes. I'm certain he will do, Thibault. Call him in."

The archbishop opened the door. "Thomas, please join us."

The tall man with the dark hair and open smile, he of the familiar look, entered the room. He walked with just the proper amount of respect, not too eager but not too subservient, Eleanor judged. And suddenly she remembered why she knew him.

It was long ago in Paris when she had first come from the Aquitaine as Louis's queen, a marriage arranged by their fathers. Bored, lonely and cold that first winter in Paris, she had begged Louis to let her attend the famous Abelard's lectures at the expanding university faculty. She promised to go in disguise as a youth, not as queen. And with trusted companions. Thomas Becket had been there also, young and eager, and challenging Master Abelard whenever he could.

"Thomas is the son of Gilbert Becket, now of London but formerly of Normandy." Thibault was droning on, his voice intruding into Eleanor's thoughts. "Thomas, the king has agreed to take you on as Chancellor when he forms his government after the first of the year."

"Indeed, I have," Henry said, striding forward as Thomas bent his knee. "Please, none of that. If we have such bowing and scraping, we'll never get the Chancery formed and the work done." He took him by the elbow, none too gently, and raised him. "From now on, you work for me."

Henry clapped him on the shoulders and moved to the table, passing his seated wife as he did so. Suddenly mindful of her, the king stopped and made a graceful gesture in her direction. "And this is the queen, Thomas. You will be working with her as well, as she is my regent while I am seeing to things in France."

Thomas again bowed, and Eleanor smiled back, extending her hand. He bent his lips to it and then looked up, but she saw no flicker of recognition in his face.

"Your Grace, Thomas of Becket and I have met before." The queen rose from her stool.

Henry looked up from pouring a goblet of wine. "You have?" Suddenly alert. "Where?"

"In Paris, My Lord," Eleanor said. "At Master Abelard's last lectures. Many years ago."

"Well, well," Henry said, looking from one to the other of them, beaming. "What a coincidence. Is not the world a wonder?"

Part Two: The Friendship
1155–1157

2 January 1155
Bermondsey Palace

Thomas Becket had been waiting some time, but he understood from Thibault when he accepted the assignment that waiting for the king was a hazard of the job. He sat at the large oak table in the king's outer privy chamber and reviewed once more the documents he had been asked to bring. He was shivering. The festivities for the coronation had been followed by the Christmas court, and now Twelfth Night was still in progress. Fires were lit in every chamber, but the stone walls were cold under the tapestries, and truth to tell, Thomas's bones ached with the constant travel from his lodging house in central London to the outskirts and this old, drafty castle.

His reverie was suddenly interrupted by the guards who threw open the double oak doors to the chamber. A servant appeared.

"His majesty, King Henry" was barely out of the man's mouth when Henry strode in, nearly knocking over his herald. He moved quickly to the table, throwing down his gauntlets and shaking the snow off his short, fur-lined cloak as he tossed it to the waiting servant. This poor footman nearly missed the catch, so quick was the movement of the king.

"Thomas! Or perhaps I shall call you Tom. Thanks for coming today. I know it's still Twelfth Night, but the business of state never waits." There was mulled wine on the hearth near the fire, and Henry helped himself as he talked. He gestured to the cup the servants had already provided Thomas, but the new chancellor shook his head.

"I cannot when there is work to be done," he said earnestly. "Your Grace has been hunting?"

"Ah, yes. Since dawn. It stirs the blood in a man. And I have new gerfalcons from Norway, glorious birds! The only birds fit for the use of the king, it is said. A pair of them. They need exercise." He returned to the table and plopped his stocky body into the sturdy oak chair at the head of it, stretching out his legs. "A good morning, too. Five birds for me alone and a dozen in all for my party."

The king eyed Thomas keenly. He saw a tall, thin and suave-looking man, his black hair and startling blue eyes a contrast even in the light of the torches placed everywhere along the walls. His clothing, Henry noted, was of the very latest cut and fabric, the doublet of the new velvet of which Eleanor was so fond. The sleeves were fashionably full and possibly silk. Yes, Henry had heard that his father was rich and a merchant to boot. But he had also been told the man under all that show was a fine scholar, and he hoped that same man would make a good clerk for the king.

"A good morning for you indeed, My Lord," came the rejoinder. Not disrespectful, but not obsequious, either. This was a man whose *amour propre* fit his clothing. Henry became mildly curious about his new chancellor.

"Do you hunt?" he asked, more to see the response than any expectation that Thibault's scholar would ever engage in such activity.

"Oh, yes, My Lord. Indeed, I do," he began, then paused, seeming to rein in his enthusiastic response. "That is, when there is time."

"I thought you'd been locked up at Canterbury abbey these past years. Does Thibault encourage his clerks in such pursuits?" Henry was amusing himself.

"I did not learn hawking at Canterbury," Thomas smiled. "My father often entertained visitors from Normandy, sometimes from other lands, for he was in trade. Some of these men were fine hunters, and they taught me the skill when I was still a lad in school."

"Sometime, then, you must hunt with me." Suddenly Henry sat forward, all business and Thomas straightened as well, assuming a serious expression. The new chancellor had heard that the king held little patience with casual conversations. He was already in awe of the queen, whom he observed constantly smoothing over the ripples caused by the king's abrupt manner.

"I would like that, My Lord," Thomas's rejoinder was simple. He, too, pulled his chair closer to the table and picked up his quill, ready for orders. "I have brought a copy of the charter of your grandfather, King Henry, as you requested."

"Good. Then we shall begin. It is my intention to issue my own charter immediately after Twelfth Night is finished. The people of this realm have lived for nearly twenty years under uncertainty and whiffling policies. Now that I am king, I shall re-establish the law as it was before the lawless took over."

"Yes, your Majesty."

"You, Thomas, are to draft this charter for me. I expect it to be finished by week's end so that I may review it before it is published."

Thomas wasted no time in speech, simply punctuating Henry's words with his own nods. He was writing very fast, taking down the king's own words.

"There are two simple things I want to emphasize in my charter: First, the politics of the land and the ownership and titles are fixed from my grandfather's time."

Now Thomas paused, looking up at the king.

"But that means. . ."

"Indeed. All the titles and land that Stephen gave away to knights to get support are now canceled."

"I see." Thomas already knew better than to express an opinion on this startling news.

Henry rose and began to pace with his customary impatience, talking more to himself than Thomas.

"Men will not give in easily, but they must see that there is a public authority operating here. Once they see that I mean to keep the peace, above all, to root out the causes of warfare that Stephen allowed to flourish, earl against earl, they will come 'round. It must be made clear in my Charter that is my aim here."

"Yes, Sire." Thomas was writing furiously now.

"The second thing is that we shall now have the king's peace in this land, and whosoever breaks that peace will pay the price."

"Yes, Sire." Becket waited.

"Further to the king's peace, be it known that the Fleming mercenaries will all leave the country by Springtide. The people will be glad of it. These foreign men are unruly and cause trouble in the shires."

Thomas tightened his lips to hold back a grin. The king saw it and flashed him a quick look, but without rancour. They both knew that the Flemish had only come at the beck of Henry to aid in his fight with Stephen.

"And further, to the barons that Stephen created and the castles he allowed in order to gain support, we shall specify outright that all the grants and titles given by Stephen are null at my command. Those made barons by Stephen must give up their castles. They belong to the crown. I will decide who may keep what and which castles shall be destroyed."

Thomas took a deep breath and looked up. "Is that wise, Sire?"

Henry stopped pacing and regarded his new chancellor as one might look at an importunate frog. "You spoke, Chancellor?" Henry's questions, like his prayers to the almighty God, were often issued in the form of a challenge. Thomas had been forewarned.

"As chancellor, sire, I need to be able to explain your policies to the barons and earls. I only meant, how can you enforce this last policy? It may mean further war."

"Thomas, do you take me for a fool? Think you that I will have to enforce this edict with the sword?" Henry came round the corner of the table and dropped into his chair. "These barons are Normans. They all own land in Normandy and will want no part of my hostility. I am still duke of Normandy, and they know it well."

"But Sire. . ."

"War and conflict are no part of my intention. We need this charter to set up a legal framework for what will happen next. And I want every baron to understand that he operates at my sufferance. Trust me. They will accept this. There is too much at stake for them."

Henry, his voice was strong now: "Stephen took land from some and gave it to others. I will make it right. I need these local English conflicts settled so I can get back to Normandy and to the Aquitaine, where I must manage those unruly subjects that came to me with my wife." He picked up a paperweight, a polished stone, and turned it over and over in his hand. "I mean to manage all my lands myself, even if it means I never rest."

"Yes, Sire." Becket continued writing, one corner of his mouth still twitching. Either this new, young king was a victim of his own phantasms, or he was a marvel. Only time would tell which.

"And I want a clause in this charter on the relations of the church and the crown."

"What shall such a clause say?" Thomas kept his gaze on his paper this time.

"Umm, say that we intend to return relations of the church and the crown to the status of my grandfather's time." Henry waved his arm. "Leave it suitably vague. We'll sort it out later."

"Yes, My Lord." Thomas could scarce keep himself from shaking his head.

"Finally, I am creating two justiciars who will work with the queen regent in any absence of me from this land."

"Do you want them named, Sire?"

"Yes. Richard de Lucy and Robert of Leicester." He chuckled. "One is competent, the other well born. They should complement each other."

"Is that all, Sire?" Thomas began to gather the sheets he had filled with his fine, clerk's hand.

"No, there are two more items for you, but not related to the charter. First, I want a royal seal struck."

"And what design shall we direct the silversmiths?"

"On one side, I will be martial." Henry eased back in his chair, stretching his legs as he looked up at the ceiling. He stretched his arms and folded his hands behind his head, thinking. Then he smiled with satisfaction. "Yes, I want the people to see a working king."

"And on the other?"

"Show me seated, with the trappings of kingship, a scepter and orb, that sort of thing." Henry's interest was waning. "Think of the stuff at the coronation ceremony. Put something like that together."

"Yes, Sire." Thomas waited a suitable moment. "And you said there was one more thing."

"Yes, yes, there is. The queen is not fond of this drafty castle here at Bermondsey. She feels we should be more accessible to London, and London to us, of course. So we want to move into Westminster before the spring. See to the work yourself so that she doesn't complain when we get there." Henry pushed himself up from his chair with a definitive movement, signaling the conference was ended. He stood with ease for someone who spent so much time on horseback.

"Westminster? Finished in the spring?" Thomas showed, for the first time, an astonished expression on his handsome, regular features. "But My Lord, that is a major project. The palace has been in disrepair since before the civil war."

"I know that, Tom. But you can do it. See the exchequer, du Hommet, for funds once you get an estimate. Let's say you'll have it ready by Whitsuntide." Henry slapped his new chancellor on the shoulder as he passed by him. "Now I'm off to the Twelfth Night revels. The queen has insisted that I attend, and this time she means it."

Thomas sighed and rose. As he finished packing the papers into the leather sack he had brought against the winter snow, he shook his head and sighed. "Yes, Sire."

But the king had not left. He had paused at the door, and when Tom turned, he felt he was being examined by those sharp, grey eyes, moving over the new chancellor from head to toe.

"Well, Tom. A good beginning for us." Henry rubbed his hands, whether against the cold or in satisfaction, Thomas could not be sure.

"Indeed, Sire," he answered with alacrity, nodding to his sovereign.

"Oh, and Tom . . . I want to see the great seal when it is done. But you will be the keeper of it as chancellor. I will give it into your care as I give the heart of my court, the chancery. Better see to your office and, Tom . . ."

The beleaguered clerk paused yet again in his turning as the king continued, ". . . get some help. You will need more clerks than ever Stephen had. He never quite got the hang of governing."

September 1155
King's Forest outside of London

"Du Hommet, what word on the birds? Have we bagged what our falcons have taken?" The king was in good spirits, as he always was when on horseback and losing his giant raptors in the great forest. His great bird was now back, resting on his wrist and hooded once more.

"All done and bagged, Your Grace. You will be pleased at the total today." The chancellor of the exchequer's long, sun-lined face was animated for once. He had been only too happy to accept the invitation of the king to join him in an early morning hunt, where they could discuss matters of the treasury in private.

Du Hommet was older than de Lucy, and not as close to the king in friendship. At nearly thirty-five years of age, he seemed positively mature next to the youthful king and his circle. He was solid and thoughtful, but the long scar down the side of his face testified to his battle experience. He was always happiest when on horseback with the falcons. And his loyalty to the king was never in question.

"Good." Henry turned up to examine the sky. "See there. Those dark clouds are rolling in. We should be off to Whitehall Palace."

"Not Westminster tonight?" Du Hommet was surprised.

"No, I understand Thomas Becket is entertaining again. I thought we'd surprise him."

"Ahh," said the other, his tone noncommittal.

Richard du Hommet had been with Henry since his first attempt to regain his mother's crown when he was only sixteen. The other man had been perhaps ten years older when he signed on to the venture. Henry often sought his advice as that of an older counsellor.

"You are not overfond of Becket, are you, Richard? The king's tone was casual.

Du Hommet shrugged. "Not fond, not hostile." Never one to involve himself in the complicated politics of the chancery, Richard du Hommet saw enough of the chancellor to know they were very different from one another and would never be friends. If the truth were told, he found Thomas Becket a bit too showy for his taste, fond of impressing people. On the other hand, the man seemed to be a hard worker and loyal to the king, so there was no reason to trouble the sovereign with his mild doubts. Besides, he knew the king understood he was a man of few words, so it would not seem untoward if he did not expand on his opinion.

"How is Becket coming along at the chancery, do you think? I know you are in and out of the offices discussing our finances." Henry, riding more slowly now as they left the forest, was not about to let the question drop. Du Hommet was forced to rein in his own horse. "I hear we now have more than fifty clerks working day and night."

"I think that is accurate, Your Grace," du Hommet's tone remained laconic, his eyes fastened on some point straight ahead.

"God only knows what they could be writing," Henry muttered, but du Hommet caught mild amusement in the king's voice.

"I think Your Grace has said himself that your grandfather's government ran well because there were charters in place, and people knew what their rights were and what were the rights of the crown and its representatives in the shires."

"Very good, du Hommet," Henry spoke heartily. There was a pause.

"And how do you think Becket is doing as chancellor?" Henry repeated his question for the third time, stopping his horse and forcing his companion to do likewise. Du Hommet cursed inwardly. He knew Henry's native shrewdness missed nothing, knew all along his question had not been answered. This time there was no avoiding it.

"Your Grace, Becket is an able chancellor for you. In the space of less than a year, he has organized your chancery and found the clerks to write as many charters and proclamations letters to popes as no doubt your majesty can think up." He stopped.

"But . . . ?" Henry pushed. The falcon on his wrist flapped its wings once, sensing the pause.

"What more?" du Hommet shrugged, scanning the sky through the trees as if searching for answers.

"The rest," said Henry simply. "What people say. What they think. Where are the danger points, if any? I need to know, Richard."

Du Hommet nodded. So, it wasn't simply poking about to see if the new favorite had been accepted by the old guard. It was the king, in his usual fashion, checking out the weak spots in the dike, anticipating how much trust to give, how far to let out the line for the canny trout."

"Then I will tell you. His clerks seem to like him well enough, or at least respect him. They grumble about being put two to a chamber the size of a writing closet and not enough fire in the grate as autumn is upon us, but I think they get the work done. I have heard no noise of overt mutiny."

"What else?" Henry's horse Pendragon pawed the ground; no doubt surprised that his rider had been still this long.

"He dresses well, Sire, a bit beyond the station he just came from. He's fond of deep red dyes, and they don't come cheap here in England. Nor the velvets he often chooses."

"But not beyond the Chancellor of England?"

"No." This time du Hommet couldn't hide his toothy smile as he launched a small barb. "Certainly not beyond the keeper of the Great Seal."

"Is there more?"

"He lives well, entertains frequently. Nearly every night his table is laid, and there are a dozen or more important people to fill it. Although, oddly," du Hommet shook his head, "it is said he himself does not eat much but is just engaged in the conversation. To tell you the truth, My Lord," du Hommet paused here.

"—although it pains you to say it," Henry's tone was dry, anticipating a compliment from someone he knew disliked Becket—

"—that Becket does seem to live for his job. He entertains not out of frivolity but so that he can know what is going on in the circles of men that matter in this kingdom. He is always searching for information, opinion, that sort of thing."

"So what troubles you about him, du Hommet?" The king was now most direct because he knew all along his exchequer had reservations.

"How did you—never mind," said the knight. "All right, then, Sire. Here is my concern. He is too much a part of his role. He has no other life. No women, no wife or mistress, no children. Nothing that ordinary people concern themselves with."

Henry flicked his riding crop restlessly against his leg. "You could say the same for military men. You and I have been on a dozen campaigns already, and I am not yet thirty summers. You are not much older. Look how focused we both were then. On Stephen when he was intent on keeping the throne of England. On Louis right now in France, absorbed by the Vexin. On the roustabout nobles in the queen's lands in the south. To be single-minded is often productive."

"But when the fighting's over, we have other lives. Court life. Family and friends. Women and love. Politics. I swear, it's only that last that interests Thomas Becket. He's like a goddam monk."

"Hah," Henry said, at last loosening the reins of his horse, and turning him back to the road, ready for a swift ride. "God's blood. Here's a thought! So then. Let's take ourselves to Thomas's table and see how elegant the conversation is tonight."

Henry spurred his horse and reached the road in a matter of minutes. There the band of men who had been hunting with the king waited patiently. Du Hommet, a fine horseman in his own right, was hard-pressed to keep up as they all galloped behind their sovereign. But no one knew what the king was thinking.

And so, Thomas. You live for your work, do you? Well done work, it seems. Still, England is all to you? So soon after your assignment? It's true, I've seen the change myself over the past months. Your tall, ascetic form straightening up with power, the slight stoop you displayed in our first meeting gone. You give orders, you know they will be obeyed. Everyone knows the king stands behind you. You know your business. You have organized my chancery well. And I trust you. Our destinities are intertwined.

Some hours later
The Whitehall Palace, Westminster
Residence of Thomas Becket

The servants appeared startled to see the king, unmistakable with the royal insignia on his accoutrements, clatter up the steps of White Hall Palace and ride directly into the Great Hall, du Hommet on horseback right behind him. The others of the group dismounted outside and gave their horses to the grooms who appeared from the shadows in the mews.

Henry, laughing and talking over his shoulder to du Hommet, rode directly toward the table, which was spread in a large, open square directly in front of the roaring fire. The nearly thirty barons and merchants seated around the table looked up, astonished, from their dinner. All conversation ceased. Henry cantered into the center of the gathering and swung easily from his horse. Du Hommet, who had some sense, paused at the outside of the arrangement and slid down, throwing his reins to the groom who had just taken the king's bridle.

Becket, seated at the center of the longest table, had looked up when the noise first reached him. He rose quickly to greet the king, who had slid to the ground and was approaching him, hand out in greeting. Suddenly everyone at the table were on their feet, and there was a great commotion of welcome. Becket reached across the table and offered his hand to the king. Henry, with a grace that belied his bowed legs and stocky body, placed his hand on the table and vaulted over to stand in front of Thomas Becket. He clapped his chancellor on the shoulder and shouted over the uproar: "How now, Tom? I hear you keep a lavish table. Is there still food left for your king?"

Becket was smiling, but he was not laughing. Though he struggled to hide it, the unexpected spectacle the king had created clearly did not please him.

"Your majesty," Becket finally found his voice. "How good of you to join us!" This last, with some effort on his part, at least had the ring of welcome.

"Yes, yes. I hear so much about your table, Thomas, and have had so little time to sample your cuisine myself." The seat next to Becket had been quickly vacated, and the chancellor made a graceful gesture toward it even as the king was already seating himself.

"My Lord, I've often told you. The seat next to me will always belong to you should you choose to take it." Becket called for wine for the king and a basin and water so he could wash his hands. The nicety was not lost on Henry, who could be quite formal when it was a question of respect.

"Sire, I believe you know my guests. Henry, bishop of Winchester. Waleran Beaumont and his brother Roger, the earl of Chester and their cousin."

Thomas progressed around the table, leaving out no one, careful to name the title of each as if the king might not remember the man without the office. But of course, Henry did remember, not only every man there but when, exactly, each of them had deserted the sinking ship of Stephen's reign and come over to the side of the Angevins. Although he always seemed dismissive of politics, Henry forgot very little of real importance.

When he was finished, Henry noted dryly, "And I believe all of you know du Hommet, my Chancellor of the Exchequer." There were some embarrassed nods. Most of the nobles at that table had borrowed from the crown at some point or other.

"Your majesty," Thomas began, as the king's wine cup was filled and the joint of roast venison brought forward to him, "we were just talking of affairs in Normandy."

"Were you so?" Henry could make even a rhetorical question sound like a challenge. None of the men present could pretend to have his confidence. "And what were your thoughts, bishop?" He turned to Henry of Winchester, former bishop of Blois, brother of the late King Stephen.

"Your majesty, Sire, I have no opinion on Normandy." The bishop of Winchester, one of the most politically astute men of his time, gazed at his king openly, his face innocence itself. He spread his hands as if inviting a prayer and murmured, "I'm a simple churchman, Sire. Affairs of state remain a mystery to me."

There was a moment of silence. Then the king burst into laughter so hearty that the entire company joined him, even, finally, the bishop of Winchester himself. Such a patently silly answer had broken the ice, and everyone was delighted to see the king in such good humor.

Early May 1156
On the King's ship sailing from Southampton to Barfleur

The king leaned his elbow on the rail of the ship and watched the coastline of England recede as they sailed out into the channel. Thomas Becket stood beside him. The king spoke quietly.

"I always watch as the land moves away from us, Tom. I want to witness it and to remember, to carry with me that picture."

Becket was astonished at his monarch's meditative statement, but then the king continued, and Becket was reassured that the king was, indeed, still himself.

"It's the movement forward or backward that gives me life, Tom. Knowing that I'm leaving, but that I'm coming back. The same for the Normandy coast when I set sail for England. My movements are the bond between the two now."

"Indeed, Sire. You speak the truth." The chancellor leaned further out over the water, but all sight of land had disappeared. Only the gulls that dipped and dived and squawked gave evidence that land had been there. "But I'm still not sure why you wished me to accompany you on this trip to Normandy."

"Ah, fretting over how the chancery will get its work done while you are away?" Henry clapped Becket on the shoulder. "I want you to see Normandy and understand the way we Normans govern. You are my close advisor. A fortnight in Normandy at my side is essential for you. After that, you can return to England." He paused, then added, "You see, I have plans."

"You honor me, Sire." Becket turned to the king, ignoring the spray coming up from the water as the ship gained wind. "I am but a humble scholar still learning the business of the chancery."

"Nonsense, Thomas. We both know better. You were made for this work." Henry gestured toward the small cabin door. "Come, we'll have a game of chess while the men work the sails against this wind. I've ordered hot mulled wine in the hold."

Henry's cheeks were still ruddy from the ride he had forced them all to make from Winchester early that morning.

"Do you never sit still, Sire?" Becket asked, following the king into his comfortable redoubt. A table stood nailed to the floor in the middle of the small space. Carved oak chairs, well cushioned, surrounded it and a board with chess pieces sat inviting play. Becket noted that the chess pieces were tagged to the board by slight pegs, allowing play even when the ship was rolling about. The invention of the pegs was obviously one of Henry's delights, as he gestured to the board by touching one of them.

The only other furnishings were two cots along the sides beneath extra quivers of arrows stored on wooden shelves. Windows gave a view outside to the bleak, grey weather, clouds forming in the west and waves chopping around the boat. A lone candle sputtered on the table, held fast by metal brackets against the movement of sailing.

"At least we're sheltered from the wind here." Becket gave his cloak a look of distaste as he threw it onto a chair. It had become spattered with mud on their gallop through the Sussex countryside.

"Finding the task of accompanying your king challenging?" Henry was evidently amused at the expression on Tom's face. "All that work in the Chancery is making you soft, Tom." The king poured wine for both of them.

"Henry, I've always been soft," Thomas replied, his good humor equaling the king's. They had established this rapport in such a short time, this friendship in which the king allowed his chancellor the right to call him by his given name when they were in private. "That's why you made me chancellor. It's perfect for me."

"And why, exactly, is that?" Henry threw himself into his broad carved oak chair with such force that the chair was in danger of tipping over, but the king took no notice.

"I can read and write, and I don't like taxing horseback journeys!" Becket sat straight and tall, with more elegance than his monarch, and faced him across the table.

"But you do like chess. That I know." Henry made the first move as he said this, moving a pawn forward. "And you are very skilled in it."

Thomas took a long moment and then moved his own piece to face the king's.

"Tom," Henry suddenly looked up. "Have you ever thought of what you might be if you were not you? If you could choose what to be?"

The chancellor was caught, his hand hovering over his bishop. He dropped his hand, frowning. "No, Sire. Never. Why would I?"

"Just wondering." Henry sat back in his chair and looked out the window to his side.

"Have you pondered such a thing?" Becket did not make his next move on the board but followed the king's gaze.

"Yes, I have. And more than once," Henry said, all trace of levity banished from his voice.

"And what was your conclusion? What would you be if you were not Henry, King of England and Duke of Normandy?" Becket was genuinely curious now. He propped his chin on his hand, his elbow jostling a bishop slightly.

"I'd be a peasant, Tom. Pure and simple." Henry turned from the window and gave his chancellor a long look. "Such a life appeals to me more than all of this," and with a sweep of his arm, Henry seemed to go beyond the ship to the lands that bordered the channel.

"I would not have thought it," Becket said. A seagull flew into the window, fell back, then gained his wings again and flew off. Both the king and the chancellor were silent for a long moment.

"Only consider, Tom. The peasant behind the plow is in the sun all day, takes plenty of exercise, becomes strong and self-reliant and has no other duties. At night he takes his woman to bed and satisfies himself. The next day, it begins all over again."

"Unless it's raining, Sire." Becket gave a snort of laughter. "Or the food runs short. Or the peasant's lord goes to war, and soldiers run over your land and take your wife. I think you have a fine idea of the life of the peasant, based in fantasy and not as things are." He fastened his attention on the chessboard once more.

"That's as may be, Tom. But the crown is heavy, and there is never a minute when I am free from worry. You have the right of it, though. It is but a fantasy I have created to amuse myself." The king, too, returned to the board, pursed his lips in thought, but then looked up. "The burden of state and the welfare of its people never leave me. I can never rest."

Then he moved, this time a bishop. The game was entering a new phase. "I do not often speak so freely, Tom. It is a mark of my trust that I can do so with you."

"Sire, I am honored," Becket murmured, stroking his chin as he considered his options on the board.

"But come now, I've shared my dream, silly as it is. What about you? You must have some idea of what other place in life you would have if you had your choice," Henry wheedled. "Who would you trade places with? What would it be."

Becket looked up, and a brilliant smile spread across his face. "Why, Sire. I seize wholeheartedly upon any role fortune offers me. Hence, at this moment, I am completely fulfilled as your chancellor. There is room for no other dream."

At this statement, Henry erupted into a series of guffaws that shook the table. He spoke when he could catch his breath. "The perfect answer for a chancellor and a diplomat, Tom. It's as you said at the beginning of the game here. And I am so happy that it was I who appointed you, my friend, to your current role!"

Becket joined in the laughter; his chuckles more restrained than the king's. In truth, he did not quite see the humor in what he had said.

Part Three: The Strains

1157 April
Southampton, England

"Good of you to come to Southampton to welcome Us, Tom, but not necessary."

The king had been jovial in his greetings at first when he saw Becket among the cluster of men come to welcome him back from Normandy. Becket stood beside de Lucy and Leicester, the king's appointed justiciars and, together with Queen Eleanor, Regent, the only officers higher than the chancellor. The king embraced his leadership team warmly, as soldiers were wont to do with their comrades, and he made no exception for Thomas. They had not seen each other since the trip to Normandy a year earlier, and the chancellor had returned to England after only a few weeks, as planned.

But Henry had been away from England for a full year, and that was a long time to be gone. As the little group rode toward London, Becket managed to stay at Henry's side, eager for an opportunity to lay out his suggested reforms not only for the chancery but also for the whole structure of the government. He had developed these plans while the king was away. At first, the king was impatient, not interested, but gradually he began to listen. He grew more thoughtful as Becket embellished on his suggestions.

The English winter was reluctant to release its hold on the countryside, and, when his people came out to meet the little group on horseback, Henry saw the harsh effects of the long season. The ground was still too frozen for planting, food was scarce, and his subjects looked thin and ragged.

The two men rode across the London Bridge together and into the dense lanes of the city. They made a startling contrast in appearance. Henry, the king, was in his stained traveling clothes, doublet under a somewhat ragged cloak against the April winds. He was unshaven from his journey and, as usual, totally uncaring about his appearance. Becket, the chancellor, had improved on his cleric's clothes mightily, wearing a cloak and hood lined in fur. Even his gloves, which were of the finest Belgian leather, silently rebuked his master's torn gauntlets.

In the last hour, Henry had become very quiet, listening to Becket's earnest suggestions. His expression grew somber, almost mournful. This was a mood that Becket, even in their brief acquaintance, had learned to fear. Finally, the chancellor ceased his stream of recommendations and waited for some response. The king's comment on Becket's suggestions, when it came, was stiff.

"Let me be certain that I understand what you have just said to me, Chancellor. You think it is unnecessary to have the justiciars, that you can handle the business of the crown when I am away? That's what I understood you to say in your roundabout, learned way."

"Sire, when you put it that way, it sounds impertinent. What I actually said was . . ."

"What you actually said was the justiciars were an extra layer of government when the queen was regent and could be dispensed with, leaving only you, carrying out my orders, and the queen to oversee all. Is that not accurate?" Henry barked the last sentence, and Becket took a long breath before he replied.

"In essence, yes, Sire." He sighed. No arguing with the king when he was in his black temper. Becket only prayed the conversation would not get worse, or at the least not louder. He looked around for help. If only de Lucy would ride forward.

"I don't think you understand the system I am trying to set up here, Chancellor." As long as the king used his title rather than his name, the tenor of the conversation would remain charged. The horses picked their way through the slush of the city as Thomas averted his eyes from the king.

"I am not setting up an absolute authority. I am trying to decentralize. It's the only way to manage this land, especially when I can't be here. I've been on the continent for a year trying to settle things down. You should take a turn at an attempt to calm Eleanor's vassals in the south. They're a bunch of unruly thugs, as far as I can see. But I must try."

"But Sire, we could make everything so much simpler, to flow like a brook here, if we didn't have all those court hearings, those juries you insist on, the appeals."

"Chancellor," now Henry pulled up his horse and the entire group behind him, even the stragglers, also stopped. "The basis of everything is the shire and a hundred, the administrative divisions We have set up to collect taxes and mete out justice. The sheriffs handle the local problems and collect the taxes. But there must be a system of appeal. And that's where the justiciars come in. You manage the Chancery, they manage the justice system, and du Hommet and the Exchequer staff manage the taxes. We are not about to relinquish that system until We see that it does not work."

"Yes, Sire." Becket gave up. "Of course, you are correct."

"Of course I am," the king repeated, kneeing his horse to go forward. "Then let's hear no more of dispensing with the justiciars. Now, Tom, I must say things are going well for you in my absence. Your cloak, for example. It's new. You must have replaced the one caked in mud that you discarded in my cabin last year." Henry moved his horse closer to Becket's. "I have envied this cloak since I stepped off the boat from Barfleur."

Becket felt a flush rising to his cheeks and hoped the king would put it down to the sharp April wind. "Your Grace is welcome to the cloak. I hadn't thought. . ."

"No, no, I wouldn't deprive you of your cloak. I can have one made if I choose." A light freezing drizzle had started, but a few hardy souls had braved the weather to catch a glimpse of their sovereign and his entourage. They lined the road as the king and his men rode past. Henry pointed to an old man propped up against a stile, huddled against the wind. "But look at that poor fellow over there, dressed in rags and barely that. He looks neigh on to freezing in this sleet."

"He does indeed, Sire. Shall I have one of the servants fetch him a cloak from the baggage?" Becket half turned on his horse to call one of the servants.

"No, wait, friend Tom." Henry put a hand on his arm. "I don't think he should have just any cloak. I think you should give him yours."

"Mine?" Becket swung around, incredulous. "You want me to give him my cloak?"

"Yes, think what it would mean to him." Henry's eyes twinkled with mischief. "Not just any old cloak from the baggage train, but a fine cloak. One that will keep him warm all the winters of his life."

"But Sire, I had this cloak made especially for the occasion of your return. It is valuable." Becket was backing his horse away from his king, but Henry moved right with him.

"*Certes*, Tom. That is what makes the gift so much more pleasing to the Almighty." Henry began to tug on the ties of the cloak and they loosened. Becket was protesting now, forgetting Henry was king, pulling the cloak back toward himself even as Henry's strong grip was pulling apart the silken cords that held the garment on Becket's shoulders. "Come, now, Tom. An act of charity. Not so much to ask."

De Lucy and FitzStephen and the others had drawn forward to see what the fuss between the two men was about. They watched the horseplay, but no one dared to interfere. Was it serious? Was the king angry? What was Becket thinking to defy the king, no matter how fond of him the king appeared to be?

Finally, Henry had the cloak, swirling it triumphantly around before he cantered over to the bent figure of the old man who had drifted into the side of the stone house alongside the lane. The villein cowered against the wall as the king approached, not knowing who he was or what a gentleman on such a fine horse wanted with him. He was shaking now, expecting to be made fun of, or worse, by this company of lords. All could see it.

Henry threw down the rich cloak upon him. "Here, old man. This is a gift from the Chancellor of England. He sees your plight and wishes to alleviate your suffering. He is willing to give you his very own cloak against this bitter wind. Wear it in good health."

By the time Henry regained the center of his group, Becket had appeared to have recovered his equanimity. He was even chuckling. A groom rode up with another cloak from the baggage train, not so fine but warm enough.

"Well, My Lord, you certainly won that battle." He quipped. "You must have sharpened your fighting skills on those southern nobles last autumn."

The king's good humor had been restored by his prank, and he jostled Becket's horse as he rode close enough to give him an affectionate slap on the back. "It's always easier to take something off a man if he doesn't have a sword at the ready. But cheer up, Tom. We are only minutes away from Westminster, and I'll wager the queen has ordered fires in every chamber for us." Then, as if in afterthought, he turned again to his friend, "And I'll find a cloak for you to finish your journey out of my own garderobe."

"That's what I fear, your majesty," Becket tossed back, "you well know what I think of your wardrobe." Henry guffawed loudly. The group rode together the last two miles, the talking subdued, and all were relieved the king had been having sport and not angry at all.

1157–1161
April 1157, some hours later
Westminster Palace Nursery

The king never simply entered a room: he made an entrance. He was always accompanied by his closest advisors and today was no exception. Richard de Lucy, du Hommet, William FitzStephen, Robert of Leicester, as usual, they all clustered around him. The men he trusted. And he was forever engaged with them while walking, to the point where some of them—absorbed in the king's words—would inadvertently trip on the uneven stones of the castle passages.

At the moment the nursery doors were flung open to admit him, the king was leading a discourse on the morals of war. His new favorite, Peter of Blois, monk, chronicler, and a recent transplant from Normandy, was thoroughly engaged with him in argument. Something Henry said in response to a comment from Peter led to a boisterous laughter from the others just as the group entered the chamber.

Eleanor turned at the noise. She had been watching the fire from a low, well-cushioned bench with a strong back. The dance of the flames was lulling her and she was almost dozing, although her hands kept a firm hold on the infant lying on its back in her lap, her head on the queen's knees and her little legs propped upward on her breasts. The mother was softly humming and rocking the baby back and forth.

The arrival of the busy group of men startled the queen. Fully awake now, she turned back to the fire. Although she had not seen her husband for three months, it was not her style to make a fuss.

"Where is the queen?" barked the king impatiently, as if the nursery attendants were hiding her from him. One of the women, stuttering, pointed in the direction of the fire. The lead servant bustled in and, after bowing, ushered the group toward the fire.

But at this point, Henry waved off his coterie of followers. They were meant only to accompany him so far, they suddenly realized. With mumbled good-byes, they took their leave one by one, only de Lucy lingering, until the king turned from him and approached his lady.

She looked up as she heard his step and gestured at the babe on her lap as an excuse not to rise. He leaned down and gave her a perfunctory kiss on the cheek, then slid down onto the bench with a grunt.

"A rough crossing, My Lord?" Queen Eleanor asked with a smile. Henry was indefatigable on horseback, but he was not a good sailor, and the constant trips across the channel to attend to his continental domains could make him tired and crabby. It was her private joke to tease him whenever he had to take a ship in boisterous weather. "If you weren't so impatient, you might have waited for clear weather to make your crossing. April is never calm."

"Ahh, Eleanor. Do not start. You know I hate sitting around in Barfleur waiting for the Almighty God to pay attention to my prayers for good weather. We've not had a boating accident yet. And you know we've sailed in every kind of rough weather." The king opened his broad hand and ran it across his eyes as if to wipe away the memory of all his difficult crossings from Normandy.

They suddenly looked at each other, but neither spoke for a moment. They had the same thought, as so often happened between them. The white ship. The fatal accident on the channel that took the life of young William Audelin, the son of Henry the First and uncle to Henry of Anjou. The man who should have been king, Mathilda's brother. It was the loss of his life that led to the decades of war between Stephen and Mathilda for the throne. Both Henry and Eleanor knew that kind of accident could happen again at any time.

"But now, my dear Elle, how are you?" He turned to her with a softness of tone, the habit of abrupt change that marked all his interactions and that still disconcerted her, even after five years of marriage. "And the babes? Where is little Henry?" He suddenly looked around as if his heir had been misplaced, not right there to greet him.

"In bed, My Lord, where he belongs at this hour!" Eleanor replied tartly. She was both amused and irritated when he addressed her as Elle, a shortening of the English version of her true name, Alia Aenor. She had been named for her own mother, Aenor, but the English did not seem to be able to cope with that southern and Roman name. Elle was also the word for "she" in French, which she suspected was a private joke of his. Still, he always used it with affection, and it often signaled his amorous intentions. Not so tired tonight, after all, she thought.

They looked at each other quietly in the flickering fire for a long moment. The king had thrown his arm across the back of the bench, and she leaned against it for the moment. All of the travels she had endured in the past three years since their coronation as sovereigns of England, the births of her three babes, the death of their son little William only the year before, the journeys with Henry tearing through her own lands of the south to quell her unruly nobles, all of these memories faded. She looked into his square face, still youthful despite a few lines that had gathered around the eyes, the freckles illuminated by the lively fire, the grey eyes she knew so well, and she was—for the moment—content.

"Well, my love. We must go to your chamber soon." Henry had no sooner spoken these words when little Mathilda woke and began to scream. He suddenly stood and beckoned the wet nurse over, who quickly took the little princess from Eleanor's arms. The mood was broken for the moment.

"I have some affairs I want to discuss with you," Henry said, pacing behind the bench. Since Eleanor showed no signs of rising, he stayed within earshot, but still, his restless temperament began to fill her space, making her weary.

"I thought we would meet tomorrow with the justiciars and go over the affairs of England at that time." She considered just rising and moving toward her chambers, but the swell of feelings she had just experienced was quickly dissipating under Henry's rapid-fire commentary. It seemed almost more restful to stay where she was and endure his energetic plans.

"Louis and I have been getting along so well ever since I did homage for the northern duchies and for yours as well." He turned, aware that he was moving out of range of her hearing.

"I know that, Henry," she pointed out. "My interest in the politics of France and the continent are focused on your relations with my former husband."

"Of course you know," he waved his hand. "I'm just reviewing the situation so you'll understand where my thoughts are on making that relationship permanent."

"What do you mean?" The queen turned to him, now somewhat alarmed. The further she and Henry stayed from her former husband, the king of France, the better off she thought they would be, the homage ritual notwithstanding. "I thought you said that was a political necessity. Now you want a closer relationship with France?"

"Ah, my dear, hear me out." Henry flopped back onto the cushions beside the queen. "I think this idea will please you. After all, you were the one who first suggested it to me."

Eleanor frowned. "I cannot recall ever saying I thought it was a good idea for you and Louis to become fraternal!"

"Ahh, but you did. And it was the moment you said it that I knew our lives were entwined. You have the dreams, and I have the force."

The queen was now fully engaged in Henry's words, leaning forward to listen. "Henry, do stop that pacing and come and sit down and speak plainly."

The king pulled up a stool in front of his wife and perched on it. He was grinning with pleasure to remind his wife of her thoughts from long ago.

"You know Louis has a daughter from his marriage to Constance of Castile?" Henry propped his torso on his elbow, intent, focused on the queen as an archer on the target.

"Yes, I heard the news when the birth occurred. It must be almost two years ago now. Poor Louis. Still searching for a son." Eleanor's smile was not entirely sympathetic.

"Well," Henry was rubbing his hands together in his usual gesture of pleasure at some political news, "His 'superfluity of daughters,' as he calls it, may be our good fortune."

"In what way?" Eleanor's face was lined with puzzlement.

"You must have forgotten, Eleanor. It was you who first proposed the idea when we met the day of our nuptials."

"The idea that . . ."

"Yes, indeed, my love. We have a son, and he has a daughter. The little one, Marguerite, would be the perfect match for young Henry. And Louis has led me to believe he would favor the marriage." Henry laughed, a booming sound that echoed throughout the nursery chambers. Somewhere behind closed doors, a babe suddenly cried, but the sound was quickly smothered by the nursemaids.

"So I did. That seems so long ago. I had put the idea aside in the press of so many other things." The queen paused. "What do your justiciars think? De Lucy and du Hommet?" Eleanor was rapidly digesting this idea. Conflicting emotions flitted across her face, half smile and half frown now. Marry her son to Louis's daughter? Would they have to get a dispensation from Pope Alexander? The pope would surely see it as another in a long line of outrageous Angevin ideas. And the emperor, how he would smolder at this alliance. Suddenly, picturing the astonishment in the courts of Europe to this plan caused her to dissolve in laughter.

"I can't wait to hear the news of the emperor's curses when he sees a new marriage alliance of his powerful opponents."

"Becket thinks this is a good idea also. I discussed it with him riding up from Southampton."

"You've already told Becket?" Eleanor's laughter faded. "Why would you tell him before discussing it with me?"

"The man's got a damn good head on his shoulders. We rode most of the way down from Suffolk together. I was thinking out loud with him. I tired of hearing his recommendations for simplifying the justice system and introduced this as another topic." Henry was sitting forward on the bench, but he turned his head in his wife's direction. "What is it about Becket you don't like."

"It isn't that I don't like him, Henry." The queen heard her own tone, sharper than intended, and she softened somewhat. "I know he runs your chancery well and that he is very intelligent."

"Is he disrespectful of you as regent when I'm abroad in our lands over the channel?"

"No, on the contrary. He is almost too respectful."

"Meaning what?"

"I can't get an answer out of him on anything before he thinks about it. It's as if he is afraid to offend me in some way."

"That's a damn site better than not paying attention to you. So, what is your reservation?"

"I don't know. He's too political. Too calculating, if you will." Eleanor bit her lip. "You know, I watched him in Paris when we were in Abelard's class."

"Go on. I'm intrigued." Henry sat back, catching his knee with his hands, winding his other foot around the legs of the stool. He looked as if he could comfortably endure a long story, should the queen choose to tell it.

"He had a good mind. He was very smooth in his attack on the master. But attack it was."

"What do you mean by attack?"

He challenged the master often, almost as if he needed to prove he was as intelligent as Abelard. The master was older in those years, near the end. He always rose to the occasion, but it seemed to me, and to those sent with me, that Becket felt a need to kill him."

"Kill him? Did he ever threaten him?" Now Henry sat bolt upright.

"No, you misunderstand my meaning. Not physically. Not in the body. But to prove himself, Becket seemed to need to prove Abelard was less in the discourse between them."

"And who won?" Henry asked, cocking his head to one side. The two candles on the table behind him sputtered, coming to the end of their tapers.

"I cannot say," the queen said quietly. "The winning was not important, it seemed to us. Only the battle."

"But why do you tell me this now?

"You confide in him?" The queen had unwittingly been using her hands, moving them in a rolling motion. The king, distracted by the movement, glanced down at them. "And now you consult him on matters of our children before me? Can you really trust him as you trust me?"

"My love, there is no one before you," Henry said soothingly, moving to sit beside her. He placed one large hand on the back of her neck while with his other, he covered her two hands as if to put them to rest. "And there will never be anyone before you. I only consulted him on our journey tonight because he has an interesting mind. I assure you, it was entirely casual."

The queen sighed. The king pulled her to him and planted a long and passionate kiss on her lips. She resisted slightly.

"Don't worry. I know where I place my trust. It is always with you first."

"My Lord, I thank you."

The king rose and held out his hand. "The best way you can thank me is to move with me to your bed chamber."

Before dawn, the next morning
The King's bedchamber

God's teeth, it's good to be back in my own bed. Good thing I'm still young. Body's starting to show the wear, though. Countless hours on horseback, hard to stand when it's over.

Elle, Elle, what a woman. Magnificent in every way. Formidable, as my mother would say. Maybe the equal of Mathilda. Huh, my mother would not like to hear that she has an equal. But it's true. I married for land, but I married well.

I'm doing better in bed with her than I am with her vassals on land. God's holy blood, what is the trouble with those Poitivens? I think the dukes, those vaunted ancestors of Elle's, held the reins too loosely. And when she was married to Louis, no one was paying attention at all. They were all bundled up in Paris. Did he ever go there? Must have. But still, those southern petit nobles all think they can do whatever they like. Pay homage to me as their overlord? Not the counts and viscounts of the south. At some point, we shall have to show force to bring them to heel.

But not yet. There is more to do in Normandy first. And I've been away from England far too long.

Great idea to marry young Henry to Louis's new daughter. Talk about cementing relationships. If he never has a son, and it looks like he won't, my sons—mine and Eleanor's—will rule France along with England and Normandy . . . and the recalcitrant south, no matter what they think now about their independence, must fall into line.

I think Louis will accept the idea of this marriage. She didn't like it when I said I'd told Tom first.

And what she said tonight about him in Paris. Always bucking authority. Maybe that is his soul. Wonder how well they knew each other all those years ago? Comes with marrying an older woman, I suppose.

Bah. Ridiculous. She was only seventeen. Bored in damp, cold Paris with a husband who should have been a monk instead of a king. That was all it was. Still, anything's possible.

What Elle doesn't know is that Thibault also suggested the marriage alliance between Louis and me the day of my coronation. Old Thibault. He didn't hold on to the post of archbishop of Canterbury all those years without having the wiles of a fox. He could see the advantages. A Byzantine way of thinking he has, like the politics of the sultans, to create a plan linking my family to Louis through the children, France and England together forever in the future. And with Normandy and the Aquitaine, the first empire in Europe. I'll bring Ireland in, too. It's just a matter of time. If I live! Aah, I can feel all that riding in my back.

Tom, a valuable man. Intelligent. A dandy for certain. But he's ambitious. Like his suggestion that I rid myself of the justiciars. What was he thinking? So he would be sole regent when Eleanor comes with me to the continent? The chancellor unchecked, running the country? This land still moans from Stephen's war with my mother. Chancellor Becket might finish it off, left to his own devices. Yes, a smart man who loves power. A dangerous man. But possibly my most valued counsellor. As long as he remembers who is king.

Henry turned on his side and willed himself into slumber.

April 1157, the next morning *Westminster Palace*

The queen did not wait to be announced but flung wide the doors herself, striding like Henry himself into the smaller of the council chambers. Her anger was apparent from her first words, her hands spread wide, already in argument. Her feeling filled the room and stopped the discussion. De Lucy trailed behind her, tall and apologetic, shrugging in the direction of his king.

"You said nothing last eve about convening this council nor about your leave-taking so soon from this palace. Why was I not informed? As Regent while you were away, I should have proper notice." She walked right up to Henry, her accusations preceding her like arrows. The king rose so as to be equal in height when she came near.

"Madame, you did not ask my plans last evening. You know they change frequently. I have received an urgent message early this morning, and I must not tarry here. I have business to settle in Bury St. Edmonds." He gestured to the carved and cushioned oak chair that footmen had hurriedly placed for her next to the king, removing the smaller one du Hommet had just vacated. "And, anyway, did I not send de Lucy just now to summon you to this very meeting?"

"And ill-prepared am I for it," she snapped, nevertheless seating herself beside the king, and carefully arranging the folds of her gown around her. "But continue. I wish to hear your council."

She scanned the table briefly. De Lucy, whom she liked best, had resumed his former seat, his tanned, thin face showing just a hint of his amusement at the royal couple's verbal *jeu de palme*. She suppressed a smile herself, her irritation fading. De Lucy was the only one of the king's close counsellors that both royals liked. He was straightforward and honest with her at all times. And when, as this very morning, he was placed in an impossible situation, of course Henry had sent him to fetch her—he always acted with respect, never excusing Henry, never criticizing either the queen or king to each other.

Unlike Leicester, who sat glowering at the end of the table, his thick neck pulling his heavy face further into the scarf he had wrapped around his throat. His nose was red, the queen noticed, so he was ill again. That would not improve his irascible disposition.

Nevertheless, she had to admit to herself that, as justiciar, Leicester had worked well with her in Henry's absence. Young, blonde FitzStephen sat next, his open, ruddy face almost a mirror of the king's own freckled countenance, except for the open part, she thought. She often thought Henry favored that young man because he reminded him of his own younger brothers, Geoff and William. Next to FitzStephen sat Peter of Blois, balding, round-from-head-to-toe cleric and Henry's new favorite, scribbling away as the men talked. Henry, who was all action, had suddenly taken a liking to having a record of these meetings. He must have a reason, she thought.

Finally, her gaze landed on Becket at the foot of the table, and he returned her questioning look. They rarely spoke except to do the business of the crown when Henry was away. He had acquitted himself admirably as chancellor, she had to admit, at least to all appearances, but there was still something unsettling in his demeanor toward her.

Memories of Paris crowded in, even as she half listened to the various voices around the table. She had been so young and so bored in her first winter as queen of a cold, damp Paris. When she heard the famous Master Abelard was to lecture again, she pressed Louis like a badger into letting her attend his sessions. All the world knew of Abelard's famous love affair twenty years earlier and the punishment of castration that had been visited on him by the guardian of his beloved Heloise for his carnal sins.

But, *mirabile dictu*, here he was, back teaching in his old age. Eleanor had desired to attend class just to see what such a man as Abelard looked like: a man who gave up all for love.

And in those classes she first encountered the handsome, dark-haired, smooth-talking young Thomas of Becket, regularly challenging his master's argument but never crossing the line into impertinence. A neat approach, she thought. A diplomat's talent. The same talent he employed so well with Henry.

"Perhaps the queen would favor us with her opinion, Sire," Becket said, looking at Eleanor.

A favorite trick Eleanor had learned when young was to wait a moment for the question to echo in her memory when caught unawares as she had just been. Oh, yes, it was about the conference at Bury St. Edmonds.

"I think the king has the right of it," she said slowly. "His judgement in these matters has been proven many times." She was struggling to remember why the meeting was so important.

Henry turned to look at her, a grin playing just below the surface of his assumed grave expression. He was peeling an apple with his poignard, the skin rolling onto the table in one long strip.

"Madame, you do me great honor," he said.

"But Sire, with respect, I disagree. If you handle these two powerful lords with such discipline, you could foment more problems in East Anglia," Thomas said, his gaze focused on the king.

"Listen to me, Thomas," Henry said in clipped tones. "There are already problems fomenting in East Anglia. That is the point of this meeting. I can't be everywhere at once, but I can enforce my royal prerogatives to try to straighten out the mess Stephen left. He let these barons build castles everywhere. In East Anglia, his by-blow, William of Blois, now William de Warrenne thanks to his marriage, and Hugh Bigod, think they can keep these castles and fortify them against me should they so choose. These are the last two holdouts of all the barons. They need to understand. This practice of castle-building and private armies will stop now." And the king stabbed his poignard into the table to emphasize his words.

"But Sire, if you exert the heavy royal hand against these two powerful men, how do you know the next time you leave for the continent, disaffection will not break out again?" The chancellor held on to the dialogue like a dog pulling on a bone. The others glanced nervously at one another. How long would the king stand for this?

"Well, Thomas, I'm surprised your diplomatic skills have not presented you with the obvious answer." Henry sat back in his heavy chair. "As I told you years ago when I ordered you to prepare the original writs, I shall re-grant most of the castles back to the lords. And they know it. But after that, they hold them at my royal suffrance."

The men at the table fell silent. Henry's strong-arm policies just might work. And the show of strength and determination from the young king, at this critical juncture, might be just the thing.

"Everyone is tired of war. What they want now is to get on with their lives. Even the earls want that. I'm going to bring the order that makes that possible." Henry paused. "And don't forget, these men all hold lands in Normandy. They will swallow hard and accept what I offer. They won't want to risk my wrath against their Norman holdings."

The men around the table nodded, one by one, seeing, at last, the total net the king was spreading. He knew what he was doing. All those hours at chess had not been wasted, Leicester thought grimly, but he had to smile.

Meanwhile, the king gathered up his cloak and stood, buckling on his sword. "We are finished. De Lucy, du Hommet, Leicester, let's to our work. I need my justiciars with me at Bury St. Edmonds."

"Sire, do you want me to accompany you?" Becket's tone had a tinge of petulance. He was smarting from the rejection of his suggestion, Eleanor thought. Good luck with that approach with Henry, whose sensitivity was on a level with that of a wild boar. Thomas, Thomas, you are not at university anymore. I hope you are up to your master's vigor.

"Yes, fine, Thomas. Of course. We shall have need of your pen to record the nobles' agreement with my offer." The king was brusque, but his demeanor softened as he turned to the queen and leaned down to speak privately.

"Madame, a word," Henry's voice broke into her thoughts. He gave her his hand to rise and lead her from her chair, his men falling back discretely as they knew how to do.

"Henry, why didn't you tell me last night you were leaving today? You've only just returned." She reached out and straightened the ruff of his cloak, which had folded under. "Can't you find more imposing clothes to wear for this important conference?"

He waved off the suggestion. "I'm a soldier, not a courtier, not one of your poets." But his tone was good-natured. "Anyway, I can't tarry long enough to make myself presentable. As for last night, you will recall, we had other affairs to distract us." He grinned. She supposed this passed for flirting in Henry's peripatetic world, but she managed a smile in return. His youthful exuberance spilled over into his lovemaking and was certainly a remarkable relief after Louis's perfunctory performance. "And anyway, I want you to join me as soon as you can ready your entourage. Bring the children."

Eleanor sighed. "Will this be a repeat of our progress north before you left for the continent?"

"Yes, I want to cover every hamlet in England before I have to leave again for France. It will be good for both of us. See how the people live. See how the sheriffs are administering the king's local justice. And how the shire and the 'hundred' system I organized is working out. We must have order. There has been chaos for too many years. And I cannot be everywhere at once."

"As you wish. I need several days to prepare the household."

"Yes, I understand. Women." He meant nothing by it, but the queen's glance rose swiftly to his, and her eyes flashed.

"Not that women are slow," he amended hastily. "I mean only, the children and nurses, the baggage trains and all. I do understand. We'll ride on ahead and get this castle exchange business done." He turned to go, then suddenly turned back.

"Elle," he said, "I have a favor to ask of you."

"What is it?" she said, a bit alarmed. Why would the king ask for a favor?

"I haven't found the time to tell you, but I have a son."

"Yes, you still have a son, despite William's sad death. And a daughter."

"No, another son. His name is Geoffrey, for my father. Older."

Somehow that last word reassured her. It was not that she expected faithfulness when they had their long separations. Henry, after all, was a lusty young man in addition to being king. But still . . . another son. Would this be a threat to her own eaglets?

"I want to bring him to court."

"His mother also?" she asked with intended irony.

"No, of course not. She was a common woman. She gave him up shortly after birth."

"You never said . . ."

"It wasn't intentional. We always have too much to talk about when we are together. But now is the time. The boy has almost six years. It's time he came to court and was educated. Have you any objection?"

Eleanor was overtaken with conflicting emotions that played across her face like summer lightning. An older son. One acknowledged by his royal father. A danger. Possibly an ally. A child, only. Perhaps.

"Sire, if you want this, it is my wish also," she said slowly. "I hope we do not regret this."

"I know we won't. I've seen the boy. He has enormous potential." Henry gave her a quick embrace and turned away, saying as he did so, "Send word when you are on the road."

He beckoned Thomas to walk with him, his way of making up for the dismissal of the chancellor's ideas in the meeting. Becket stopped and bowed low as he passed the queen.

The king was gone in a swirl of men, cloaks and swords, always worn on the road. The queen stood for some minutes, letting the entire scene settle in her heart.

27 May 1157, one week later
On the road from Bury St. Edmonds to Chester

Becket was far enough back in the entourage to be denied an unfettered glimpse of the king, which he badly wanted. For some reason, he had been assigned to ride in the second section of the king's men this morning as they rode out of Bury St. Edmunds. His companion today was William FitzStephen, the younger son of a landed family, who kept Henry's legal records for him. Not a cleric, not a member of the Chancery, not one who kept chronicles. Still, Henry mentioned in passing that he would like Tom to get to know the young man better.

This was proving difficult. Young William seemed to have nothing on his mind but idle chatter, and Becket was fuming inwardly that he was denied the king's ear this very day when he was longing to discuss, nay to take apart, the scenes of the previous week where the king confronted the nobles.

Henry had been right, of course. A firm hand was needed. William of Warenne, King Stephen's bastard son, was happy to yield his castles and to receive the most important ones back from the king. Hugh Bigod, much older and tougher, at first was less amenable, but when faced down by his king, who roared that he would not have his barons in fortresses that threatened the peace of the land, Bigod too finally agreed. And was promptly rewarded with the return—at the pleasure of the king, Henry emphasized—of his key pieces.

The king had good instincts despite his youth, Thomas saw now. He would bear watching. These men at Bury St. Edmonds were the last of the great barons and earls that had protested the loss of their castles, which Stephen had allowed them to build in return for their support for his cause as king. Henry was gradually knitting up a nation from a scattering of powerful lords, each with their own militias. A remarkable achievement in one so young, Becket had to admit.

As they rounded a curve, Thomas could lean out from his horse and spot the king, riding as he had suspected, with de Lucy and du Hommet. Becket was aware that de Lucy did not like him. And du Hommet liked no one. Yet these were the men the king chose to keep close, together with Robert of Leicester, his most trusted advisor. All of them young, younger than Becket for certain. He had fifteen years on the king, was his chancellor, yet Henry most often turned to those others, named them as justices in his absence.

Still, Becket held the Great Seal, and that was as good as the king's word. He had the power, next to the king, by virtue of that fact.

FitzStephen took a note from a young page and reached out an arm to shake Becket to attention.

"What is it?" Becket felt his annoyance rise. He had ceased listening to the younger man's ramblings miles back without even a pretense of courtesy. FitzStephen had taken no notice, still maddeningly cheerful of countenance.

"The king has just sent a page for you. He wants you to ride on ahead, now." The young fair-haired knight was grinning, which irritated Becket even more. Had the man no envy in him? Did he not wonder why Becket was chosen to accompany the king instead of himself?

Shaking his head and without bidding his companion farewell, Becket galloped to the front of the line. Du Hommet, alongside the king, yielded his place smoothly, and Becket's horse fell in step with the king's own Pendragon.

"Well, Tom," Henry said. "How are you finding young FitzStephen's company?"

"He seems to prattle about a great many things, Sire. But it's difficult to listen when there is no strategy about his thinking."

"He's young, it's true," the king said easily. "But I think he shows promise. I want you to get to know him better."

"Sire, he's a knight from a landed family. He's no scholar. Surely you cannot mean to suggest him for the chancery?"

Henry's hearty, bellowing laughter when he was in a good mood was as compelling as his manic shouts when he was in a rage. "No, of course not. He's well suited to his role as knight, and the work of a scholar would only frustrate him. But I think he may turn out to be a leader of men. I just want to get your ideas on what he might be fitted up for in the future. You know I value your assessment of my men."

Becket felt uneasy. On the face of it, it seemed the king was offering him a compliment, but behind it, he feared, lurked some sort of test. Of acumen? Of loyalty? Still, he was flattered that the king wanted to know what he thought of the others.

"However, that's not why I summoned you. I want your opinion on another matter." Their horses had settled into a trot, the pace led by Henry and one that allowed the conversation he had initiated.

"How is Thibault's health?" The question came abruptly, and Thomas nearly reined in his stallion. Why bring up the archbishop of Canterbury so suddenly?

"As far as I know, excellent, Sire. He may live to a hundred years." Becket chuckled even as he spoke.

"You know him best," Henry said. "You have been as close as father and son."

"It's true, My Lord. He took me when I had finished at Merton and made me his secretary. He even took me to Rheims to the Pope's Synod in '48. He has taught me everything I know that you find valuable."

"And he is aging. No one, not even the giants of our time, escapes the hand of time." The king's voice was matter of fact.

"What are you saying, Sire, exactly?"

"As I am cleaning up the mess that Stephen left with my nobles, I want to keep good relations with the church. It's because of Thibault that the crown and the church are in such accord. In truth, the archbishop and the king bring the rest of the nation with us. I get along with the bishops, with Foliot, with Roger Pont l'Eveque and the others. But Canterbury is key. In my grandfather's time, the king and the archbishop were respectful of each other's position." The retinue was fast approaching the formidable castle of the earl of Chester. The long, dusty road ahead wound uphill to the stern, square Norman keep at the top, surrounded by a stone wall which hid, Becket could only hope, chambers with clean featherbeds.

"Indeed, My Lord. You have the right of it."

"But when I think of Canterbury and the value of Thibault, I ask myself what will happen when he dies?" The king was staring straight ahead now, not looking at Thomas, almost as if he were scanning the future. "Thomas, the church assumed great leadership when the country was in turmoil under Stephen's rule. Perhaps too great. Many customs were bypassed as the church became the stable force for people. But now, the monarchy has been revived. The king must be seen as resuming his proper role."

Thomas paused for a moment before answering, searching for his words carefully. "My Lord, since you have named me chancellor, I have little to do with the abbey or with the politics of the monks therein. If you ask me for advice, I must say I am not the person who is qualified to counsel you in this matter. Surely any of the bishops you have named, Foliot or Pont l'Eveque, would be an adequate successor."

"Ah, yes, Tom. Insofar as running the abbey is concerned, you are right." Henry pulled his horse in slightly, slowing down the entire line as he did so. Becket realized suddenly that the king was making a point. He listened more intently now.

"But I have needs beyond the abbey." Henry now was completely stopped, and he leaned toward Becket intently, placing one hand on the other man's pommel and the other on his arm. "I want to nurture harmonious relations with the church here in England. I need someone to succeed Thibault when the time comes that can help me with that."

As if to accent his words with his actions, Henry abruptly turned and resumed riding, with Becket hustling to catch up with him.

"Sire, what exactly do you mean? Do you want a puppet at Canterbury?" He risked something with his plain speech, but the king's meaning was eluding him.

"Of course not, fool." The king snapped, frowning. "Do you see Thibault as a puppet? I only want someone who sees the advantages, as I do, of church and state working together. As in my grandfather's time." Now Henry was riding as if there were a burr under his saddle, and Becket was hard-pressed to keep even with him.

"Forgive me, My Lord, but I am just wanting to be clear on your meaning."

"We'll talk no more about it now." Henry's tone was still abrupt. "Just give the situation some thought. Meanwhile, I have other things on my mind." He glanced upward to see the worn, oak drawbridge clang down over the steep ditch around the earl of Chester's castle. "Ah, here we are. Some good wine shipped over from the Loire, a hot meal of good English beef and a ready bed." He turned again to his companion with another of his remarkable about-face mood swings, a smile on his face. "And tomorrow, good Chancellor, you and I will lead our men in the best hawking of the season. The earl is known for his forests!"

With that Henry, suddenly applied his spurs and galloped up the hill, joined as if from out of nowhere by de Lucy and du Hommet, always with him when the time came to greet the noble host of the evening.

And Becket let his horse walk slowly, a bit apart from the line of men and baggage, as he pondered the king's meaning.

September 1157
Oxford, England: The King's own forest outside the city walls

They don't like it when I ride alone, but de Lucy understands and holds back the others. Of all my men, I trust him the most. Even more, perhaps, than I trust Becket. Although I rely on Becket's advice, which he offers constantly. Sometimes I feel crowded by him. Oh, he is endlessly amusing. And it pleases me to tease him about women, of whom he seems to have none, or his finery and the table he keeps, which far exceeds my own—or so FitzStephen keeps telling me. That young man will turn out to be as much of a sybarite as Becket if he does not take care.

There is no one I'd rather ride and hawk with than Becket, not even du Hommet. But today, I want to be alone. Today I am free. This day my lineage is assured. The Queen has given me a great gift, once again. De Lucy brought me the news at Lincoln, and it took me only a day to reach here. I told him as a reward, we would name the prince after him, which quite took him aback. But Elle is as fond of de Lucy as I am, and she agreed when I saw her yester e'en. We don't differ on such minor things. The boy will be called Richard.

I need to think this through. The whole effort with Louis can be revised, a double matrimonial tie knotted. Both the little princes of ours to both the daughters of Louis. After all, he's the one who complains of a "superfluity of daughters." I'm happy to take them off his hands and take France in the process.

He's signaled he is interested in the prospect. He knows I've nearly got him surrounded, with Normandy and Anjou and then Elle's lands to the south, as far south as Toulouse. Though I need to settle that situation soon. Count Raimond is not behaving as the vassal to our empire that he is. But that's for later.

I need to meet with Louis in the new year as soon as possible. We should settle all our differences. I won't bring Elle, though. Even the thought of those two meeting is unsettling. She has a temper, I've discovered. Not like mine, of course. But still, I don't cross her unless I have to.

Never understood why she doesn't like Louis. I think he's a good enough fellow. Should have been a monk, she says. Always pious and praying, listening only to Abbe Suger. Suppose that would get old for a young, spirited bride like Eleanor. Well, they trained him for the abbey until his older brother died. Then he had to step into the palace shoes. Fate chooses for us. Louis never wore boots in the field like I did as a lad. Wonder how they got along when they were first married before things went bad. They were scarce more than children when their fathers made the union.

And boots in the field reminds me: Becket shall go to Paris to finalize the agreements on the marriage of the children once Louis and I have worked out the details. Just his kind of thing. No one can put on a show like Tom when he wants to. That'll impress the Parisians, who may still remember Eleanor's abrupt marriage to me after the annulment of her marriage with Louis as a betrayal. Tom'll dazzle 'em. It's what he does best, pomp and glory.

But what truly matters is the empire Elle and I are building, our common dream. Now there are two sons and the possibility to extend the borders of my lands to the very banks of the Seine. From the border of Scotland to the Mediterranean. I'll be knocking on the doors of Berengar's Barcelona before it's over. And for a start, I'll take the Vexin off Louis for a dowry for his little girl. He can't refuse. And, anyway, the land between Louis's royal demesne and Normandy has always been in dispute between us. He may be glad to be rid of the argument.

Henry's gerfalcon pecked at his gauntlet, a gentle reminder that the king had been still for a very long time. Henry sat, mounted, on a slight rise, overlooking the River Cherwell. The gerfalcon grew impatient. Henry smiled and pulled the hood off the large bird. It sailed upward, circled, then plunged downward into the woods and was lost to sight.

January 1158
Westminster Palace, London

The king looked around the table at the dozen startled faces, all staring at him, nonplussed.

"So, you are all agreed," he stated this decisively, not a question at all. "The offer of marriage with the daughter of the king of France . . . What is her name again, Madame?"

"Marguerite, my lord." The queen, who sat to the king's right, spoke with clarity, her tones clipped and dry. "I did not hear one soul disagree with you."

In truth, they were all so stunned no one had spoken, either for or against the proposal. Only Eleanor and Becket had been in the king's confidence on the matter before the council meeting, and, in his typical style, Henry left the astonishing news for the end of the session. The usual business had taken up most of the morning. Henry was leaving again for the continent to lay the offer of marriage before King Louis. Eleanor would be regent in his absence. Only a small number would make up the party. The destination and purpose of the trip were to remain generally secret.

"May I not accompany your party, My Lord?" Becket, who had been sitting with pursed lips throughout the meeting, broke in as the king began to gather up scrolls and maps that lay strewn in front of him. He had expected the king to give him credit for the idea, but that had not happened. The entire meeting had gone forward without a mention of him, nor was he named among the group that would accompany the king on this, the idea he had put forward months earlier.

"No, you may not," Henry said in his abrupt way, causing FitzStephen, a gentle soul, to flinch visibly. The rest looked at the ceiling or down at the table.

"But I wish the queen and you to remain as the others depart. I have further business with you."

Taking their cue, the others rose with relief. Henry was excited and volatile this morning. They could all see it. No telling what might happen if Becket pushed him in council. Becket, they had agreed privately, had the king's ear but sometimes had trouble keeping his place. Henry's mood could turn on a farthing, it was said. They had all seen it happen.

As the heavy oak doors closed behind the counsellors, Henry tapped his fingers on the table, then picked up the stone paperweight and massaged it with his restless fingers. After a moment's thought, he pushed back his chair and propped his knee against the worn table. The three sat in a semi-circle, the queen and Becket turning their chairs toward the king in the middle. He began to speak, then paused. Finally, he turned to Becket.

"There are reasons why you should not come with me to the meeting with Louis, Tom. I want to be clear about my plans."

Eleanor's brows arched, her green cat's eyes looking from one to the other of the men. Henry never held "private" conversations without purpose. She knew the story behind the plan to marry their young prince to Louis's daughter, but she wasn't certain what Henry was up to with Becket. Mollifying him for some reason? This seemed unlikely to her seasoned mind.

"I need to meet with Louis alone. He must be sold on this idea without any pressure from the past. This is one reason I am taking such a small group, only my immediate officers. It will not be a formal presentation. We'll simply talk man to man."

Eleanor turned away for a moment to hide a smile that was slipping out in spite of itself. Man to man, indeed, as if they were villeins meeting in a tavern. More like England to France. But Becket was listening intently, trying to discern his role.

"There may be reasons why Louis might balk at this arrangement, so I have to help him see how this will work to his advantage."

"One of the reasons being he is asked to accept as his son-under-the-law the child of his former queen and wife," Eleanor put in. The king made a small wave of his hand in her direction, and now she smiled openly.

"I want my sons on the throne of France. Louis is unlucky. He has no son. If our luck holds and his does not, my sons will include France and all of the continent in their domains," Henry stated.

"Our sons," Eleanor corrected him tartly.

"And I want the rest of the Vexin as a dowry."

Becket gasped. "Do you think he would agree to that? It's his buffer against your Normandy lands and Anjou and your southern provinces as well." He nodded to the queen. "Yours and the queen's," he amended.

"Louis is tired of fighting."

"He never was a fighter, except that once in Champagne when he was trying to impress me." Eleanor couldn't resist another comment.

"He wants peace. This offer is the perfect out for him." Henry suddenly dropped his propped-up knee and sat up straight as if ready for business. No longer casual, he scraped his chair to the table. "No, our larger problem is that his counsellors, and the people of France, were not happy when the queen and I combined our lands so soon after the annulment of her marriage."

"What can you do about that, My Lord?" Becket was following the king but frowning, not certain where this trail of planning would lead. "This was all decided years ago."

"That's where you come in, Tom. And why you are not going to Normandy tomorrow." Henry turned to him. "If Louis and I come to an agreement, it will be private. Then I will send you, my Chancellor, the most dashing man in England, to publicly finalize the marriage plans in Paris."

"Why me, Your Grace?" Becket was puzzled, but suddenly hopeful as he saw his stature improve with this possibility.

"Because no one but you, Thomas Becket," said Eleanor, standing, "can cut such a splendid figure at the court of the Capets. You are elegant, educated, handsome, resplendent in every way." She laughed and said, "Henry, it's brilliant! Only you would think of this."

"So you can start planning now, Tom," said Henry. "Get yourself a retinue. Buy another garderobe for your new finery. We'll have this done in six months, and we'll cut such a fine figure the people of Paris will think they have been invaded by the Milanese."

"But, Sire, you also will need to plan." He nodded in the direction of Henry's rough tunic and worn cloak. "You, perhaps even more than I, will need refurbishing."

"Oh, I won't be with you when you make your grand entrance. I do the deals, you do the show, Tom. That's how we work so well together."

And Henry's own grin lit up his square, bluff face. They were all three laughing now, as if they were children planning a game. But there was an undercurrent also, each one having private reservations that must be examined later.

The king turned to Becket and motioned him to rise. "Now you will leave us. The queen and I have other business to discuss." Becket nodded and gathered the scrolls he had used in the meeting. "Take the Great Seal for keeping at the chancery while I'm gone. The queen may need it."

Becket made his bows to the king and then the queen and backed away from the table.

"And, Tom!"

Henry's voice boomed across the large hall.

Becket turned at the door. "Yes, Sire?"

"Do remember, when you get to Paris at the head of that delegation, that you are there on my behalf."

"Of course, Sire." Becket's face remained impassive. He was never certain when the king was making a joke. "Do I have leave to retire now?"

"Yes, indeed." Henry turned his attention back to the queen, sitting to his left. The door closed behind the chancellor.

"Henry, be careful," Eleanor said. "Do not bait him."

"Bah," Henry slammed his hand on the table. "Tom is all right. But he needs to be reminded from time to time that he is not a king. Sometimes, he assumes too much."

He looked at Eleanor for a long time. "You don't like him as well as I do." He was announcing, not asking.

She returned his look and chose her words carefully. "He is a talented man, and you have a strong friendship with him." She closed her eyes briefly. "I neither like nor dislike him. He has my respect as your chancellor, and I have always admired his keen mind. I have observed, however, that he conceals his true feelings under his diplomatic face when you tease him in public. But Henry, if you poke a snake long enough, even in good humor, it will eventually strike back."

They sat, briefly, in silence. Then the king said, "And, speaking of true and honest feelings, I ask you again, what are yours about this marriage proposal with your former husband's daughter?"

She thought for a moment, inspecting her fine hands that lay folded and resting in her lap before she raised her gaze to meet his. "This marriage, should it come to pass, will give you a realm the equal of the emperor Barbarossa."

"And it will be the making of you as the first queen of Europe," was the rejoinder. The king did not laugh.

February 1158
Courtyard of Westminster Palace, London

"Make haste, make haste," the king was already mounted, pulling on Pendragon's trappers to hold the restless horse. "We certainly do not want to miss this opportunity. It's not every day we can sup with the devil and leave as his friend."

The rest of the king's men were nearly mounted, the same coterie around him, Becket noticed. All his best men: even Leicester, who did not like to leave England anymore as he complained his old bones ached when he took ship across the channel these days; even the other two justiciars, de Lucy and du Hommet, although Henry almost always left at least one of them in England riding circuit on his courts. Only the queen as regent and Becket as chancellor were left to guard the kingdom.

Becket felt the stiff wind coming up. They'd have grim weather on the ride, he thought with some satisfaction. The king hated riding in the heavy rain, though he often did it. Becket still chafed at the king's refusal to include him in this most important diplomatic mission, worrying that Henry's impatience and quick temper would foul up the plan. But he was somewhat mollified as he watched the riders leave the courtyard in a cloud of dust. The most important role, if the king kept his word, would be his own diplomatic mission to Paris to formalize any agreement. Then would his true colors show; then would all the courts of Europe see what the English chancellor was made of. He could use this time well, in Henry's absence, to develop his plans. The king might balk at the budget, but Thomas knew well what it would take to impress the sniffy Parisians with their English marriage offer.

He stood on the battlements long enough to see the dust of the small entourage disappear outside the walls of Westminster Palace. Then he took himself off to his study to begin the outline of plans for his own trip to Paris.

February 1158, four days later
On the road in Normandy

Eleanor understands, or at least I think she does. Who would have imagined six years ago, when we were wed in defiance of Louis and his whole Paris court, that I'd be riding to make peace with him through our children? It's his chance to wed our countries and stop the carnage in Normandy and the constant bickering. Don't like having to raze villages. People don't have anywhere to live, and Louis's appetite for land is growing. He won't stop until he has a reason. Well, I'm about to give him one.

I don't blame him for being reluctant to meet, but this time I said it was urgent. Perhaps he expects me to retire from Normandy? I didn't give him a hint of what was on my mind. Want to surprise him before Suger and that crowd get a look at the proposition and warn him off.

I remember when I did homage for Normandy to him, with my father present. It just complicates things to have both of us ruling. How much simpler would it be to unite our lands, even if it will only come to pass in the future?

Louis is so predictable. He'll raise the spectre of French anger that Eleanor took her lands and then united them to mine. But I have the strategy. Becket can persuade them. He has a talent for that sort of thing, a chance to cut a fine figure and strew someone else's silver around Louis's capital. Even Louis has to prefer that kind of show to war.

I like Louis, even if he more resembles a monk than a king. Elle doesn't understand why, but then she had to be married to him, and I don't. I just have to sup with him and get along to get what I want. I'd happily sup with the devil to get what I want. And Louis has a form of integrity. He never goes back on his word. He's not a bad soldier, either, for someone who didn't take the field in his youth. Brave, sometimes fool-hardy. Wonder what it would be like to deal with the older brother if he had lived. Rumor has it he had a practice of exploding when displeased. No monkish ways, that one. I think I prefer Louis, especially if the task is to make peace.

Suddenly de Lucy was at his side, breaking into his thoughts. "There's a hostel nearby, Sire. I suggest we stop for the night. Bec is a short ride in the morning."

* * *

When Henry saw the sun as he left the inn the next day, he took the weather as a sign from heaven that his plans were favored. His spirits rose. They arrived at the abbey of Bec, welcomed by the abbot no less, a doughy, rotund man who appeared to spend more time in the dining hall than in the chapel. He had a cheery face, however, and a generous smile, which promised plentiful wine and calvados. That alone, thought Henry, should soften even Louis, the most serious of kings.

The abbot himself showed the king and his men to the great hall. A table had been laid with refreshments, and Louis was already there, pacing and looking nervous.

Henry approached the king of France with his arms extended, and Louis, looking suddenly startled, allowed himself to be enfolded into a surprisingly strong embrace. Over his shoulder, Henry glimpsed the aging Abbe Suger, looking somewhat the worse for the travel. Suger was Louis's teacher, his constant counsellor since his youth. Henry didn't mind. Better to have Suger here than second-guessing his offer when alone with the king of France. Henry had some sympathy for the mild-mannered Louis, who had spent his young years in St. Denis under the abbe's tutelage, preparing for a career in the church that was cut short by his older brother's death. Louis was called to kingship and marriage with the young duchess of Aquitaine in that same summer, as his own king-father lay dying in Paris. Not an easy passage.

Once Henry had released the surprised Louis from his bear hug, he turned to Suger, who bowed only as low as required by strict etiquette.

"Duke Henry," Suger murmured, reminding Henry of his vassalage to Louis for Normandy.

"Your Eminence," said Henry cheerfully, holding out his arms. For one startled minute, both Suger and de Lucy thought Henry might embrace the aging abbot, but he merely took his elbow with one hand and clasped his hand with the other. De Lucy breathed a sigh of relief, even as he knew Henry had stage-managed this gesture deliberately.

"Well, Abbot," the English king turned to the host of the abbey at Bec, "thanks to you for this meeting place and," he gestured to the largest table groaning under the weight of many platters of meat, fish and sweetmeats, along with flagons of wine laid out for the important travelers, "for your generous hospitality. And now, if you will excuse us, King Louis and I have important business to discuss. Have you a private chamber where we could meet for an hour or so?"

Startled, the abbot nodded. "You may use our chapter house, your majesties. It's yours for as long as you may need it. Please follow me." He turned to his provost and ordered him to manage the meal for the travelers. Then he led the two kings out of the Great Hall.

De Lucy knew better than to follow Henry, but Louis's key advisors trailed after the kings until Louis, prompted by Henry, who had tucked his hand companionably under the French king's elbow, dismissed them gently.

When the two kings had obtained the chapter meeting room, the abbot announced that he would have food and drink brought in for them. Then the monarchs were finally alone. Henry motioned to the smallest table, set under a broad opening in the stone wall. The tapestries had been pulled back to admit the weak, northern light through the wind-eye. They faced each other for a long moment, each reading the other's face: the older king with the long, mournful Capet countenance, lined with years and wars and worries about succession though he had not yet forty summers, and the bluff, square-faced, freckled, red-haired, cheery young man opposite him, whose startling grey eyes held his own.

Henry met Louis's gaze without a blink, then looked expectantly around the room while he gathered his thoughts. This small chamber was the place where he hoped his empire would finally take shape. Everything hinged on the next hour. He wanted to remember the limestone walls dripping with the damp February air, the empty fireplace with last night's cinders still on the hearth, the candles and torches that had been brought in hurriedly when Henry asked for a private chamber. Yes, this was a place of destiny. Henry wanted to mark it well.

Louis waited with his customary, irritating patience.

"Louis," Henry began, "It's time to settle the issue of the Vexin once and for all."

"The Vexin belongs to France now, Henry." Louis sounded a bit testy. "Anjou yielded the final portion to us when you did homage for Normandy five years ago. That was the trade-off that allowed you to inherit the dukedom your father claimed earlier. Your own father, Count Geoffrey, witnessed the agreement." Louis pushed back his chair and made as if to rise. "If that is all you wanted to discuss . . ."

Henry held up his hands in protest. "Wait. Hear me out. Please. I have a proposal for you. I know you will be interested if you would only listen." He looked upwards, theatrically organizing his thoughts.

Rats in a bin! I should not have started with the Vexin. I know how Louis reacts to any threats to his lands. Should have started with the advantage to him, not with something to take away. This is the kind of thing Thomas does so well. But I couldn't involve him. This is for me to do. Must needs back up and start again.

"I promise you that my proposal will be to your advantage, Louis." Henry pressed forward as he saw the older man pause. "You will be happy with my offer. At the least, listen to it. You can always refuse."

Louis sighed, but he dropped back into the heavy oak chair, more in weariness than agreement. He rested his long, bony arms on the table, leaning across the space toward Henry. "Let's have it then."

Henry poured them each a goblet of dark red wine from the flagon as he prepared new words, exercising uncharacteristic patience.

"You have, as you have been overheard to remark, a 'superfluity of daughters.' I have sons. We each have children that survived." He silently reminded himself not to bring up the new child Eleanor would bear him in the autumn.

"Yes, I heard of the death of your young William. I am sorry for your loss. . ." he paused for a beat ". . . and Eleanor's. But you have two surviving sons. There is no shortage of boys in your nursery, Henry." Louis sounded more rueful than irritated. He had to fight his inclination to like this cheeky upstart, almost young enough to be his son, who had stolen not only his wife but her vast lands from his overlordship. "I cannot see how you could be sympathetic to my problem."

"Aah, but my bounty should become your benefit, My Lord King." Henry twirled the gold stem of his goblet in his broad fingers.

Go slow. Remember Tom's advice. "Your advisors cannot always follow your swift thinking, Sire," Tom was wont to say. "Slow down. Explain. Give them time." He was right. If I am to snare this royal prey, make him see our mutual advantage, I must not push too hard. Louis does not respond well to forceful propositions. And he's canny. I must remember not to underestimate him because of his mild manner.

"And how might that happen, I ask myself?" Louis took a sip of his wine. Like Henry, he was not above the political pause. His eyes, over the goblet, were watchful. Henry shifted in his chair. "In a way will benefit you. But for me and my interests, I'm not so certain."

"God's teeth, Louis. Are you always this suspicious?" The challenge erupted despite all Henry's good intentions of diplomacy. "It's a wonder you have time to run the Capet kingdom if you are searching for stoats in every corner."

Suddenly Louis burst into honest laughter, shaking his head.

"Henry, we find ourselves in a strange situation. You are king of England, yet you remain my vassal for Normandy and Anjou. You stole my wife and her lands, yet here I sit talking as if we were family. Worse yet, I can't help myself. I like you. We have skirmished over villages and borders for the past four years, and yet we meet here as friends. Can you fault me for a bit of cynicism?"

The flush receded from Henry's face as he suppressed the urge to chuckle. "No, Louis. I cannot. That's why I wanted to cut through all the messengers and heralds and offers and sit down with you alone. It is time we stopped chasing each other's armies all over Normandy like demented mice and instead build something together. Hear me out."

"I'm willing to listen. But I promise nothing."

"Suppose we aligned our considerable forces. . ." Henry began.

"I cannot imagine it, but go on," Louis responded dryly. "Only speak plainly, as you usually do. As far as diplomacy goes, I can tell you now, it's never been your bailiwick, and you are not likely to acquire the talent at this point in your life."

"All right, I take your point. So, then, plainly, here is my offer: I have sons, you now have a new daughter. Let's combine our houses. I want to betroth your young daughter, Marguerite, to my oldest son, Henry. They are well suited in age. I believe she is but two years and Henry is now four. If they marry, it will keep us from stirring up the countryside every few moons to try to gain a bit of ground. And you would no longer see me as a vassal and a threat but as a brother." Henry's hands, which had been engaged in reinforcing his words with gestures, fell to the table. He waited.

Louis must have thought this was coming. He'll take his time responding. If he doesn't take the offer, Becket will have to come back and repeat the diplomacy. I will have this marriage, one way or another.

After a silence that was longer than usual, Louis said, "So you envision your descendants and mine sitting on the thrones of both France and England."

"Such a situation," Henry took another swallow of the red wine, "would eliminate a lot of fighting and strife."

"Hmm. I'm not so certain of that," Louis said absently, his right forefinger tapping restlessly on the table. For once, Henry waited, reining in his desire to pile more arguments.

"But it would surely be to our advantage to unite all of the vast lands we both hold," Henry finally said.

"Including Eleanor's lands in the south?"

"Of course, everything. No county, no dukedom, no village would be held back."

"And what is your immediate trade for this betrothal?"

"I've thought that through," Henry said.

"I'm sure you have," the older king murmured.

"I want the Vexin reunited with Normandy as dowry for the child. The castles of Gisors, Neufchattel and Neaufles would be part of the land parcel."

"Go on." Louis had not lifted his eyes from the table and was now engaged in examining his long, immaculate nails and the many jewels on his fingers.

"The child would come to our court to be raised with Henry. When the time comes, they would be formally married."

"I'd never agree to let Eleanor raise my daughter!" Louis hissed.

"Fine, then the child can have a guardian of your choosing and rest on a border town for the time being. I'll give her Avranches as a dowry."

"What else do you want?"

Henry wiggled a bit in his chair. The next part was delicate. "I have trouble in Brittany."

Louis looked up, surprised, and said, "I thought your brother Geoffrey was Count of Rennes after his marriage to Constance of Brittany."

"Well, that part is true, but Conan is back in the county and styles himself Duke. He's taken up residence in Rennes and is growling at Geoffrey from his perch there. I fear blood may be spilled. The situation is tenuous."

"Didn't you give Conan some English title to appease him?" Louis has good information from somewhere, Henry thought with admiration.

"Yes, Earl of Richmond. And I didn't oppose his return to Brittany, but I never dreamed he'd breach our agreement and begin to make overtures of war for the entire county. If he tries to take Nantes, as well, there will be war."

"Aah, Brittany, the end of the earth," Louis sighed. "I've always just left it alone and hoped it would go away."

Henry had forgotten Louis's fine sense of irony. "Well, that's not happening," he snapped. "And it's creating a lot of trouble for me. I cannot just leave my brother Geoff hanging there without help."

"What does that have to do with this betrothal?" Louis prodded.

"Oh, I have an idea about that. If you could give me a title, say . . . Seneschal of France, that would give me some leverage to address this problem." He paused, eyebrows raised. "You will remember from your dealings with my brother Geoff that he is not easy to control, either."

Now it was Louis's turn to look abashed, reminded that only recently he had taken Geoff's side against Henry. Yet, what could he do now, under the circumstances?

"All right, the marriage, the Vexin, you can be Seneschal and sort out Brittany. But we still have one problem."

"And that is . . .?" Henry could scarce believe his own hearing.

"My people love you not, nor can they forgive Eleanor for leaving us and taking a portion of our country with her." Louis's voice had hardened. Clearly, Henry thought, neither had the king forgiven her. "I don't know how they will receive this news of marriage."

"Oh, that," Henry waved his hand as if brushing away a pesky insect. "I've thought about that already. Here's the plan: We'll keep this agreement secret for some time. Later this summer, I'll send my best diplomat, Tom Becket, to Paris for a formal agreement. He'll put on a great show of liberality. He's very good at this diplomacy stuff and also loves to dress up and give alms. Even you will be impressed. By the time he leaves Paris, your people will all want to move to England to be near him!" Henry sat back and beamed at the startled Louis.

"If you say so," was all the king of France could manage after a long pause. "Suger will have fits when I tell him what I have agreed to," Louis added glumly. "He will say I gave away France. He's quite frail now. The shock could finish him off."

Not all that bad an idea, but no, be charitable. Henry brushed away the thought.

"Louis, Louis, present it to him as the best of all possible plans." Henry reached across the table and clasped his new friend's forearm in a grip that made Louis wince. "You are not risking France, you are gaining the crown of England!" Henry poured more wine and raised his goblet. "To our family for generations to come."

Louis's mind was already racing ahead to the thousand things that could go wrong and raised his glass with considerably less enthusiasm. But raise it, he did.

August 1158
The Chancery at Westminster

The entrance of the king into the small, stone offices of his Chancery was, as usual, chaotic. He arrived with no advance warning, striding down the long hall bellowing for Becket. Startled clerks looked up as his party passed the small, crowded rooms where they labored elbow to elbow. Thomas, in the larger chamber at the end of the long hall, saw Henry coming and rose. The coterie trailing him were his closest advisors and two unfamiliar faces.

The king's short cloak swirled on the top of the large oak writing table that served as Becket's main bureau of affairs. As the king turned to greet his chancellor, papers flew, several onto the floor.

"Your Grace," Becket bowed quickly, then discretely signaled one of his clerks to attend to the displaced documents. They all knew he hated clutter.

"Well, well, Thomas. All in order for your trip to Paris?"

"Indeed, Your Grace." Becket looked around at the small group of men, all of them soldiers. Their large, bluff presence seemed to bring an unknown element to the very air in his carefully kept chancery. Still, he put a good face on it.

"I was not expecting you, My Lord," he added.

"Yes, yes, well, if I took the time to announce my every move, I'd never get anything done," Henry said amicably. "You may not know these men." He gestured to the two newcomers. "Richard of Ilchester, a marvel with the German tongue, is my envoy now to Barbarossa. We hope our new gifts soften him up in case something goes awry with our Capet agreement. I am also thinking of offering him the child, Mathilda. A man can never have too many allies, Thomas. Remember that."

Becket raised his eyebrows slightly. It was out of character for the king to lecture him.

"And Simon of Apulia, just in from Sicily, with interesting news. It seems someone has leaked the details of our impending alliance with France and all the nobles of the south are astir, all the way down to Berengar at Barcelona."

"*Certes,* they would be, Your Grace. Sicily itself is not that far from the queen's, pardon, I mean your, southern counties."

"Indeed, which is why we need to cultivate Barbarossa. With his holdings in the northern Italian states, we may need help in our south. But to my purpose now, have you the plans for your official visit to Paris? We want a good show." Henry threw himself into Becket's cushioned chair and waved the rest of his group into stools and chairs around the room. Becket pulled up a stool next to the king and reached for a cluster of parchments.

"Here, Your Grace."

"Read it so all can hear, Thomas." The king leaned against the tall back of his chair and stared at the ceiling, the better to listen.

"Yes, Sire," Becket said in his fullest chancellor voice. If the king wanted a performance, he would give him one. Standing, Thomas read off his plan in a sonorous voice, an unmistakable imitation of Archbishop Thibault's drawl and tone at his most pompous, sending Henry in spasms of muted merriment.

"Becket, as representative of his most exalted majesty Henry the Second of that name, King of England, arrives in Paris with the following accompaniments and accoutrements: "Eight wagons for his personal possessions, other wains to carry his private chapel, his cross and vestments of liturgy."

"A chapel? A cross? What's all that about?" Henry broke off his laughter, wiping his eyes with the back of his serge sleeve. "Vestments of liturgy?"

Becket smiled. "You forget, lord, that I still hold the office of Archdeacon of Canterbury."

"God's teeth, Thomas, quite a contrast to have eight wagons for personal possessions and then carry a chapel. The Franks will think you're praying to keep your possessions," Henry muttered, but with a broad smile.

"To continue, Sire: Wains carrying the chancellor's bedchamber, bed, curtains, featherbeds, then loads of English beer for the Franks and gifts, of course, for all the important people at court. Several barrel-topped wains for carpets and silver plate." Thomas paused to reach for his goblet of wine.

"Must you take all that?" Henry ceased his laughter as a small frown appeared. The expense was beginning to dawn on him.

Thomas took a long draught, then turned to the king. "You said you wanted a good show." He grinned. "I believe you used the term 'magnificent show for the Franks, to help them forget all about Queen Eleanor's desertion.'"

"Right. I did say that," Henry admitted, twitching slightly.

"We need armed guards, of course, for protection. Twelve will do. And the dogs to protect the protectors. Falconers and grooms. And then I have a special treat designed."

"I'm sure you have," Henry said ruefully, wondering what du Hommet and the office of the exchequer would say about all this when they were in private.

"We will have troupes of solid English villagers performing their native songs in every village we pass through from our landing on the coast to our arrival in Paris. I've instructed my servants to round up two hundred of them to help bring a slice of the good English life to the people of the Frankish kingdom." Thomas tossed the parchment back onto the table. "When those villagers see how merry a people we English are, they will welcome this alignment and marriage with open arms."

Henry, sitting casually with one leg slung over the arm of his solid chair, leaning back against its high, carved back, cast his eyes to heaven as if searching for help. "Do you think you might be overdoing it?"

"And then, as you might expect, we need the knights, squires and grooms to support all of this pageantry." Thomas continued, now in his ordinary chancellor's voice, as if toting up columns of figures.

"God's hair, what is all this to cost?" Henry finally roared with his customary change of mood. "You'll have everything but elephants from India!"

"Your Grace, I have not finished working out the sums. But I put the question to you: Is it not worth it to gain the crown of France?"

De Lucy and du Hommet exchanged glances, and du Hommet could not suppress a grin. Becket always had just the perfect argument for what he wanted to do, and he really wanted to do this show.

"And, Your Majesty," Becket seldom used that title except in highly formal situations, "Louis's subjects will ask themselves, 'If this be but the Chancellor, how grand must the King of the English himself be?'"

Henry sighed and turned to de Lucy. "Make a note that we must double the tax on those two castles I gave back to Hugh Bigod. He will fuss, but he is behind schedule."

"Yes, My Lord," de Lucy said, not daring to look again at his compatriot du Hommet for fear of bursting out laughing. Henry was, in this case, a fish well and truly landed by this chancellor. And a victim of his own scheming to boot. Still, he seemed overall content with the plans.

"My Lord, one more thing." Thomas stopped Henry when he rose to go. "Do I bring the infant back to your court here, to the Queen?"

"Good Christ, no," the king snapped. "I'm going to collect her myself in the autumn. Your job is to formalize the agreement on behalf of my government. And besides, she'll not stay here. Louis will never allow Eleanor to have the raising of his daughter. He'll appoint a guardian, and she'll be in his protection. Probably Avranches. I've decided to name Avranches her special city."

Thomas was thunderstruck. "But if I'm not to get the infant, what is the point of this voyage?"

"The point, my dear Chancellor," Henry threw his arm around Becket's shoulders, "is to persuade our Frankish cousins that they want this alliance. We are going to accomplish this with a great deal of theatre, for which you have already demonstrated a great deal of talent." The king took his other hand and fingered the fine velvet of Thomas's robe. "Very fine, indeed." He patted the chancellor on the back as he released his hold on him.

"This will be well done, Thomas. Wish I could be there to see it." And the king's cloak swirled across the table again as he turned quickly to go, dragging the scrolls to the floor as he had on his entrance. Oblivious, as usual, he beckoned his men and waved to Thomas as he left the room. He did not see his chancellor bend, himself, to pick up the scrolls before his clerk could do so.

Oh, yes, this will work. Louis will get more than he bargained for, but this show will bring the Franks around to accepting Eleanor's son for their eldest daughter Marguerite. The French queen is enceinte again, I hear. Perhaps in the near future, Louis will agree that his younger daughter Alix might also marry into my family. That would be un embarras de richesses. But it would seal the bargain for certain, assurance that if something happened, God forfend, to either of the older children, there would still be a dynasty to follow for a united France and England. Yes, this show of Becket's, this brilliant game, will be well worth the candle.

Late September 1158
Paris, Île de la Cité

It was a bedraggled group of a dozen men that cantered across the flimsy bridge over the Seine and onto the Île de la Cité, the river island on which Louis had built his redoubt. The late September rain dragged down the leaves from the trees and slashed into the men's faces as they rode.

William FitzStephen caught up with Henry, who was in the lead, riding beside the faithful du Hommet.

"Is it far, Sire?" The young knight tried to sound casual as he pulled his cloak closer around him.

Henry turned to him, chuckling.

"Getting wet, are we, Will?"

"Yes, Sire, but that's no matter. It's Peter of Blois. He's about to drop off his horse. He's not used to the pace that is your habit, Sire, begging your pardon for the impudence." FitzStephen took liberties that others might not due to his youth and the special affection which the king showed him.

"Yes, we're nearly there. Tell the scholar to hang on and not die. We need him to write about this portion of our alliance. I want this all recorded."

"As you wish," FitzStephen bowed and, laughing himself, fell back to offer what comfort he could to the drenched scribe.

As they reached the island, Henry saw, scarcely visible through the sheets of rain, the bulky stone building that served as the royal residence for the king of France. A small party of men on horseback emerged from that direction, dimly visible in the descending dusk. The oriflamme of France, the sign of the king, was carried by their leader. Henry raised his brows. "De Lucy, this is indeed an occasion. They've brought the flag!"

"Maybe they just wanted to alert us that they were not brigands making to rob us, Sire," de Lucy shot back.

Louis' scouting party brought their horses to a stop in front of Henry and his men, and the English king allowed himself to be welcomed in the formal, French style, although it meant additional wetness for all as they parlayed politely in the rain. Then the French force led the small royal party to the palace. Henry bowed slightly to Louis, who stood with his Spanish queen Constance on a veranda, watching.

"Quite a difference from the expansive retinue Thomas Becket brought last month," the queen observed in her Castilian-inflected French.

"Indeed," Louis said thoughtfully. "But this is more like Henry. A dozen men, no baggage train to slow him down, all business." He turned to his wife. "You may enjoy his company, but never forget his open ways conceal the cleverest of men." The king chuckled ruefully. "But even so, I've no choice but to trust him in this alliance he has proposed."

They turned to walk together to the Great Hall, where the English king, once dried off, would be royally welcomed.

* * *

The king of France, the Spanish-French queen and several of their closest retainers entertained Henry and his men at supper in the refectory, closer to the kitchens than the Great Hall and a more intimate setting than the cavernous formal chamber. Henry's men had bathed and dried their clothes before fires in the room set aside only for them, an honor as Louis's men slept in the Great Hall at night. Louis tended toward the Spartan, Henry recalled, but the feast laid out for the English guests was plentiful and hot. Lamb, goat, wild boar and almond rice coupled with hot spiced sauces, good wheat bread, sweetmeats and cakes satisfied the weary travelers.

After the meal, the men were excused, and the queen also retired, leaving the two kings together, alone, for the second time that year.

"So, Louis, what are your plans for the care of the infant? I trust you've had ample time to make arrangements."

"Yes, the plans are settled."

"Good. Then I'll take her with me and deliver her to her guardian. Who have you chosen for her safekeeping?"

"I've settled on Mantes as the place, on the marches. Robert of Neuburgh is your seneschal, justiciar and dapifer. He is thoroughly trustworthy and assures me he has wet nurses and women who will nurture the infant. She is, after all, still a babe." Louis's voice carried a hint of regret.

Henry moved the conversation quickly forward. No time for sentiment or second thoughts. "Even better than I had hoped. Mantes is on the way back for us. Neuburgh is an honorable man and will safeguard the infant well." Henry paused, his restless hands playing with the salt cellar, then with the fork in front of him. He tapped the fork against the cellar several times. Louis, whose nerves were always on edge, was on the verge of asking him to stop when Henry finally did.

Then he said to Louis, "And when can I take possession of the castles on the far edge of the Vexin, the castles that make up her dowry?" Henry wanted that small strip of land that lay between the kingdom of France and his Normandy. It could shift the balance of power between the two kings.

Louis sighed. "When you get the castles, you will have the Vexin in its entirety. But, Henry, we did agree they would come into your possession only when the marriage was formalized. And the church will not agree to the marriage of infants, as you well know." The tired voice of the French king contained all the notes of resignation he could muster.

"Yes, yes, I know. But I think there is a way they should leave your ownership, even while not arriving at mine. A token, perhaps, of good faith." Henry smiled. Louis's experience with that smile had not always been pleasant.

"No doubt you have a plan," Louis said, his fine mouth drawing into a thin line. This vassal was indefatigable when it came to possessions and land.

"Yes, I do," Henry said honestly, looking up. "And it's quite simple."

"Which is?"

"You give the three castles into the care of the Knights Templar. Their book is impeccable. We both know this. They can hold them for us until the marriage is solemnized."

Louis took a deep breath. He could argue with this young upstart, but the fact was the plan was brilliant. It placed a major part of the dowry in the hands of the richest and most holy faction in France and England.

The warrior monks had already developed a reputation for the protection of pilgrims along the route to the Holy Land while amassing a fortune in trading rights along that same path. Their fiscal performance was, as Henry said, impeccable. They were bankers themselves and had no need to plunder the goods of others. And they would have no need to alienate either king. Reluctant as he was to part with a single castle, if the Templars held them and the alliance fell apart, he had every confidence they would be returned to France. So why not?

"Done," he said simply to Henry. "How long will you stay with us?" The question, from any other host, might be seen as rude, but Henry was beginning to understand his new-found friend and took no umbrage at the abrupt request.

"Only until Sunday. I want to visit your shrines, move about your city alone, by your leave, of course, let the people see we from England are not monsters."

Louis laughed softly. "And distribute alms," he put in.

"Absolutely!" Henry rejoined, getting into the spirit of the thing. "Eleanor told me I must see the great church at St. Denis. Does the saint still walk about carrying his head?"

"He's been seen there recently," Louis replied dryly. "You must go investigate." He poured more wine, and the two men smiled at each other. Perhaps, Louis thought, there really will be peace between us.

Late October 1158
Mont St. Michel, Normandy

"Your majesty, you are well come to our abbey." Robert de Torigny, arms outstretched, spoke even as he hastened down the last few steps of the high fortress known as St. Michel in Peril of the Sea. His black Benedictine scapular flapped in the wind around his thin body as he greeted the small party of Henry, King of England, Duke of Normandy and Count of Anjou. This noble was a well-known visitor but never had he come at the same time as the king of France. The abbot was beside himself with delight and importance as he made his bow to Henry. This meeting would be something to write about in the chronicles he kept as a meticulous history of his abbey.

De Torigny had good cause to celebrate, for all knew that a historic event was taking place on this day. The alliance between France and England, between the king of France and his vassal for Normandy, Duke Henry, was to be finalized. The abbot's tall frame shivered in the wind that swept off the sea in a cold wave. Winter was coming. But for all that, he was happy. Finally, it appeared there would be peace in Normandy.

The abbey looked out over the brave, roiling sea. The long causeway road leading to the mainland was no longer under water. Nothing would stop this day from being an utter triumph. One year earlier, when he had been in Calais, he had caught a glimpse of the white cliffs of Dover from the top of the hill leading to the French port. He thought it was a good omen at the time for peace between France and England. And now, today, here were the kings of these two countries who had chosen his own monastery to parley. He was deeply honored.

Coming on fast, as his scouts had reported, was the small troop that carried the flag of France. The party would soon be complete, and all was ready.

* * *

Not long after Henry and his men had been installed in their chambers, the king of France arrived and with a much larger contingent than Henry had brought. Robert had a moment of a clutched heart when he saw their numbers, but the Benedictines valued hospitality above all, and his monks rose to the occasion. Some even volunteered their cells for the most important of Louis's counsellors.

Now the state dinner was to begin. A grand table had been set up in the Great Hall and fires laid in the two, huge fireplaces. The kitchens had been preparing for weeks, and even though it was late autumn, large quantities of fresh meat, salted fish, game and every kind of grain were laid ready. A host of cooks worked in front of the big fires.

The young king Henry, he of the ruddy, square face, grey eyes and the disconcerting directness of conversation, vied for the abbot's attention with King Louis. The French king was greying now, his thin face more lined than when Robert had last seen him, but he was still quiet and regal in appearance. They sat in high-backed oak chairs on either side of the abbot in the great hall, with their men ranged in front of them at trestle tables covering the vast room. The mighty lords, their closest advisors, were near them. The men were as rowdy as always, but they fell silent when the gong rang, and the abbot stood for the opening prayer and reading from the Rule of St. Benedict, as was the routine of the monastery.

It only took a moment after the lector's voice fell silent, St. Benedict now honored, for the noise level to rise again, but all seemed in good humor as the men fell to.

The monks, seated at their own tables along the walls, were cheerful as their lay brothers poured measures of the local red wine for them and their guests. Later came the delicious cups of the special calvados Normandy was known for—a secret recipe of apples distilled into a fine brandy that the monks treasured in their competition with the southern mountain monastery that produced the famous Carthusian recipe. Robert de Toringy helpfully confided the story of this competition to the kings. Course after course of hot food appeared, first the kid, then pigeon, followed by meat, interspersed with sweet almonds in milk and the crushed fruit-and-ice the monastery was famous for in winter.

Robert de Torigny had hoped the conversation would produce some tidbit of interest for him to include in the chronicles he was secretly keeping, but no word was given him about the purpose of this odd meeting.

It was not that Mont St. Michel was not an important place. Set on the rocks of the hook of Normandy, a strategic point that was important for both Normandy and France, it was not untoward that two kings would meet there. But this seemed almost a state occasion, yet with a contingent of men, at least for the king of France, enough to start a small war.

Robert had a feeling there was something deep about this meeting. It was the conclusion of some final negotiation, that much was clear. But the talk at the table was all about the hunting in the Vexin as opposed to the glories of the King's Forest outside London and the marriages of Louis's two daughters by Eleanor to the Counts of Blois and Troyes, nephews of Stephen. These were, Robert knew, ancient family enemies of Henry from the times of his mother's war, yet the king seemed almost jovial at the mention of their marriage alliance, teasing the king of France on his good fortune. Once or twice Robert winced at the mention of certain topics, but the two kings seemed intent on discourse with equanimity.

At the end of the dinner, Henry turned to the abbot and said simply, "Abbot Robert, is there a small, private room where the king and I could converse?"

"Of course, my lord," the monk replied with alacrity. "You are welcome to my own private chamber. I will send wine and fruit compote to you."

"No, do not leave us, Robert," Henry said in that sudden way of his. "I think King Louis would enjoy a private talk with his long-time friend." Robert always forgot: Henry was a native of the Norman-Anjou territory and knew all the friendships that had developed among the educated classes there.

"Nothing would please me more." The abbot could only smile broadly. His curiosity about this meeting was about to be satisfied, it seemed.

And so, half an hour later, the three were ensconced in the abbot's cozy chamber, the small fireplace blazing behind them, the bustle of the men at arms bedding down in the Great Hall finally shut out by the heavy, carved oak doors.

Servants materialized quietly and set flagons of wine, a bowl of winter fruit and sweetmeats on the table.

"I have had enough of the good wine of your region this eve, Abbot Robert," Henry stated flatly, stretching out his legs and lengthening his body against the back of his chair, his habit of late. His legs were already bowed from his constant travel on horseback, even at his young age, and they ached in the damp air of the Norman north. Then, surprisingly, for the young king was not known to overly imbibe, he added, "But in honor of the occasion, I'll have one more, a glass to raise to our important new venture."

Louis smiled benevolently at his former queen's husband as Robert raised his hand to the steward, motioning toward their goblets.

To Robert's delight, the English king then said, with his usual directness, "So, Louis, why did you want to meet me here at Robert's abbey? Is there something on your mind. And why bring so many men?"

"I've made a brave and successful *chevauchée* through my domains. I stopped to visit my infant daughter Marguerite, now your ward, and I can report that she is flourishing. But I thought it would not go amiss if I showed my northern subjects something of a king's retinue, so I brought a host with me."

Henry threw his head back and laughed. "I doubt that you have need of the show, Louis. Every one of your vassals is aware of your power. Including this one."

"Yes," said the canny older man, tilting his head toward his most important vassal, "but it hurts nothing to bring out an occasional reminder."

Henry's mirth told the Abbot he was anything but intimidated. "Did you make your progress through the Vexin? That is, our Vexin," Henry couldn't resist adding.

"Yes, and everywhere there were questions. But when the marcher lords understood our arrangement, that the marriage of Marguerite with your young Henry will not take place for years, and that the transfer of the Vexin to you will wait until then, they were satisfied." Louis paused. "For the most part."

Henry caught the final phrase, but let it pass. Now was not the time to press on the issue of the satisfaction of the lords who would eventually come under his domain.

"Let time do its work. We have plenty of time." Henry's restless fingers, as always, were playing with the bric-a-brac on the table. He twirled a salt cellar in his fingers, all the time watching Louis's face. Then he turned to the abbot.

"Robert," the English king said in an abrupt change of topic. "How is your magnificent history of the Northern Times coming on?"

"Very well, Sire. Very well indeed."

"Ah, you are about writing then, Father Abbot?" Louis asked, taken by surprise at the new direction of conversation.

"It seems to me someone must record the events of the times," The abbot said. His narrow face had lighted at the mention of his project. "How will anyone know in the future what has taken place if someone does not record it?"

"By all that's holy, man. Much of what has taken place in my lifetime is best forgotten," said Louis.

"Louis is no doubt thinking of the wars in the Holy Land. The expeditions of his youth." Henry said, grinning. "Perhaps those bloody scenes would be enough for any man, especially one trained at St. Denis for the monastery."

"It's true," Louis admitted, shrugging. "I was not intended for either the throne or the army in my youth. But when my brother died, there was no choice. It was my duty."

"Well, I admire you, Louis, and your sense of responsibility. But here sits one soldier who will not bleed on the sand of the Holy Land. There's enough work here in my realms to occupy me. I hear rumbles of a new crusade in the works. Well, the church may preach and storm, they may offer to save my soul if I go on this next one, but I'll resist. Making government, not destroying it, is my work on earth." Henry thoughtfully plucked a couple of dried grapes from their wooden bowl and popped them into his mouth.

"But Holy Mother Church surely knows best." The rejoinder of the French king was a statement, not a question. His hands were clasped on the table as if to strengthen his words. It was exactly the kind of pious statement that made Henry roll his eyes to heaven, but he restrained himself in the moment, merely emitting a noise that sounded suspiciously like "bah" to the abbot.

Robert looked from one king to the other.

"Aah, Louis. We each have our burden to bear. You have your training in the church and, consequently, your memories of the Saracens you killed in Outremer. And I…" Henry gave an exaggerated shrug, pausing, "I have Eleanor."

Robert suppressed a gasp. The French king looked startled, blinked, the words hanging over the table as if suspended in space. Then, without warning, he threw back his head and gave forth a huge guffaw. Robert could not recall ever seeing the restrained older king so amused. Henry joined in bellowing as if the comedy were contagious. Suddenly, Robert began to chortle as well. Soon all three men were speechless, laughing until tears rolled at the outrageous fortunes of life.

Eventually, they quieted down. Louis spoke first, still chuckling. "I hear that Peter of Blois has joined your court."

"Indeed, a first-rate scholar," Henry said, his body yet twitching with mirth. His private merriment was all the greater as he thought of what Eleanor might say should she hear of that comment. "He's most welcome. We have amassed a good number of scholars. Even Gerald of Wales joins us now and again."

"I would watch out for that one," Louis put in. "He has a venomous pen."

"Is it Becket who draws them?" Robert asked.

"Not really." Henry grinned. "Tom is more for the good wine, good company, good conversation. He's not that interested in the scholars. Told me not long ago he finds them rather dull at dinner."

"Well, why are they all coming to you then?" asked Louis. "It can't be the climate in England."

"Some of it is Eleanor," Henry admitted. "It's known she adores scholars. Took in lectures in Paris when she was a young queen." He frowned. "The famous Abelard, back for a couple of years before he died. Becket was there too. She knew them both."

"I remember," Louis murmured.

"And then there is a natural affinity, the brotherhood of scholars." Henry continued quickly. "Once you have someone like Peter of Blois or Walter Map, others come to join the fun. They know they are welcomed by me, too. That I read and respect their learning. They are well-fed and hold sessions for the younger nobility. The kind of thing I had in Angers. We had one of the early universities there, you must remember." Henry pointed his finger at Louis. "Paris wasn't the only bright light. The count, my father, encouraged knowledge and reading, collecting the books the monks copied. I hated my Latin lessons, but now, when I have time, I read."

"I'd forgotten your interest in books," Louis said quietly. "In another time, if we were each not so busy with our duties, we might have had time to compare our thoughts."

"And so you can right now," Robert interjected. "Have you read Boethius? Or the new translations of Aristotle by Averroes from Spain?"

The three men sat together, talked of ideas, of ethics, of the power of learning. And then of politics, of what the popes might be up to (there being three at the time), of the German emperor Barbarossa and which side was favored in the Italian conflicts.

Suddenly Henry rose without warning. "It's after the midnight hour. We sail the Channel at dawn. I must rest a few hours with my men."

"When will we see you again in Normandy? Or perhaps even Paris," Louis asked, rising also.

"We'll be back before Christmastide. Eleanor and I will spend it in Cherbourg. We have some trouble in the south."

"Ah, yes, Toulouse."

"The count of Toulouse seems to forget his fealty belongs to my wife's Aquitaine," Henry said, looking knowingly at Louis.

"Yes, so I have been told."

"Is your sister Constance writing to you, then?" Henry asked. "Her marriage to the count might prove a liability in the future."

"Ah, well. Families. Our first loyalty." Louis smiled to take the bite out of his words. "Really, Henry, you would expect no less of yourself where your own family interests lie, *n'est-ce pas*?"

"Indeed, Sire," Henry said, using that title deliberately to remind Louis that he had sworn fealty to him for Normandy, Anjou and Maine. "But of course, now, with the promised marriage of our children, you and I are also family." The smile on the younger king's face reminded Robert of a wolf's head he had once been given.

Henry came around the table and hooked his arm into the older man's as the latter was fastening his cloak. In this manner, abbot Robert saw the younger man lead the elder from the room, all the while still speaking to him. The king of France bent his head to meet the other's, and they looked almost the same height, although the abbot could have sworn that the elder was half a head taller only a moment earlier. He followed them from the room as Henry continued his cheery discourse on the pleasures of their new family connections, Louis nodding and occasionally emitting a slight chuckle.

Abbot Robert had no doubt that Louis knew exactly what Henry was doing, but still, he enjoyed it. The English king had his own rough charm, Robert thought. Part of it was his directness, and part his keen mind. Yes, Louis was definitely no longer thinking of his own sister's husband.

Outside the room, Henry dropped Louis's arm. They stood facing each other, a farewell. With the fortunes of kings, who knew when they would meet again. It was Louis who moved to embrace the younger man. "We were meant to be brothers," he said, just audible to Robert's keen ears.

Henry turned to the abbot. "I bed down with my men in the Great Hall, Abbot Robert. We sail at first light. Many thanks for your hospitality." He pulled a purse from his tunic and pressed it into Robert's hand. "For the poor and the scholars," he said simply.

The abbot bowed deeply in Henry's direction. Instead of kissing the abbot's ring, which was, after all, protocol, Henry clasped both his arms in the gesture of friendship his knights used with each other. The clasp was warmly returned. Then Henry casually pulled a torch from its wall sconce and, moving lightly on his feet for such a sturdy man, disappeared into the dark.

Suddenly the French king seemed smaller, quieter, as if without the turmoil and energy of Henry's presence, he had retreated into his usual shell of restraint. Robert offered the older man his arm. "Shall I see you to your chambers, My Lord? I have a place set aside for you."

"Yes, I would like that. And you can also send in my valet. I do feel as though I drank more wine than was good for me. As usual with Henry." King Louis was not unsteady, but he seemed suddenly almost fragile.

"Aah, but My Lord. What a conversation! The wine only helped us range over all the topics fitting for kings." Robert was smiling with the memory.

"It's true, Robert." Louis turned to him. "I have never been allowed, or perhaps never made time, for such a conversation among equals since I left my schooling at St. Denis. And I tell you, I love no man so much as the king of England, who brought us to this moment."

* * *

Henry dropped onto a pallet beside de Lucy in front of the fire, but sleep refused his invitation. Thoughts chased themselves like rabbits inside his head.

Louis is not a bad sort. He does tend to the pious from time to time as if he slips from ruler to monk in his head. The monk used to drive Eleanor mad, she's said. Maybe he never made up his mind what he truly is. But his memories about Outremer: for certain he's not a soldier.

My gut will not be silent. Christ's bones, it must have been the eels. Why do abbeys near the sea always have a need to show off by serving fish? But are eels fish? There must be another name for them. God only knows. Still, it was eels that killed my father, I'm certain. I should avoid them.

This matter of Toulouse is worrisome. The count of Toulouse insists he does not owe Eleanor homage, and since his marriage to Louis's sister, his actions have become more outrageous. Sometimes he claims sovereignty, sometimes he hauls Berengar down in Barcelona into the conversation, says Berengar's his true overlord. I'm told he says whatever suits him when my messengers approach. I know Eleanor wants him settled.

Too many other matters to attend to in London. We'll discuss it at Cherbourg. I promised Elle we would be back in Normandy at the holidays. Tom can join us for Christmastide, and we can all discuss our approach to this situation. We should do some statecraft in the midst of all the music Eleanor loves to bring on for celebration. Yes, then we can plan.

Christmastide 1158
Cherbourg, Normandy

The royal children had been bathed in hot water tubs for the Christmas festivities, to which action they had objected mightily, their howls heard all the way into the queen's chamber where the king and queen entertained a special visitor. The chancellor of England was attending them for Christmastide at the king's expressed wish.

"Madame," Henry raised his eyebrows at his wife across the small table, "Can you not quiet your children?"

"My children, My Lord, are quiet. It is yours who create the stir," she replied with the edge of a smile. Henry caught that impulse, Becket saw, and it quieted his own impatience. So, they were still in tune with one another, he thought. That must mean that Eleanor had something to do with his invitation to join them.

"Well then, we must have yours teach mine their manners," Henry said. Now they both grinned. Beckett was familiar with their repartee. For them, it was a form of amusement. Becket sat between them, looking from one to the other for all the world as if he were watching a *jeu de palme* match. When his two sovereigns went at it like this, he was never certain who had the service side and who the hazard. Usually, it was good-humored and sometimes verged on phantasy as they traded jibes and *bon mots,* but he had also seen a sharpness from time to time, which disconcerted him.

Now, though, all seemed calm. The three sat in comfort despite the strong wind beating around the small castle walls, and they enjoyed the warmth of the mulled wine and the fireplace. Excellent mulled wine, Becket thought. For someone who cared little for elegance in dress or table, the food was exceptionally good in the royal household. But then, Becket bethought himself, that improvement had come with his sovereign's marriage.

Eleanor was elegant, as always, in her holiday attire, the rich-looking new wools dyed a deep red coming out of Bruges, her blonde hair braided and piled high on her head, a brilliant tiara adorned with rubies and the requisite veil providing the modest covering. The king, as usual, had not bothered to change after the hearty hunting party of the afternoon. Becket had enjoyed the hunt immensely and had been well-rewarded when he felled a buck Henry claimed to have missed the previous day. That was one thing about Henry: he carried no grudges and was always generous in his praise. If he was quick-tempered when things went wrong, he was just as often equally fast with good-humored friendship.

"What do you think, Tom? Both the queen and I value your opinion on this matter."

Becket whipped his thoughts back into the present. "I'm sorry, My Lord, I was thinking on another matter altogether." He had learned early on never to lie to Henry. If he wasn't listening, admitting it was far preferable to trying to bluff his way through. Henry, who appeared so careless for so much of the time, was actually always paying attention. At the outset of their relationship as king and chancellor, Becket's lessons on this point had been painful and, consequently, few.

"Good! At least you are thinking on our matters," Henry groused, but not ill-humoredly.

Eleanor smiled, but without warmth. Her feelings about the chancellor remained mixed. She admired his wit, his competence and knew he served his king loyally. She remembered him as the handsome cleric just out of Merton's priory when they were in Paris twenty years earlier. Had she fancied him then? She could not remember now.

She had never forgotten the stunning picture in her mind's eye of his challenge to Abelard in front of all the students. Pierre Abelard, the master philosopher, who had returned to the university years after his fatal romance with Heloise and his castration, to teach again for a mere handful of years before his death. And there was Becket, nearly a match for the master, point for point, a great game for the rest of the students to watch. The master was the victor in that run, but only just. He accepted the gauntlet his prize student had cast down with something almost like amusement. But Becket had been in deadly earnest.

Still, there was something intangible missing in Becket, even then. His debates with the master all those years ago had been invigorating for the mind, but without passion. Abelard had passion, but not Thomas. And Becket had not changed. All that service to Henry as chancellor, impeccable, competent, above reproach. But withal, Becket was the coolest person she had ever seen. Eleanor did not trust him. But should she share these reservations with the king? When he clearly did place his trust in this man. Perhaps not now. That action might have unintended consequences.

No, she did not trust Becket, but his opinion was always well worth the hearing.

"What is the problem, My Lord?" Becket was saying.

"The problem is that my queen cannot control her subjects." Henry glanced impishly at Eleanor, who had opened her mouth to protest, then saw his expression. She shook her head, but Becket could see she was amused.

"Henry thinks everything that happens that involves him must be blamed on someone," she said dryly. "No event, no matter how small, is the result of circumstances or external forces. The fault for it must be assigned."

Here they go, thought Becket. The poignards are out, even though the humor was still evident. He began to wonder how he could bring this conversation to a close before royal tempers rose.

"My queen and wife has long wanted to settle the issue of Toulouse. Admit it, my dear. You even tried to push Louis into making the run at the recalcitrant counts of Toulouse."

"What if I did? The county rightfully owes fealty to the Dukes of Aquitaine," she shot back quickly. "I said so then, and I say so now. It is time the matter was settled."

"But you know what *they* say," Henry continued, slouching back in his chair and apparently unruffled by his wife's passionate tone. "*They* say that they loaned the ninth Duke William of Aquitaine, your grandfather, money for his adventures against the caliphate and that the Duke never paid the loan back. They claim they have earned their independence."

"That is an old tale that bears no repeating," Eleanor stated firmly, her open hand delivering a flat slap to the table. "Raimon has yet to produce the document by which my grandfather agreed to any such loan. And Toulouse belonged to my grandmother Philippa, who was the lawful wife of my grandfather Duke William, the troubadour. He received it in her dowry. So, whatever he owed the count there, he was still the lawful overlord."

"God's teeth, Eleanor." Henry rolled his eyes. "The hot blood of the south will out in the politics of it all. You are living proof of that."

"Better our hot blood than the cold Normans you come from," she rejoined just as quickly. "Bred in the snow, they were."

"Aah, wait one moment, Majesties. I need to get a clearer picture of the problem," Becket interjected smoothly, suddenly brought back to the present. His diplomatic skills had already been well honed on this royal couple, even if he had difficulty keeping up with their repartee.

"What, exactly, is the issue here? If there is trouble in the south, if it's the Lusignan family again, you've settled them before, Henry, with a quick trip and the show of force. Why not do it again, just that same way?" He paused. His sovereigns looked at him, puzzled. "What, exactly, is the problem?" he repeated weakly as they stared.

"Haven't you been listening?" Henry's tone was sharp. "The problem is Toulouse."

"Hunh. Toulouse is big." Becket muttered. "Toulouse could be a problem. What do they say?"

"Well, it's Raimon, of course. That endless chain of Counts Raimon, those southern hotheads…"

"You are repeating yourself," Eleanor interjected.

"First he claimed he was independent. When my messengers came with threats if he did not submit to the House of Poitiers and our realm, he claimed he owed allegiance to Berengar of Barcelona, then to Pierre of Aragon." Henry was working himself into a state, his face red now, his voice rising.

"Sire," Becket said in his quiet chancellor's tone, "Calm yourself. This can be addressed."

"Yes, well, all right then. Tell me how, Thomas. Get me out of this." Henry, in his agitation, rose and paced the length of the room once. Then returned to flop back into his high oak chair. The fire spit cinders onto the hearth. The three listened to the snapping sound as Henry took a few deep breaths.

"It's not as though I have time for this," the king finally continued. "I have so many claims. We are setting up the king's justice system in England. I've got Louis still snapping at my heels in Normandy. Anything could happen there, even with our new-found friendship." He paused, then took time for a smile. His quicksilver moods, thought Becket, not helping this time.

"Anjou is fine, but south of that is always trouble. Limoges, Chalus, Perigeux. I put out one fire and there is another. Poitiers itself, the seat of the dukes of Aquitaine, has malcontents stirring. I leave a small contingent of men to deal with the problems, and they constantly call me back to help." Henry adopted the look of a long-suffering shepherd whose collies were no longer working well. "It's a wonder anyone would want to be a monarch. And I must make time to deal with Ireland. Yet, I'm always called back to the continent."

It wasn't exactly a whine, gruff Henry would have been incapable of such expression, but Becket felt his master's misery acutely. And Henry was no fun when he got into this state; no fun to hunt with, to sup with, to goad the scholars at his court into engaging dialectics. All the fun left him when he became morose over problems of state. No fun at all. This must be handled.

"My Lord, I see a solution," Becket said, suddenly full of vigor. "Simply treat these unruly vassals as you would any other. Do what I suggested a moment ago. Raise an army and present yourself at their gates. Make an example of Toulouse. I guarantee they will fold their tents and accept you with gifts and open arms."

Eleanor had been silent for some time, her head bowed, her hands folded deep in the wine-colored velvet of her lap, listening. Now she raised her head.

"There is one small problem with your solution," she said, her voice carrying a hint of steel that put Thomas on alert. Her right hand, with long, slender fingers, extended toward Thomas as if to offer him some gift or as if to forestall further comment. Her sleeve fell away from the wrist, a cascade of green silk beauty onto the table.

"Raimon, the current count, the fifth of that name in the counts of Toulouse lineage, is married to Louis's sister, Constance," she stated with a fine, cat-like smile. "You, with your well-trained diplomatic eye, can readily see the complication. We are now family again, Louis and I, *grâce à* Henry, as our children have been espoused." She arched her fine brows. "Surely, you recall your trip to Paris for the official signing. In great style. Cost the exchequer a fortune, but apparently enough to make the French forget their antipathy to their former queen."

Indeed, Becket thought, it had been enough at the time.

"Aah, yes. Right," he said. Silent for a minute, he thought. Then he turned to Henry. "My Lord, despite the family connection, I still think you should treat Raimon like any other recalcitrant vassal. Raise an army, go down south and force the renewal of his allegiance."

"Brave words, Thomas, for someone who will sit in London while we're on the road to a hassle with Louis's sister!"

"No, not at all," Becket said with sudden inspiration. "I plan to raise my share of the army and join you."

"You?" Henry and Eleanor said in unison, finally surprised at something their chancellor said.

"Indeed. How could I do other? Besides, I think, My Lord, you have never seen me in the field." He grinned. "I do not lack valor."

Henry was nonplussed. He stared at his chancellor, then burst into laughter.

"Well said, Tom. I never believed for a minute there was not a soldier in you somewhere." He talked through his mirth. "Not the way you hunt."

"And how is that, My Lord?" Eleanor looked puzzled.

"With great vengeance! Especially when thwarted by the animal at first go." Henry shook his head, but Eleanor had fastened her attention on Thomas.

"So, you secretly long to take to the field, Chancellor." She made a statement, not a question of it, but there was a hint of skepticism in her tone.

"There is nothing I would like more, Madame," Becket replied, sitting forward in his chair, turning quickly back to the king. "Now, My Lord, we must plan to raise enough funds to pay an army. It must be a larger host than you have taken to Normandy, arms and men enough to impress. I have a suggestion."

"I'm certain you do," Eleanor murmured, her lips pursing as she confronted this new version of Tom Becket.

"God's teeth, let's hear it," Henry said, now well hooked into the game.

"We set a levy, by shire. Each household will have a share. Each shire must send so many men or so much money to replace the men. We'll have enough in a fortnight to pay the mercenaries from the Belgium colonies to fight our battle for us." Becket was now nearly on his feet, so passionate was he.

Eleanor watched him through narrowed eyes.

Henry sat upright and leaned forward. "I like that plan well, Tom. But rather than the shires, let's place it on the lords. I say five shillings for each knight in their service to buy them out. We'll use the money to hire the Belgians again. They fight like demons once in the field. And this way, English knights can stay at home. We'll organize the army."

"Why the lords? They might protest." Becket frowned.

"No, no, no. They'll love the plan. It gives them a chance to look good in front of their knights, buying them out of service. Breeds loyalty. Trust me, I know them well. Meanwhile, I place no further burden on the shires, as I am trying to get the justice system working at a local level. Which reminds me," Henry turned to Eleanor with his rapid change of mood and topic, "How did the hearings come out on the use of the king's forest at St. Albans? Were you able to settle that dispute in my absence?"

"I sent a writ to Robert of Valognes, reiterating your earlier judgement and instructing him to stop cutting down the abbot's trees until the matter was adjudicated. Leicester is to hear the case in the next fortnight. The sheriff tells me that Valognes' men have stopped destroying the wood."

Henry made a fist and knocked his knuckles on the smooth maple table three times. "We must have a system. We cannot be present for every dispute in the kingdom, so let us create a law we can enforce, one that everyone respects." His mouth pulled into a firm line.

"Sire, I fully agree. But presently, we must lay plans to raise an army and move on the Count of Toulouse, Constance Capet marriage or not, to reinforce our queen's rights over her people."

"And don't forget the plan we discussed to meet with Raimon Berengar of Barcelona." The queen interjected. "We must start with diplomacy."

"Ah, my clever queen," Henry smiled and turned to Becket. "You know her plan for betrothing our youngest babe, Richard, to Berengar's daughter? Could be quite fruitful, in every sense, ha, ha, and certainly, the hint of it will neutralize the count of Barcelona in our dealings with Toulouse."

Before Becket could offer a rejoinder, the queen appeared to stifle a small yawn with the back of her hand. "The hour grows late. I will withdraw to my chamber," she said. "You are welcome to use the anteroom as long as your ideas flow. But please do not be loud, or I will not sleep tonight."

Both men rose as she did, and the king bent over her slender hand, lingering scarce a moment, a perfunctory gesture. Before Eleanor had reached the large oak doors, the rising voices behind her indicated the two men were already in full tilt as masters of the Norman-English invasion. She glanced back to see Thomas now making notes and figures on the parchment that Eleanor had left lying on the table.

An interesting side to the former scholar, she thought mildly. Behind her, she heard the king's voice bark, "Enough of this, Tom. Let's do real battle on the chessboard. I've been waiting for a week because the queen's given it up for Christmastide. I've new ivory pieces from an artist in Norway."

Much later, Thomas finally took his leave, the king waving him off casually. As the chancellor entered the corridor leading to the Great Hall, he cast a glance over his shoulder just in time to see the king—after a moment of hesitation—turn toward the queen's sleeping chamber and quietly enter it.

September 1159, The Aquitaine
Henry's camp before the walls of Toulouse

It was not the first time Henry had found himself in a tight spot in the field. The rain had been pelting down for three solid days, and his men were soaked clear through. The tents were soggy, inside and out. Although his mercenaries did not complain—they were, after all, paid to do this—he could sense that much more of the combination of rain and military inaction, not to mention the dysentery sweeping the camp, could produce a mood of rebellion. As their captain had put it to him not an hour earlier, "The men are paid to fight, not to sit in the pissing rain for days." Although the man's attempt at Norman French was close to unintelligible, Henry understood his meaning well enough.

The king had made his way through the mud from the War Council tent to his private quarters, cursing for the hundredth time that week the fortunes that had brought him Eleanor's land and recalcitrant *petites noblessse*. He flopped on his bed and thought it all through again.

This enterprise seemed such a good idea when Eleanor and I and Tom talked about it at Christmastide. In the event, however, it is a disaster.

I'm in a tight spot. When I came a fortnight ago—God's bones, was it only that? — it had seemed the sun was shining on my plans. I had a goodly number of paid men at arms—thanks in part to Tom's brilliant scheme of allowing my nobles to buy their knights out of service—and I was heartened by Tom's wondrous powers of raising his own small army, 2,000 men paid for by himself. This is a new side to Becket, and one that I like. He is more like me than I could have thought possible. He is not the dandy and dinner-party-giver he's always appeared, but a true soldier. He is like my brother.

But all that is not saving us. Let me think on what has happened. . . . It all started with the arrival of Louis and his army, come in support of his sister's husband. I didn't think he would defend the count, but there it is. That's Louis where land is concerned.

He had plenty of time to pull back when he saw my arrival. And he must have known I meant business, to come all the way down here with this army of my own. I didn't think it would come to this, Louis and I facing off one another outside the walls of Toulouse.

There was the meeting in Tours in late winter. Louis came, all right, but said he would not give me his promise not to interfere, which he had (I pointed out) so generously given me last year in the affair in Brittany.

Then the meeting at Heudicourt, just weeks before my host was set to march to Toulouse. And still no agreement. Barbarossa no help. Too close to his ambitions in Italy for his comfort.

Louis has changed. Is the old nettle of Eleanor's lands coming to me with our marriage still pricking? Or is the difference for him here that his sister is involved in this one? Or does he just dislike the fact that the sum total of my lands already overwhelms his?

When we arrived, Louis was in his tents with his men, arrayed on the opposite field from me but well within sight. He had a far smaller host than mine, that was evident. The fleur de lys fluttered from his tent, and I immediately sent a message asking for a parley. Louis responded warmly, was even open to a meeting, the first since our enormously amicable encounter at Mont St. Michel. He embraced me as a brother when I entered his tent.

But then things went wrong.

Louis announced right off that he was entering the city. He said I could do what I liked about it, but that he had an obligation to defend his sister and her city (not to mention that good-for-nothing count of a husband of hers). He said he was done talking, but he wanted to give me that message in person.

He could not have been more polite. He's probably sincere. The man has no artfulness in him. Incapable of nuance, much less deception. He really should have been a monk.

But now, what do I do? If I attack the city with Louis in it, I am effectively attacking the lord to whom I have sworn fealty for Normandy and Anjou. That could call into question all the lords who have sworn fealty to me. If I don't respect the code of honour, why should they. Could be a damnable mess. God's right ear, what to do.

And now the troops are either ill with the flux or coughing from the rain. How could I even win if I breached the city walls now? I have only half an army or less with which to do it . . .

There must be a way out.

Becket entered the tent, pushing back the flap Henry had closed against the rain. "Sire, they said I would find you here." He shed the heavy blanket that had shielded him from the worst of the weather, and Henry was surprised to note the fine linen tunic and woolen leggings covered only by a leather jerkin of considerable value.

The king swung his legs over the edge of his cot and stood. He scratched his buttocks in several places, now cursing the fleas that didn't seem to mind the rain enough to stay out of the pallets. He had not changed his clothing for several days and was miserable for it.

"Things do not look good for us, Tom."

"No, I admit there are problems," Becket said with a solemnity that made Henry emit a tough little laugh.

"'Problems' scarce covers the situation. I have a sick army, terrible weather and a decision as to whether to attack my liege lord, the king of

France and fly in the face of every code of honor accepted in our times. I would call this set of problems rather a catastrophe."

"Sire, none of those issues are insurmountable. I have called the captains to a conference with you in just one hour. But I wanted to talk with your first about your strategy."

"Go ahead, I'm listening." The king sounded morose as he shuffled toward the table that held the wine and bread brought for his repast. He lifted the pitcher in the direction of Becket, who shook his head. Henry poured a liberal amount of wine into his earthenware goblet before turning to his chancellor. He did not invite Becket to sit.

"I think this is our opportunity." The chancellor was clearly excited.

"For . . .?" Henry said, raising his brows. Any opportunity in his present dire situation had escaped his notice.

"The count of Toulouse will obviously expect us to pass. To fold our tents as it were and steal away. He'll have a wager going right this very moment that you'll not attack him because the king of France is within these walls."

"Yes. And . . .?" Henry gazed at him over his goblet as he lifted it to his lips.

Becket beamed at his king. "This is the perfect time to take them by surprise. Attack. Confound them by doing the exact thing they expect you not to do."

"No," Henry said simply, wiping his lips with the back of his hand.

"But Sire, I believe …"

"I said no—absolutely not." The king paused. "I'm pleased you've called the captains. They should be gathering now, so we'll go to the command tent and give them the news."

"Your majesty," Becket rarely used the king's formal title, "I ask leave to speak as your chancellor."

"You may speak, but I'll not alter my decision." The iron in the king's tone should have warned Becket, but he was focused instead on his chance of persuasion whilst he had the king alone.

"As your chancellor, I oversee the good of the kingdom." Becket moved a bit closer to the king in his enthusiasm, as close as he dared. Henry raised his hand.

Sensing that he might be pushing the royal temper, Becket stepped back a bit. Henry finally looked at him. His gaze was intense, and there was a set to his square jaw that carried a warning Becket ignored at his peril. Yet the chancellor pushed onward.

"Sire, I have brought seven hundred men here to fight for our cause at my own expense. Let us not waste those good fighting men. We have the opportunity here to take two magnificent actions: we could capture Toulouse, bring the counts to heel as you have with others who have ignored your and . . ." His voice rose on that last word, and he repeated it, "and capture the king of the Franks. Louis would be your captive, Sire. Think of it."

"I have thought of it, Chancellor," Henry said in a much lower voice than his colleague, forcing Becket to lean forward to hear him, "and I can think of nothing I would less rather have in this world than the king of the Franks taken by my forces and in my custody!"

"But . . ."

"Do you not hear me?" Henry's voice rose. "Is this what you are advising? Against all the laws of chivalry, I make war on my overlord, the king of the Franks? I have done homage to him for my lands here. Take him prisoner? A fine situation! And then what? Take the king of France back to England? Or to Normandy, where his barons would come at once, and I'd have to spill honest English blood to keep him? Start a war that could last for one hundred years?" By now, the king was red-faced and shouting, and it was Becket who was looking away, looking down, looking anywhere but at the enraged face of his king. "And what of those who owe me fealty? What will my vassals make of such a move? That they may do the same to me?" He paused, letting his words fall on the charged air.

"By no means will I allow myself to be put in that situation!" and with these words scarce spoken, Henry hurled his goblet at the oak chest that stood in the corner, smashing it into many pieces, red wine flowing over the carpets in the tent. "Go to the Command Tent. Tell the captains I will arrive shortly. Do not tell them of my decision, I warn you. Do not seek to contravene my will, or by God's head, I'll have yours. Go." This last command was a growl as if it came from the throat of an enraged bear.

Becket knew that any words he spoke would be lost on the king, who now appeared fully in the throes of the famous Angevin temper. The king picked up his scabbard and cast it in the direction of the beleaguered chest, the only solid thing in the tent. The chancellor knew well the next item jettisoned could be directed at him, and there was still a heavy shield standing in the corner. He grabbed his blanket and left quickly, the shield flying out the flap of the tent behind him. He picked it up from the mud and tossed it back into the tent, which generated another heavy stream of invective from inside.

Thomas Becket ran through the heavy September rain of the Toulousain. He had weathered many of Henry's rages in the six years they worked together, but never had one been directed at him. Something was changing.

He had been right in his advice to the king, he knew it in his heart, and instead of listening, the king had dismissed him out of hand, like some ignorant cowherd. Henry had not even given his strategy a proper hearing.

Becket seethed, but he also knew he could not ignore Henry's warning. The man had an uncanny ability to see something amiss. He dared not warn the captains of the king's decision to abort their mission. And anyway, they themselves were disheartened and probably would be glad of the chance to take their money and disband. It was an ill day, indeed, for Normandy and for England. The chancellor no longer noticed the pelting rain.

Christmastide 1159
Falaise, Normandy

Henry looked remarkably well-groomed on Christmas afternoon when he appeared at the foot of the castle's stone staircase, just outside the Great Hall. Falaise, though one of Henry's smallest, was also one of his favorite castles. It was the home of his Norman ancestors, and he often felt a kinship with the past when he rested here.

The king was cleaned and newly barbered, his short red beard and combed hair complimenting his leonine face and powerful shoulders. He wore a long wool tunic from Bruges, the color of rich Bordeaux wine, and woolen dark green hose—a costume that, for a change, actually looked royal. Around his neck hung the medallion of the king of England, a copy of the great seal which he had commanded be put on a chain for special occasions. All he needed to complete the outfit was the orb and sceptre, but even Henry, in his drama, knew that would be a step too far. After all, he was simply greeting his wife, whom he had not seen for four months, not holding a state ceremony.

Still, this was an important meeting, their first since he had pulled out of the conflict outside Toulouse and left Louis to his own devices there. He had gone south to discipline his wife's vassals and left without any accomplishment on her behalf. How would the queen react? Her messages, when informed of his actions outside Toulouse, had been noncommittal. But he knew from experience in her person her reactions might be more astringent.

His court stood arrayed in rows along the hallway, torches blazing in a way not usual in the royal castles when the queen was absent. She adored light, and Henry knew it. From the Great Hall floated the sounds of lutes and a recorder or two, musicians brought from England, with uncharacteristic thoughtfulness. They were providing the melodies of the south, of which his wife was so fond. Peter of Blois, standing next to Walter Map, noted all in the scene carefully. He leaned over to his fellow scholar and whispered, "The King has outdone himself tonight on every level."

Walter Map threw an amused glance in his direction, cocked his head, and then said, "He has to. This is the first time Eleanor has seen him since his retreat at Toulouse. He wanted their meeting to be this public. A private one may have involved a royal tongue-lashing."

Peter of Blois grinned. "Maybe we'll see it here?"

"Not bloody likely," Map said. "Henry's too smart to create a scene with Eleanor that could go into my chronicles. By the time they are finally alone tonight, Eleanor will have had time to mute her anger. And even the hot-headed devil can be charming when he chooses."

Eleanor had arrived late the night before, and she, too, looked thoroughly royal as she descended the stone stairway in the castle to meet her king. Her tall, still-slender figure was captured in a gown of the new velvet fabric, dyed in woad and the deep blue set off her high color and green eyes to perfection. She moved like a queen, Henry thought, as she came toward him. Yes, she was every inch worthy of being *his* queen. Then he noticed her expression, face lined and mouth firm. This did not bode well for their reunion.

"My dear, your beauty outshines the stars this cold night," Henry said as he extended his arm to her. She had bowed first, ever so slightly (Walter Map noted the restraint with interest), and he had raised her hand to his lips. Now he took her elbow and guided her into the Great Hall.

"You are turning poet in your older years, Henry," Eleanor said with some amusement, although an edge of anger lurked in her tone. The king was warned.

The royal couple took their places in the center of the head table, and the marshall pounded his staff three times into the floor to announce their seating. The court flooded into the room and, with great noise and laughter, took their chairs, some above the salt and some below according to their rank. The Christmas Court of the King and Queen of England had formally opened. This, Christmas day, was the first of the twelve days of celebration.

The royal couple talked quietly for a few moments, then were joined at the table by de Lucy and Leicester. These nobles were accompanied by their ladies, a rare occasion for usually the justiciars were at the court alone, their business with the king being foremost in their minds.

The great feast of Christmas, however, was a family affair.

"So you think Becket can handle the business of England alone whilst you and the queen are here with me?" Henry turned to de Lucy, who was obviously taken by surprise at the question.

"Well, Sire, of course he has du Hommet still there to ride herd on him. I think no harm will come to the country in our absence." De Lucy smiled at the king, somewhat puzzled. "Was there a reason you inquired about Becket?"

"Not particularly. We parted outside of Toulouse, and I haven't seen him since, although he writes regularly. Seems to be managing the chancery in my absence. But he was not happy that I did not take his advice to attack Louis at Toulouse."

De Lucy pursed his lips, his narrow face settling into its natural lines north to south as he thought. He was a deliberate man, was de Lucy. Then he shook his head.

"I've not seen nor noticed any difference, Your Grace." Di Lucy gave a small smile. "He still entertains lavishly, still hunts much of the time, but his clerks in the chancery work hard, and the writs are going out on time, at least as far as my work is concerned."

Eleanor had brought many of her own ladies in attendance with her, and they were arrayed below the great table. A large space had been left in the middle of the hall, below the royal table. Eleanor raised her brows in question to Henry, who responded with a self-satisfied smile.

"Just wait, my dear. A surprise for your Christmas court. You will see during dinner."

Eleanor pursed her lips, then lowered her voice and took the plunge with an abrupt question.

"Henry, despite your elegant letter, I remain puzzled as to why you would leave the field at Toulouse without settling matters with Louis. Now I would like to have the real story. What, exactly, happened to cause you to retreat?"

He was taken aback by the question and perhaps by the word retreat, but the queen knew better. He was always prepared, and he knew this moment would come. No doubt, though, he expected it later when they were alone.

"As I wrote you, Elle, it was an impossible situation." He cleared his throat and gestured to the steward for more wine.

"Yes, I know what you wrote me, but I heard a slightly different story from Thomas."

"Did you now?" The king, waiting for his drink, turned his attention to his wife, who was looking full at him.

"To be plain, when he returned to England shortly before I did, he wrote me his own account of what happened. I received it even before I left Poitiers that month for England."

The response was abrupt. "I'm surprised he took it upon himself to do that."

"He said you could easily have taken the city, that Louis didn't have sufficient troops and you had more than enough men."

"Did he so?" Henry turned to his plate of stewed mutton in piquant sauce, which his taster had just replaced in front of him. "Well, he was mistaken. He was mistaken in his advice at Toulouse, and he was mistaken when he wrote that to you."

"What makes you so certain?" The queen waved away the servant now hovering at her shoulder, anxious to pour her more wine.

"Madame," Henry turned his entire upper body to face the queen, and his brow was knit fiercely. "Kindly do me the honor of respecting my superior experience in politics, especially in the field of battle, and allow me to make judgements that a first-time soldier like Becket would be incapable of rendering." He turned back to his plate, and added half under his breath, ". . . no matter how fine a hunter in the forest he may be."

Eleanor responded in a low voice. Only those close around the couple heard her. "Well said, Henry. I will give you that honor. But I think you should know what your chancellor said to me. When I returned to England, he asked for an audience. He told me in person what his advice had been to you. And instead of taking it, he said you flew into a rage."

"Tom is a fine chancellor, and I'm certain he has our best interests at heart. But he is neither soldier nor military strategist." Henry raised his head from his dinner and stared out at the crowd. "Did he tell you what Louis did that shifted the balance?"

"He said Louis had apparently boxed you in by joining his sister and the count inside the city walls so that you would appear to menace your overlord if you made a foray on the town."

"Becket wasn't present when I held the council with Louis. He and the others were asked to remain outside the tent. Louis wanted only me. My chancellor, for once, does not know what was said there."

"And?"

"Your mutton is getting cold," Henry said, nodding in the direction of the queen's silver plate. "You are holding up the next course by not eating. And Walter Map is staring at us, so please smile and eat something, or he'll go back to his chamber tonight and write that the king and queen quarreled."

Eleanor looked quickly out over the crowd, caught Walter Map's glance and then raised a spoon to her lips with a broad smile.

"Louis challenged me directly," Henry continued as he attacked his venison. "One king to another. He said he was going inside the walls of the city without his men. He told me he had commanded his men not to stop me from entering the city. He looked me right in the eye and said, 'If you can attack the city knowing that your liege lord, from whom you hold Normandy and Anjou, has gone inside for safekeeping, then all of feudal society is at risk. I leave it up to you.'"

"Louis said that?" Eleanor seemed almost ready to laugh. "Louis? He was never so brave when he was married to me."

"Ah, my dear. Perhaps you do not know your former husband as well as you think. Or perhaps he has changed since you knew him." Henry waved away the rest of his meat, quaffing more wine instead as if this exchange with Eleanor was giving him a great thirst. Now nuts and fruits were placed in front of him.

"So it would seem." She was grinning in earnest now. Louis! Who would have credited such a report? Suddenly so manly and statesmanlike.

"Louis was always smarter than you gave him credit for." Henry said thoughtfully, popping a few almonds into his mouth. "And this scheme was positively ingenious. He had me. If I could attack him, my overlord, it would open me up to the same attacks from my own vassals. And you can be certain he would make sure they all knew about it."

"What happened?"

"Louis can be very dramatic . . ."

"As can you."

". . . as I was saying, Louis has a touch of the theatre about him. Always has. Must be that religious training he got at St. Denis when he was headed for a church career when his older brother was in line for the throne. But after he laid this out for me, and before I could argue with him, he turned and walked out of the tent. Of course, I followed him. I couldn't imagine what he was going to do."

"And?"

"He simply walked up to the gates of the city and knocked on the gates three times with his staff. It was all pre-arranged. A messenger had been sent. They were ready for him. The door opened, he walked in, the door closed. And we all stood there and watched it."

"Becket said you had enough men to attack and win." Eleanor had recovered her appetite and was tearing at a pigeon now with her fine teeth, speaking between bites.

"Becket, my dear, was not in the tent with Louis. He didn't hear the challenge, nor did he have the responsibility. Forgive me, he is a fine chancellor, or so it seems, but he is not the diplomat he thinks he is, or he would never have pressed me to attack. He doesn't think long term."

"Well, don't be cross with him for coming to me with his complaint. I believe he borrowed a lot of money to secure those knights of his, and he wanted to see some action for it all."

"I don't believe we should produce war and mayhem to compensate him for his army expenses," Henry said tartly.

"But do grant him the right to his inexperience and frustration," Eleanor said in return.

"I do believe you are becoming the chancellor's champion, my dear wife." Henry turned to her, a smile of amusement chasing his scowl away. "Quite a *volte-face*."

"I just believe I am beginning to understand him better. We are working well together in England, and that ought to be some comfort to you." The king responded with a slight tilt of his head.

Trumpets blared a fanfare. Eleanor sighed. "Louis may be dramatic, but I believe we are about to endure a theatrical event of our own."

Four chamberlains walked in with flaming puddings on their heads. They came up to the head table, then parted. A single chamberlain followed, carrying on his head a giant pie. This was placed on the table in front of the king and queen. Upon a signal, the marshall approached and, with his sword, sliced open the pie. A number of small birds flooded the room, to cries of "bravo, bravo," from the delighted court.

Eleanor rolled her eyes toward heaven: "Did you order this? Were you deliberately trying to distract me?"

Henry's expression told her everything, but it was just not in her at this point to berate him.

"Just trying to have a festive occasion, for once," he mumbled as she shook her head. But by now, he knew he had her. The cloud that had hung over their meeting had been blown away. Or so he hoped. Her good humor was returning.

De Lucy, who sat on the other side of the queen, leaned forward. "Sire, did you have time to read the dispatch from Thibault of Canterbury?"

"Indeed, I did. But not time to compose an answer."

"I saw him when he had his conference in London. He promised me no firm recommendation on which pope to back until you had made your decision." Eleanor spoke to both of them.

"Yes, but he gave advice in the message. And I had come to the same conclusion. I'm backing Alexander over Victor in this dispute. Alexander will make a far more reasonable pope, and we have long ties with him."

"And I think Thibault was inclined to back Alex, also, from what he said to me," Eleanor responded. "But he had enough sense to hold off the bishops from a formal statement until you had weighed in."

"I tell you, Eleanor, that archbishop is sent by God to promote the peace of the kingdom. It is as if we operate by one mind, Thibault and me. He wants the church and the state to be at peace, and he is a consummate diplomat. There is no one to match him, and I don't have to worry about conflicts. We work together."

"What will happen when he is gone?"

"Gone? Why should he be gone? He is in good health, not that aged . . ." Henry's voice trailed off.

"He looked very tired when I saw him just days ago," Eleanor said quietly. "He is aging, Henry, and you just don't want to see it. You might put your mind to a plan of what should happen when he dies."

"Ilchester is just back from Germany. He says Barbarossa has allowed a new practice. His chancellor has now taken on the title of Archbishop of Mainz. In effect, he's uniting church and state through one person."

"Something to think about," Eleanor murmured. "Goodness, what is this?"

Henry looked out over the Great Hall.

"Oh, I had them bring over some actors to perform from the troupes in England. They are reported to be very entertaining, and they sing and dance as well. I thought it would please you." The king glanced at his wife's face, now fully emptied of the concern he had first noticed. "After that, we have some *trouveres*, not quite your troubadours, but local to our north country and quite talented. And here comes the venison as well."

"Henry, this is quite a feast. The exchequer will not be best pleased." Eleanor laughed as she made her comment.

"Anything for your amusement after you've come all this way for the great feast of Christmas. And later in the evening, perhaps, my love, we may prepare to welcome another prince next autumn?" Henry was so seldom coy that his remark caused his wife to take a second glance in his direction. He kept a very straight face, and she turned her attention back to the stage. She had to suppress her smile.

Late October 1160
Argentan, Normandy

The three of them, with their attendants, arrived nearly at the same time, but that was totally accidental. Still, it created a courtyard mess, a chaotic swirl of men, horses, baggage, and a few of the queen's women. Henry had just a slight edge in time. He had been hunting in the nearby forest and only had four archers with him, so they were able to dismount as the other parties flooded in, and their horses were taken away to the stable.

Eleanor was next, with the three little princes, Henry, Richard and Geoffrey, a sleepy group in one cart. They were held in place by their minders, still in the care of nurses. Henry, the eldest at five years, was straining to see his father while Richard, only three summers, and Geoff, a year younger, were crying for milk.

Eleanor had brought more baggage to Normandy than on any previous visit. She had ridden horseback the last five miles, no doubt to be awake when confronting Henry. She reluctantly allowed du Hommet, who had accompanied her, to assist her in dismounting. The three little princes were helped down from their wagon and, hunger complaints forgotten, were running and shouting. Even Geoff, who had just learned to walk upright, toddled after young Henry, his idol. A very small girl who was the same size as Prince Richard—not yet three years of age—was still in the cart, screaming with fatigue, a state which, apparently, her nurse could do nothing to assuage. A stone-faced male servant picked the howling little girl out of the cart and carried her, the Princess Marguerite of France and the future queen of England, gingerly into the castle.

Becket came riding in behind the cart carrying his young charges. Almost unnoticed in the rush, he slipped from his horse and threaded his way through the crowd to the side of the king. Eleanor joined him there. William FitzStephen rounded up the little boys who followed him when he promised he had sweetmeats and nuts and bread and cheese if they would only come up the stairs and see. And they could look at the bows and arrows in the king's own arsenal if they were good afterward. The boys' nurses trailed behind, looking tired and somewhat dazed.

Henry grasped both his wife and chancellor by the elbow and guided them into the castle and up the stairs behind the children. The three headed for his privy chamber as he peppered them with questions, Becket first.

"Was there any trouble when you arrived at the castle to collect the infant, Princess Marguerite?" Henry asked as he hustled them toward the open door. He still had the sheen of the hunt on his brow, and Eleanor wrinkled her nose slightly as a breeze wafted his earthy forest scent toward her. "What did Robert of Newburgh say when you demanded her?"

"Sire, he was not at the castle. The Templars were there, but their leader was not of a mind to argue with me and the dozen knights I brought with me. He asked to see my papers, and the writ with the royal seal on it was enough for him. He recognized your imprint. Said he had spent some years in England under the war between your mother and Stephen and that he was glad of a chance to assist Henry Fitz-Empress."

"Let's hope he stays glad when Robert of Newburgh returns. Or better yet, when Louis hears I've taken possession of his daughter."

They reached the room, and Henry threw his cloak onto a chair as he made his way to the table. Refreshments had been laid out for the tired travelers. Wine from Bordeaux, fruit and cheese and breads were on silver plates, and goblets for the water and wine.

"So, sit, we must make our plan." Henry poured himself a full measure and stamped his glass on the table.

"I thought the plan was to marry young Henry and princess Marguerite as soon as possible." Eleanor's voice was sharp through her fatigue.

"My dear, it must be done correctly so there are no repercussions. We have not really had time to consider all the ramifications of taking possession of the princess."

"It's not our fault Louis acted with such unseemly haste," Becket said. "Who could have predicted Constance would die producing yet another daughter and that the King of France would marry again within a month. And marry Adela, the sister of the House of Blois."

"Yes, yes, regrettable. But I must say I admire the dispatch with which he conducted this operation." Henry said, talking through a full mouth of cheese, into which he had also crammed a small piece of bread. Hunting always raised his appetite.

"He must have had some inkling that things were not going well for poor Constance as she prepared to deliver her child. We even had reports in England that she might not survive the birth," Eleanor interrupted.

"Whatever went on, the alliance with the House of Blois is a disaster for our dynasty," Henry said quickly. "Henry, Count of Blois and Thibault, Count of Champagne are now the brothers-in-law of the king of France. They will be more of a menace than ever now. And they have the land and knights to back up their posturing."

Becket also had taken some food, and now he joined the conversation. "Yes, Louis could have another child within a year, and it could be a male. And . . ."

"And there go all our plans to unite France and England under Henry and Marguerite," Henry finished for him.

"But don't you think this plan is quite extreme? Taking the princess from her caregivers? That a conversation with Louis first might have been advisable?" Eleanor looked at both men. Becket looked down after meeting her eyes, but Henry had no such problem.

"And that would accomplish exactly what?" The king tore into a crust of bread. "He'd have a clue to our plans and could fortify the marches. He will understand perfectly well what I have in mind when he finds his daughter in my care. As soon as the marriage is accomplished, I'm taking the dowry. At least the Vexin will be all mine. One good thing out of this disaster."

"Henry, you just signed peace with Louis at Whitsun this very year. We just got past the disaster of Toulouse. Now it will start up all over again. Surely you don't expect him to do nothing when you seize his castles."

Henry got up, his sudden movement slopping wine from the goblet, but the cup steadied itself. He began his pacing, throwing his arms wide for emphasis as he talked. Eleanor sat back in her chair, taking deep breaths. She had just lost another child in the womb and should not even have been traveling so soon. But Henry had insisted.

"Well, yes, of course there will be a fuss. He always makes a fuss! But it never amounts to much." Henry was talking very fast now. "You'll be surprised when you consider how all this back-and-forth posturing between Louis and me results in so little bloodshed. The brothers of his new bride, Blois and Champagne, will squawk and some small castles will change hands. Then it'll be over. Meanwhile, at least I'll have the Vexin. As was promised me." He stood at the end of the table, arms akimbo.

Eleanor and Thomas said nothing. Henry conveniently took this for complete assent.

"Good," he said as if continuing a conversation and in agreement with only himself. He came back to sit across from them. "Now then, I have two papal legates on their way here who will, out of gratitude for my support for Alexander, who is now acknowledged pope, witness the ceremony of the children's marriage. We must do this right. There can be no question, when I go into the Vexin, that the marriage has taken place legally and the dowry is forfeit."

"No, indeed," Eleanor murmured. "None whatsoever."

Becket remained silent.

Later, Henry found sleep eluding him. He tossed around on his pallet, as he reviewed the conversations of the evening.

Well, what did they expect? That I'd sit still for this betrayal? Louis making marriage alliance with the House of Blois, the descendants of Stephen who tried to wrest the crown from my mother? What was the king of France thinking? He must be desperate to have a son, but the unseemly haste with which he wrapped up this event will be remembered. And the balance of power is shifting for him with these new relatives.

With Louis's new connection, the house of Blois might even revive their distant claim to the throne of England. Wouldn't that make a mess? Louis has left me no alternative. I have to get something out of this marriage of the young ones. And it might as well take place now to cement—so to speak—our relationship with the reluctant throne of France. Once the marriage is done, Louis can't undo it, no matter how he sputters. Nor can he deny me the Vexin in its entirety. He promised it as the dowry. That's been written and witnessed.

Becket was unusually subdued tonight. Did he say anything at all? I don't remember. Maybe a fit of pique because I didn't ask his opinion on this marriage. But surely it's plain as day. There are no drawbacks that I can see.

Thibault is waning, that's the news de Lucy has brought me from across the channel. I need to have a plan. I must have someone I trust, like I trust Thibault, at the head of Canterbury. I can't be distracted by wrangles with the church over this or that petty law or crime. Thibault thinks Becket is his natural successor. Ilchester says the emperor did something like this in Mainz, made his chancellor archbishop. Becket doesn't have holy orders, but that's a minor detail. If I make him archbishop, he can take holy orders the hour before his election, and it will be legitimate. And best of all, he'll still be my chancellor and my man. And it might pull him out of whatever doldrums he has been sunk into since Toulouse. Yes, he might actually like it.

My gut is giving me trouble. I wonder if I should get more fresh air. Maybe another hunt tomorrow, just a short one. Tom might enjoy that.

April 1161
Argentan, Normandy

"I gave orders not to be interrupted." Henry's unhappiness at the disturbance was evident in his quick bark. The messenger who breached the security of the meeting cowered. He was a young page from the area, a round little fellow of twelve or thirteen summers, whose parents had "donated" him to the service of the castle when the king and his court were in residence. His face could not have been whiter if it were a snowball.

The king could feel the gout in his swollen foot as his boot pressed upon it. The potion his physician (trained at Salerno with some expense to the treasury) had prescribed was not effective. It was probably not effective because he had decided not to take it this early Spring morning since he wanted to be alert for the meeting with his counsellors on several matters. Nevertheless . . .

The messenger. He dragged his attention away from his aching foot.

"Sire, the marshall told me I should bring this to you straightaway. The messenger just arrived, but the man rode so hard to bring this, he collapsed when he dismounted."

Du Hommet took pity on the boy.

"Henry, the boy is just doing what he was told." Du Hommet lifted the battered scroll from the lad's hand and replaced it with a coin.

"It's from the queen," the page added, emboldened no doubt by the coin.

Du Hommet passed the scroll to the king, who cut the red wax seal with the small knife he had been fiddling with. He waved the page away.

"What news, Sire?" Thomas Brown was new to Normandy and English to boot, but he was a man Henry was coming to trust. He looked around the small table.

"Thibault of Canterbury is dead. The queen is sending Becket to confer about a successor. She believes the post should be filled soon." Henry tossed the parchment on the table. "I'm not so sure."

"And what is your thinking on this matter, Sire?" Du Hommet was a man of business and wished never to leave a matter undecided. "Why wait?"

The king pursed his lips and looked off in the distance for just a moment, gathering his thoughts. The counsellors were unused to any pauses from the king.

"I think the monks will have their own candidate." He finally said. "It is their prerogative to elect their own leader. But..."

They waited.

"I would prefer it if I could have someone like Thibault. Someone who understands the crown, who is familiar with how government and justice work together."

"That would be someone not currently a monk, then," William FitzStephen ventured without humor.

"Exactly so," the king said.

The men in the room stayed quiet. A single thought had entered the room. Becket. None had to ask.

Suddenly the king looked around and, as if the topic of Canterbury had never been mentioned, said, "I'm told Louis wants to talk peace in the early summer. I've had enough of the skirmishes we've endured ever since the marriage of the royal children. I'm for entertaining his invitation. Everyone agreed?"

Du Hommet, Thomas Brown, Walter of Coutances, William FitzStephen and even Walter Map, who had been invited to keep the minutes for the king's records, they all looked at one another. Silent, grinning somewhat ruefully, they nodded assent.

* * *

When Becket arrived at Argentan two days later with his usual retinue of pages and valets, the counsellors had finished their business. The king had waited with uncharacteristic patience for his chancellor. With the swelling of his foot diminishing, Henry announced that he had time for a ride and a chat with his chancellor just as soon as the visitor had time to rest. They left together, alone, early the following morning.

They were in the forest surrounding the castle, and each held a gerfalcon on his wrist. Henry, unusually, was more interested in the conversation than the hunting this time.

"What news besides Thibault's death?" he inquired. "What does the queen say?"

"She just returned from a progress through the Yorkshire dales," Becket reported. "The queen had been gone two weeks. She came back just before the archbishop died."

"Let's follow this trail. I think there is better hunting down by the water." The king led the way, giving himself time to choose his words carefully. He still had not decided on Canterbury but was leaning toward Becket as his choice. Should he tell him?

The two men had left the castle early in the morning in good humor. Henry was encouraged that the ill feelings caused by Toulouse seemed to have diminished in his chancellor, and the old Tom, his friend and comrade, had returned. Hence the decision to hunt alone with him and have the chance for private conversation.

"Queen Eleanor asked me to tell you that she thinks . . ." Becket paused, seeming to choose the correct words. The king did not like to be ordered about. The chancellor corrected his verb. ". . . That she *wishes* you would consider returning to England. You have been away three years now. She feels you should make an appearance."

"Are there problems that you see?" Henry was quick to pounce.

"No, of course not. All is running smoothly. The queen is amazing as regent. I've gained great respect for her. And your justiciars are hard-working. When they are not reporting to you here on the continent, they are traveling the circuit in England, hearing the cases in the courts you have set up. And, by and large, their decisions are respected. The system of the king's justice is working."

Henry glanced up at Tom. When they were on horseback, the difference in their height was lessened, but the stocky king still must look somewhat up to the tall chancellor. Yet it seemed to disturb Henry not at all.

"The queen thinks that Canterbury should be filled soon."

"I'm certain the monks are waiting for your permission before they make their choice," Tom said, his dark hair ruffling in the wind. He was staring out over the river. The king noticed, for the first time, slight silver streaks in the black.

"They damn well better. We need to have a concord between church and state, and I have to have someone I can live with." The king turned his attention to the sky, scanning it. His gerfalcon twittered a bit on his wrist, head suddenly up as if to catch the scent of a bird. Henry noticed. That's absurd. How can a bird know when there is prey from that far away? Then he spied the great eagle the bird had sensed, coming into view skimming down the river on the opposite side.

"Who's the front-runner for the monks' choice?" he asked absently. "You must know the gossip."

"Foliot in London, I'm told. He's the most notable scholar in England." Becket turned to Henry. "I understand they think Roger Pont l'Eveque in York is too much your man."

"Those devil monks," Henry laughed. "Always after their own independence. Well, more power to them. I don't mind. Just as long as we can get along."

It seemed as though the king would make to release his falcon when he turned once more to Becket.

"And who is your candidate?"

"Me?" Becket's face showed honest surprise.

"Yes, you. You're still an archdeacon of the order, are you not? You never resigned that post, to my knowledge."

"No, but . . ."

"Then you must have an opinion for your new leader."

"Sire, I honestly haven't thought about it. What happens at Canterbury has so little to do with our business, and you and Thibault have been in concord for so long, it hasn't occurred to me that it might not always be so."

"Hunh." Said the king, suddenly releasing his great bird. The gerfalcon circled overhead for a moment, then headed directly downriver. Good bird, Henry thought. Good hunter.

Late April 1162, one year later
Falaise, Normandy

This morning the king was the last one to appear in the courtyard, hurriedly running down the stone steps. He was dressed in his hunting clothes, although no one had seen him leave the castle that morning. His clothes were in greater disarray than usual, a sign that he had thrown them on at the last minute. He looked tired.

Queen Eleanor herself had only just arrived moments before. The children, Henry now seven, and Marguerite of France, having recently had her fourth birthday celebration, stood huddled near Becket as the king and queen approached from different directions.

Eleanor noticed the children were holding hands, the little girl grasping onto Becket's travel cloak with her other glove, and she had a sudden and unusual flood of warmth near her heart. They were so young to be hostages to fortune in this way.

"So, all is well for the departure!" the king announced rather than asked, as was his habit. His ruddy face was still flushed with sleep.

"Yes, Sire, I believe so." Becket was his most solemn self, taken with his responsibility for not one but two royal children on the journey back to England and, more importantly, in the afterward. The young Henry had been in his care for some years, and he held affection for the lad, who was bright and quick at his lessons. But now he would also have the princess of France in his household and the proper guidance of the two of them until they were old enough to consummate the marriage they had been forced into a year earlier. At that point, they would have their own household. But that was at least eight or nine years in the future.

"Do have your attendants watch the princess carefully," Eleanor said as the five of them stood in a circle, the wind ruffling the king's full rust-colored hair and the queen's light blue silk veil, held down with a simple coronet of small jewels. "She is still so young."

The king was always impatient when he saw sentimentality on the horizon. He waved away the queen's remark.

"Remember, it is absolutely necessary for you to take the prince to Westminster and have my barons renew their vows of fealty. And I've had a further thought on the matter. I want you to contact my goldsmith when you arrive in London and have a small circlet made for the occasion, for the prince. I want there to be no mistake about the meaning of this ceremony. He is to be acknowledged as the heir to my throne."

"Yes, Your Grace." Becket bowed.

"We must act to secure the barons of England and the counts of Brittany and the south to our succession." Henry was speaking more emphatically than necessary since they were all standing so close.

"My Lord, I'm certain Thomas remembers all that you have been at pains to convey to him in the past three days. He is, after all, quite astute, as you have often pointed out." As always, Eleanor's gentle but wry announcement of the obvious slowed the king down, Becket thought, and he worked to keep the smile from appearing on his own face. The king never seemed to mind when such gentle teasing came from her. They did have a certain understanding. Becket himself, notwithstanding his close relationship with Henry, was wary enough not to try the same technique. He was quite certain the king's response would have been immediate and unpleasant to any familiarity from his chancellor.

"Yes, yes, I know. Just reviewing for the common benefit. I wish I could be there myself, but I'm needed here. I place my trust in you to carry out this important ritual."

"Henry, you must consider coming back to England," Eleanor said, placing her hand on the king's left arm. His right hand had been resting on his sword handle, but he raised it and took her hand in his own, a gesture of gentleness that surprised the chancellor. "You have been away too long. The people need to see you, not just your justiciars or your queen."

"I shall return as soon as I've settled things here in Normandy. I have the government to run here. Since Robert of Neubourg died last year, I've no seneschal. Many projects to conclude, some roads and parks. The people need more than battles and alarms." He looked at her steadily, and she nodded slowly.

"Sire, My Lady, with your leave, we should begin the journey. Although we have the day, it is but spring and the light does not last." Becket broke into their exchange. "The little ones will be tired enough, and we hope to reach Barfleur before nightfall."

"Quite so, quite so," the king said. "I've decided to ride with you as far as the coast, see you safely on your ship."

"But, Sire, there's no need," Becket began, but seeing the group of six archers coming up from the stables, now mounted to ride with their king, his voice trailed off. He knew Henry well enough to know there was no purpose in remonstrating with him. Suddenly the king turned and waved at one clump of his courtiers standing a discrete distance away. The tall, lean figure of Richard de Lucy detached himself from the others and joined the king and queen. He, too, Becket now noticed, was dressed for travel.

"Are the grooms bringing our horses 'round?" Henry asked gruffly, a tone of annoyance that his exact moment of departure had not been anticipated in the stables.

"Here they are, My Lord," de Lucy replied as the king's destrier and his own were brought on the run by the young grooms. Becket was clearly surprised by the addition of a man of de Lucy's importance for the short ride. The king was unaccustomed to traveling with an entourage when it was unnecessary. A few archers for protection always suited him well enough. It was a short ride to the coast. But perhaps he had extra care for the little French princess with them, and for his own heir.

Becket directed the squires to help the royal children into their cart and gestured his men to form their line. The castle gates swung open, the drawbridge lowered with a huge clang, and the line began to move. Becket and de Lucy brought up the rear, the king riding between them with the six archers close behind.

Usually, the king was out in front, setting the pace. Today Becket had deliberately held the king back with conversation, fearing that his challenge would be to trick the king into riding slowly enough that they did not leave the children's cart in the dust behind them. Henry, in one of his rare bursts of sensitivity, seemed to understand this. He appeared in no hurry this day to deposit his chancellor and his queen and children on the boat rocking somewhere in the calm waters of Barfleur harbor.

When the party finally reached the high cliffs overlooking the Barfleur, the king held up his hand and stopped. He drew Thomas aside with him, "A word in private, Thomas, if you please," as he edged his horse toward the summit of the hill looking down on the port. They sat side by side, watching the boats bobbing in the water.

"Your ship is ready—I've seen to that. You may board now and still take advantage of some daylight remaining." Henry began after clearing his throat. It was almost as if the king did not know how to proceed. Becket was puzzled.

"You have my thanks, Sire." Becket waited. If it was a private conversation the king desired, he always had his reasons.

"I've thought for months, since Thibault died, about the succession at Canterbury. I've come to a conclusion."

"And?" Thomas forced a casual tone, although his heart began racing.

"My choice for archbishop is you, Thomas."

There was now a full moment of silence.

"Sire, I'm overwhelmed," Becket began carefully.

"But not surprised?" Henry cut him off. No use to lie. Henry could practically smell a partial truth.

"Not altogether," Becket responded uneasily. "It had crossed my mind when you delayed making your wishes known to the monks."

"I can't name the archbishop. It's the monks of the cathedral chapter who have that responsibility," Henry said flatly. "They choose their own leader."

"But we both know they have waited to see what you will recommend. My sources tell me they have delayed their selection solely on account of your silence."

"Did they so?" Henry looked skyward as if for answers from the heavens. Clouds were moving in from the channel waters. "You must have excellent sources. Better than mine," he added.

"I doubt it," was his chancellor's quick rejoinder. Then: "Why do you want me to take on this office? I serve you well as your chancellor. I have enough to do on your behalf with affairs of state."

"But Tom, you are the perfect candidate from the perspective of the monks. You were trained at Bologna in canon law, you still hold the post of archdeacon in the Canterbury community, and best of all, you are still chaste, are you not, Thomas?" The king playfully poked his chancellor in the side with the handle of his dagger. He had been playing with it, tapping it on the front of his saddle as they spoke. "And you know the business of the crown. In fact, I got this idea from old Barbarossa. He took his archbishop in Mainz and made him chancellor. And, from all reports, it's working beautifully."

"Sire . . ." Thomas began his protest anew.

"Now, now, I'm simply listing your assets. I hold no grudge that you would not join me in occasional lustiness when we were young . . ."

"I never intended . . ." Becket began, his thoughts racing between the past and the future.

"Chancellor, please," the king interrupted. "Please, I do not say this to make you uncomfortable. And understand the queen never minded my occasional conquests. We have long ago come to our arrangement. She married me for property, not for love. And anyway, I am not such a sybarite as that worm Gerald of Wales puts about in his published records."

"Sire, no one would . . ." Becket paused. "And how did you . . ."

"I, too, have my sources," Henry's mouth tightened. Becket left the topic.

"Still, My Lord, look at my finery." He suddenly fingered his sleeve, laced with small pearls and jewels. "What kind of figure would I cut as archbishop with my love of clothes and food and cheerful company?"

"You will manage, I'm sure." The king considered him for what seemed like a long time, his chin slightly lifted, his jaw firm, his grey eyes inscrutable, almost cold in the late afternoon light. Thomas met his gaze honestly, looking down at his sovereign. "I've seen you rein in your senses when there was work to be done."

Finally, the older man spoke to his lord formally, "If I am to be your candidate, your majesty, what would you expect of me?"

"Expect? Expect?" Henry repeated, shaking his head as if swatting away a group of gnats. "I'd expect you to do the job like Thibault did. With diplomacy. With honesty. With honor."

"Things may not work out as you plan," Thomas said. "I would have the responsibility of the church in England, as well as the state. What if there is a conflict?"

"Well, work it out, man. You're currently archdeacon at Canterbury, but you managed to come up with the idea of the levy on the abbeys and bishops for the army to take to Toulouse." Henry's voice was now growing impatient.

"Do not do this, Sire. I fear for our friendship if you do." Thomas spoke with impulse that even Henry could see.

"Nonsense. Things will go on as they are, only more smoothly as your power expands."

Becket was silent. Something in his posture altered slightly, a slight raising of his spine, the smallest movement, but it caused the king to arch his brows.

"Do you say you do not want this?"

There was no pause. "No, Sire, I do not say that. I will accept the decision of the monks of Canterbury right gladly."

"Good man," Henry said with relief, clapping him on the back. Then, without another word, he began to redirect his horse back to the group, waving for Thomas to come with him. He did not look back to notice with what reluctance Becket followed.

As they approached the others, the king put his hand on Thomas' reins and stilled his horse. He then spoke his last words to his chancellor. "The message to the monks of Canterbury is going on the same ship you will be on. De Lucy sails with you to bring news of my choice personally to the Chapter House. As soon as the ritual is completed at Westminster for the young prince, I urge you to appear at Canterbury. Have no fear. By that time they will be ready for you to make your case."

He offered the kiss of peace, and the chancellor responded, with their horses so close they rubbed against one another. Into Becket's ear, the king whispered, "Go with God, Tom. This is a splendid opportunity. And do not forget those who are your friends."

A brief, last set of instructions privately delivered to de Lucy, and then the king shot forward, waving his archers to follow him back to Falaise. He left his chancellor behind with turmoil in his heart. A splendid opportunity, the king had declared. Indeed. But all decided in advance, Becket thought. All decided without even knowing if he, Becket, would agree to the job. The king had all the power.

Part Four: The Election
1162

Late May 1162
Kent, England: Canterbury Cathedral Chapter House

The Augustinian monks of Canterbury were gathered in their Chapter House when Becket arrived. They had not yet been called to order, although the chairs were in the neat circle arrangement they used for their formal meeting. He strode into the small stone room, set somewhat apart from the imposing cathedral structure, acknowledging in his heart some conflicting emotions. But he put a bold face on it.

As archdeacon, he would have been welcomed at their regular chapter meetings where all decisions by the monks were taken, but he had never attended. He told himself it was for lack of time, but there were other reasons, complications of loyalty to the king and secrets that must be kept on matters politic. Thibault had often encouraged him to come, to get to know the new monks better, but Thomas had visited the monastery only rarely and then only to converse with his mentor, the archbishop.

Today the black-robed monks glided about the room, speaking in low tones—the way monks do—in groups of two or three. In the center of the room, Becket was not surprised to see Gilbert Foliot, scholar and Bishop of London, and Roger Pont l'Eveque, Bishop of York. They made a comical-looking pair, he thought, standing side by side, with ruddy-faced Roger short and stout and Foliot tall and lean, the preoccupied look of the true scholar lining his face. Henry of Blois, Bishop of Winchester, was also present, but he kept somewhat apart from the others. As the former King Stephen's brother, he no doubt saw himself a cut above his brother bishops, Becket thought. I might if I were in his place. The bishops of the province, as they were called, had been invited to attend to certify the election of their archbishop to Rome. But somehow, their presence unsettled Becket. He was still only chancellor, had no part in this ecclesiastical hierarchy, yet here he was asking, no, demanding in the words of Henry his king, to be made head of all these monks, the chief among all these bishops.

He was glad to note de Lucy's absence—he'd been to dinner and had met with the chapter the night before. His presence today would have been too much pressure on behalf of the king's choice. Becket was relieved for a moment, but then his eye lit upon Arnulf of Lisieux sitting quietly in the corner. This must be Henry's idea of subtlety, he thought grimly. The king's closest ally, the bishop of the largest city in the northwest corner of Normandy. Who would not see him as the king's eyes and ears? There was no question: The monks were under duress to elect him. Would this affect his relations with them for years to come?

The prior gaveled the group to order before Thomas had a chance to speak to any of his fellow canons. He took his place in the front of the group beside Foliot and Pont l'Eveque, nodding to them cordially.

The opening prayer, *de rigeur* for this group, droned on, and then the business of the day was entertained.

The acting prior rose and made the proposal: That Thomas of Becket, Archdeacon of the Cathedral at Canterbury, would take the chair of Saint Augustine as the Archbishop of the Cathedral and head of the church in England. The floor was opened for discussion.

A storm of comments ensued, with the unlucky prior calling for order, again and again, using his gavel of office to enforce order.

"Four of our members and one guest have been given leave to speak. We will then have the voting," the prior announced. Fortunately, he was a relatively young man with a powerful voice. Maybe he could be archbishop one day, Thomas thought with grim humor.

"As you all know, the chapter members and bishops who will speak are chosen by lot. Our guest, Bishop Foliot, newly appointed to the chair at London, will speak first."

Gilbert Foliot at this time was nearing fifty summers of age. He was the foremost scholar in England and, indeed, considered so in Normandy and elsewhere. His tall figure nearly rivaled Thomas' own height. His face was arranged without expression of any kind as he nodded to the chancellor.

"I come here today to oppose the election of Thomas Becket to the chair of Canterbury," he began. No surprise there for Thomas, as he heard the catalogue of reasons why his election was a bad idea for church and state alike. Well, Foliot would say so, he thought. He himself had made no secret that he was available for the spot.

He expected his four brother canons to gainsay Foliot's objections, and the first three did so vigorously.

But then David of Wales approached the front of the room. He was an older man, short and unreasonably stout, a monk with the face of a large, unpleasant animal, Becket thought. Maybe a wild boar. He was somewhat new to the community, and Becket had been told his humor was as choleric as his appearance. The look on his face did not portend well for the chancellor's election.

"Now, then," Brother David began quietly, always a bad sign Becket knew, for he used that rhetorical device himself quite frequently to calm his audience in advance of unwelcome news. "We are gathered here today to review the proposition that the Chair of the Archbishop be given to our brother, Thomas a Becket, current chancellor to the king."

He paused and wiped his brow with a square of the whitest linen. Becket was just musing on how difficult it must be to carry that much weight wherever one went when David's voice changed, became charged with something as if it were an entirely different person speaking.

"But is he really our brother? Is he at all? Yes, he studied with the monks at Merton and here in Archbishop Thibault's household, and he was named to the post of archdeacon as well. But, my brothers, look at him. He sits before you like a lord, the chancellor of the king, not a humble servant of God as we consider ourselves."

A pause while the speaker cleared his throat. The room had fallen silent, except for the buzzing of the bees outside the open window. Becket felt distinct discomfort, his hearty dinner rising in his sternum, moving toward his throat.

"He wears fine clothes, he dines with kings, he serves the king of England, not God. Yes, he does some good works, but my fellow canons, he does those always in the sight of others." Brother David's heavy voice was rising in the room. "This man . . ." he shook his pudgy finger in the direction of Thomas, now sitting stiffly upright. "This man is a man of the world, not a man of the spirit. He does not deserve to lead us. He will never be one of us."

Then to everyone's utter amazement, Brother David stalked over to stand in front of Becket's chair, "Lay aside your worldly self, get you a tonsure and a robe, look like us for the sake of God, and then come back and ask us to elect you."

The old man turned, and, for a moment, it seemed as though his legs would give way. His power wafted from him, and he nearly staggered out of the room, exhausted with his undertaking. Becket sat, stunned.

All was quiet for some time. Then Becket rose, and Foliot and Roger Pont l'Eveque sat forward expectantly as their colleague made his way to the front of the room. Becket's face was flushed, his eyes flashing. Here stood a different man, no longer the unflappable chancellor they had both come to know. Even the aged Arnulf of Lisieux snapped his head up from his nap to watch the drama.

"All right," he said finally, in a strong voice everyone could hear, a voice laced with anger. "The election is postponed for one week. I will go to Merton's, where I was a student. I will be tonsured and robed and will meet you all here on Sunday next. You will all have visible evidence of where I place my loyalty. Then you make your decision." And with that, he strode from the room.

Exactly one week later, on June 2, a tonsured Thomas Becket was ordained a priest, and on June 3, 1162, he was unanimously elected Archbishop of Canterbury at Westminster Cathedral. The young prince Henry, only seven years of age, sat in the stead of his father. He was swallowed in the large throne, but he sat still for the entire ceremony, his eyes wide and watching. When the mitre was placed on his master's head, the young prince smiled. His father would be pleased.

The king had triumphed; the monks had yielded. But at what cost? And to whom?

Part Five: The Falling Out
1162–1164

July 1162
The Castle at Rouen, Normandy

It was full summer in Rouen, and de Lucy was enjoying relief from the heavy, wet English weather he had endured, even into June of that year. He and William FitzStephen had ridden hard from the coast, scarce waiting for their boat to dock, only to find the king himself had not arrived yet from Anjou. This welcome reprieve allowed de Lucy a rare moment of leisure, and he and his traveling companion, young William FitzStephen, were lounging on pallets in their chamber.

FitzStephen was tossing a ball into the air as he lay on his back and then trying to catch it with his foot. De Lucy was sitting up, reading some correspondence that had arrived ahead of him. His once handsome face was showing the lines of fatigue and worry that accompanied his position of chief counselor to the king and his justiciar in his absence in England. There were additional things to worry about today, not the least of which was the king's reaction to an unpleasant bit of news he carried with him.

After a brief scratching noise, the door to the small chamber flew open and a head popped around. It was the apple-cheeked serving maid who had brought them food and wine earlier. FitzStephen immediately brightened.

"I am to alert you, my lords, that the king is even now close. He will be here within the hour. He sent a courier to tell you he expects you here and ready."

FitzStphen sprang to his feet, all thoughts of a dalliance flying from his mind. He began to pull on his tunic and buckle his sword. De Lucy was slower, his years and the number of months he had spent in the saddle in the service of his king weighing more heavily on him now. But he, too, wasted no time in unfolding his long frame, assembling his knightly ware and making himself presentable.

As he left the chamber, he picked up the heavy, worn leather bag that had never left his side since he departed England a week earlier. He had had a smooth crossing of the channel, but he was now preparing himself for the storm to come in the next hour.

Indeed, Henry always entered a room as if he, himself, were a storm and today was no exception. Throwing doors open impatiently, not being announced, dispensing with all the niceties, de Lucy had to smile at the expected performance. They were meeting in the smaller of the two reception halls in the Rouen castle. The room was cool, despite the summer heat without, as the damp stones never lost their winter chill. De Lucy had kept his cloak on, but Henry shed his as he came across the hall to them, not waiting to be approached.

De Lucy and FitzStephen made a brief obeisance, and Henry, as de Lucy knew he would, raised them immediately, clapping de Lucy on the back.

"Well, well, and how was the channel for you this week."

"Not a difficult crossing, Sire. But you might invest in some new straw for the pallets we use on night journeys. I thought my back would break in the morning."

"Hah, de Lucy. If your back was breakable, I'd have done it for you long ago," the king was in a jovial mood. He gestured for them to take chairs at the table, settling himself at the end. The servants, whom he had evidently accosted on his way up the broad stone steps from the courtyard, were quickly entering with wine and bread, oatcakes, nuts, dates and grapes for them, in heavy earthenware bowls. The king waved them out of the room, the steward closing the door after backing out.

"I had an amusing thought, Henry, as we were waiting for you."

"What was that, Richard?"

"This is the only court in Europe where the king is always off running around and the staff waits at home for him. All the other monarchs, I am told, send their men out and relax themselves at home."

Henry laughed, as de Lucy knew he would.

"I had business in Angers. The empress is not well of late, and she had some matters to discuss with me. She no longer wants to travel from her familiar surroundings." Henry paused as if he were following other thoughts, perhaps his mother's advancing age, but then he caught himself and turned to give de Lucy his total attention. "So, tell me all the news. Becket's consecration as Archbishop of Canterbury went off without a hitch, right?" After the king had served himself, he poured from the pitcher for de Lucy and FitzStephen.

"You've had that message, Sire," de Lucy stated. He knew the queen had written immediately after the event.

"Well, done, de Lucy. The queen said there was some trouble, some grumbling among the monks, but you managed to persuade them."

De Lucy took a deep breath. "I wouldn't say trouble, exactly. At the first election, an old monk from Wales got up and berated Becket for not being monastic enough … no tonsure, no robe."

"Fair enough. He warned me his finery might be a problem."

"Yes, well," de Lucy paused as if searching his mind for the correct words. "At the end of that tirade, Becket stood up and addressed the monks with great dignity, I'm told."

"Weren't you still there? Did you not hear his address?"

"No, I'd supped with the monks the night before. I was able to make your wishes known at that time in such a way that there was no mistaking your support of Becket. I thought it best not to be too heavy-handed at the actual election. But I was clear the previous evening the royal favor would be withdrawn from Canterbury if this election did not come to pass."

"So, how did you have news of the Welsh monk's tirade?" The king was popping dates into his mouth by the handful, spitting out the pits onto the rushes on the floor.

"One of the younger brothers approached me the day before, made certain I knew he was willing to act as my eyes and ears in return for a favorable mention to you. The next day he sent a note by courier with a complete description of the scene."

"But Becket was elected."

"He delayed the election for a week, went down to Merton's where he'd studied as a boy and returned tonsured and robed. The Canterbury monks loved it."

"I'll wager they did." Henry smiled slightly, but an inscrutable expression was passing over his usually open face. He stopped chewing and frowned. "Tom was always a bit of an actor, so no surprise that he put some theatre into his accession. I see he still knows his audience. I should know. He read me right for years." The king's tone had lost some of its joviality, acquired a slight edge. "So go on, the consecration took place at Westminster the day after Becket was ordained a priest, all done right and proper. Thomas Becket, my chancellor, is now a priest of God, a monk of Benedict and the Archbishop of Canterbury."

"That is correct, Sire."

There was a pause. "What aren't you telling me?"

Damn the man, de Lucy thought. He's got God's own clear vision.

With a sigh, de Lucy reached down to his feet and hauled up the leather saddle bag, which he thumped onto the table.

"The archbishop," de Lucy's voice emphasized the title and paused, "sent for me the week after he took office."

"He sent for you?" the king's brows rose slightly. "He sent for a justiciar of the realm?"

"Yes, Sire," de Lucy plopped the dark, stained bag on the table in front of the king. "He gave me this and instructed—instructed — (repeated as if the king might not have heard the word the first time) me to bring this to you."

The king, sitting back slightly, looked at the leather travel sac for a moment as if it might contain a dead rat.

"Do you know what it is?"

"Yes, Sire."

"So do I," said Henry, rising as he bit off the end of every word he uttered. His chair tumbled backward with the force of his movement.

"You had word from the queen ahead of my arrival?" de Lucy asked in surprise.

"I need no word from the queen to tell me what has transpired." The king swept the bowl of fruit from the table in anger as his arm moved one way and then it swept back and caught the goblet half filled with wine, sent it flying, spattering FitzStephen in the process. Well trained, the young knight did not move a muscle, riveted as always by the sight of his king possessed by his anger as if he had been taken over by a wild boar.

"One," the king shouted now, "You come in these chambers to meet Us carrying a heavy bag and a hang-the-dog look. Two, you unobtrusively place the bag where you think I won't see it, at your own feet. Three, you've just come from England with current news of the mission we sent you on to get Thomas Becket elected Archbishop of Canterbury. This was a mission we designed to bring greater harmony to relations between church and state. It appears you succeeded all too well."

FitzStephen could not believe his ears. Was the king blaming de Lucy for his successful mission? He sat up straighter and leaned forward. Wait until Walter Map hears about this!

But the king simply rolled onward in his ever-faster monologue. "Now the subject of our efforts has decided that, thank you, he'd rather just run the church, never mind the state at all." In delivering this soliloquy, Henry's pacing became more frenetic as his voice grew louder. He reached the door to the chamber and slammed his fist against it. FitzsStephen and de Lucy glanced at one another. There was no stopping him now.

But then, suddenly, the king stopped himself. He turned and leaned against the door for a long moment, his head down. De Lucy and FitzStephen looked away in embarrassment. Would the king actually cry? A long, shuddering sound came from the bent figure, and then Henry straightened up. It was as if he had come back to himself by some superhuman effort. He strode back to the table.

Grabbing the leather, he jerked at the drawstrings. Gradually he drew out the great seal of England, the very one he had designed and given to his Chancellor for safekeeping eight years before. He stared at it for a long moment, turning it over in his hands to see both engraved figures: the king as warrior, the king as ruler. Then he dropped the heavy object on the table, shook his head and sighed.

December 1162
Cherbourg, Normandy

The three royals—the king, his mother and his queen—were finally alone. The servants and counselors had been dismissed, the business of state and province set aside for the moment, the festivities of Christmas at abeyance for a few hours.

The king's privy chamber was the warmest room in the drafty castle, and the fires burned brightly in the three fire-chimneys that dotted the room. A small table had been set with a light supper, the main meal being always in the forenoon unless the king had not returned from his morning hunting.

Henry quaffed his warm, mulled wine newly poured from the pitcher sitting on the hearth and observed the two women most prominent in his life: his wife and his mother. Matilda had consented to leave her rooms at the castle in Angers and keep Christmas with them. He did wish the two, queen and empress, got on better. Or at least could see how alike they were one to another. On the other hand, perhaps it was better they did not see what they had in common. He found that last thought amusing.

"Queen Eleanor, it's been too many years since we have had a chance to sit at table and talk together." The Empress Matilda's body may be shrinking, Eleanor thought, but she has lost nothing of the force in her voice. Take care, take care, do not rise to the bait.

"Indeed, too long, Empress Matilda." Eleanor smiled her most enchanting smile, and Henry shifted in his chair. He'd rather face an angry pope or a choleric Emperor Barbarossa than these two women at the same table. It was almost worse when they endeavored to be polite to one another.

"When are you going to return to England, Henry?" Matilda demanded, her lined face arranged in a frown. "I'm told that you are needed there. It's been more than four years since you have set foot on the land, and yet you are the king. For once, I agree with Eleanor."

"Thank you, Lady Mother. I'm aware of where I have been for the past four years. I do not need reminding. You both seem to forget that I have been looking after my continental domains, looking after my wife's domains, settling things in Normandy, dealing with Louis and his many faces . . ." Henry stopped, aware that his voice was rising.

"Yes, I understand," Matilda said in a surprisingly firm voice. "But the throne of England was won only after hard fighting. You must not lose it for lack of attention." The empress was never one for subtleties, Eleanor thought, the corner of her mouth twitching slightly.

"Much of the hard fighting was mine, Empress, if you will recall," Henry said with little feeling. "And Queen Eleanor has been regent in my stead and done marvelously well," Henry contended. "She has spent days traveling the country. When the people see their queen, they see their king. She is his appointed regent."

He took a breath. Matilda seemed about to speak, but he raised his hand off the table slightly, stopping her. "I have excellent justiciars, who ride circuit for my courts of justice which are working very well, thank you for asking. My chancery is amazingly organized and working well, with writs and charters forming the backbone of the nation. All is well in England, and I have had work to do here in Normandy."

Eleanor broke in this time as Henry paused. "Empress, Henry is ready to go back. We have been trying to take ship for England for several weeks. The storms have been relentless. It's why we're here in Cherbourg rather than a more comfortable castle. We sail as soon as possible after Twelfth Night."

"And speaking of the Chancery," Matilda proceeded as if Eleanor had not spoken, "what do you propose to do about Becket?"

A silence fell upon the little group. The king made a great task of dipping his bread into the stewed fruit that sat before him. He swept the bread through, raised it to his mouth and took a great chew of it, then wiped his hand on his sleeve, at which Eleanor winced. She had never quite grown accustomed to the blunt manners of the Normans.

"I propose, at the present moment, to do nothing about him." He had finished the bread and now, taking the small knife from his belt and aiming it at the heart of the cheese slid the knife down. Eleanor winced.

"But he's resigned his chancellorship, I understand. Sent back the Great Seal. What could your relations possibly be with him now?" Matilda tapped her finger on the table impatiently. "Now you've made him cock of the walk. I hear he thumbs his nose at you. He's insulted you."

"It's true the seal was sent back, but there was no letter with it. I have not received an official resignation, and if I do receive such a document, I plan not to accept it."

"The work of the Chancery proceeds well, Matilda," Eleanor interjected. "I can attest that, as regent, the clerk's service is still prompt and correct. Geoffrey Ridel is every whit as competent as Becket, and with much less drama about it all. The work of the crown has gone on without a hitch, as the English would say."

"And," Henry added with a grin, "although I haven't appointed Geoffrey Chancellor, I have taken my right to appoint him Archdeacon at Canterbury, since that is a title Becket no longer uses."

Matilda was not to be mollified. "You can jab at Becket all you like, Henry, appointing Geoffrey Ridel to a title at the cathedral. But Thomas Becket is a dangerous man. All this posturing since his election. I was told he declared the day of his consecration a new feast...Trinity Sunday or some such thing. A sign, I believe, that he believes himself to be moving closer to the godhead as he moves away from his king."

Henry had been picking up his forks, twirling them, discarding them as they spoke. Now, even that outlet of movement was not enough, and he rose restlessly, began walking, speaking over his shoulder. His voice was rising, whether from irritation or so he could be heard. Eleanor was not certain.

"Lady Mother, I'll admit Becket has been provocative. The whole matter of demanding a ceremony of obedience from Bishop Foliot when he was moved from Hereford to York was calculated to annoy Us. Even Becket later admitted such a formality was unnecessary."

"The worst he has done is to ignore the royal courts," Eleanor interjected. "In the matter of Tonbridge, he sent to Roger de Clare and demanded the castle back, as the right of Canterbury to claim it, rather than taking the matter through the crown's good courts."

"That's exactly what I mean. The man's dangerous. He is expanding the power of the church at every turn and ignoring the king's system." Matilda seemed to grow taller in her heavy oak chair as her indignation rose. Her voice, too, was fuller with indignation and Eleanor grew wary.

"But Empress," she said smoothly, "I think the king has taken the reasonable path. He is not there, he has not spoken directly to Thomas since he was elected, and we will be in London as soon as the channel storms subside. Then Henry can talk with Becket, get his direct words, and only then decide the meaning of these actions." Eleanor tried for syrup in her voice, which was not her usual way. Matilda glanced sharply at her.

"Are you trying to calm me, Daughter?"

Eleanor winced at the familiarity. There was not that much age difference between her and her mother-in-law, and she knew the term daughter, as used by Mathilda, was not one of affection. It was intended to make her more diminutive. Eleanor did not react kindly to the attempt. Her tone grew firmer.

"I'm simply stating the fact that Becket has been acting as archbishop for only six months, and Henry has not had a chance to ascertain his mind in these matters. He will have that chance soon." She rose. The king had paused at the far end of the room to listen, perhaps glad to let Eleanor handle his difficult mother for a few moments. "I recommend patience in this matter until we know what this all means."

"Patience has never been the strong suit of the Counts of Anjou," Mathilda stated flatly.

"Don't I know it!" Eleanor said. "I bid you a good evening, Empress." The queen made the slightest of bows to the aging empress, who sat stone-faced, looking straight ahead and who gave only the slightest nod in return.

"Husband," the queen nodded to Henry as she passed him, and he acknowledged her. With that, the conference ended. Henry decided he was not up to discussing matters with his mother on his own, so he rang for the servants to see her to her bedroom.

The king slept fitfully. Swarms of confused images haunted his dreams, one after the other, none of them pleasant. Near dawn, he awoke, sweating, and the random dreams coalesced into disturbing thoughts about Becket.

The empress has reason in her assessment. Becket's actions in the last six months are not only mysterious but dangerous. But I really don't care how he parades his new office. He always was a lover of show. He may no longer be in tunics with pearls sewn on the sleeves, but I'll wager when he is in full dress as archbishop, his robes are every bit as glorious as the threads he wore as chancellor. Hah! Good for him. That's what he loves—show.

Extravagance is not the worrisome part. It's these little shoots of church power in places where he need not extend it. The whole business at Eyensford where Tom appointed the clerk Laurence, while the lord William there claimed the right to name the clerk. A modest difference that might have been settled easily in the courts. But Becket escalates every chance he gets. He excommunicated William! God's holy grief! An excommunication over the right to appoint a simple clerk of the church. Not even a priest. Not even a deacon! A clerk! Under our customs, William had every right to appoint his own clerk. These prerogatives of nobles to appoint church officials have been in place since my grandfather's time. They should be respected.

Eleanor counsels patience. It's well she does. Hah again. But what is going on with Tom? And why no letter of any personal sort since his election? Maybe he doesn't write personal letters? Or doesn't write them anymore, now he's grown so important.

It seemed like such a good idea to appoint him, to close the gap between church and state, to get along. I don't think I was wrong. But why all these little things? When I see him face to face, we'll talk it out. A good hunting party, a ride in the fresh air and the woods he loves so much, that will settle everything. Eleanor's right. For once. Tom, Tom, are you still there? Will it be as it once was?

January 1163
Southbhampton Port, England

Henry was on deck, leaning on the side railing long before land was sighted. When the sailors called out "Land Ho, starboard," Eleanor appeared with their small children in tow: Mathilda, Richard and little Geoffrey, who had kept Christmas with their parents. They joined Henry as their nursemaids hurried after them to wrap the children in large woolen cloaks against the fierce winter wind. The spray from the waves chopping at the barque's side flew up in their faces as the fine prow cut through the water propelled by the east wind billowing the high sails. The sky was nearly clear of clouds, but it felt as though the wind were possessed by the devil himself.

It was a miracle they had been able to cross safely, but Henry's small store of patience, Eleanor knew, had come to an end. He was, he announced the previous evening, finally, for England, weather or no. She could come or she could stay. Of course, she would come. She would not miss his meeting with Becket for all the world. It promised to be a clash of titans. Eleanor was looking as intently as her husband at the two figures at the front of the small group huddled on the wharf in welcome.

"There they are. And look at young Henry, still hanging on to his master's hand," she said. The king squinted against the spray interfering with his keen sight. "Do you take that as a good omen, My Lord?"

There stood the archbishop, tall, in his plain monk's robes, the cowl visible over the heavy mantel he had put on against the weather. The young boy beside him, the prince Henry, not yet nine years of age, looked small and vulnerable. The wind had blown his cap away, but he did not make a move to retrieve it, hanging on to Becket's hand as his hair was tossed about. Eleanor wondered, not for the first time, if she had made a mistake allowing Henry to give Becket the boy at such a young age.

"At least that relationship has not been fractured," Henry said as if reading her thoughts. "We'll have to see if that is a good omen, will we not?" Henry turned to face her, leaning his arm on the rail. "It could just be another complication."

She nodded. Amazing, sometimes, they did not need to explain what they were thinking in full. As if there were two minds at the head of the realm instead of one.

The royal couple remained on the deck, although Eleanor finally ordered the children below as they were in danger of becoming drenched by the waves slapping against the side.

The crew, with much shouting and to-ing and fro-ing, managed to lay down the gangplanks, as the Normans called the long, wooden boards that stretched from the shore to the ship and allowed the king and his party to disembark.

The king bounded off the ship first, as was his wont, and headed right for Thomas and the boy. Robert of Leicester and du Hommet were crowding forward, but it was Becket the king embraced jovially.

"Tom. It's been too long," he said. The archbishop, still holding the hand of the young prince Henry, extended his other hand in the king's direction. Eleanor, who was close behind the king frowned. This extending the hand for knights had become the new way to show a greeting and to demonstrate that the greeter held no sword in his hand. But it was an odd gesture for the archbishop to make, almost as if he were the equal of the king.

The king brushed aside the extended hand and fully embraced his former chancellor with words that surprised the two justiciars crowding behind the pair.

"Come, Tom, no formality. Give us the kiss of peace." And without further ado, the king kissed Becket on the mouth, as was the custom. The archbishop, who pulled back slightly for an instant, had no choice but to return the kiss of peace, or rather submit to it. All who saw knew this as a sign of complete friendship in the manner recommended by Augustine in his sermon. De Lucy was watchful. He knew the king's developing reservations about Becket but had no idea what was in his mind at the moment. Why force the kiss of peace? Why not show his concerns openly?

"Your Grace, I am overwhelmed," Thomas said when he could break free. The boy prince had dropped his tutor's hand and now stood between the two men, propelled forward by Becket's hand around his shoulder. The king separated from Becket and looked down on his oldest son.

"Prince Henry," he said, affecting a stern tone that fooled no one, "have you been a good student for your master in my absence?"

"Yes, Sire," the boy replied stoutly, making a kind of bow as he had been taught.

"Good," said the king, ruffling his hair. "Now go and greet your mother." Henry turned his attention from Becket to his justiciars and the other men, shouldering among them easily as a soldier would move among his troops, calling most of them by name and grasping hands more in friendship than in formality, waving away royal protocol and rituals by his actions, giving them permission to be his men. Eleanor, watching him, marveled not for the first time at his ability to be so at home with anyone, no matter what their station, when he chose. Perhaps this talent rose from the years when he had taken up his mother's fight for the crown of England, shipping with hired men across the channel when he was not yet twenty, sleeping by their side in the open, sharing their rations, listening to their stories.

Henry was shouting some orders as the horses and carts for the children were brought to the slight rise above the shore. The group began to move, *en masse*, toward the place where they could mount and begin the journey. They were led, of course, by the king.

Eleanor overheard Becket say, as he caught up with Henry, "Sire, I'm happy to see you. The prince and I have waited these five stormy days for your ship. But now we ride to London with you. I say it was all worth it."

"Hey, Tom?" the king turned to him as if he had forgotten him for the moment. "But we ride not to London tonight. The weather is wretched, and the children are too tired. No, we'll stop at Southampton Castle. I've sent a messenger on ahead to warn them. They'll make ready, I'm certain."

The children are tired? thought Eleanor. Since when had Henry noticed the fatigue of his children?

"Southampton?" Becket sounded unsure. "If that is your wish, Sire. I had set up a welcome in London, but . . ." The king was moving forward at a fast clip. Becket added hastily: "I'll see that my retinue is advised."

"Yes, Tom. Do that. The queen and I will expect you to dine with us upon our arrival. Of course, there will be a chamber for you, but your retinue may have to make do with the local hostel." And the king plunged forward, engaged in an active conversation with du Hommet about the value of the Norway gerfalcons as against those bred in England.

It was only later that Eleanor noticed a distinct change in her royal spouse. They sat at the high table as usual in Southampton Castle, Eleanor on one side of Henry and Becket on the other, as they had so often over the previous years. But something was different on this evening, the queen sensed. Something that must be apparent even to Becket.

Oh, the king was cheery and attentive to his former chancellor; that much was clear. Perhaps too cheery and perhaps too attentive, Eleanor thought. He seldom turned to her side, which was not his custom. She had a good conversation with de Lucy, who sat to her left and was caught up on the state of affairs in the kingdom since she had departed for Normandy. But there was something off about the king's conversation with Becket, something forced. She could feel it.

After the many courses, the *trouveres* appeared with their small troupe and melodic if mournful offerings. Their presence was a nice touch, Eleanor thought. Henry could not have found traveling singers here in the south of England. He must have sent them from Normandy long in advance of their coming and without her knowledge. He knew how much she loved music. Finally, they finished and bowed out, and the king rose, a signal that others understood marked the end of the formal dinner. They also stood and waited for the king to depart. Henry gestured for Eleanor and the archbishop, as she now thought of Becket, to follow him.

Ensconced in the royal privy chamber, the three took cushioned oak chairs in front of the largest hearth, sitting in a semi-circle, the king in the center. The chairs had been arranged before their entry, which struck Eleanor as odd. The king was acting in extraordinary ways. Nevertheless, giving no outward sign of surprise, she settled herself in for what promised to be an entertaining exchange.

She could see Becket's chiseled features in outline when she glanced his way. Still the same handsome cut to his face, the rather firm chin, but the full head of black hair had given way to the monk's tonsure, and that gave his features a stark, unyielding look.

"So, Archbishop, are you liking your new duties? We have heard little from you this past six months." Henry turned casually toward Becket, who could not refrain from pulling back slightly, perhaps defensively, into the recesses of his cushions. The king leaned his elbow confidentially on the arm of his chair, creating an ambience of friendship between them, a technique Eleanor had seen him use before. It was quite powerful in generating awe in lesser men. But would Becket be intimidated? She waited to see.

"My Lord King," Thomas began stiffly, "The responsibilities of the leadership of Canterbury have been far larger than I anticipated. I have endeavored to fill them to the best of my abilities, that is, to rise to the office that has chosen me."

"Ah, the office chose you," Henry said, keeping his voice light. Eleanor winced, knowing what was to come. "And here all along, I thought it was I who chose you. Did not my justiciar and trusted (here a slight rising of the voice) officer, Richard de Lucy, carry my express views to the monks of Canterbury in person?"

"Yes, Sire. He did." Becket held his tongue with some effort, having seen Henry use this rhetorical device on others. He put you in a position where the more you said, the deeper you dug the hole, sometimes as deep as your grave.

"And did these same monks not, understanding the future of my pleasure depended on it, act on my views and elect you?" The cheeriness had dropped from the king's voice, a hardness there now.

"Yes, Sire, but . . ."

"But what?" the king interrupted him with a roar.

Becket took a deep breath. "Your wishes, as conveyed to the monks of Canterbury, indeed caused them to elect me archbishop of the cathedral. But I have since come to feel I have been called to this office by a power higher than you or I, My Lord King." Thomas leaned forward, turned in his chair to face Henry now, increasingly passionate as his thoughts took shape and words. "Just as chance of birth made you king, but you—acting as king—have demonstrated that you, too, have been called to your office."

Henry sat back, nonplussed. Eleanor, too, took a sharp breath. Bold, indeed. Knowing the Angevin temper, she was surprised to hear Becket bait the king in this way, unless—she thought with astonishment—unless the cleric actually believed what he was saying.

When the king finally responded, his voice was amazingly calm.

"Let us set aside the idea that chance made me king, a proposition that is completely in error to its foundations. I fought for this throne, in a way you did not fight to gain your office and in a way you will never understand." Henry paused and took a deep breath, collecting himself. "I believe I must know what you are thinking, Thomas. You are now telling me that you are called to be Archbishop of Canterbury by some higher order?"

"Indeed, My Lord. That is exactly what I am saying. When the monks murmured amongst themselves that they did not want to accept me because I was not like them, I went to Merton's to be tonsured and robed. The monks were correct. I must be like them to be their leader."

"And now you are their leader in all that is done?"

"Absolutely. And not only them. The other bishops accept my primacy, down to Roger of York, who struts the stage too much for my liking. But even he has acknowledged that I lead not only the monks but the bishops and, thus, the entire church in England. By virtue of my office, I am the church in England."

Eleanor waited for the explosion, but it did not come. Just another several minutes of silence and the cracking of the fire in the hearth, spitting out cinders that quickly died.

"I'm calling a council meeting in March at Westminster. We have items of law and land that need to be addressed. Also, I must settle the matter of the Welsh uprising. These things must not be allowed to fester."

Thomas murmured agreement.

"As you know from our former (a slight rising of the voice here? Eleanor couldn't be certain) relationship—that is, when you were acting as my chancellor—I desire clarity, both in what the crown intends and what the landowners, the barons, in particular, understand. We shall all return to the customs that were in place when my grandfather was king. Before that miserable war and chaos that Stephen inflicted on the land."

The king stopped, but Becket said nothing.

"Does the church wish to be represented at this council?" The king tipped his head to Becket in question.

"I think," Becket spoke hesitantly (did he sense a trap, Eleanor wondered), "that what you propose would be a council on issues of the land and state, Sire. It does not seem that it will touch on ecclesiastical matters. I see no need for the church in England to be formally represented."

"Probably not," Henry said thoughtfully. "There will no doubt be later meetings. If any questions arise, particularly because you, I mean, that is, the church in England, is a major landowner and tenant-in-chief of the crown. If such questions do come forward, I'm certain you will want to be there to answer them."

"Yes, very much so." Becket waited, and when no further word came from the king, he added, "Sire, there is the matter of the church council Pope Alexander is calling at Tours this year."

"What about it?" Henry asked, somewhat absently. He seemed to be occupied with other thoughts, gazing at the fire.

"Will you prevent me from attending?" Becket regarded Henry with a grave look.

"Why in God's sweet name would I do that?" Henry looked up.

"You have the power. Stephen prevented Thibault and I from crossing to a papal council when there was turbulence in the land. This time there is turbulence in Rome, what with two of them claiming to be pope."

Henry shook his head. "Victor's claim won't last. And anyway, I've already given Alexander all the assurance he needs of my support. You are free to go to Tours."

"That's a great relief." Becket smiled. "I'm planning to propose Anselm of Canterbury for sainthood at the conference."

"Ah, proposing saints already, are we?" The king rejoined in apparent good humor. "Well, thank the Lord Almighty, it's an Englishman! We can't have too many English saints." He smiled and murmured, "And another archbishop of Canterbury to boot."

The king rose abruptly, and Thomas hastily followed suit. Henry threw his arm around Becket's shoulders and pulled him close, but not for another kiss of peace. Instead, in a voice so low even Eleanor could not hear, he whispered in Becket's ear, "You may think yourself the church in England, Thomas, but We are the Crown. Forget that at your peril."

Then, making a great show of yawning and stretching, the king nodded to his wife and announced he was off to bed.

"We leave at first light tomorrow, my Love," he said to Eleanor. Then, to Becket, "No need for you to ride up to London with us. The prince can come with us. You'd best get back to Canterbury. Do let us know your plans for Tours." And with that, he walked out with that rolling, horseman's stride that so marked him. Becket stood still, astonished.

Eleanor had risen and observed her husband's bizarre behavior with alarm. Both his cheeriness and the fact that he had never before retired before she did, caused her eyes to widen. She watched him go until he disappeared from the chamber.

Then Becket said, "A word, my Lady, if you please, before you leave. I seek some advice."

* * *

It was more than an hour later that the small door to the queen's sleeping chamber opened quietly.

"Elle, are you sleeping?" the king was making some attempt to soften his hearty voice, used to shouting orders rather than approaching women in their chambers.

"Not anymore," she replied dryly, in a voice from inside the heavy curtains surrounding the bed.

"Good. I want to talk." Henry piled into bed beside his queen without further ado.

"I am tired tonight, Henry. That was a rough crossing." Her protest was mild, however. Children were their best safeguard against their enemies, and she knew her duty.

"Yes, yes. I understand that." Henry brushed aside words as he settled into the featherbed. "It's about Becket."

"What, pray tell me, was your performance all about tonight?"

"What performance?" She could feel him frowning in the night.

"That apparent heartiness you affected with Becket when we arrived, the clapping on the back, the kiss of peace. And then telling him he need not accompany us to London. Almost shunning him."

"What makes you think that was all performance?" The king adopted an injured tone.

"I know you, My Lord, to the bottom of your theatrical heart," Eleanor said almost affectionately. "And then, after you left, Becket said you threatened him."

"Did he say so?" Henry sounded amazed, then chuckled softly. "Well done, Tom. Well done."

"He asked to speak to me before I retired. And what was that particular scene all about? Leaving me alone with another man? Almost as if you wanted to start a scandal in the household."

"I never thought of that," Henry said with contrition.

"Henry, let's have an honest conversation."

"No, it's true. I left you alone with Becket because I knew he would confide in you if I were not there. In truth, I've come to find out what he said."

"I was just in the telling of it if you would stop interrupting. He said you threatened him."

"I simply said he might think of himself as the church, but We are still the Crown."

"And you added something about his peril."

"I did. I told him he forgot that important point at his peril." A pause. "And I meant it."

"But why bait him needlessly? Wait and see what he does at the councils you have called. You don't know his mind yet. He gave away nothing tonight. And you let him know you felt threatened." Some of Eleanor's exasperation infected her voice. Henry rolled on his side and faced his wife, propping his head on his hand, elbow on the pillow. He had deliberately left one edge of the heavy bed draperies open and the light from the wall torches invaded. He could now see his wife's face.

"Eleanor, I already know what he's thinking. He sent back the Great Seal without so much as a thanks for all the years I've kept him in the most important office in the state, saving yours and the justiciars. Without so much as a letter of explanation."

"But you didn't ask him for an explanation today."

"I shouldn't have to. God's hair, the man is a cleric to his bones, with or without the archbishop's crozier. He understands how the state works. And what about a common courtesy? I'll tell you what I think."

The king had forgotten all about making love and was now totally absorbed in the topic of Thomas, which may have been a good thing. The queen was beyond fatigued and satisfied not to be called into conjugal duty this night.

"I think he doesn't want to resign any power. I suspect he wants it all." Henry's voice was louder now.

"That's absurd, Henry. He's only a churchman." Eleanor was becoming alarmed, sensing the famous Angevin temper would shortly create a scene in her bed that would bring her women sleeping in the small anteroom.

"Eleanor, mark this. I insisted on the kiss of peace when we met. If he could have denied me, there, in public, denied his king the kiss of peace, he would have."

"How do you know this?"

"I felt him pull back, just the slightest, as I came close. God's breath, I could taste his resistance when I kissed him. I could. I could taste the poison rising from his heart."

"My Lord, you must calm yourself." The queen was now facing him, also lying on her side. She put her arm around his bulky shoulder and stroked his neck and back. Gradually she could feel the tension beginning to subside. "This excitement of yours serves no good purpose. Wait and see what happens. You have only just re-met. You cannot judge from one day what the future will bring."

"I have a bad feeling about all this. As if there is now a scorpion in my nest."

"Wait and see, My Lord. Wait and see. I do not think Becket will cross you in any serious way. Just let him be." She waited a moment, then spoke again. "I had a chance, while undressing, to speak with Betsy and

Alice, my London court women who came in the entourage to greet us. Becket has a following now, they say. He is considered quite holy."

"Is he so?" The king's tone was skeptical.

"It will not do to make a fuss. Wait and see. You have time, and there are other pressing matters—the laws and the Welsh. Wait and see what Thomas does next."

"You have reason in what you say," Henry murmured. His breathing was eased with her affectionate touching. In silence, they edged closer together.

Part Five: The Crisis
1163–1164

July 1163
Woodstock: The Royal Hunting Lodge, near Oxford, England

The king's good humor was apparent as he strode into the Great Hall of his hunting lodge at Woodstock. He had risen at dawn and rode out gaily with only du Hommet and the earnest Thomas Brown, gloves on their hands and hawks on their wrists. They rode back a few hours later with at least one bag of birds, it was reported by the grooms in the servant's hall outside the kitchens. The king was always pleased when the hawks had taken birds enough for dinner.

Henry had fed his honored guests well at the usual eleven o'clock hour, and now, at nearly one o'clock, they were assembling in the largest chamber of the castle for the promised council, to which they had been invited by the king.

Henry was all joviality as he entered the large chamber, speaking casually to most of the men there as was his wont, a clap on the back here, a handshake there. When he came to Becket, he extended his hand with a smile, and the archbishop responded in kind, his face inscrutable and grave.

The thrones of the king and queen were at the head of the room, but both were empty. Eleanor was in London attending to the business of the realm in the king's absence, and Henry rarely held with the trappings of power except on certain royal occasions when he felt the need to make a statement to his people. Today, as usual in these conferences, he sat at the long table, Geoffrey Riedel at one side to keep the record of the meeting, and de Lucy and Robert, Earl of Leicester, on either side of them, in attendance as justiciars of the realm. Piles of scrolls were in front of them. The small leadership group faced a crowd of barons on one side, nearly three dozen, Geoffrey counted, and the church men arrayed on the other.

Henry took his place in the center of the head table. The nobles sat on the left, in two rows facing the king and his counsellors, but at a slight angle so they could observe their ecclesial counterparts. All the important landowners were present, Geoffrey noted, as he copied names onto his parchment for the record. The earls of Salisbury, of Lincoln, of Chester, even Robert, Earl of Gloucester and uncle to the king, appeared, though he was so frail with age, he could scarce make his way to his chair.

On the right side were the major bishops of England—Roger Pont l'Eveque of York; Gilbert Foliot, recently named Bishop of London; Henry of Winchester, aging now but with eyes still alert; and the new bishop of Hereford, whose name Henry had temporarily forgotten. Also with them was Josceline de Bohon, newly installed as Bishop of Salisbury. Several of the abbots were there, although the monasteries had not been required to participate in this discussion. In the center of this group sat the acknowledged leader of the church in England, Thomas Becket, Archbishop of Canterbury.

Like the nobles, the churchmen also sat at an angle to see not only the king and his advisor but the other participants. In the back of the room were two rows of chairs set carefully and filled with the black habits of the Benedictine monks of Canterbury, admitted as observers only with no rights to speak.

Henry finally stopped fiddling with the various pens laid out in front of Geoffrey Riedel, took a deep breath, and opened the session with minimum formality.

"We welcome you right gladly to this council. We suppose you all know why you were invited. After the chaos of the wars caused by the battle for the throne of England, we believe part of our royal responsibility is to bring a return to the customs of my grandfather, King Henry's time. Our purpose is to provide order in the land and clarify the law."

The barons murmured quietly; heads nodded in what appeared to be assent. In truth, they had all grown tired of war and chaos that had ended only a decade ago, and some of them had even willingly returned castles they had taken from Stephen, with the understanding that Henry would re-grant them under his domain. The king had mostly kept his word to this point, so he had the goodwill of the barons. Nevertheless, as he spoke, he scanned their faces for signs of discontent.

The churchmen, on their side, were quiet, waiting, as it were, for how the particulars of Henry's "customs" would affect them and their land.

Geoffrey Riedel read off the list of "customs," more than a dozen, to acquaint the assemblage with them. The barons and the churchmen listened silently.

The king then looked around. "Are there any questions?" he asked as if the vote of support was to be summary.

There was a moment of pause as the men took stock of how the meeting was going. At this rate, they would be free for a ride through the forest before nightfall. Some might even start for home.

The archbishop of Canterbury had been the center of a flurry of whispers in his group. Now he rose with confidence, holding on to the staff which carried his insignia of office.

"My Lord King, we beg leave to speak."

"Yes, Archbishop. Please, you have the floor." Henry sat back in his chair, his forearm pressed against the table, his full attention given to his former chancellor.

"Your Majesty, we beg leave to differ on the point of the sheriff's aid bill."

"How so? It seems straightforward enough." The king frowned, deliberately misunderstanding, as if somehow any objection to this proposal must arise from ignorance and not difference. Becket took a deep breath, but before he could speak, the king interrupted him with a fuller description of the matter.

"We are proposing that the church, as a major landholder, pay a portion of the sheriff's tax directly to the crown rather than to the sheriff himself. This will increase the crown revenues without putting an added burden on the sheriff to come up with the increase." He spoke patiently, as if to a child.

"We understand the meaning of the item, Your Grace. But we object to the entire practice. As a group." He looked around for support and the other bishops, murmuring, nodded assent. Even the abbots, who ordinarily did not prefer to differ with the crown in public, appeared in concord with the archbishop.

"And what is the objection, pray?" Henry said with ominous pleasantry.

"We will pay aid to the sheriff if he deserves our aid by his service. But we will not pay it directly to the exchequer. Tax the sheriff further, if you must. But we will pay no further tax to the revenues of the crown than we pay now."

The king rose in sudden anger.

"By the eyes of God, it shall be given as royal revenue and entered in the royal rolls. It is not fit that you should gainsay this, for the sheriffs are my own true men. No one here would oppose aid for your men and against your will!" the king stormed.

Becket raised his voice so all could hear him. "By the reverence of the eyes by which you have sworn, My Lord King, there shall be given from all my land, or from all the property of all the church in England, not one penny for this sheriff's aid bill which would pay to the crown what is due the sheriffs directly!"

The king stared at Becket, who stood tall and unbowed, his chiseled features brought into relief by his tonsured head, his staff held in front of him like a weapon.

The king threw down the stone paperweight he had been holding upon the table. His justiciars looked anxious, expecting a famous display of the Angevin temper. But Henry mastered his emotions, as he could in extreme situations, and in a voice close to normal, announced, "This council is in recess. We shall take up these matters in autumn at Winchester."

Then he strode from the room, signaling his displeasure only by the force with which he slammed the door behind him, startling his men at arms standing close outside.

1 October 1163, The First Great Council Gathering Westminster Abbey, London

With solemn demeanor, the marshall proceeded the king and queen down the aisle of the great abbey, his steps measured and precise. The king was arrayed for once in all the glory of his state as sovereign, his heavy robes laced with gold and the crown of gold and jewels, his grandfather's crown, upon his head.

Eleanor was likewise dressed in elaborate finery she ordinarily disdained, willing to set aside her personal dislikes for the occasion and dress for her part as queen. The brocaded train that trailed behind her required four pages to lift and carry, so heavy was it with rubies and gold thread. She, too, wore the crown of England. The royal couple took their thrones, not used since their coronation ten years earlier.

Behind her marched the royal children: Prince Henry first, tall for his age of nine years, then the others, Mathilda, a year younger, Richard, already showing the rust-colored hair of his Angevin forbears, blond Geoffrey, each one a year behind the other. Watching the parade, de Lucy thought of Eleanor, for whom he had great sympathy. She was a strong woman, but she must be physically exhausted, with all her queenly duties plus bearing a child almost every year. Not for the first time, he marveled at her spirit. He noted that the little French princess was not present. But perhaps that was due to her age. Hard to control the little ones at state occasions.

Last of all in the line came the eldest son, another Geoffrey, the bastard Henry had brought to court to raise with his own brood. There could be no doubt of his paternity. At eleven years and with rust-colored hair and freckles, identical to the king's own, he was the very image of Henry.

Prince Henry made a deep bow to each of his parents and then, remarkably, walked to his tutor and master, Archbishop Becket, who was standing in front of the high altar watching the procession. Young Henry bent low to honor him, a gesture nearly as deep as the one to the sovereigns. He then followed the marshall, who was leading the other royal children (each of whom bowed in turn to their parents but not, notably, to the archbishop) to their places. Meanwhile, the singers had moved in and taken their seats in the quire, all the while chanting the antiphonal plainsong that the church had adopted as its own.

The great nobles followed, taking their seats between the quire and the high altar, as allowed. When they were seated, de Lucy turned to FitzStephen and muttered out of the side of his mouth, "I think the king and the archbishop endeavor to outdo each other in regalia this night."

But surely judgement between their presentation was nigh on impossible, for the white of the archbishop's vestments glittered with gold thread also and albeit he wore no crown, his white archbishop's mitre yet sparkled with jewels. His crozier, the bejeweled bishop's staff with the heavy silver cross on top, was almost as impressive to the gathered crowd as the scepter the king had trotted out for the occasion; at least to those who could see in the crowded church. All the lords of the land, without exception, and their ladies, were present.

"So, it would seem," FitzStephen answered. "Are things still as bad between them as they were left at Southampton?"

"No," de Lucy whispered back. "Henry is always willing to make a public scene, but he's much more reasonable in the doing than the saying. There were some messages back and forth, and he got Thomas to lift the excommunication on William of Eynsford and to withdraw the monk Laurence . . . a monk Becket had no business placing in that church without the lord's permission. That is if we are to follow the ancient customs of the first King Henry's time."

"Don't mention that phrase to me," FitzStephen shot back. "It portends nothing but trouble, at least between those two." To which de Lucy emitted a short grunt of concord as he turned his attention back to the front of the church.

Becket had mounted the high altar and was proceeding with the order of the day. The occasion of this great gathering was the transfer of the bones of Edward the Confessor, the first king of that name, from under the altar to a larger, more open shrine behind the high altar. But every actor on the stage that day, it seemed to de Lucy, had some other purpose in mind. The king and queen intended to demonstrate royal power and connection to the sainted King Edward of centuries earlier.

This would remind everyone of the customs of the king's grandfather's time. Becket was there to show his pre-eminence over the church in England, even into Westminster Abbey, the ancient seat of the kings of England. De Lucy would have had further proof of intentions if only he knew the silent thoughts of the king, sitting on his throne, motionless for once, watching the archbishop with keen interest.

These items of jewels and gilt are not the matter for kings, nor is an archbishop made so by the heavy cloak and mitre he wears. We are like actors, playing roles written for our shades. Well, I can play my part, Tom, I can play it well. As well as you with your crozier and mitre, and central role on the altar.

We have exchanged notices on certain subjects. The issue of sheriff's aid we will set aside for now. You lifted the excommunication on William of Eynsford. Well and good. That is one mistake you have corrected. But how about the banishment of the canon Philip de Brois? True, he killed a knight, but you have no right to banish. Nor to brand the clerk who stole the silver chalice and was caught. Branding? It's a form of torture. To be used only in severe cases, if at all. But always and only to be used by the royal courts, not you.

You and your church courts are not the law. I am told reliably that over one hundred criminous clerks have committed murder in the past year. Yet your courts routinely absolve them, claiming the protection of the church. Protection for these n'er-do-wells who have broken the king's peace and inflicted death on his subjects. This situation will end. We will end it.

You are usurping the rights that belong to your sovereign, Thomas. You have over-reached in your attempt to ingratiate yourself with your brother bishops and supposedly raise the rights of the church itself in England. But the laws and customs of my grandfather's time cannot be rewritten, no matter how many canons you set to busying themselves writing up the church's law. You are not the king, Thomas, not even king of the church.

13 October 1163, The Second Great Council Gathering Westminster, London

The first thing the participants noticed as they entered the great royal hall at Westminster this time was the presence of the thrones in the front of the chamber. After the great oak doors had been thrown open, the king and queen led the nobles and bishops into the massive chamber. The royals seated themselves as the rest of the retinue filed in.

The justiciars and chief counsellors were next, following in double file. Du Hommet turned to de Lucy as they made their way down the aisle between the seats for the bishops and the barons and muttered, "Haven't seen the thrones used in the Great Council since the coronation. Apparently, today the king wants to make a royal statement."

"You know what he plans. He told us yesterday in our council," de Lucy said back, out of the side of his mouth as they made their way to the head table.

"Yes, but I didn't know he was going to make a theatrical piece of it," du Hommet replied, but with a slight grin. "He's going to have to join the actors' guild if he keeps this up."

"Henry deserves to be king. He always knows how to play the sovereign to his audience when his back is against the wall."

The two men took their place at the head table alongside the faithful Geoffrey Riedel, nervously arranging his ink pots.

The barons filed in, talking among themselves but with noticeable restraint. The churchmen entered by another door, the same bishops and abbots that had been at Woodstock only months earlier. Thomas Becket was in the front row of the churchmen's side again, surrounded by his fellow bishops.

The queen sat, elegant and upright as always, nodding at the barons as they, one by one, made a brief bow to both the king and queen. She had a cheery word for a few of them, bright smiles for others. To a few, she gave her hand for their obeisance.

When all was settled, barely settled de Lucy noted, the king stepped down from the throne and stood at the head of the assembly. The marshall pounded his staff three times on the floor to call for order, but he need not have bothered. As soon as the king left the throne, all murmuring ceased.

"You all know why you were invited here today. We had decreed that We would take up the matter of the primacy of the see of Canterbury over York."

There was another wave of sound that appeared to be a general assent.

"But We have decided to dedicate this discussion instead to a matter most grave and dear to our hearts." Henry began his usual pacing back and forth in front of the two groups. No one showed more surprise at this turn of events than Thomas Becket unless it was Roger Pont l'Eveque, the bishop of York, who had been led to believe his case for independence from Canterbury would be heard today.

"As you all know, we are striving for clarity in the kingdom on matters of justice and the courts. And we are aware that, while we have been away some years settling affairs in Normandy and the south of France, matters here have come somewhat out of hand."

Robert of Leicester, sitting on the far side of Geoffrey Riedel, leaned forward and caught the glance of de Lucy. Here comes the trebuchet lobbing the rock, his look said. De Lucy nodded almost imperceptibly.

"We need to have a system for justice for offenses against the king's peace that is fair to all. But it has come to our attention that many clerks, priests, but even those who have minor orders, call for protection of the ecclesiastical courts when they have offended against the law of the land. We called you here today to propose a remedy."

The barons began to murmur, a sound that Eleanor took to mean support. But the bishops sat stunned as stones, not even looking at one another, clearly astonished at this turn of events.

"Over one hundred murders have been committed in the last year alone by those who then fled to the church for protection from Our laws. These criminous clerks hope to evade a just punishment by claiming their connection to the church. This situation must cease immediately. They will no longer be tried in the courts of the church and receive a light sentence or a verdict of not guilty when they have broken the law of the crown and kingdom." Henry finally stopped pacing. His last statement nearly shouted out, fell like a thunderbolt on the ears of the barons and bishops. The room was entirely still. The king then dropped into his chair at the long head table among his counselors. His acting chancellor, Geoffrey Riedel, was scribbling every word.

"We propose a revision of the current practices, going back to the laws and customs of my grandfather's time," Henry said after a moment and in a much calmer voice. "Those who offend against the king's peace will henceforth be tried in the king's courts, regardless of any connection to the church."

Then the king motioned to the marshal, who pounded his staff three times and shouted, "The king has declared a recess while you all consider these words."

Suddenly the silent room was astir with murmurs and low voices. No one dared speak with a loud voice at this moment. Henry watched all with keen eyes, slightly hooded. Nothing escaped him. A servant came in to offer the queen a wrap, as the room was quite cool.

The bishops flocked like birds around Becket's chair and the barons, with less movement, also consulted among themselves. Many of the barons present had suffered when a minor cleric or parish priest had stolen from them or harmed their peasants and then fled to the protection of the Holy Mother Church. They were generally in favor of the proposed clarification. But the churchmen on the opposite side of the room were clearly alive with protest. Their prerogatives were being invaded.

After some minutes, the king gave a signal to his marshal. "Order, order," he shouted now, pounding his staff upon a signal from the king.

The room fell silent as the archbishop rose straight as an arrow from the little group of bishops huddled around his chair. He pushed his way gently from their midst and walked, leaning heavily on his crozier to stand before the king.

"My Lord King, we must protest this proposed change in the customs and practices of the law of the land. We, the church, have always had our courts of justice, even in your grandfather's time. You must admit that." Becket stood taller than most men and today robed only in his simple monk's habit, the cowl resting on his broad shoulders, he had a certain dignity that could not be denied.

The king looked up at the archbishop from his seated position like an inquisitive bird and cocked his head before speaking as if in a questioning mode. His voice was measured and reasonable. His counsellors glanced at one another. This quiet voice was their king at his most dangerous.

"But Archbishop, no one disputes your right to your own courts for misfeasance of your own clerics of your own laws. What we are talking about here is the privilege the church has taken, over time, to extend its protection into the matters that concern my realm. That is what we seek to remedy here today." The royal voice carried, but it was contained and entirely persuasive. "Further, I seek not to interrupt your right to trial of those who claim your protection, but only that—if convicted of crimes against the king's law—their punishment would then be decided by the state."

"My Lord King, on behalf of my fellow bishops and the abbots here, I do protest that you are infringing upon our rights." Becket half turned as he spoke these words and the bishops in the front row of churchmen nodded assent, a few of them reluctantly. "We have the right of both trial and punishment, and the crown has no business interfering. After all, the crown takes its power from the church."

Henry had been writing as Becket spoke, or pretending to write, but his head snapped up at this last comment.

"Do you say then that you refuse to agree that the realm will return to the customs and practices of my grandfather's time in the justice system?" Henry had risen now and stared across the heavy table at Becket.

"My Lord, give me leave to consult my fellow bishops," Becket said, and, receiving a nod, he returned to his group. Again, they clustered around him like magpies, speaking with intensity and occasionally, a voice was raised. Finally, at a nod from the king, who had remained standing, the marshal's staff pounded the floor.

Becket once again detached himself from the others and came to stand before the king.

All this time, Eleanor had observed the interaction from her good perch upon her throne. After all, Henry had told her he needed her there to watch, to assess, to advise him when this difficult encounter was complete.

What she saw now were two men on their way to becoming implacable enemies facing each other. Her keen sight took in Becket's expression, not sorrowful but rigid, and Henry's rising color, always a bad sign. It was clear Becket was no longer interested in working things out. Could the king ever compromise? Not very likely, she thought. Had things gone too far between these men already?

"My lord, my fellow bishops and I have conferred, and I speak for all of them as their leader. We wish no disrespect, but we cannot agree to the invasion of our authority as it pertains to those who have a right to our protection." Becket announced this in sorrowful but firm tones. There could be no mistaking his meaning.

"Archbishop, We have been silent awhile and have meekly observed the attitudes you bishops adopt toward our royal authority and the government of this country. And as We have listened to your views, We have been wondering and humbly searching our mind as to what fault you should find in us," Henry's voice was slowly rising along with his color, not a good sign, Eleanor thought, "that you should deem us less worthy than other kings, our predecessors, to wear a secure crown."

"Your majesty, the wish of the church in this matter is to agree to all the customs and laws of your grandfather's time," a collective sigh came up from the baron's section of the room at this admission until Becket added, in a loud, clear voice, "*salvo ordinae*." The queen heard the sigh replaced by a gasp from the barons' front row.

"That means . . ." Becket began to elaborate but was interrupted by the king.

"I know what it means, man. I, too, know Latin. It means you will agree to anything as long as you don't agree to anything that changes your current reach of judicial power because you want to keep your privilege as churchmen. In fact, it means you agree to nothing!" The king spat out his last words.

Becket began to protest, raising his arm as if to speak further, but he was forestalled by the king's next statement.

"If that is your position, there is no point in continuing here today." The king had moved to the counsellors' table and was pulling together scrolls, usually the task of his chancellor. But his restless hands needed an outlet for his rising temper, and he shoved Geoffrey Riedel aside, his face flushing dangerously.

"I declare this council adjourned." Henry pushed a heavy chair out of the way, and it toppled backward.

"My Lord, wait for the blessing of the bishops," the marshall said, hurrying after the king as he strode from the room.

"Fie on the bishops. They care naught for my office, so I care naught for theirs." Henry threw these words over his shoulder as he strode through the doors.

The assembly sat, waiting for a sign from the queen. The marshall, turning from the king as from a lost cause, looked toward the queen for some signal as to what to do. De Lucy rose quickly and approached the queen, lifting his head as if to ask a question. She read his gesture and signaled the marshall to pound his staff three times to formally end the conference.

De Lucy offered the queen his hand to assist her descent from the throne dais as the meeting came to a tumultuous end. She allowed him the honor, but all smiles had fled her face. They were replaced by a frown, an expression of deep concern. She looked neither to the right nor to the left as she made her exit. Behind her, a storm of conversation broke out as the lead barons descended upon the churchmen in outrage.

25 October, twelve days later
Northampton Hunting Lodge

Eleanor's arrival that morning at the king's Northampton hunting lodge was unexpected. Henry had ridden hard, his sweaty horse breathing heavily as he entered the courtyard of the castle. He was unprepared for the sight of the small entourage, several attendants and archers still milling about. The insignia on the blankets covering the two riderless horses bore the queen's own crest.

Only half a dozen archers rode in the rear, a worrisomely small retinue for the queen to be about with, the king thought, after his first surprise. *Well then, I suppose Elle has come to settle me down and encourage me to make it up with Becket. She's in for a surprise this time. We've reached the end of the road. Or maybe he has changed his mind at last. He is willing to see reason, drop all this "I am the church" nonsense. Huh. We'll see.*

Henry did not pause to stop at his chamber and change his tunic and hose, soiled with the morning's hearty riding. He tossed the bag of birds he had felled with his expert bow at du Hommet, still by his side, and mounted the stairs two at a time.

As he expected, his visitors, also still in their travel clothes, stood talking together near the stained-glass windows at the far end of the Great Hall. The king stripped his gauntlets off and tossed them on the long oak table in the center of the room without pausing.

"Eleanor. De Lucy. What brings you here? Have you news? Has Becket finally come around?"

Eleanor looked at her husband. She had not seen him since he roared from the hall at Westminster a week earlier, throwing himself on his horse as his grooms and personal archers snapped to attention and looked around for horses to join him. He rode out of the lanes of London with only a straggling handful of retainers at his side, bellowing instructions to du Hommet over his shoulder. The general idea, as du Hommet understood these wind-swept shouts, was for him to gather the king's household and follow him to Northampton. For his wife, he had no word.

But now, finally, she had come to him. His face, flushed from his morning ride, was lined with fatigue, his eyes deeply shadowed, the residue of sleepless nights. The queen scanned her husband's face keenly. She recognized the signs, and she knew the cause. The scene at Westminster was no passing drama for Henry. Becket had struck him at the core of his kingship with his refusal to comply fully with the challenge to support the "customs" of the land. The queen felt some pity for Henry, but she also felt her old, familiar annoyance at the triumph of his choleric temperament over reason. He was ever his own worst enemy.

"Henry," she said patiently. "We are here for serious conversation. We have ridden since early morn to see you this day. But you have just now come in. Do you need time to refresh yourself?"

The king waved away her comments, watching her face. Since when was Eleanor willing to delay serious business for anyone's toilette, even her own? This was just Eleanor setting the stage ready for her performance.

"My Queen," he said unctuously, "do not fret. I am delighted you are here and have no need to change my garb or bathe. I am curious as to what brings you here." Then he turned to de Lucy.

"If you have come as well, Justiciar, this must be serious indeed." He was making a feeble attempt at humor, Eleanor thought, and his manner was uncharacteristically jovial for someone who had thrown a temper tantrum only a week earlier in front of all the lords of the realm.

"But where are my manners? Please, let us sit. We can dine here rather than in the crowded hall." He turned, gesturing toward the table behind.

"Send in some refreshments," he ordered his steward, who was hovering nearby. Then he turned apologetically back to de Lucy and Eleanor, who had drifted towards several chairs pulled back from the table to sit more informally near the hearth. "Dinner is never ready until an hour past the middle of the day here at the lodge. I suppose they have adjusted to my hunting schedule. Well, well, sit down and tell me what you have come for. I can read your face, Madame, and I know it is not good news."

The queen perched delicately on a chair under the remarkable window Henry had obtained as a gift for her only the year before. A large square made of the new colored glass the Venetians had invented. It was a mullioned piece that he had installed in the stone walls of this, her favorite room at Northampton. The sun behind it now cast a blue light over the queen as she sat straight in her chair.

She settled her skirts around her, then glanced at de Lucy, who gave a mild shrug. This news was hers to tell.

"Becket visited me," she began.

"Did he, now," Henry threw himself into a chair opposite her and stretched out his legs as if making himself comfortable enough to hear a long story. De Lucy finally sat, also, deliberately a bit apart from them. Long experience had warned him how to avoid the crossfire.

"He brought Prince Henry with him," the queen continued, watching him for signs of the usual fit of temper.

"Ah, yes. He holds our son and heir hostage. I had quite forgotten," the king said sourly. He had not, of course, forgotten, but Eleanor let that pass in the interest of getting on with it.

"The prince is quite disturbed at your argument with his beloved Master Thomas. He said."

"Who said? Becket or his hostage, my son?" the king interrupted.

"Henry, could you just forbear commentary until I have finished?" The queen could put iron into her tone when she chose, and she did so now. Not for nothing had she been duchess in one province and queen in two countries. The king settled back, his chin in his hand, his elbow resting on the large oak chair arm. The veneer of patience did not fool his wife, but as long as he kept silent, she was gratified.

"The prince explained to me, quite formally, that he wished me to intervene with you and speak for his former master. Even though the prince has his own household now, he is still concerned for his tutor. Master Thomas, he explained, was only standing up for the church at the Westminster Council. He meant, our son said, no disrespect."

Henry threw his head back on the high cushions and gripped the arms of the chair. He rolled his eyes in his head heavenward.

"Sweet hair of God! Now he has persuaded my son that I am the unreasonable one. And you two have been tapped by him to deliver that message."

"Henry, just listen for a moment," de Lucy interjected, using the king's Christian name as he seldom did. "The queen and I are not here as Becket's envoys."

"What then?" The king's head snapped forward. "Is there some other reason for your spontaneous visit? What malfeasance is this man thinking up now?"

"It's not Becket, Henry. We come on behalf of the Privy Council, your closest advisors. They met at the White Hall the day after the Westminster conference. You remember, the one you abruptly departed?" Eleanor could inject irony into her voice as well. "Flinging insults at the bishops over your shoulder as you went . . ."

"Who was at the White Hall?" The king wrapped his knuckles on the arm of the chair in agitation.

"De Lucy and du Hommet and Leicester were all there, four of the great earls and the three main bishops. I, of course, was not, but your justiciars attended me afterward. Meanwhile, I had the visit with Becket and the Prince, our son." The queen kept an even tone as she continued. "In conference, your justiciars and I decided that de Lucy and I would ride to see you here."

"I'll not let that man's manipulations with my son interfere with the business of the crown. Nor will he prevent me from bringing the rule of law to this country," Henry growled.

Eleanor rose and moved behind her chair, where she could look down on the king and de Lucy. As the king looked up at her, the firelight playing on her face now, he saw how tired she was, and the sight roused some vague feeling in him. All this was no fault of hers. She was only trying to bring it to a workable conclusion. He sighed.

"Henry, for the good of the realm, for the good of all the plans we have made for our sons and daughters and for this magnificent patchwork of counties and countries you and I have knitted together, this business of battle with the church must stop. There must be an accord between you and Becket. Too much is at stake." The queen took a deep breath. "You could damage our legacy for generations to come."

"What is it you and the Privy Council want from me?" Henry grumbled, looking from one to the other of his visitors. "There must be a request in all of this verbiage somewhere." De Lucy looked hopeful, but the queen knew better. Henry could appear perfectly reasonable one moment and throw himself rolling on the ground in a rage the next.

"Becket asked if you would see him here. To talk this out." The queen presented her request calmly, but her fingers, picking at her gown, were trembling.

The king did not respond for a long moment.

"He just wants to meet, Sire," de Lucy added helpfully.

"And where is he now?" Henry asked, although he already knew the answer well.

"He is at Oxford, waiting word as to whether or not you will see him," the queen said.

"Did you stay at Oxford last night?" Henry asked bluntly.

"Yes," the queen replied without hesitation. "He rode that far with us yesterday."

The king sighed as he rose from his chair. He was still a young man, but he seemed to have aged in this conversation. He seemed older than when Eleanor had last seen him. Was it only days earlier? The queen watched carefully as Henry turned his back on them, made for the doors of the hall. She knew him so well. He was considering his reply as he walked, wanting to hide his open, bluff face from the two of them.

When he was nearly at the entrance, he stopped and said over his shoulder, "Send word to Becket that I will see him day after the morrow at our favorite hunting spot in these woods. He knows where. Ask him to come as early as he can, but not to spend the night here. I don't want him under my roof."

With that, the king went out and slammed the great door behind him.

"Is this a good sign?" de Lucy asked the queen. "That he's willing to meet?"

She shook her head. "I don't know, Richard. I don't know what is on his mind. He is unhappy we brought Becket with us to Oxford. Maybe he senses that he cannot trust us." She gathered up her cloak and gloves. "He is beginning to see betrayal everywhere. Anyone even giving Becket a hearing will be judged harshly by the king. Henry's will is being thwarted, and he does not suffer such conflict easily. His judgement may be clouded."

His voice quiet, de Lucy said, "I understand."

"Yes, you always do. He is lucky to have you at his side. Stay with him," Eleanor said, looking full at de Lucy for a long moment. Then, "I'm going to my chambers. I'll have the servants find quarters for you. I'm certain Henry will appear at dinner. Here at Northampton, it's usually held long past the noon hour. After all, the king is here to hunt, and the schedule revolves around him."

With that, she turned and left the room also. De Lucy stood for some time staring into the fire.

October 1163, two days later
Northampton Hunting Lodge

"Your Grace, Archbishop Becket seeks you. He said you had sent word to meet him here." The deep voice of Henry's aide de camp, the faithful Roger Lagrange, preceded his crashing bulk through the trees. He arrived, breathless, on foot. The sight of the king sitting still upon a log, his faithful horse Pendragon nosing around the forest floor, brought the heavy Roger to a halt. The king signaled for silence, raising his finger and shaking his head. Two squirrels sat near a large tree trunk, observing the king.

Henry sat facing the small river, and it appeared he had been tossing pebbles and odd pieces of wood into the stream. A small pile of such a nature lay assembled at his feet. After the motion for silence, Roger's monarch proceeded to toss in two more small stones, the second landing farther than the first, watching them part the stream for a moment.

"Sire," Roger whispered, "The Archbishop waits for you at the crossroads of the forest path."

Henry finally turned to look at his servant, nodding. He said, in a very quiet voice, "Bring him to me on foot and alone. We must not disturb the animals. After all, it is their forest."

Roger concealed his surprise and answered in an equally soft voice, "Yes, my lord. He is not far."

The king continued his game against himself, testing each little piece of forest detritus for weight before tossing it into the stream. He did not look up when he heard the gentle swishing of the monk's robes. He had been certain Thomas would appear before him in the robes of the cathedral monks. Thomas, so predictable once he set upon a path.

"So, you are come," Henry said without looking up.

"Yes, Sire. The queen sent word to Oxford two days ago that you would see me here this morn." Becket stood, apparently at respectful attention, but the king was not fooled. Henry began to rise also, preferring to stand rather than conduct this conversation in the familiarity of sitting side by side. Becket moved to extend a hand to his king, but Henry waved it away, grasping at the convenient trappings of his patient horse to pull himself up.

"Did you ride from Oxford this morn?" Henry occupied himself by brushing the leaves and dirt from his doublet, then attending to his arms and legs. He had yet to meet the archbishop's gaze.

"No, Sire. When I got the queen's message, expressly telling me to be here but not stay at Northampton lodge, I went to Berkhamstead for the night. It's closer and the ride from there takes less time."

"Aah," Henry said, finally looking at his archbishop. He moved to face his former chancellor and, in so doing, moved slightly uphill so that he was almost equal in height to Becket. "Yes, I recall giving you Berkhamstead castle as a mark of gratitude when you were in my service." The king pointedly refrained from using the title of office, chancellor. Becket said nothing, looking at the king intently.

"I see you are not dressed for hunting. It would be difficult in those skirts." The king raised his brows.

"Sire, I did not think you invited me here to join you in hunting," Thomas said solemnly. Then, "And in my present office, I have foresworn those former pleasures that are of the world."

"Have you indeed?" Henry raised his brows. "God's sore feet, you're beginning to sound more like Louis every day!" His laugh was genuine but not particularly friendly.

"Yes, the pious aspect of Louis always rubbed on you, if I recall," Becket responded in a light tone. "But what was it you wanted me for?"

So, it was Becket bringing the conversation to its head on his own timeline. This lack of deference was a change, the king thought. His eyes narrowed.

"The queen seems to think you and I have something to talk about," Henry made a flat statement. "I am not certain I agree, but I did allow that I would speak with you."

"Sire, that which happened at Westminster last week, I regret."

"Which part of it do your regret, Archbishop?" It was the first time in the dialogue that Henry's voice became hard. "Betraying your king or betraying your friend?" Henry's square jaw jutted out ominously.

"Sire, I . . ."

"No, Thomas Becket. Not you. Not 'I' spoken by you. It is We who are in charge. The royal prerogative. We are the nation, and you are but

Thomas Becket. And yet you stand against Us on Our major project of bringing law back to this lawless land." The king's voice had risen as he spoke. Becket had heard this tone before, and he knew it could turn into a roar in short order. It was the first time the royal wrath had ever appeared dangerous to him. Not for effect on a royal audience now. Thomas Becket himself was its only object.

"Sire, all the bishops . . ."

"Yes, yes, you are their leader. They must follow you. Or do you follow them in order to be their leader? It is a question, isn't it?"

"If you would let me speak, my lord," Becket began again, and when Henry didn't interrupt as expected, he had to pause briefly to assemble his thoughts. "I am the church in England," Becket finally said. "You are the king, but I am the church."

"Aah, yes. So you wrote to the pope this summer." Henry turned away slightly, gazing for a moment at the running water of the stream.

"Sire? I wrote to Alexander?"

"Yes, after Woodstock. He sent a message to me, asking what this quarrel was all about. Now let me see . . ." Henry scanned the sky as if to find help in recalling the exact words.

"Ah, yes, I have it. You wrote 'The clergy in England was hitherto, by special privilege, exempt from lay jurisdiction.' Yes, I think those were your exact words, as quoted to me by the pope himself."

"Well, I was only trying to . . ."

"I know exactly what you were trying to do, Thomas," the king snapped, his tone indicating that the use of Becket's given name was no sign of affection. "You were trying to manipulate the powers of Europe against me, using the pope for your own political ends." Henry's restless hand toyed with the small dagger at his waist. "And that is the thanks We receive for all of the favors We have bestowed upon you." Suddenly he sighed and walked a few paces away. When he faced Becket again, his face had altered, now possessed by an almost sunny expression.

"Tom, Tom, can you not see what I am trying to do?"

"I can see that you want to breach the independence of the clergy in England by dragging our people into your courts." Becket had seen these abrupt *volte-faces* before. He kept his enthusiasm in check.

"Well, that is one way to look at it. But you are deliberately misunderstanding my purpose. You can still try your villeins in your church courts. But if your courts find them guilty, they will be stripped of the protection of the church and handed over to the crown's courts for punishment. Is that so unreasonable?"

"It's the principle of the thing," Becket said doggedly. "You are infringing on my . . . on the church's traditional rights. On our honor. On the honor of God."

"God's holy teeth," Henry shouted, using one of his favorite personal oaths and apparently so angry he was unaware of the irony of the juxtaposition. "Infringement is a matter of your opinion, yours, and your fellow bishops. I notice even Roger of York has come to your side on this. Hah! And to think Woodstock was originally called to settle your quarrel with him."

"Forget Woodstock. What we speak of here, this is no puny difference. We are talking about matters of vital concern to all the church in England, unto the generations to come," Becket intoned.

"Will you stop this nonsense!" Now the king's voice had reached a roar. "You are creating a war out of a difference in a taste of wine! You are puffing yourself up in this contretemps, making it something it is not. Cease it now!"

Becket straightened himself further and placed his hands definitively inside his sleeves, in the manner of monks when pacing or at prayer. He now looked over the king's right shoulder, refusing to meet Henry's angry stare.

"You well know that the church's prerogatives you are so eager to defend are not traditional rights. During my grandfather's time, they followed Roman jurisprudence. Things got confused when the war between Stephen and my mother turned this land into chaos. I'm trying to turn it back into a land of law and courts and shires where my subjects can live in peace." This last line was uttered almost in hopelessness, the anger draining from the king as he turned away again.

"And so they may." Becket suddenly placed his hand on the monarch's arm to gain his attention. "We respect all your laws. But we will not stand for an infringement on the rights of the church in this land. We take care of our own."

Henry's mood shifted abruptly once more. "Who are you that you stand against Us? Have I not raised you, Thomas Becket, from your poor and humble station to the pinnacle of honor and rank? It hardly seemed enough for me unless I not only made you father of the kingdom but also put you even before myself. How can it be that so many favors, so many proofs of my affection for you, which everyone knows about, have so soon passed from your mind that you are now not only ungrateful but oppose me at every turn."

The archbishop looked at the king for a long moment, silent. Then he said softly, "I am not unmindful of the favours which, not simply you, but God the bestower of all things, has deigned to confer on me through you, so far be it from me to act against your wishes in anything, so long as it is agreeable to the will of God. Submission should be made to temporal lords, but not against God, for as St. Peter says, 'We ought to obey God rather than men.'"

"I don't want a sermon from you. Are you not the son of one of my villeins? The king spoke in disgust as he began again to jettison the forest stones and wood chips into the river. He positioned himself as if to block the sight of Thomas from his vision.

"Sire, I am ready to serve your honour and good pleasure in all things, saving the good of our order and the honor of God."

"Get out of my sight," Henry hissed, throwing his arm sideways without looking as if to strike anything that stood in his way. "If I never hear that phrase again until my deathbed, it will yet be too soon. Get away from me before I call my men and have you arraigned for high treason."

The king's voice held a new note, one of unmistakable menace. The archbishop was suddenly and, for the first time, physically afraid. He bowed and backed slowly up the hill as if afraid to turn his back on such a dangerous animal. He watched his king as he felt his way with his feet to the path opening, where he turned and disappeared into the forest.

Henry sat down on the log and waited for his anger to cool. He had been close there, at the end, to a sudden murderous impulse, he knew it. That would accomplish nothing and turn Becket himself into a martyr, but the man was beginning to ask for martyrdom. How could things have come to this between old friends? Henry sighed and buried his face in his hands. He began to weep in frustration and loss.

Some time passed. Henry was not certain how long he had been sitting and staring at the river, but finally, he rose stiffly from his perch on the old log. He stretched to get his muscles moving, first one arm, then the other, then stamping his feet on the ground to get his blood moving in his legs.

The river was flowing as it had been before, still issuing an invitation to play to a tired monarch. A slight breeze rustled the trees, and leaves were drifting down, a sign that winter would come. Henry sighed and moved toward Pendragon, who lifted his head in welcome at the approach.

At least someone is dependable. I can count on Pendragon. As for Becket, he may be lost to me. Not only lost as a friend but become my implacable enemy. He has finally become greater than himself. He has become the church. There is no difference now. He thinks he is the pope of England. Thomas Becket, what hast thou wrought? I knew when you gave me the reluctant kiss of peace that we would never find our fellowship again in this world. I should have always known this might happen. You were so eager to please, grateful for the favors, my right hand, my loyal man as chancellor. Why did I imagine that would continue once you had power of your own? Why did I not see your character? Because I didn't want to see it, and we both know that. It suited me to be blind to your innate concern for your own matters, blind to that element in you that wants not to serve but to be served.

The past is gone. You want to play power games? I'm all for it. You will rue this day. You are no Louis, no Barbarossa, not even Alexander. You are now only a monk, a monk that I created. You will not get in my way as I try to set down the practices of justice in my realm. You think you have Rome in your pocket, but you are mistaken. You think you can out-fox my canon lawyers, but you are mistaken again. You think you can stare down your king, but there you are very much mistaken. This will not end well, but you have brought the end, when it comes, on yourself.

December 1163
Christmas Court at Berkhamstead, formerly the castle of Thomas Becket, now the property of the King

The hour grew late. The small group of men sitting around the large oak table in the stuffy council room at Marlborough Castle were shifting in their seats as the king motioned for the next sheaf of parchment to be placed before him. Du Hommet sighed, Robert of Leicester rolled his eyes toward heaven and William Fitzstephen stretched his arms upward and cracked his knuckles high in the air. Walter Map, in place to record the events, had propped his head on his hand and appeared to be dozing. Geoffrey Riedel sat to the king's right and was working his shoulders to relieve the stiffness. Only de Lucy maintained decorum.

The king was much too occupied with the business at hand to notice any of his counsellors' indications of restlessness. The monarch was like a man driven this day.

"Wales is settled for the moment. We must get on with Ireland. I cannot wait much longer. Every report says the princes are ready to welcome our arrival, to align with us. We will be the balance between the princes and the priests. But I must be there in person to receive their allegiance and with some show of force." The king unexpectedly raised his head from the documents, and every face immediately assumed a look of assiduous interest.

"De Lucy, how many knights can we call up for such a voyage to Ireland? If we can't get what we need, we can pad the corps with our trusty Belgians. They are always ready to carry bows for money."

"We can safely plan on nearly what we took to Toulouse. I suppose we must again give the barons the choice of a levy or the knights' service." Henry paused. That had been Tom's suggestion, and a good one it was. "Yes, well, let us think on it."

For a moment, the king paused, overtaken by memory. During the planning for Toulouse, Thomas sat by his side. He knew immediately the numbers and the cost of every ship and every archer. His judgement was unerring in these matters. But now he had removed himself, was gone forever from these councils.

The men waited expectantly for the king to continue. This hesitation was unlike him. Finally, he spoke with an abrupt change of subject.

"On the matter of Thomas Becket, former chancellor of England and now Archbishop of Canterbury, I have something to report," Henry stated.

The small group straightened as if they were one. Gone was fatigue, gone was the urge to sleep. Even Walter Map came to life. Only Geoffrey Riedel, who was, to all intents and purposes, currently filling the role of chancellor, did not look surprised. A small smile played upon his lips.

"The chancellor, I mean archbishop, visited me at Woodstock only a fortnight ago. He was dismayed that we had recovered our castle at Berkhamstead and the manor at Eye from him. He had assumed they would remain as part of his estate once he had left my service. The archbishop expressed sincere regret that I had removed Prince Henry and Princess Marguerite from his household. He has rethought his position, been persuaded, let us say, by the Holy Father Alexander, to come around to Our proposals. He will no longer oppose Our will to re-establish the customs of Our grandfather King Henry's time." The entire group sat open-mouthed at this news, delivered unexpectedly and with some apparent hesitation, so unlike their sure-footed monarch.

"The archbishop (now the voice was stronger, no stumbling over the title) apologized to me for his recalcitrance and, at my urging, agreed to make his position known publicly. So," Henry continued, "after the celebrations of the great feast of Christmas, we shall formalize these agreements at a council called for my hunting lodge at Clarendon. All the barons and bishops have been summoned to attend Us there. After that formality, our courts may once again become the sole, active justice system in this land. And We shall no longer be distracted by these matters." The shift to the royal "We" was as much a surprise as the announcement itself. It signaled the king speaking as king, something this informal monarch rarely did when he was with his privy council.

"You have only to mention Becket, and Henry puts his crown on," de Lucy muttered sideways to Leicester, who nodded. Glancing at his colleague, Robert of Leicester noted how the black hair was streaked with grey. He wondered if his own face had aged as much in the past months over this interminable quarrel of church and state.

Louis Lagrange, the Steward of Berkhamstead Castle, chose just that moment to enter the chamber by a side door. This aide of the king could not have made an unobtrusive entrance to a room if he had tried, which he never did. His mere bulk demanded notice, and the bustle with which he walked added to the interruption. He leaned down and whispered extensively to the king, who nodded several times.

"Very well, gentle knights." The king looked almost relieved as Lagrange made his way out of the room after bowing. "The queen sends to tell me the court has been assembled this past hour, and the dinner is in grave danger of burning in the kitchens if we do not postpone the rest of our business." He rose, and the others, most gratefully, followed his example.

"Mayhap we'll have Christmas cheer after all if Becket is giving in," du Hommet muttered to the two justiciars as they moved to flank the king.

"I'll believe it when I see it with my own eyes," de Lucy shot back.

Leicester laughed. "Christmas is supposed to recall miracles," he said good-naturedly. "Let's all believe it for the moment."

25 January 1164, day two of the Conference
The Hunting Lodge at Clarendon

The king entered the broad meeting chamber with his entourage of servants and the faithful Geoffrey Riedel beside him. It was the second day of the meeting, and things were going well. Henry appeared in full regalia, having cast aside his traditional hunting and riding outfits for the day in honor of the majesty of the occasion, and although he wore no crown, there could be no mistake that he was king. His cloak was trimmed in ermine, the sleeves of his tunic in deep red velvet with gems beaded on the cuffs. He wore his medallion of state around his neck on a thick gold chain. His justiciars could not recall ever seeing him wear that symbol since his coronation at Westminster more than ten years earlier. Here indeed, was the splendor of the monarchy deliberately brought out for the barons and the bishops and, most especially, for Archbishop Thomas Becket, finally brought to heel.

As Henry had announced at Berkhamstead, Becket had indeed made a formal acknowledgement in front of the entire assembly the previous day, an agreement to accept the customs of the days of King Henry the First of that name, Henry Plantagenet's grandfather. A few of Becket's brother bishops had been clearly unprepared for the about-face of their leader and muttered busily among themselves when the archbishop made his statement publicly. Henry could not be certain they knew this move in advance, but he was not concerned about their murmurs. Henry had recently met privately with Roger Pont l'Eveque and Gilbert Foliot and knew that their envy of Thomas Becket could be turned to good use in this matter. They could always criticize him later for his positions at this council. But the important point was to tie these agreements down today, to make them concrete in front of all, so there could be no misunderstanding in the future.

The chamber was cold, as could be expected of middle England at the end of January. The barons, sitting on one side, were clothed in furs against the weather. Few had even shed their riding cloaks. On the other side, most of the bishops were no less sumptuously and warmly robed, although a few from the outlying dioceses wore only woolen cloaks. Henry, as he sat on his throne watching the crowd of worthies, secretly paid respect to the simplicity of the rural bishops.

Ah, yes, the men of the church will dress according to their station whilst their humble charges may go in rags or lack enough to cover their young against the wind. That time I forced Becket to give his cloak to the shivering beggar, it was a joke to him, well maybe a joke, but he failed to see the point. His wealth as a man of God as opposed to the needs of the common man. But he learned nothing from it, for look at him now, with all the trappings of his office and his power. Even his brother bishops treat him gingerly. They are confused. Is he their leader? Or their competitor? Or their enemy? Even the best of them, Gilbert and Roger, are divided within themselves. Thomas, Thomas, the only man who ever trusted you sincerely was myself. And look how that has turned out.

Fires burned in all three fireplaces, but the fierce English wind could be heard whipping around outside, even slicing in gusts through the arrow openings to rustle the heavy tapestries against the walls. Torches lit the assembly. Most present had slept well, and why not? This fight between king and archbishop was finally resolved with Becket's agreement. And on the first day of the conclave!

Becket entered the chamber last among the bishops, with a small boy carrying the episcopal cross ahead of him. His long, handsome, dark-shadowed face bore no expression whatsoever. If the barons had hoped for some sign of sincere repentance for having caused so much mischief in the realm, they could not read it in his demeanor.

Henry, sitting alone on the slightly raised platform, acknowledged his archbishop's bow with a nod. He watched the jewels on the archbishop's staff sparkling and the gold winking in the light thrown from the torches. Such was the church become today, the king thought, bemused, interested in a show as grand as his own. For himself, display held no power except to remind his people of who was king. He much preferred the battle won, the enemy's castle taken, or the courts of justice settled. That way only lays peace for the realm.

He bore no envy of Becket's riches now that he had his agreement on the division of justice in the courts. He had seized Becket's castles in the autumn only to teach the archbishop a lesson—what the king bestowed, the king could take away. That was the point of holding the royal Christmastide celebrations at Berkhamstead. But he had no need to further humiliate his former chancellor. That is, if Becket were sincere in his agreement to comply with the Constitutions. Somewhere, though, in the back of his mind, something in Henry worried like a dog over a bone. The expressed compliance of Becket before Christmas seemed, somehow, too easy. He had reconfirmed it the previous afternoon in front of all here at the great council of the realm. But would his agreement hold? Today would tell, for Henry had a surprise in store.

After his bow to the king, Becket took his usual seat in the front row at the center of the bishop's side. The justiciars were arranged at the long table, along with several canon lawyers from the chancer and the lawyers for the crown, men well-versed in Roman law as well as canon law.

The marshall pounded his staff three times on the floor. The room continued to hold a low buzz, so he repeated the action with greater energy. Gradually, a cloud of silence descended on the group, and even the murmuring drifted off.

"My lords and bishops," the king began, nodding to each side as he acknowledged their presence, "We have reached agreements in the council yesterday that should provide for peace and lawful justice process in this kingdom for many years to come and for the end of confusion between what is the realm of the church and what is the right of the state."

There were some murmurs from the barons' side of the room. Some of them had suffered wrongs at the arbitrary justice process that delivered thieves and murderers to the bishops' courts in the past. They were clearly on the side of the king. The bishops were silent. Even Roger of York and Gilbert of London were frowning. Although they had given their word to Henry that they would back him, he could see writ on their faces that they still felt some threat to their ecclesiastical rights. He hoped their private agreements with him held up through the surprise he had arranged for the day. And now he would deliver it.

"In order to make these agreements formal, we have had our chancery draw up the document to which we will affix our signatures and our great seal," here he smiled at Becket, a wolf's smile du Hommet would say later, "as the sign of understanding and agreement on the part of all here."

The room fell silent. While no one was actually surprised that the king, with his need for detail, would have something written down, an agreement in writing could present a problem. What would the actual wording be? The barons were glancing in the direction of Thomas Becket, but since he was in the front row, it was difficult for most to see his reaction.

However, it was not at all difficult for the king, sitting on this raised chair and leaning toward the archbishop on his elbow, watching him like one of the hawks they used to release in their hunting days watched its prey.

Becket half rose from his chair, his face dark as an approaching thundercloud. De Lucy, facing him from the head table, closed his eyes and muttered a prayer, or perhaps a curse, as he saw this. It only took a moment for the thunderclap to descend.

"What is this, My Lord King? You have said nothing about agreements in writing. We had the discussion yesterday in this very chamber, and my fellow bishops and I agreed that we would respect the intent of the customs of your father's day, except as it would show menace to the laws or dignities of the church. You have, in turn, promised that the customs would not." Becket's voice, usually so urbane, was shaking with rage.

"Naturally, We understand your position," the king said as he pushed himself out of his chair and descended the three steps to be on equal footing with Becket, even as he invoked the royal pronoun for the upper hand. "And were things to continue as they are today, you would be entirely in the right of it in your preference for giving your word to Us. But as you well know," the king was pacing now in front of the entire assembly, his hands locked behind his back as he so often did to keep them still, "the peace of the kingdom cannot rely on you and I in our present roles forever."

Becket opened his mouth to speak, but the king released one hand long enough to hold it up and forestall him.

"We have lived through near anarchy under the late King Stephen's England, and such a situation, God forfend, could occur again should you and I pass on to our heavenly reward." Now the king came to a full stop in front of his archbishop and swung his powerful upper body directly to face him.

"So we must make provisions for just such circumstances. Here is our offer. Merely sixteen constitutions laying out Our decrees of clarity between the church and state. After all, you bishops," and here Henry made one of the grand gestures he often affected in his royal public appearances, sweeping his arm toward the entire left side of the chambers where the bishops sat, swiveling their heads to see first the king, then their primate's response, then the barons' reactions, "are both holders of the power of the church and also, at least many of you, my feudal lords through your land-holdings. We must have clarity on your various roles above all."

Becket drew himself up to his full height. In his ecclesial robes and with his brightly jeweled staff, he was equal to the king in the power of his presence and slightly taller on the physical plane. But his face was a picture of conflicting emotions. It was clear he had been caught entirely unawares by this ploy of the king's to write the agreements in sixteen parts.

"My Lord King," he began stiffly, in a strong voice that could be heard around the hall, "I beg you for time to consult with my fellow bishops. I know you and your advisors," here he bowed to the royal table of counsellors and canon lawyers assembled by the king for the purpose of this meeting, "will grant us the right to discuss these matters outside this chamber. Perhaps a slight recess?"

"Indeed, indeed," said the king, with a generous smile and another royal sweep of the arm. "We are approaching the dinner hour. We shall dine in the great hall and return to this chamber before the winter sun sets to finish our discussion. But, Archbishop . . .," the king paused, his bright eyes narrowing and his wide face, usually so open, closing somehow in expression as he moved toward his quarry and dropped his voice considerably, ". . . do not tarry too long. It is Our will that these sessions will not continue indefinitely. Do not force Us to make the decision for you on this matter," Henry allowed one of his exquisite pauses, "that is, for you and your fellow bishops."

With that, the king gestured to the marshall, who in turn pounded three times on the floor with his heavy staff. Those at the head table gathered up their scrolls and papers and made ready to leave, Leicester casting a knowing glance in the direction of de Lucy. The king left first, accompanied by Geoffrey Riedel, an honor that was not lost on Becket as they swept past him.

Then the archbishop took his right of precedence, taking his crozier from the lad and leaning on it himself as if for support. He was followed closely by Gilbert Foliot and Roger of York, muttering between them, the others clustering behind them, with the barons joining in the informal recessional. De Lucy now understood: Becket, and even Foliot and Roger Pont l'Eveque taken somewhat into the king's confidence, had not known, not had an inkling, was that these constitutions, these sixteen agreements, would be presented in writing, casting them into the practice and record of English common law as it was evolving. The role of the church, and of her bishops, would be circumscribed by them.

No one heard Robert of Leicester instruct William FitzStephen as the head table followed the participants out, "Stay in the anteroom. That's where the bishops will talk. Come back to us with news."

"Yes, good thinking," the young FitzStephen, fond of gossip, jumped at the chance to overhear the discussion. "I'll present myself as an errand boy if they notice me, there to run messages to the king if they have questions."

"Aye, that's a good thought." Leicester grinned, "and maybe they'll be too busy to notice you at all."

25 January 1164, day two of the Conference, in the evening
The Hunting Lodge at Clarendon

"Henry, have you finally gone mad?" The queen swept into the royal privy chamber without warning, slamming the heavy door behind herself and discarding her cloak as she came, a veritable whirlwind. This is unlike her, de Lucy thought, looking up from the game of chess he was playing with the king. And with a look at her face, he could see why. Her usually calm demeanor, the beautiful diamond-shaped face he had always loved, was pale and pinched with anger. He looked quickly at the king, whose head snapped up at the slamming of the heavy oak door. Everyone in the room rose in respect and surprise.

"My dear, what brings you to Clarendon? I thought you were at Salisbury with the children for the week." Henry pushed himself back from the heavy table and stood to greet her, extending his hands to take hers, which she snatched back.

"What brings me here is a messenger dispatched by your archbishop this late morning with the gravest of news. What are you thinking to force this issue with writs signed in blood?" She waved the other counsellors back to their seats.

"Now, now," the king responded mildly. "Scarcely signed in blood. You know how dramatic Becket can be."

"Henry, when Thomas came to you at Woodstock, he said he would agree with your basic will to make the customs of your grandfather's time the law of this land. I was present when you and he made that agreement."

"That's true, my queen. He did say so." The king, still standing, picked up the bishop from the chess board, the one he had just taken, and fiddled with it.

"His private agreement was not enough for you," the queen went on, coming around the table. De Lucy could not remember seeing her so overwrought. "You insisted that he had rejected this proposition earlier in public and he must reverse himself in public."

"Yes, all that is true." The king met his queen's challenging gaze for a moment as they stood face to face. Then, slowly, he turned from her and moved to the hearth and propped himself by extending a straight arm and grasping the thin oak mantel. He looked absently into the dancing flames as he addressed her. "What is the point of your review here?"

She ignored the edge creeping into his voice and moved to his side, her voice becoming more urgent. Despite her earlier permission to sit, the counsellors remained standing and alert. None of them wanted to miss this show. They knew when the king and queen disagreed in front of them, the performance was worthy of the guild awards for actors in the touring theatre groups.

"The point to my words is that Thomas agreed to all that you requested, and then today, you come up out of nowhere with this written document. These . . . these sixteen demands of him. . . . These so-called constitutions. They have put him in an untenable position with his fellow bishops. They are urging him on one side to resist, and you are demanding on the other to give in."

"Is that what Becket is calling them?" The king straightened up and faced his angry wife again. "Demands? And demands of him?" Henry's voice rose on the last note. "How like my former chancellor to see everything in the light of being directed toward himself. Madame, I did not commission these constitutions for the benefit of tormenting my former officer. They have nothing to do with him personally. They are to protect the order of law in this land."

"Oh," the queen threw her arms up dramatically as she turned away. "You are impossible."

"And your evidence for that, Madame, is?" The king no longer sounded calm, his face coloring. "It is the archbishop who is impossible to deal with. He persists in seeing everything as it affects him, and him only. He wants to be the head of the bishops, but he wants to have all the power himself. He wants to pacify the choleric temperament of the king, but he wants his sovereign to bend to his will. He wants laws and justice as long as they are his law courts and his justice system."

The king was advancing toward the queen on these words, his right arm now extended with a fist turned upward, a bad sign, thought de Lucy.

"By God's beard, this is my answer to him. He is not the sovereign of this land, nor shall he ever be." Henry's voice, rising, turned into a shout on his last words. "He will not usurp the king's power."

The queen, who was used to the king's temper, did not step back, and Henry stopped just short of her. The counsellors all sat wide-eyed, waiting for the outcome of this royal battle. The king had never been known to strike the queen, Indeed, he depended on her often for advice and left her regent of the kingdom in his absence. But this scene, her apparent defense of Becket, aroused the anger of the king against her, unlike anything they had ever seen.

The room was silent as the king's last words echoed. The fire crackled, spitting cinders onto the hearth.

The queen stood calm before him, her narrow shoulders straight and her hands clasped together behind her back, as was often the king's habit. De Lucy knew the king was perfectly capable of throwing himself on the floor and chewing the rushes if he thought it would serve any useful purpose, although they had never witnessed him doing this in front of the queen. Still, there was always a first time for anything.

After a long pause, the counsellors realized as one that the king was going to wait it out, that the queen must speak next. Like a game of chess at the end, the next move was hers. None dared intervene.

Eleanor, at forty summers, and a mother many times over, was still tall, still somewhat slender, and still regal. De Lucy watched in awe as she drew herself up to her full height, nearly the equal of her husband, preparing to speak. She was the more mature of the couple, nearly thirteen years older than the king and far more levelheaded. Her cool nature was a welcome antidote to the king's frequent outbursts. De Lucy chewed his lower lip thoughtfully.

"Henry, if you pursue this revenge, you will wreck everything you and I have worked for. All this wonderful realm you and I have crafted together," here she swept her right arm sideways, magnificently, the point of her long sleeve nearly trailing in the rushes, "will blow away like chaff in the field. An illusion, like a magician can create. It will only last to the times of our sons if you cannot master your anger and use reason if you cannot listen to your canon lawyers and your counsellors and release this terrible hostility toward Becket. It will take two of you in this realm to save a breach between church and state that will echo all over Europe."

The king looked at her for a long time without moving. It became clear she would not speak again, but nor would she turn and leave without his response.

When he finally spoke, his voice was unexpectedly soft. "Madame, you may have the right of this situation. But Becket and I have passed the turn in the road where it is possible to mend the fence."

Only now, after a long moment with the king's words echoing in the air, did the queen finally turn away. Nodding to the counsellors, Eleanor, Queen of England and Duchess of Normandy and the Aquitaine gathered her train and swept from sight with as much regal grace as any of those present had ever seen. After a moment, the king turned back to the table, rubbing his hands together as if in anticipation.

"De Lucy, we must delay our finish on the chessboard until later, although I know I have you now. Needs must return to our real game, establishing the laws of this realm. There is sure to be more trouble before this council is ended. We must anticipate all scenes and plan for them."

He threw himself into his capacious chair at the head of the table, the chessboard still sitting. The men, who had stood scattered about the room in a daze, suddenly stirred themselves and took their customary places at the table.

The king continued as they all composed themselves. "FitzStephen, tell the others what you heard as you listened to the bishops while you were lolling about in the anteroom when they met with Becket. They need to advise Us on this matter. We all need to understand our opposition."

"Sire, as I reported to Your Grace when I left the anteroom this afternoon to come to this council, it seemed the major bishops were beginning to urge Thomas to compromise. At the very least, York and London were reasoning with him."

"And what was Becket's demeanor?" Henry asked, his eyes narrowing.

The earnest, round face of young William FitzStephen shone happily to be able to report good news. "The archbishop was still sitting in the middle of the group, but as I passed, I saw him nodding to his brothers as they exhorted him."

"Well done," said the king. "Well done, indeed."

Some hours later, the counsellors' meeting finally adjourned. As they bid each other a good night outside the door, de Lucy observed the king heading in the direction of the queen's chambers. "Now," he thought, "how will that encounter play?" And, not for the first time, he considered that the king and queen always knew exactly what they were doing in public.

27 January 1164, two days later
Clarendon

The patience of the barons was wearing thin, de Lucy noted as he entered the council chambers. There were restive murmurs from that side of the Great Hall as the counsellors strolled down the aisle. De Lucy took note. He was in sympathy with them. They had not expected this conference to go on for days, but none of them dared leave before the outcome of this mighty struggle was known.

Today the king had elected to enter after everyone else, including the archbishop, had joined the conclave. Thus, when the bishops entered, York first, then London, then Chichester, and finally the primate Becket preceded by the choir boy bearing his staff of office. But today, there was no king to bow to, no ceremony to be observed. This deprived the archbishop of his right of drama. Once again, de Lucy thought, Henry's astute sense of managing public scenes was put to good use. Not for the first time, de Lucy wondered if the king's occasional temper tantrums were simply a larger part of his control stratagems.

And here he came, once again in the royal regalia he usually disdained. Robes flew out behind him as he hurried in, preceded by a page bearing—could this be true—the royal scepter? Maybe Henry was overdoing it this time. He must have sent to Winchester for the jeweled icon.

The king took his seat on the raised dais and signaled the marshall to call the meeting to order. Then, without preamble, he stood and motioned for Geoffrey Riedel to hand him the parchment on which the sixteen constitutions had been written.

"Gentle knights and lords, good bishops, we have been engaged in discussions long enough. I entertain a hope that today we shall reach agreement and that both the archbishop, for the church in England, and myself, as the crown, may sign these sixteen agreements clarifying our feudal rights." Henry flapped the parchment open, unrolling it as if it were the ten commandments. He then passed it to a page standing near his chair, who carried it over to Geoffrey Riedel sitting at the long table facing the barons together with the other counselors.

The archbishop rose slowly. "My Lord King," he bowed in a mockery of the ceremony that had been denied him when he entered, "My brother bishops and I have reached an agreement." The bishops waited expectantly, anticipating a final end to the long discussions.

"I cannot sign that document," Becket stated in a loud and hostile voice. A collective gasp echoed from both sides of the room. Clearly, his brother bishops were surprised. They had expected something else altogether.

"You cannot sign? You agreed before we recessed yesterday that you would sign these agreements."

"I know, and I should not have done so." Becket turned halfway to his brother bishops. "I ask you all to forgive me for agreeing to something that could be used to our detriment in the future. You know I dispute five of these stipulations, especially those that pertain to our rights to judge our own people in our own courts without interference from the king and the rights that belong to us feudal landholders." He turned back to the king. "I am invoking the rights of the church as I refuse to assent to your plan."

The king took the three steps from his platform in a bound and was close in front of Thomas before he could step back. Du Hommet and Fitzstephen both stood at the same time, but de Lucy held out his arm to bar their progress. This scene belonged to the two men at the center of the stage. Whatever must happen would happen.

"By the teeth of God, you will regret this." Henry hissed into Becket's face, spittle flying from his mouth. "You have led us on a merry dance here, keeping the lords of the land and your fellow bishops captive all week whilst you leaned this way and that, teasing the officers of the realm like a whore in the alley. But now," he thundered, "you have gone too far. Leave this assembly before I have my men truss you up like a pheasant and hang you from the rafters."

When Becket did not move, the king shouted, "Get out of here, by God's hair, before I change my mind and hang you for treason."

De Lucy blanched at the monarch's vulgar phrasing. Word of this would certainly get to Alexander, who was lurking in Sens until he could get back to Rome as pope. Alexander took a dim view of insulting his bishops, even if he did need Henry's support. De Lucy was always thinking ahead.

Becket stood still as Henry spoke, gathering himself as if in the face of a storm. Then he turned, apparently calm, and signaled his boy to carry his jeweled crozier ahead of him as he made his way through the crowded benches. Becket was used to Henry's temper, but never had it been turned so completely in his direction. He must have thought on some deep level that the king, in his present state, might well carry out such a threat, for he turned and began to walk with a measured rhythm toward the heavy doors that still remained closed. The marshall hastened ahead of him to signal the guards to open the doors.

Henry, who also understands the power of drama, waited just a fraction of a moment after the door closed behind Becket before he turned to de Lucy and said in tones that reverberated around the chamber, "Close the ports. I want the archbishop in England. This is not finished between us."

Late September 1164
Winchester Castle, England

"Still no word, Sire," du Hommet reported as he entered the king's large privy chamber. The king was already seated with de Lucy and Geoffrey Riedell, working as usual when he was not hawking or hunting. De Hommet slid into his chair beside Riedell, who was writing assiduously, scratching the pen across the parchment like a chicken scratching for feed.

"He's got to be somewhere. We discovered where he was those first two nights, then pouf," Henry flicked his closed fingers open as if to let a dove fly away, "he disappears."

"Except for those two attempts to cross the channel," de Lucy interjected. "He knows now all the ports are closed against him."

"Yes, the last thing I need is Becket running to Louis or Alexander. Things are fragile enough on the continent as they stand. I don't need the rebel archbishop stirring up France against Us." Henry drummed the table with his restless fingers.

"Let's get on to the next topic. What do we hear from the North? I need to take my mind off the church and attend to the military threats. The Welsh are quiet now, but William the Lyon of Scotland seems to have slipped the leash." The king frowned. "And what news from the pope, from Our pope, that is. I always forget to specify since Victor is still lurking about in the background."

"Sire, the response is back from Alexander on your request to him to make York temporarily the primate of England in the absence of the archbishop of Canterbury. Have you read it?"

"Yes, I have." The king slouched into the back of the chair and steepled his fingers for a moment, then sat forward suddenly.

"Send the orders back to Alexander with our thanks. They are of no use to Us."

"Sire, he is giving you almost everything. He agrees York may temporarily be primate of England. The only thing he denies is giving Bishop Roger power over Becket."

"But that is precisely what I asked for. It's no good for me to mess around with bishops and archbishops if it does not deliver Becket's head to me. Send them back with our thanks, but for now, we will leave the situation as it is."

Leicester and de Lucy exchanged glances. They both had the same thought. The king's obsession with Becket was getting out of hand. But what to do? At this moment, du Hommet raised the issue of the emperor, and Henry brightened.

"Yes, yes, the queen and I have talked it over, and we agree to offer Our daughter Mathilda to Barbarossa for marriage to his prince. Henry the Lion of Saxony."

"Very astute, My Lord," Leicester murmured. Among all of them, he was the most sensitive to Henry's stratagems because, as the oldest of Henry's counsellors, he knew well the ebbs and tides of fortunes on the continent that affected the king of the English. His sovereign's rise had been spectacular in the past dozen years, but he was also ringed with enemies as a result, both without on the continent and within, in the church. "This will also put Alexander on notice. Barbarossa still backs Victor for pope, but some commerce with Germany will alert Alexander that you may not forever back him."

"Yes, I thought you'd see it that way," Henry said, turning Leicester's way. "This business with Becket and the church could unsettle much of what I have built in Normandy and Brittany and even the south as far as Toulouse. Things are quiet, but how quiet will they remain with Becket on the loose? The German princes are needed to shore up the East for me. Louis needs to feel that I am not alone, not vulnerable, no matter which way Alexander takes the church opinion in this matter."

For the next hour, the group talked and worked, plans were made, and writs were written. Henry appeared to have forgotten the renegade archbishop altogether, but just as de Lucy thought he would dismiss the meeting, he turned to Geoffrey Riedell and made a surprising statement: "Geoffrey, I want to draw up a writ summoning the magnates and all the bishops to Northampton in early October. When the leaves turn."

"Sire, what is the matter of the call?" Riedell looked puzzled. It was clear the king had not discussed this with him earlier, de Lucy saw.

"I am disturbed that Becket did not appear as summoned last week to answer the complaint from Sir John the Marshal, who has not received justice in the archbishop's courts and is now appealing to me. The call is to witness the answer of the archbishop to the charge that he has not given justice in his courts. By his attempts to flee, under the Constitutions of Clarendon he has forfeited his own right to be heard in the church's courts."

Nicely done, Henry, thought de Lucy. You have snared the archbishop coming and going on this one.

"But Sire," said the immensely practical Geoffrey even as he scribbled down the king's words, "Becket did respond to your summons. His men testified that he was too ill to appear."

"Indeed." The king smiled grimly. "Let us see if he is too ill to appear before all the barons and bishops in October. We shall settle this matter once and for all. If he does not appear, he will be named fugitive from the king's justice and hunted down by my men." His voice was low with violence. "I want him ruined."

The men sat in silence. Each one of them prayed within that they would never be the object of this king's hatred. None of them offered a soothing rejoinder. This battle between king and archbishop was beyond words. It was going to be a primal fight to the death.

6 October 1164, day one of the Conclave Northampton Hunting Lodge

The king stood on the balcony of the hunting lodge at midday, but far enough back so as not to be easily seen from the courtyard. He watched from afar as the clusters of knights and barons came down the old Roman road and watched again as they gathered inside the walls of the lodge. The manor was capacious, and many of the nobles would stay for the night while their retainers would have to ride back to the town for shelter. The bishops would lodge in the outbuildings on the land, which had been carefully prepared for them. With any luck, the convocation would not last more than two days.

Henry was musing on the fates that had brought him here when he saw the archbishop's staff nestled amidst a small group of servants as they rode into the courtyard.

Well, well, Thomas, now we come to it. You would not be satisfied with the care of the Great Seal and the bishop's staff. You thought you could have more power if you made the church equal to the state. You think when I summon you to account, you can play sick, that there will be no accounting. You think you can defy me because you hold the ultimate weapon of the church, excommunication. But you are very much mistaken, my former friend. As you will see, no one crosses Us without penalty. I will not rest until you beg for mercy.

"He looks ill," said a quiet voice beside him. The king had not heard the queen approach him, so intent was he on observing his opponent, dismounting now, with help from his aides. "His face appears haggard even from this distance."

"He does look thinner," the king agreed without turning his head. "And he will be a mere shadow before I am done with him."

"Henry, I want to talk with you before the opening ceremonies." The queen put her hand on his forearm, a rare gesture for her—touching the king when they were in public view. He turned his head and looked straight at her, their eyes at a level. She was, he saw, magnificent as ever in her forest green wool gown, her hair covered with a white muslin veil so thin it looked like a cloud, looked like it could float away were it not for the slender, jeweled coronet holding it down in the breeze. Their gaze met, her green eyes deep as the sea off Ireland and his large, grey eyes that could appear so candid but always hid his true feelings.

"I know what you are about to say to me, and I don't want to hear it again." Henry suddenly broke the mood. He turned to look down at the gathering bishops, who all seemed to be arriving together, some collecting around the archbishop as he descended from his horse and made his unsteady way to the entrance. He seemed more frail, perhaps even ill.

"But you must think ahead before you go through with this theatre of cruelty against Thomas that you have arranged for these days." She hardened her voice and forced him once again to look at her.

"So you know?" The king cursed inwardly but kept his voice neutral.

"Yes, if I am to open the ceremonies today as you insisted, I must know what is to happen. I demanded to see the order of business. Do not blame Leicester. He and Geoffrey Riedel had no choice."

He should have known the queen would be relentless in her pursuit of her intentions. Henry saw that he must deal with her. He sighed. In her own way, she could be as powerful and insistent as he was. He knew it. It was only fortunate that they frequently thought alike. It was that similarity that had prevented many open clashes of wills on his marriage front.

Taking her elbow, he moved her to the iron rail along the balcony, now careless of who might see him. He released her and gestured to the gathering crowd below.

"In an hour, you will call this conference to order in my name. If Geoffrey gave you the order of business, then you know that today Thomas Becket will be called to account for his treatment of Sir John Marshall in his courts."

"Yes, but that's not the whole of it, is it?" She placed both hands on the railing, and he noticed her skin whitening as she tightened her grip. These signs of choleric temper were unusual in her. "It's what you plan for tomorrow that is to be the surprise, isn't it?"

The king nodded, giving up. "Yes, I plan to take this occasion to call my former chancellor to account for his past sins as well."

"Going back even to his years in the service of the crown? At this point in time?" The queen arched her fine brows, still gazing at the cluster of bishops below. "I wonder how that will sit with his colleagues. Where do York and London stand on that? They defended him at Clarendon." The queen was tapping her fingertips on the iron balustrade. "And he still leads the church in England, thanks to your intransigence with Alexander when he offered you a partial victory there."

"Don't worry, my dear," the king said with a dry, humorous tone. "Roger Pont l'Eveque and Gilbert Foliot have moved places on the chess board since January. I have their firm assurances that their loyalty is with me."

"Henry, you must let go of this *idée fixe* that Becket is an enemy who must be crushed. You will rue the day if you hunt him into the ground. You have humiliated him enough. He has received your message. Let him answer here for Sir John's complaint and then go safely back to Canterbury. After tempers cool, you can resolve your differences."

The king listened to this speech patiently and then sighed deeply. "That might have been possible at some time. But no longer."

"And why not?"

"Because we do not have a difference, the archbishop and I. We have betrayal on every level. And as king, I do not tolerate betrayal." The king turned again to his wife.

"Henry . . ." she began, but he cut her off.

"Eleanor, how well did you know Becket all those years ago in Paris?"

"What are you implying . . ."

He cut her off again. "I am just asking how well you knew Becket when you attended Abelard's classes as the wife of Louis, as a young queen. Were you impressed with him? Did you enjoy his careful logic? Was he favored by the great master? Did you invite him to the palace? Was he handsome in his youth?"

"Henry, have you finally gone completely mad?" The queen raised her voice, careless of who might hear. "I saw him once, never met him, never had anything to do with him. You will let this demented jealousy destroy our family. Stop it now!" Eleanor turned on her heel and stalked away. After a few steps, she turned back and addressed him, pointing in his direction.

"I no longer recognize in you the noble man I married."

He watched her go, then turned again to watch the courtyard below, but the little circle of bishops had disappeared into the fortress. Becket was no longer in view.

7 October 1164, day two of the Conclave
Northampton Hunting Lodge

In the months since Clarendon, Becket had aged. The life of a fugitive had done him no favors. Henry now stood at the front of the hall to watch his former chancellor as he approached, seemingly held up only by the jeweled crozier on which he leaned. This time he held the staff himself; there was no boy servant.

As if he carried the cross on Calvary, himself. He's a man of drama to the end. Maybe this is a Greek play.

Becket had slept poorly. That was the next thing Henry noticed when the archbishop limped slowly down the aisle. As he approached, Henry saw that his adversary looked, if possible, worse than he had the previous day—haggard and with shadows ringing his eyes. The archbishop approached his king and made a deep, silent bow. He then retired to his seat.

The other bishops had followed him in and took their accustomed seats after the proper acknowledgement of the king's presence. Several of the lesser bishops sat around Becket, but Henry, now taking his seat on the dais, noticed that York and London, and even Henry, Bishop of Chichester, sat in the row behind the archbishop. As if to distance themselves from someone who might have a disease that was catching.

Yes, Thomas is hurting. The day yesterday did not go well, but it was not bad enough. He had fines levied by Leicester in my name, 3,000 silver marks for his treatment of Sir John, but several of the bishops and even two barons stood surety for him.

Today will be different, my former friend. There are charges coming that you have not foreseen, and the cost will be much higher. Today, you will pay in every way for your betrayal of our friendship, for your overweening pride, for your o'ervaulting ambition. Today I will break you.

After the marshall had pounded three times, the group again gradually settled into silence. The archbishop rose and turned to half face the barons while including the king.

"Your majesty, honored nobles and bishops, we have settled the matter of the complaint of Sir John against my ecclesial courts, the fines have been levied and surety provided. My thanks to those who support me now in my need." The proud archbishop bowed slightly in the direction of the barons. Then he turned to the king.

"I am uncertain why the conference was not adjourned yestere'en, Sire. You have made the complaint and judgement has been rendered by your court. May I now retreat to my rightful home?" There was no note of pleading in the voice, which seriously annoyed Henry. What would it take for this man to understand what was about to happen to him? Was it not enough to insult him by summoning him through the office of the sheriff of Kent rather than by personal writ? Did he truly have no idea what was to happen?

"We have not finished with you," the king said in a voice he worked to make cheerful. "Leicester, as chief justiciar of the land, will you read the civil complaint against the charged, Thomas of the house of Becket?"

Robert, Earl of Leicester seated at the head table with his fellow justiciars, rose slowly. The complaint he read was as follows:

"Thomas a Becket, we call you to account for your handling of the finances of the crown when you held the office of Chancellor, specifically:

- Your failure to account for the funds spent on refurbishing the castles of Eye and Berkhamstead when they were in your care as chancellor
- Your lack of fiscal accounting for the abbacies and bishoprics you held while chancellor, in all more than 200 silver marks
- The money you borrowed from the crown to equip your expedition to Toulouse while you were chancellor.

Leicester droned on in a voice that could not have been more impersonal. In truth, Henry had to admit, Leicester had never liked the archbishop, had been ever jealous of the attentions the king had showered upon him as chancellor and hunting partner. But even so, Henry knew his justiciar took no pleasure to play his role in this piece of theatre. The humiliation was too complete. Leicester was astute enough to guess that the bishops and perhaps even the great earls would not stand for this without some pushback to the power of the crown. Still, Leicester understood politics. With his office came some unpleasant duties.

Suddenly, the reading was complete. Leicester had finished by stating flatly:

"Thus, Thomas Becket, you are so charged by this court on behalf of the crown. How do you answer these charges? How do you plead?"

There was a collective gasp, louder from the barons than from the bishops. Silence fell like a heavy stone upon the group.

Becket, still standing, appeared to have shrunk under the onslaught of charges. He held on to his crozier for a long moment, slightly bent as if taking support from it. His face and his unwavering gaze turned on the king. Those intelligent eyes sought some answer from Henry's, and it was the king who looked away first.

Why? Why? So now you, too, know the sting of betrayal, my former friend Thomas. Now you know what it feels like when the person in whom you placed the greatest trust turns on you like a dog. The person, a brother whom you thought you knew well, whose bread you shared and who would have given you his bed if necessary, his very crown, casts you down into the mud.

Henry's brief reverie had not gone unnoticed. But before the king had looked away, Becket had seen his face and now, finally, understood his fate. There was no turning back now, no throwing himself on the mercy of the king's court. He addressed his tormentor directly.

"I answer the charges thusly: Every one of those accountings was rendered when I was chancellor. And if they were not rendered in writing, the king knew. And if the king did not know, they were all forgiven by Church law at my consecration. There is not any basis in law for these charges of past deeds." He paused. "And the king knows it!"

Another gasp went up, this time from both sides of the main aisle. Bishop and baron alike were as astounded at the defiance of the archbishop as they had been of the charges. Gradually, they realized they were witness to a struggle so large, so beyond any they had seen between men in all their years of fighting and war, that they were silenced once more.

"That remains to be seen." The king sounded amazingly nonchalant.

"I will not remain here further. I have been summoned to answer the charges of Sir John Marshall, and judgement on those has been rendered. Others have stood surety for the fine." Becket made as if to turn away.

"Archbishop," here the king's voice hardened and stopped his opponent. "It is fit that you retire to the anteroom while the court deliberates. But do not, I repeat, under pain of treason against the crown, do not leave the hall until these matters have been settled."

The archbishop retired to the anteroom to await his king's next move. Leicester presided over the discussion of the barons and bishops, which turned rowdy at times. Becket could hear the voices rising and falling, and even some shouting, when the servants brought him bread and cheese and wine, and he realized he was hungry. A few of the bishops moved from the inner chamber, where they had no vote but could add voice to the proceedings, to sit with Becket and report the discussion. Then, restless also, they would move in small clusters back to the closed meeting chamber. Like small flocks of white birds on the beach near Dover, Becket thought. He listened to their chatter to him but kept his own counsel as to his next move. As the autumn sun was setting through the arrow slits in his chamber walls, he reached a decision.

The torches were lit along the wall by a pageboy when the doors to the Great Hall were finally thrown open and Leicester, flanked by Henry, Bishop of Winchester, and du Hommet, entered the antechamber where Becket waited. Three of the highest barons followed, crowding in close behind. The king was not with them, nor was Becket invited back into the Great Hall.

Becket understood that a fellow bishop would be designated to announce his sentence, hence the presence of Henry of Winchester. He had been found guilty of the offenses concocted by the king to ruin him. He felt nothing; his heart was numb. All was lost. All was finished. Now there was no turning back and no way forward of his choosing.

Leicester held an official scroll. Behind him crowded the barons of the land, as many as could squeeze through the great oak doors. This was drama they were unlikely to see again in their lifetime. The major prelate of the land brought low by the king, who was himself nowhere to be seen. He must have left the chamber by the side door, Becket thought to himself grimly. No point in seeing and owning the carnage he had wrought. But there was one play left to checkmate the king, and Becket had it.

Leicester had only just begun to read the sentence when Becket held up his hand with authority and shouted, "Stop, my lord. Go no further on pain of your soul."

Surprised, Leicester did stop and looked up at the tall, dark man facing him down.

"What is this you would do?" Becket's stentorian tones rang out, filling the anteroom of the great hall the way they once filled Canterbury Cathedral. "Have *you* come to judge *me*?"

Leicester blinked, his hand holding the scroll suddenly unsteady. Becket continued, seizing on the earl's pause.

"You have no right to do so, not under the king's law." Becket's voice was strong and full. Everyone crowded closer to the small group in the center of the throng.

"Judgement is a sentence after trial, and today I have not had a trial on these charges. I have not had the opportunity to answer them point by point. I have said nothing in a formal lawsuit, made no defense as required by law, on these past grievances the king has chosen to bring forward."

The crowd was silent. All the great lords were listening, and some of the lesser ones were pushing in the rear to get a glimpse of the archbishop as he was speaking. He knew he had his audience and continued, his tone growing ever stronger.

"I have only been summoned here in the case of John Marshall, who has not even appeared to prove his charges. With respect to even this, you cannot pass sentence. Furthermore, such as I am, I am your spiritual father, and you are only magnates of the household, lay powers, secular persons." Du Hommet, listening in amazement, almost grinned. The archbishop's tone made "secular persons" seem an insult. Wait until Henry heard this!

"I refuse to hear your judgement." The archbishop thundered his conclusion and, belying his frail appearance at the start of the trial, turned and swept from the room. No one barred the door to him. He disappeared into the gathering dusk, and suddenly they heard the pounding of horse's hooves. In a flash, he had gone. Apparently, he had been prepared for this eventuality.

None of his fellow bishops dared speak, nor did any follow him. The entire gathering stood amazed, Leicester most of all. Finally, the earl rolled up the parchment on which the judgement and sentence were written.

He turned to the group and, tapping his thigh nervously with the document, said, "What has been said here today should not be spoken of abroad. Not until the king has made his announcement." Which, du Hommet thought, was like telling drunk men to pray. The news of the drama would be everywhere before daybreak.

Leicester had the sense to speak no further, and he threaded his way back through the barons to find the king and report. The archbishop had played the trump card: his power as spiritual father. No one could gainsay that he was still Archbishop Primate of England. And that fact was down to Henry's game.

Henry was standing at the large window in the second story. None of his people saw Becket ride away, but Henry had a clear view of a figure about Becket's height darting from the doorway below him and springing with some agility upon his horse tethered in the courtyard. The king had no need of an explanation from Leicester as to what had happened.

It was said that it took the king several days to recover from the spell of choleric temper he produced upon seeing the figure of his former archbishop ride off under his nose and unhindered by his men.

As for the archbishop, moving from monastery to monastery under assumed names, he managed finally to gain a port and a ship across the channel and on November 2, he landed at Flanders. For the time being, he was out of reach of the English king. But he found a warm, if careful, welcome from the French one. Louis offered him sanctuary in France.

The Battles

August 1165
Marlborough Castle

The sun was settling in the west, and a mild end-of-summer cool breeze played over the grand bed of the king in his castle. He turned on his side and regarded his queen as she lay naked and drowsy beside him.

"You are as beautiful as the day we married," Henry said.

"Mm, such compliments are rare from you, Lord King. You must want something." Eleanor turned on her side now to face him and propped her head on her elbow.

"It's been too long since we have lain together." It was a statement, not of sadness but of fact. "We have not seen each other since we kept Christmas last year. You are very busy now with all your diplomatic efforts. And I am busy with the children."

"Do you want me to leave again so that your duties as regent would be added to your duties as mother?" Henry chuckled.

"No, that's not what I'm saying. But the boys are getting older, and I think you should see them more."

"I'm occupied now with affairs of state. Trying to bring some stability here so I can get back to Normandy. We have trouble again in Brittany, and I need to gather some knights." He sighed and flopped on his back into the soft down. "It never ends."

"I thought perhaps you were more occupied with sending missives to Alexander, trying to get him to cooperate and discipline that rogue archbishop of yours."

"Aah, Becket." Henry rolled to the side of the bed, legs over, and, in one swift movement, stood and shuffled to the long table at the side of the room. He poured himself a draught of red wine. "Don't mention that thorn in my side."

"Better that than to mention the news we received this noon from France."

Henry turned and looked down at his wife, a smile playing on his lips. She lay naked, still youthful in some ways, still desirable.

"Yes, odd that a message announcing that your former husband now has a boy-child by his new wife should have sent us to bed so quickly."

"Here is what I think," the queen said in cool tones that marked a half-jest. "I think you have always needed to show Louis you are more the man than he is. And he you, as well." She laughed softly. "And you, with all these sons, have always been ahead. But now, he has one too. And he only needs one for the succession."

Now the king laughed out loud. "I think you have the right of it there, My Lady. And so I am. He only got daughters on you, whereas I have four sons—well, three surviving."

"Well, I had something to do with that, if you please, My Lord."

Henry sat down on the edge of the bed, his broad back to her now. A chill was creeping into the room through the opening in the wall, the one usually covered with tapestries. The cool air of nightfall was arriving in stealthy gusts.

"Indeed, I cannot deny it. Nor can I deny that Louis having a son does not bear on our future. Henry will no longer be the heir to the French throne. It will be the new prince now."

"I understand they call him *Dieu-donné*," Eleanor said.

"I'm certain they do," Henry said ruefully. "After all these years and all those daughters, fortune has finally smiled on the French crown."

"What is your response to all this?" The queen was now sitting up, her back against the large, carved bed. She sensed the conversation was shifting from lovemaking and *repartee* to something more serious, along the lines of the affairs of state they usually discussed. "Are you not concerned?"

"My response will be to send a message tomorrow to Louis congratulating him and then to send for the children, his and ours. Henry and Marguerite. They are at the house in London where we sent them after I took them from Becket's household. Yes, we shall celebrate the nuptials of little Henry and French Marguerite before the fortnight is past."

"What? Henry, you cannot marry the children. They are not of age." Eleanor suddenly lost her manner of *insouciance.* The king could not be serious! "The church will not allow children to marry before they are old enough to consummate the marriage."

"Bah, a mere formality. I want that union celebrated in front of the archbishop of York, and I want the whole court there to see it. With a new heir in France, I don't want Louis deciding he no longer needs an alliance with me and calling his little daughter back."

"How will you get approval for the exception to marriage at their age?"

Henry turned to look at her and the enigmatic smile that resembled most a cat caught in the cream spread across his face. "I already have approval. It was one of the stipulations I forced Alexander to accept when he was afraid I'd move to the German side and support Victor as pope. Now that Alexander is back in Rome, he cannot take back what he has already sanctioned."

"Oh, my," was all Eleanor could say as she moved to her side of the high bed and prepared to step down into the soft rushes. She so often saw Henry as a soldier, as a lover rough or gentle, as a king holding his court in thrall by sheer force of personality and temper. But she forgot, for long periods of time, that he was also a statesman. He was rarely caught unawares. It was the part of him she liked best if the truth were known—the chess player in him.

But the king surprised her again and, with his athletic body, rolled suddenly back onto the bed and grabbed her arm, holding her fast from leaving.

"Come back to me for a moment, my love." He said in a voice growing thick with desire. She hesitated for a moment, then turned her body back to him and curled inside his arms. This time they made love slowly, warmly, like old friends. Louis and the new heir, Becket and the continental politics, even the pope and the marriage of the children, all forgotten. This was the best part of life, she thought, as she gave herself over to his mounting desire and matched it.

April 1166, The Easter Court of Henry and Eleanor
The Ducal Castle at Angers, Anjou France

"What news this morning? I heard the messenger arrive." The queen strode into the council chamber with her customary decisiveness. Leicester and du Hommet were standing behind the king, reading over his shoulder. Geoffrey Riedel, the indispensable but still unnamed chancellor of England, was sitting to the king's left, writing madly. William FitzStephen looked up and, when he saw the queen, stood.

"Not one, but two letters from Becket carried by the same messenger." The king rose and moved to greet the queen with a quick embrace.

"It's not necessary that you cease your business, My Lord. We have only just seen each other." Eleanor smiled at the small assembly. "Where is Becket now? I've quite lost track of him since Louis took him under his protection." She paused, thoughtful for a moment. "Louis was always in need of birds with broken wings to fix."

"God's feet, don't I know it." Henry turned in exasperation. "I thought Louis's piety would drive me to heavy drink," he said as he poured a goblet of red wine. "That is, in the days when we were speaking."

"And is Louis keeping the archbishop in the grand style he prefers?" Her tone was arch.

The king gestured with his goblet. "At first, I was told, he did. But Thomas always needs a retinue, and soon even the crown of France grew tired of supporting his expensive entourage. He's been persuaded to retire to the Cistercians at Pontigy, where he can continue to compose endless letters to me and to the pope."

"And to the German emperor and the courts of Europe and the chanceries and monasteries of all of Christendom," du Hommet interjected, stretching his long arms above his head, then moving to the wine table as well. His tall frame was seeming shorter to Eleanor's eyes. He had only just joined them after remaining behind in England for some months, and she noted a change in his appearance. Perhaps they were all aging now. She herself was feeling more tired with all the travel than she had felt even just a year past, and the babe she was carrying now seemed heavier than she remembered the others.

"And what does Becket say?" the queen came closer and glanced down at the parchments spread out.

"You can read them for yourself, my dear. The first letter, obviously written to cajole me into forgiveness, is rather gentle. But the next, written within a day, takes a firmer tack. That one rather lectures me. And you know how I take to lectures by churchmen. He exhorts me, as his spiritual son—son, I tell you!—to reinstate him to his rightful place at Canterbury, as is his due and as God would want."

"What will be your reply?"

"I don't think I'll reply to these letters. It's the part about his actions only responding directly to God's manifest wishes that I object to most. Becket was always wont to confuse his desires and proclamations with those of the Almighty Deity. It's not a conversation I care to have with him."

"Probably wise," Eleanor said quietly. Henry was maturing too. There was a time when such letters would have sent him into a rage, but he seemed relatively calm this morning.

"Anyway, I have sent to Rome to have Alexander name Roger of York temporary archbishop of England."

"Why do that? Why not wait until this is settled?"

Robert of Leicester joined the queen and king, standing near the hearth. April was still chill in Angers, but Eleanor was happy to be back in the castle. When she was first married to Henry, it was here that he made her his representative, that she realized she could govern even those who were not of the south. It was in this castle she had first felt a true queen in her own right, taking counsel and making decisions. That had never happened in Paris with Louis and his advisors. Yes, she had made the right decisions those many years ago. Her fate was intertwined with this soldier king.

Leicester's low voice broke into her thoughts. "The king has decided the time has come to crown young Prince Henry."

"Have you, Henry?" The queen, in her surprise, used his given name in public.

"I have," Henry said. "I think it is dangerous to leave the ceremony for later. I want all the barons there, and I want them to swear allegiance. England shall not have another divided country if something should happen to me."

"But have you thought through what this might mean for the prince?" Eleanor was careful with her words. "It puts a great royal burden on a young person. He's still a boy."

"Nonsense. He has more than ten years. When I was his age, I was fighting for my mother's crown in England. On my own."

"You were sixteen years of age when you went to England, your mother told me. Not ten. Don't exaggerate. And you went then against her wishes," Eleanor said dryly, moving to sit in a chair at the end of the table. She pulled the parchments toward her.

"Did you hear about the cardinals here yesterday, My Lady?" FitzStephen, who had been in the king's privy council long enough, took the liberty of addressing the queen directly.

"What cardinals?" Eleanor looked up from Becket's letters. Her fine green eyes narrowed slightly as she turned to the king.

"Ah," the king dismissed the topic, casting a warning glance at young FitzStephen. His young aide's color rose, and he looked down suddenly.

"Alexander, interfering as usual," he muttered.

"No, Sire, you must tell the queen the story," Leicester was chuckling.

"Please, someone tell me." The queen's voice held a note of irritability.

"Alexander is trying to resolve this matter with Becket. He sent two cardinals over the alps to talk to us, first Becket, then me. You know how cardinals travel. It's taken them two months to get here." Henry was pacing again, his hands behind his back to keep them still. But a grin had spread across his face.

"The pope, now that he is back in Rome, is terrified that I'll go to the side of Barbarossa and the schismatics, throw my weight behind Victor as anti-pope. So, he's trying to placate both me and Becket. The pope is worried because my former chancellor is pelting the European courts with his righteous position and my evildoing against the church."

"What happened when the cardinals arrived?" Eleanor was suspicious. Henry was enjoying this story entirely too much.

"They had been to see Becket, instructed to bring him to Rome."

"A mission for which I assume you have paid dearly?"

"Indeed. Much English sterling has been spread around Rome as you might have guessed. But Becket, as usual, demurred. He couldn't go, he wouldn't go, he dragged out enough canon law so that the cardinals finally left him, out of sheer exhaustion."

"And they came here to report to you," Eleanor stated this, waiting still to see what had amused young FitzStephen so heartily.

"Let me tell, Sire," du Hommet interjected, his long, serious face for once wreathed in smiles. The king nodded assent.

"When the cardinals reported that they had no luck in coercing Becket to Rome to face the tribunal, the king became, umm, quite angry." Du Hommet shook his head. "He excoriated them, as is his wont," he said, glancing at his sovereign to see if this statement went too far, "and as they were leaving the chamber to escape his anger, he threw an inkpot after them, shouting 'I hope I never see a cardinal again, any cardinal!'"

"No, Henry, you didn't!" Eleanor, by now was grinning also. "To the cardinals?"

"And that's not all, Madame," FitzStephen dared to get back into the conversation now that the king was chuckling. "They were so frightened of the king's wrath, they left without their *equipage,* riding their horses out of the courtyard at dusk like demons were after them. Their servants and baggage followed them some hours later. In the dark."

"My Lord, you must have outdone yourself," the queen remarked with awe. But she looked very amused. It was well known that Queen Eleanor had little regard for cardinals or anyone in Rome ever since her youth when Pope Innocent had tried to re-enforce her marriage to Louis by bedding them formally himself. She had also been overheard to say flatly to the king's own mother, the Duchess Matilda, on one of their rare visits, that the king deliberately staged his fits of anger to create a reputation for choler that would make men fear to cross him. The Empress Matilda was overheard not to disagree on that theory.

"Meddling churchmen," Henry said, not without good humor.

"Meddling at your request, apparently," the queen replied tartly. She stood suddenly to indicate her part in the conversation was at an end. "I still think the Becket fight is taking too much of your time, My Lord King," she added.

"Well, Madame, I disagree. It may seem that way, but I have a vast amount of land to administer, and something is going on somewhere all the time. This fight with the archbishop, which verges on a fight with the church, is only part of my work." The king spoke in his usual abrupt voice. His queen was not cowed, however.

"Yes, I understand that. But I still say Becket's rebellion occupies too large a place in your thoughts." The queen moved to her husband and placed her hand on his arm as if to gentle him. "And now, we must prepare for the Easter feast on the morrow. Tonight Arnulf, the Bishop of Lisieux, will preside over the Old Testament readings. Tomorrow, at dawn, it will be Bishop Rotrou of Rouen saying the Mass. I must go now to see that the children are ready for the rituals, and I trust your counsellors will do the same for you!"

The king smiled, moved to his queen and brushed his cheek against hers on either side, startling his men. The royal couple rarely touched in public. Leicester, du Hommet and FitzStephen bowed low to the queen. Even Geoffrey Riedel, that small, hunched figure, stopped his interminable scratching with the quill and rose to make an obeisance as the regal figure departed, leaving behind a cloud of the spice scent from Spain she often wore.

Eleanor's thoughts at the moment of her exit would have surprised all the men she left behind. Her stomach was churning. This pregnancy was making her ill, and it was increasingly difficult to keep up the appearances of strength she needed to present. She promised herself, as she swept from the room with her head held high, that this pregnancy would produce the very last of the Angevin eaglets!

6 January 1169
On the Road to Montmirail, Normandy

"Father, a word if it would please you." The young prince had ridden up so swiftly and quietly that du Hommet and de Lucy scarce had a moment to take in his request and to fall back just behind the king and his eldest son, reining in their horses to allow the royal family to take the lead of the entourage.

The young prince was fourteen years and a stronger and more princely-looking youngster it would be hard to find. Even though de Lucy preferred the brother next in age, Richard, named for himself, he had to admit that the young Henry was definitely regal material. He could be just a bit too regal on occasion, somewhat arrogant, but de Lucy had seen him in tournament in Normandy under William the Marshal's tutelage and, even then, at thirteen, the youth had acquitted himself well, showing valor and determination against much older lads.

The two close advisors of the king could not hear all the conversation, but they heard enough to know they did not want to be part of this discourse between father and son.

"Sire, I would like to know why we are meeting the king of France today. You have not explained the goal of this meeting. Master Thomas always taught me to look at the goal and be certain that what transpires moves me toward that goal." The young man spurred his horse as his father's speed increased, no doubt at the mention of the name of Thomas Becket.

"So what do we want to accomplish with this meeting, Father?" The lad was persistent; you had to give him that. "You were only lately warring with King Louis, and now we sit down to sup with him. But to what end?"

Henry finally accommodated the conversation by slowing his horse slightly and turned to his son. The prince's face set in profile was that of his mother. And he had the same disconcerting habit of insisting on knowing why, always why.

The king sighed. "Yes, the King of the Franks and I skirmish a great deal. It's always over land or villages or else over some imagined wrong dating back before either of us was born. It's what we do in feudal France. That's what fealty is all about. It's a system of lords and vassals. Why have the knights who are committed to us if not to shore up our power? And they must have something to do, mustn't they? So we must fight."

Prince Henry gave his father a sharp glance. Was he being teased? Sometimes he was not certain. He began again.

"But now here we are, going to meet him in an amicable situation. Is he our enemy, or no?" The young man's face, sunburned from the outdoors, was earnest. "If I am going to be king, I must understand these things."

Henry tried to remember if the world was simpler when he was fourteen, but he could not recall how he saw things then. Was everything either right or wrong? He was near this age when he was hiring mercenaries to fight for him in England. Perhaps he had not seen what the world looked like from Stephen's view. Henry smiled at the memory of his cheek in those days, sending to Stephen for funds to pay his soldiers so that he could return home to Angers. And Stephen had paid!

"Why are you smiling, Father?" The prince had glanced in his direction.

"I want you to listen, boy," he said, suddenly emphatic and serious. "The world is complicated. You can be fighting one day to the death, but if you make peace the next day, you must hold to the terms of it." He looked sideways and saw his son frowning. "Do not worry yourself, you will always find someone else to fight. Or you can just hold one of those dangerous tournaments you and William the Marshal are so fond of putting on in Normandy."

"How did you know . . .?" Tournaments with spears not blunted had been outlawed by Henry himself, and the young prince knew well he should not have been participating in them.

"I know everything that goes on in my realm, my son. Believe that, if you believe nothing else I'm telling you."

"But you still have not answered my question." The lad was persistent, Henry would have to give him that.

"My fights with Louis, your father-in-law, I might remind you, have to do with our arguments over borders. But there's been a larger fight recently, one we both want to end."

"The fight with Archbishop Becket, my master and tutor. I know all about that."

"I doubt you 'know all about it,' as you say." The king was growing testy. One of the young prince's drawbacks was his failure, often, to see the temper rising in his choleric father. This was apparently one of those times. That failure irritated Henry even further. "I just told you, the world is complicated. The battle between your *former* master and myself is about larger issues."

"The archbishop told me that you don't respect the church." The lad did not know when to retire from the field. The king suddenly reined in his horse, causing du Hommet to pull up short and raise his hand for the entire procession, all the way back to the baggage train, to halt.

"And did he also tell you that he, himself, fails to respect the crown? The courts of justice that administer the law of the land? That he repeatedly refers to his king as his 'spiritual son' when I made him archbishop myself? Did he tell you he uses the name of God to place himself above the state?"

The bored, rather arrogant expression the young prince usually affected was suddenly gone in the face of his father's anger, replaced by a startled expression. The king continued in the same thunderous voice.

"We will make peace with Louis, and you will do homage to him for your lands of Anjou and Maine and once again for Normandy. Richard will do homage for Poitou and the south and little Geoffrey for Brittany. We will sup with the French king and agree with him on whatever he says. We will sign the treaty."

"And then what?" the boy said.

"And then he will produce Thomas of Becket, and we will hope that all the diplomacy I have undertaken in the past four years will result in a treaty with that worthy as well."

"Master Thomas will be at Montmirail?" Young Henry's face lit up despite himself. His father turned his horse's head and cantered forward, forcing the young prince to do likewise.

"Please do not call him 'Master Thomas' in my hearing again," the king ordered flatly. "If Becket agrees to return to England and take up his post as archbishop and lift all of the interdictions on England that he has the power to lay on Us and Our people, then we shall have peace and an end to this affair."

"Master—umm, the archbishop—is also very stubborn," the young prince ventured, pressing the horse with his knees to keep up with the king.

"Also?" Henry shot him a glance that made the young prince gulp.

"Well, I meant to ask whether the archbishop is likely to take this offer of peace the king of France is arranging." Young Henry had an inquiring mind. The king took the question seriously and was momentarily thoughtful before he responded.

"I don't know. I don't think I know him anymore." They rode on in silence for a few moments. "Mayhap I never knew him at all," was the king's final comment before he lifted his arm to du Hommet and de Lucy to rejoin them in the front line. The young prince rode on with them, but he was unusually quiet and did not join in the badinage of the older men.

When the group arrived at the site, the pavilion for Henry had already been thoughtfully raised by the king of the Franks and the pennants had been raised above them. The lilies of France flew from one of the larger ones and the lions of England from another. A third pavilion, smaller and a bit further back, flew the keys of St. Peter and the tiara of the pontiff himself. That, thought Henry, would be for the recalcitrant archbishop.

Louis himself came forth to meet his acquired family, the young prince, now husband to his daughter Marguerite; and the English king, now husband to his former wife. The strange path of fate must have crossed his mind as he extended both hands to his brother king, and they gave each other the kiss and cowl of the Cistercian order. Thomas Becket detached himself from the group that was standing behind Louis and walked slowly forward.

Henry was shocked. He had not seen Thomas for four long years, and the change was marked. There had been rumors that Thomas now wore a hair shirt under his robe and abused himself with the scourge on a regular basis. The figure before him was bent as if in some kind of private pain, and the face, when it lifted as he approached the two kings, was haggard and dark. The cowl was slipped back with a veined hand, and suddenly the archbishop fell to the ground in front of his king.

Henry moved without thinking, to lift him up and embrace him in greeting. The archbishop returned the embrace warmly.

"My Lord," Becket began slowly. Obviously, Louis had given Becket leave to speak publicly to Henry at the greeting before any private conference took place. "I greet you in the name of the Lord. I come in peace before you and seek your goodwill. In the presence of the King of France, of your sons the princes and the papal representatives. I commit the whole case and all of the issues that have risen between us to your royal abatement . . ."

Henry, gratified, was nodding encouragement. This was, indeed, more than he had hoped for, but Becket was not finished.

". . . saving always, the honor of God." Becket bowed, and Henry took a step forward.

"By God's great feet," he began, "how dare you come before me suing for an end to our quarrel and then immediately use against me the very phrase that has caused our rupture. By the holy heavens, I shall . . ."

This time Louis stepped in front of Becket.

"My brother, calm yourself," he said quietly. "This anger ill becomes you at this point. Let us retire and discuss all matters after we have supped together."

"I'll not break bread with that, that . . . scoundrel. He comes only to provoke me!" Henry folded his arms and turned away. Many in the crowd began to murmur, thinking the English king too harsh on the churchman. Henry, who paid little attention to any crowd's response, happened to glance in the direction of his sons. Geoffrey and Richard were watching him without expression, but a cloud of disapproval had settled on young Prince Henry's features. The look was so adult for a fifteen-year-old lad that Henry was startled, understanding like a clap of thunder that his son's disapproval was directed toward himself.

"Sire, let us proceed with the parley. We have many issues, including the great matter of homage from the princes to King Louis and the future of your two realms." De Lucy was suddenly at the king's side, urging him to attend King Louis. Henry thought the better of a further public display of choler and allowed himself to be distracted.

"Yes, and Henry, I have more great news." Louis himself took Henry's elbow and began to lead him away from the center of the group, just as Becket's two servants came up to support his frail form and lead him to his pavilion. Clearly, they wanted their master removed from this king's temper as soon as could be managed.

"My brother, what would you say to yet another marriage between our houses?" Du Hommet and de Lucy had fallen into step behind the kings, joined by two of Louis's key counselors. All of them could hear the king of the Franks make his next outrageous political move, saying, "I think we should discuss the marriage of Marguerite's new little sister, as to your son Richard. A fine, strapping lad like that needs a princess for his wife. That would make two bonds between our houses."

De Lucy kneaded his elbow into du Hommet's ribs. France was going to get the Aquitaine back if he had to marry every one of his children to England's royal offspring. "Superfluity of daughters" indeed. Louis, the old fox. Now that he finally had a son, he was going to steal Henry's as well. Wait until the counsellors heard this one!

14 June 1170, Feast of St. Barnabas
Westminster Abbey: Crowning of the Young King

The June night air in London was fresh and cool. Gone were thoughts of winter and snow, the hard and long spring the residents had endured through the end of April and the rains that had come in May to pelt the city. Gone were all thoughts of events and weather that ordinarily occupied the city's citizens. Tonight they would be treated to a ceremony like no other they would behold in their lifetime—the crowning of their next king while his father still lived and reigned. This unprecedented event would be one they could all recount to their grandchildren.

The event was rendered all the more amazing by the fact that the man doing the crowning was not, as was the custom and right in this land, the primate Archbishop Thomas Becket, who had been languishing abroad these many years since the Great Quarrel began, but by Roger Pont l'Eveque, Bishop of York, acting Primate of England in the absence of Canterbury. Roger of Normandy and friend to the king, chubby little Roger with his cheery face and game leg that produced a limp, valiant

Roger, who had stood up for the king when many churchmen on the continent were calling for an interdict upon the king and all his people over his treatment of Becket in exile.

The fight between the archbishop and the king had rattled Europe, as far down as Rome. It was only due to the friendship of Alexander, the third of that name, finally installed in Rome as pope after the protracted battle with Victor and, in large part, due also to the English sterling King Henry was said to have spread liberally around Rome that England even had an acting primate. And that the country, so far, anyway, had escaped the pronouncement of anathema by the pope. If such a blow fell on the king for his treatment of Becket, it would fall even harder on all the people of England, for no weddings nor burials could be held in the churches, no baptisms nor church bells ringing out over the green countryside, no sacraments so no solace at all from mother church for the advent of father death, while the interdict from Rome lasted.

But that blow had not fallen, miraculously, during this whole long argument, and now here they all found themselves. Bishop Roger and his fellow bishops were lining up in front of Westminster Abbey, ancient coronation site of the kings and queens of England. All the barons and magnates and the magnificent churchmen who ruled them were present and the crowd was equally eager to see the handsome children of the king and queen sweep slowly down the aisle of their national shrine.

The long procession wound around the church, down all the aisles and through the quire in the middle of the church, snaking through the aisle between the facing quire stalls, seeking the maximum effect of the theatre, incense wafting from the censors held high by the deacons in their red cassocks covered by white surplices trimmed in Belgian lace.

The royal couple, who had robed in the rooms behind the high altar, came out to meet the procession and took their places on the thrones set in front of the church. Only God was higher, as the altar was on a slight step up from Henry's place. Very slight. Eleanor had once remarked that Henry thought about having his throne, at least, raised up to match it, but had decided against it as a frivolous expense. "Otherwise, he'd have done it," she had stated to de Lucy on one occasion in front of the king himself, who denied it vigorously through his laughter.

The townspeople, at least the dignitaries such as the mayor and some of the richest burghers, had seats in the back of the abbey. The rest of the citizens crowded around the doorways to see the show. When the king and queen appeared, the crowd was gratified to see—or to hear, if they were outside in the streets—that the king and queen wore the crowns created for their coronation. They both disdained royal show and had only been known to wear these intricate coronets once since their crowning sixteen years earlier.

The queen was resplendent in her signature forest green, this time in silk and lined with grey accents and a gold silk redingote overall, peeking through the magnificent red cloak almost completely covered in precious ermine skins brought from the north. The king was a match, in a robe of gold and a cloak that nearly outshone that of the queen with its twinkling jewels and fur pelts.

Once the sovereigns were seated on their thrones, the Bishop of York rose. It was true that Roger was not particularly prepossessing in appearance, but he did have a certain regal way that he could call upon when he was performing the rites of his office. Fortunately, this was one such time. The king and queen, ensconced in such comfort as was to be had in this situation, sat back to enjoy the show.

Prince Henry looked every inch the future sovereign, cutting a handsome figure as he made his way toward the high altar and the standing archbishop. Richard and Geoffrey were right behind him. The prince knelt with all the grace only the young could muster.

Henry rose from his throne, came down three steps and pulled out his sword. There, in front of everyone, he knighted his oldest surviving son, dubbing him quickly on each shoulder. The young prince looked up at his father at the end of the ceremony, and Eleanor saw a look of such depth on her son's face she was in awe. She craned her neck slightly, but the king's face was hidden from her.

Several hours later, after the Mass had been said and the crowning itself completed, Henry and Eleanor retired to their chambers. She was lying in bed, thinking over the evening, and forming her plan as to how she would tell the king her decision. They had not lain together since the birth of little John two years earlier. She mused on this for a moment. Partly it was due to the king's peripatetic lifestyle, to her own responsibilities as regent when he was away. The truth was, they were growing apart. She felt it with that exquisite sense of a woman leaving child-bearing years behind. Love changes also.

But the triumph of this evening would make him want her again. These types of public victories, crowning young Henry in Becket's absence to spite him, would inspire high feelings and even lust in her still-young spouse. And she would not deny him this last bonding.

Yes, she was expecting the king to her bed. Two candles were lit, casting a flickering light over the chamber that did not quite reach to the bed itself. But she could see the outlines of the

chest on which they sat. Enough light for the conversation to come.

Her only hope was that he would not mention Thomas Becket this night, please God, not once. Yes, Henry had triumphed in his wishes, had the Westminster crowning in spite of Becket's refusal to come home and take up his role as archbishop. This event was all about Henry's will again. The fist of iron, that intransigence he put on like armor anytime he was crossed. The queen felt a sense of finality flooding over her. He would not be happy to hear her decision. But this was the right time to tell him.

The small door, the private one connecting their chambers in this castle, opened softly. Henry stood in it for a moment, looking only at the queen in the shadows of the bed. She turned her head in his direction. The moon fell through the arrow slits, creating a few lines of light on the stone floor, interrupted by large areas of shadow. The queen had time for a fleeting thought that this visual checkerboard resembled her marriage years. The light had come in patches, but there was plenty of dark. Scarcely enough light for the king to make his way to her bed, but he managed. She made love to him in a manner that was almost ferocious, part anger, part farewell sadness. He did not understand, it was not like her, but he responded. They tangled, fell apart, and then made love again.

Finally, spent, they lay side by side but not touching and rested without words for a long time. When the king finally spoke, his voice was soft. "When Becket hears what we did today, he will be in a fury."

"My God," the queen pushed herself up on her elbow. Her voice was low but charged. "Can you not forget that man for one evening with me."

The king, who had been drowsing off as he had uttered his last phrase, came suddenly awake.

"I only meant . . ."

For once, the queen, usually so deferential or at least withholding of temper, lost her composure. "I don't want to hear it," she nearly shouted in his ear. She threw back the light coverlet and rose from the bed in one movement, casting a cloak over her naked shoulders. His gaze followed her figure as it made its way in the shadows to one of the arrow slits and frowned to look out.

"If I never hear that man's name again, I will die a happy woman," she said in a more modulated tone, but still intense, strong. He did not doubt what she said.

"Indulge me, My Queen. This day is a triumph for us. For both of us." His voice was even; he was back in control as king. "We have shown Becket and even the pope that they do not control the crown of England."

"What are you saying?" Eleanor turned to look at the bed and then lifted a candle from its stand. She began lighting all the tapers that sat in the wall sconces, one by one until enough light was shed that she could see Henry sitting up. She walked over to the bed and looked down on him.

"I thought this coronation of young Henry was about securing the succession should anything happen to you so that England should not fall prey again to civil war, as in your mother's time."

"Well, well, so it was." The king swung his bowed legs over and stood, unwilling to have the queen standing over him. They were nearly the same height, but his stocky frame exuded a virile aura, a spirit ready for conflict, against her thin body.

"But the main reason—you must have seen it—was to show Becket and the pope that they do not control the crown of England."

"Am I to understand this whole ritual today was about Becket?" Eleanor stood rooted to her spot, unable to move for the moment.

"Bah, he's been writing Alexander in Rome and all the crowned heads of Europe—John of Bohemia, all the German princes, the emperor himself, saying only he can crown the son of Henry of England as primate of Canterbury. That's the club they have been wielding over me. Well, it's now done." Henry jerked the sleeve on the robe as he donned it, then belted it and marched over to the chest that held wine and goblets. "Roger did good work, the coronation is valid and they can go fiddle with their church-over-state swagger."

"God's breath," she swore, adopting unthinkingly one of Henry's favorite oaths. "You are possessed by the furies, haunted by some specter of this man you hate that was once your friend. I despair of your balance."

"My balance," Henry's anger was mounting. "You think that my balance is affected because I refuse to let the crown submit to religion? Oh, no, my dear wife. My balance is not at risk. I have moved with deliberation and have achieved my goal. I do nothing in matters of state that does not have reason."

"And now what," she asked bitterly as she poured her own goblet of wine and watched the wine splash outside the rim on account of her shaking hand. "This interminable war with Becket and the church will go on as long as you and Becket live?"

"No, not at all." The king's voice was settling as he paced. "It's all about to end."

"How so?" The queen looked up sharply. In his present state, she knew the king was capable of anything, even the monstrous.

"No worries, My Queen. You should be glad of heart. Becket and I are about to reconcile."

"What?" Disbelief shattered her exclamation. For once, the elegant and fine-minded queen momentarily lost all words.

"I have already sent messengers to Louis to arrange a meeting between Becket and me at the end of the next month."

"Louis! Louis won't help you!" The rejoinder was immediate. "He'll be furious himself that you did not include the Princess Marguerite in today's ceremonies. I know him. He is a stickler for protocol."

"I know. My message explains away all that." Henry waved his arm. "We'll have another crowning when Becket returns, a ceremony to include Marguerite. That's all part of my plan. Louis is growing tired of our Thomas himself, ever since the archbishop's rude words at Montmirail. He'll be glad on several counts to help me out in my true efforts to reconcile."

"What are you offering Thomas?" The queen was becoming curious despite herself. Perhaps she had never exactly ever appreciated the canny statecraft of her young husband until this very moment. Indeed, her estimation of his abilities was rising, even as her affections were further disengaging in this interview.

"He can come home. I'll restore the benefices I confiscated in our quarrel, so he'll have a comfortable living, and he gets to re-crown young Henry."

"That will all take time," the queen stated.

"The process has already been started." Henry shrugged.

"You have planned this for a long time."

"Indeed," he said, looking at her, his eyes narrowing.

"And you never saw fit to take me into your confidence?" He could see in the candlelight the queen's fine brows lifting.

"Ah, I did not want to burden you with my decisions," he said, and then a grim smile appeared. "And, also, I wanted no hint of my long plan to reach Becket and Alexander before it was time to extend the olive branch. After I had demonstrated the power of the crown over the abbey." He paused. "I never really knew how to gauge your sympathy for Becket, you see."

With all the tapers blazing, the chamber was lit as if it were day. The two could read each other's expressions if they were facing, but Eleanor turned away. The king frowned, suddenly unsure of what would be said next.

"Henry, I've come to a decision." She spoke as she walked to a large oak chair placed in her chamber, next to a table set with candles so that she could read at night if she could not sleep. She sank, rather than sat, into the cushions.

"Decision?" He suddenly felt fatigued, felt the world shifting for reasons he could not fathom. Some awesome sense of fate, which he did possess in abundance, was giving him inner signals, and he experienced a rising sense of panic.

"I have decided to return to my lands, to Poitou."

"Yes, you mentioned not long ago that you would like a sojourn in the Aquitaine. I think that's fine. I'll go with you for a time, to be certain those Lusignans cause you no trouble this season."

But something kept Henry from moving toward his wife, kept him at a distance when he wanted now to take her in his arms. She seemed somehow more remote than he had ever known her. Her words were strange to him.

"No, Henry. You misunderstand my meaning. I want to go permanently. I want to be among my own people, away from this frozen land . . ."

"It's June, the weather is sweet," he interrupted without thinking.

"From the coldness of the people, from the weather, and most of all, from your endless occupation with the Becket affair."

"But that is only one matter among the many I face as king and duke . . ."

"So you say," she anticipated his next words. "But it is all you think about while you are doing those other things. Becket, always Becket. It is as if he is your evil twin, and you are fighting with yourself."

The king was stunned into silence at this accusation. A practical man, he had not noticed the queen's disaffection. And they had been separated so often, for so long.

"But if you stay in the south, who will govern in my absence? You have always been regent in England when I am away, since our marriage began."

"You have able justiciars in de Lucy and du Hommet. You know they are capable."

"But what about us? We agreed at the outset to build this together, this great empire, for our children."

She looked at him across a great divide. Her anger had dissipated, and her melancholy increased during the course of their conversation. Her voice was weary.

"Henry, I am tired of empire. I am weary of birthing children for the empire. I am tired of the politics of empire, of England and Normandy and Anjou and tired of France and the pope and the emperor and the dance around Becket. Aways Becket until I am sick to death of hearing the name."

"If you are angry because I did not take you into my confidence about the real reason for crowning our son . . ."

"No," she waved her arm in his direction. "I had already decided this, and I knew I would tell you tonight. Any disappointment I feel now has been gathering for years. It is time, and you know it. Time for me to retire to my own lands. The younger children may come if you choose. And Richard. Since my province will be his patrimony, he needs to know the people he will govern."

The king turned away, his own anger returning.

"I'm not at all certain I shall agree to this," he muttered as he stalked from the room. "We'll talk again tomorrow after you have thought further." The door was closed with more force than necessary. The queen almost smiled. Of course, he had to take that tack. He couldn't just agree outright. It had not been his idea.

Eleanor stood still for some moments, then moved back to the bed, which had cooled considerably. She slept soundly for the first time in months.

The king, on the other hand, encountered difficulty in slipping into the arms of Morpheus.

Well, that's that, then. It appears to be over. She was quite clear; she wants to go home, and not just for a visit this time. It shall be permanent. I cannot complain or whine. The truth is I do have competent and trustworthy justiciars here in England and a seneschal finally in Normandy, and the way is open now to move to Ireland and settle those rebellious people once and for all. But she has reason on her side: I do not need her now as I did at first. And there is the Clifford girl, all dark eyes and welcoming smiles. She knows I shall see her again. Rose of the world, indeed. And her father seems favorable.

Still, our marriage end should be by my choice, not the queen's. Eleanor's. Perhaps that is why I am restless. After all, we have grown apart. But why? We could have gone on for years as we do now. Why make such a point of it?

Ah, well. At least the crowning today was a triumph! The people will talk about it for years. Walter Map and Peter of Blois and the rest of the scribblers, they will see to it.

Thomas Becket, thorn in my side for too long. There you have it, Thomas. I don't need you. Pudgy little Roger Pont l'Eveque of York can crown as well as you. Even the pope couldn't stop me, couldn't aid you. And you will fume to think that York, never eager to bend to the yoke of Canterbury, was the bishop to crown the next king.

What did Elle mean, the "dance around Becket"? This has been no dance. We are serious, deadly serious.

And the Clifford girl. She might assuage my loneliness. It's not worth it to make a quarrel with Eleanor. I'll escort her myself to Poitiers with a kind mien, if not a quiet heart.

With that, the king felt sleep finally descending, and he gave himself over to that deep, dreamless state that only the pure of heart or the oblivious can attain.

22 July 1170, Henry and Becket reconcile Freteval, France

The small group could be seen in the distance riding up to the king and his party, who awaited them outside the walls of the castle keep. As they approached, Henry could make out the three men in the lead: William of Sens and Thibault of Blois, identified by the ornate liturgical garments each was wearing, with Thomas between them in the plain, scratch-wool robe he had affected since he arrived in France, the humble Cistercian white. Henry watched them come with truly mixed emotions but gathered himself to a hearty welcome.

The two men, the king, and the archbishop dismounted at the same time and embraced in front of their retinues. De Lucy noted there was no kiss of peace offered or given, nor was one apparently requested. Henry gestured to the inside of the castle, and the two men entered, followed by the king's men and only then the visitors.

Henry took Thomas' arm and led him to pace around the small inner courtyard, talking where they could not be heard. Thomas was seen to be nodding, and again nodding and suddenly speaking with great intensity. It was the king's turn then to nod after a moment of reflection. Thomas broke into a broad smile. Then the king led him inside for the feast that had been prepared by the royal kitchen, so certain had Henry been that Thomas would accept his terms for his return to England.

After the feasting, Thomas, the two archbishops and their small party left the castle. There was no room for accommodation for the entire party of newcomers, and, besides, Henry was not at all certain that he was yet ready to sleep under the same roof as his opponent.

He seemed fine, a bit thinner and not as importunate, yes, and older. Aye, perhaps I seem older to him now as well. But he has accepted the terms. I'll wager Alexander told him to get this thing settled once and for all and come back to Canterbury and take up his duties. All this messing about and upsetting cardinals like Bosa, not to mention the emperor, must stop. I know exactly how Alexander thinks. And Thomas is ready. He seems as tired of the fight as I am. Perhaps now all will be well.

There were two odd things, though. He never asked for the kiss of peace, which I would have refused, as a matter of course. I am not yet ready to show trust to him yet. And he never mentioned that last bitter conference at Clarendon. When he fled my kingdom. The start of our Great Quarrel. Huh. No more did I, though, so we settled the fight without ever either of us admitting we were wrong. I hope the peace holds.

I did waver on the matter of the bishops who took part in the coronation. I agreed he might reprimand them. I hope that is the extent of his intention. You never know with Thomas.

12 October 1170, the final meeting
Amboise, France

"Come, ride apart with me a little, Thomas." The king had reined in his horse as the small group of men on horseback reached the crossroads. The king would ride one way and Thomas Becket another, preparing to part after three days together. The conversation had been amiable and, perhaps, with just a tinge of formality about it. But no disagreement, none.

Three long days, Henry was thinking. Nevertheless, if indeed Thomas was to be received back into the "king's grace and friendship," he knew he must accept the course of events now, events he himself as king had set in motion.

The king's comment was not a request, and Thomas understood this. Motioning du Hommet to remain with the others, Henry rode a bit into the Touraine meadow that surrounded them a few paces, and the archbishop followed, dismounting as soon as the king did so.

"My Lord Archbishop, let us return to our old friendship, and each show the other what good he can, and let us forget our hatred completely."

"I would gladly do so, My King." Thomas took a step toward Henry. "And to seal this pact, let us exchange the kiss of peace once again."

Henry stepped back and held up his hand. "Not yet, Thomas."

"But why do you deny me now, as we are putting our differences behind us? We should show each other the brotherly love that the kiss of peace represents." Thomas extended his own hand. "I have asked for it repeatedly in this parley, and though you have granted other boons, you have resisted this, my one wish. Even this morn, when I came to stand beside you at the Mass in the chapel, you denied me."

"Thomas, Thomas, you should know better than anyone that the kiss of peace is not allowed at a Requiem Mass." Henry smiled in mock horror. "You are, after all, an archbishop."

"My Lord King, it was you who instructed the priest to sing the requiem . . ."

"For the repose of the Empress Matilda's soul, she who died three years ago this week . . ." Henry quickly interjected this, bringing the discussion to a close.

Thomas stood looking out over the broad and rolling fields, the wheat now harvested and thought how fleeting was every season of life. He sensed a restless movement from the king and turned back to him.

"My Lord, I think not that I shall see you again in this life." Becket's voice was filled with sadness.

"What?" bridled the king. "Do you then think me a traitor?"

"No, My Lord, not at all." Thomas hastened to reply, pulled from his half-reverie. "I . . . I don't know what compelled me to say that. Just a feeling."

"So we part friends, and after you are safely back at Canterbury, as we have agreed, we shall at long last exchange the kiss of peace there as you crown my son and his daughter." Henry smiled. "I have business in Berry for the moment, but I'll join you at Rouen in the middle of November, and we'll make the journey together back to England. I want to be in Normandy again by Christmas."

"Yes, Sire," Thomas murmured. "Yes, My Lord King."

But when Becket arrived at Rouen a month later, there was only a letter from the king saying he was prevented from joining Thomas on the journey and the papers for safe conduct. Oh, and one more thing: the king had assigned him a traveling companion, one scholar John of Oxford.

Eight: The Ending

25 December 1170, trouble at the Christmas Feast
Bures, Normandy

"John of Oxford? Henry, what could you possibly have been thinking?" Despite her intentions of taking up residence permanently in her southern domains, Eleanor had reluctantly joined Henry for Christmas just ahead of the princes. These young men arrived from England, and Brittany, and Richard, of course, came with his mother from the south, where he was intensely engaged in learning the craft of ruling the duchy from her. When they were assembled, together with their parents and sisters, the family was gathering to impress the entire feudal world, who were all riveted by the current chapter of the Plantagenet family drama.

"You know John of Oxford and Becket hate each other. They nearly came to blows in Rome last year after Becket excommunicated Oxford for aiding you!" Eleanor was insistent.

"Yes, yes, I know that." Henry, who was sitting at the small table in his privy chamber with his queen, gestured toward a plate of dates, sautéed in rosemary and still warm from the kitchens. "Here, try some of these. They are a marvel in this cold clime."

"Wherever did you come by them?" Eleanor was momentarily distracted as she lifted one daintily to her lips.

"They came last summer, dried, from the routes up from Spain. But once they are heated in oil, they taste almost better than when they are fresh."

"But again, I ask," she said, returning to her point, "why on earth send John of Oxford with him? I wouldn't want to be on that ship. I vow they'll kill each other before they've crossed the channel." She placed the pit of the date on the plate in front of the king and wiped her fingers on a serviette. "And to the world, those who know what has transpired, it will look like a gratuitous act of meanness to the archbishop you have supposedly forgiven."

"I don't give a rat's tail how it looks to the world," Henry said with his customary vigor. "God's hair, if I stopped to worry about what the world thought, I'd never have made a motion and I'd *certes* never have put together this realm." He rose and began his restless movements around the chamber, straightening the chess pieces from his earlier game, lifting a spear near the door and setting it down nearby. "No, I had a good reason for what I did."

"Which was?" The queen turned her head to follow his trajectory to the door and back.

"Thomas's reception in England is uncertain." He said gruffly. "It is said the sheriff in Kent, Gervase of Cornhill, lies in wait for his boat."

"What do you mean? I heard much gossip that the common people could scarce wait to get him back."

"Oh, well, yes, because it means the end of the feud between us. It means the end of the threat of excommunication from Rome, which has been a burning issue for my people. It means peace and churches safe from closing. The common people will be quite happy."

"So, what concerns you?" Eleanor saw his face as he came back to the fire and stood sideways. "You must know something else."

"I have set in motion writs to recover some of the benefices that will truly belong to Thomas again once he resumes."

"Aah, I see," the queen said. And with her customary quickness, she did. "You fear there may be antagonism from certain quarters who will resist giving back those lands which you allowed them in the archbishop's absence."

"John of Oxford, key scholar at my court, signals my support of Becket and the conciliation between us." Henry looked pleased with himself. "I told John to send word back on Becket's reception, to guard him above all things, and if there was trouble to send immediately to William Marshal for arms and support. We should have word in the next days as to how things went."

The queen gave her husband a long look of appraisal, and there was some appreciation in it for his political manipulation. "Well, what is done is done. We can only hope the outcome is as you plan." The queen rose. "Now, let us go to the Great Hall. I know the cooks wanted to serve dinner before the hour of noon since there is such a great crowd."

"Yes, a great crowd. But all our children are here to keep Christmas. It is truly a wonder that the year has gone so well. I hope to put all the unhappy events behind us in the coming days." And he held out his arm to the queen, although they both knew she was very capable of walking on her own.

In the event, however, the dinner was not the happy gathering that the king had hoped for, and the royal couple did not have to wait for days to hear about Becket's return to England. They had only been served the fish, the first course, and the pigeon, the second course, when there was a great ruckus in the back of the hall.

Despite the best efforts of the guards at the door, and to be fair, the sentries were taken completely unawares, a small group of men burst in. Bedraggled from the sleet outside, not having paused to remove their wet clothing or dressed in a manner respectful to the king, three men poured forward, followed by several knights.

"My Lord King, we beg of you redress for the wrongs done to us." The man first to reach the head table was short, plump and wringing wet, but he cast himself on his knees in front of the sovereign. To Henry's amazement, he looked down on Roger Pont l'Eveque, Bishop of York and rival to Thomas Becket.

"Roger? Bishop Roger?" the king looked down in astonishment. "What are you doing here? What in the realms of hell has happened to bring you here in such a state?"

"My Lord, terrible events have taken place."

"Roger, man, stand up." The king himself had stood. The queen, who was sitting beside him, rose as well. Gilbert Foliot and Henry of Winchester had, by this time, reached the royal dais at the head of the

Great Hall. The three English bishops flocked around the king, the dripping newcomers in their black cloaks looking for all the world like a cluster of wet ravens.

Fitzstephen and de Lucy pushed their way into the center of the circle from sheer habit, but also concern for the king being overwhelmed by the volatility of the bishops' behavior.

"My Lord King, would you have your privy chamber made ready so that you may talk to the churchmen in a more . . . um . . . convenient setting?" de Lucy, made steady by years of standing at the king's right hand, brought a sense of decorum to the small group.

"No, we'll hear this in our court. All should hear. What in the name of God has brought you to this pass? Why are you all not in England for the Christmas celebrations?" The king's voice was at its height, and the hall fell silent. All watched the scene.

"Roger, compose yourself." The king placed a hand under the kneeling archbishop's elbow and helped him rise. "Begin with your reasons for coming here in this state."

"My Lord, that man, that *ci-devant* Archbishop Becket, has arrived in England, with your blessing."

"Yes, yes, you knew that he was returning. I sent word to you." Henry's heart sank. He had known, somewhere in his heart, when he saw the parade of English bishops that Becket was behind this. But he could not gather his thoughts enough to imagine what had happened.

"You said he was returning, that you had finally made peace with him." Roger, now standing, struggled to compose himself. The king waited. He stared at Roger, a frown growing. The other two bishops closed in so that the king and queen found themselves standing in a circle of wet churchmen.

"You have the right of it, Roger. I allowed Becket to return once we had made peace. You knew the reconciliation had to come sometime. We could not live forever under threat of interdict from Rome or with the distraction of the letters Thomas was sending to crowned heads all over Europe." The king was leaning forward for this exchange, his handsome, round face lighted from the side by the growing fire. FitzStephen, more than the others, watched this scene with amazement. What would the chroniclers make of this conversation? Walter Map and Peter of Blois had already made their way to the center of conversation near the king's chair and were pushing in to hear the words of the English bishops.

"Well, the 'archbishop' . . ." here Roger gave a satirical sing-song tone to the title but looked abashed when he saw the king's face darken, "Becket, that is to say, arrived at Southampton well enough. He was greeted first by the sheriff of Kent, who had come with armed men to arrest him."

"You see, my dear." The king turned to the queen and spread his hands. "What I predicted came to pass. That local threat is exactly why I sent John of Oxford with Becket. No one would believe Becket would travel with that man unless I had ordered it for his own safety."

"It seems your plan worked perhaps better than you had thought it would." Here Gilbert Foliot took up the tale, his dry, scholarly approach a welcome relief to Roger's semi-hysteria. "John of Oxford indeed protected Becket and told the sheriff he must desist in his plan. And the party moved north. Becket collected a great crowd as he went, everyone cheering him as he moved north."

"I see," said the king, his figure suddenly straighter.

"The sheriff and his men were turned off by the cheers of the crowd. They knew they could not stop the archbishop with that mob on his side." Foliot continued. "Becket was leading them, riding slowly on his horse and bowing to the left and right. It looked like bloody Palm Sunday in Jerusalem."

"Did it, now?" The king grew thoughtful upon hearing this.

"He first announced he would make his way to the Lord Henry's manor at Windsor, but when he arrived there, your son refused to see him." Foliot stopped and peered at the king's face. "Prince Henry sent word that because the archbishop was absent, he had been crowned by another and the 'former Archbishop of Canterbury' was not welcome in his house."

"I see," the king murmured, frowning.

"The crowd grew as he made his way to Canterbury. It is said that an armed guard assembled around him."

"Archers?" the king's eyes opened wide in surprise.

"Yes, and some knights, we are told."

"By God's teeth, that was never part of the agreement." The king stated warmly. "He has exceeded his limit in this."

"We have misjudged his state with the common people, My Lord," Gilbert said, with his usual understatement. "He has more of a following than any of us imagined."

"But that is not the worst of it," Roger leaned toward the king, almost placing his hand on the king's arm before he caught himself. "Becket has issued excommunications for all three of us bishops for participating in the young king's coronation. Excommunicated! Becket is the only archbishop left in England."

"Excommunication? That was never agreed upon," Henry said, now his famous temper flaring. "I gave him leave to reprimand you for officiating at a crowning that was by law the right of Canterbury. But that was all. He was to go no further! By God's eyes, he must think himself king now."

"He has driven us out of England." Winchester chimed in now. "He has laid interdict on us and the people of our parishes. All to satisfy his own vanity."

"My Lord King, he is setting up another realm of power to satisfy his vanity. While Thomas lives, you will have neither peace nor quiet nor see good days."

"By the throne of the Almighty," Henry stamped his foot hotly, his choler now well up. He shouted to all in the hall who had stopped everything to watch this display, raising his right arm as he did so. "All of you, listen to me. What idle and miserable men I have encouraged and promoted in my household, who leave me exposed to the insolence of a fellow who came to my court on a lame, sumpter mule and now sits without hindrance upon the throne itself."

"Henry," Eleanor began, though she knew the futility of stopping his full-blown rage.

"Will no one rid me of this troublesome priest?" Henry roared.

Some hours later in the King's chambers

It was some hours later as the king, who had by now calmed down, with the aid of warm, mulled wine, sat in his chamber with de Lucy. The king had grown quiet, just staring at the table.

The queen burst in.

"Henry, there has been a report of some knights riding in haste from this hall."

The king looked up from his reverie. "What are you saying?"

"Four knights have disappeared saying they intended to arrest the archbishop. Fitzstephen reported it to me directly. The stable boy confirms it. Reginald FitzUrse was in the lead, and de Morville and de Tracy were with him."

"God's beard, those young hotheads. They'll be out for blood. You said there were four of them. Four!" The king was on his feet now, no longer torpid.

"Richard the Breton rode with them."

"He is trouble," de Lucy muttered, also standing now. "He has killed before without provocation. We must stop them."

"This is all because of your howling, Henry," the queen said, furious. "They mean to do exactly as you said, rid you of this troublesome priest. How could you be so loose with your words!"

"I've said worse before about Becket. No one believes I mean it."

"Well, someone does now, apparently," the queen stated flatly. "I've sent du Hommet and three knights after them. The sentry at the castle gate reported that they rode off in different directions. They may be going to different ports."

"Wherever they are taking ship, it's no mystery where they're headed. All of them will meet at Canterbury," the king spoke quickly. "We must stop them. Du Hommet will make the arrest, that is, no, we must send more men to the main ports. Cherbourg, Le Havre, Dieppe. They have to be at one of them."

"But Sire, the queen just reported that they rode in different directions. They might be at any of the smaller ports." De Lucy's voice was uncharacteristically intense.

"Then send men to all ports in Normandy. I want those knights stopped. Before they take action that we cannot rescind."

The queen stood watching the king, his voice now growing hoarse with commands. She bit her lower lip in thought. Then she turned, unnoticed, and made her way to her chambers, where she gave orders to her servants to begin packing her household.

Nine: The Afterward

2 January 1170, eight days later
The Castle at Argentan

"Has the king sent any orders?" De Lucy himself was restless this morning. He had just appeared from his quarters and threw himself into a large, carved chair near the others. The great men of the king's council were sitting quietly in a corner of the smaller chambers outside the king's own room. Servants moved slowly about, cleaning up the bread and watered wine and dried fruit that had served for breakfast. A small group of knights, who had not found anything else to do, were sitting playing at dice near the fire. They, too, were subdued, speaking in hushed tones as if they might wake the king in his chamber if they were too loud.

"None whatsoever," du Hommet responded, rising as he did so. "We are suspended in time here until he appears."

"How long has he been in chambers?" FitzStephen asked for the third time that hour.

"It's been two days since the messenger came with the news of Becket's death. No one can go near him. He roars even in his state if he hears the door creak." De Lucy knew. He had tried to gain entry twice. "I fear for his sanity. I have never seen him like this before."

"He must blame himself for his rash words." Leicester muttered. "If he had not spoken thus, Becket would still be alive."

"He's said worse before when Becket tried his patience. It was those drunken knights. They were trying to prove something."

"Well, they couldn't have been too drunk," FitzStephen put in smartly. "They were sober enough to split up and get passage across the channel."

"But something must be done. This news has riveted Christendom," Walter Map had joined them quietly. "The king must be brought to his senses. He must say something in his own defense."

Leicester looked at Map, his mouth twitching on one side. "Walter, you know as well as I do that no one, nor nothing, not the pope himself, can make the king do what he does not want to do."

"What does that mean?" de Lucy looked up.

"That perhaps the king will simply wait until this blows over," Leicester said wryly. "Even the pope can't stay angry forever."

"If he can, this might do it," de Lucy said, "if only the queen had not insisted on leaving immediately for the south."

"I think she knew what was coming," du Hommet said.

Leicester looked at him, his narrow eyes opening wide for once. "You think she knew those knights were heading to kill the archbishop?"

"The queen has a better feeling for what is happening in the land than ever the king does. I think she knew this was the end, that Henry could not recover from this terrible event. To kill an archbishop!" du Hommet closed his eyes.

"But the king did not kill the archbishop," de Lucy said sharply.

"It will look that way when it all gets out. Too many courtiers heard Henry shouting to be rid of the troublesome priest at Bures. I cannot think what the king can do at this point. No wonder he lurks in his chambers." Du Hommet shook his head.

At that moment, the double doors to the chamber were flung open. Heads snapped up as the cold January air rushed in from the castle hallway. Suddenly the members of the Privy Council stood with one movement as their astonished eyes beheld their monarch, clean-shaven, washed and dressed as king, stride into the room. He wore the small coronet, the one he always disdained. The informal crown.

Unseen for three days after a mighty fit of anger at the news of Archbishop Becket's murder, the king looked for all the world as if he had just presided over a state dinner. He tossed his short cloak back over his shoulder as he sat down among his men and called for bread to break his fast. They all stood staring until he looked up at them.

"Come on, men. For the sake of God's good nature, sit down and stop gawking. Have you never seen the king breakfast before?" He pulled a plate toward him that had half a loaf on it. "Someone wake up the servants and get food in here! We have work to do. FitzStephen, find Geoffrey Riedell. I have letters to be sent immediately. Then we have plans to make."

"Yes, My Lord." FitzStephen, who had sat down out of amazement, now scrambled again to his feet.

"And get those Norman bishops in here. I want Routrou and Arnulf. They must leave for Rome immediately. We can't let this thing fester with Alexander. I want them gone by noon. Signal their households." The king chomped off a large chunk of bread. "And I need those maps of Ireland. I intend finally to make this voyage. This is an excellent time to do so. And I'll return triumphant, de Lucy!" Henry turned to his trusted justiciar. "You can depend on it."

"Indeed, Sire," de Lucy said, and for just a moment, he felt the sense of impending doom that had been present ever since the four knights left was lifting—just for a moment.

"Walter Map, I want you to put the word about that the queen has withdrawn to the south. I want no more mention of her in our records."

"But, Sire," Map began. But the king cut him off.

"No, it is as I decree. See that Peter of Blois and John of Salisbury and the others cease to write about Queen Eleanor as part of the record of England."

"Yes, your majesty." Map bowed, his face still showing his startled reaction.

"FitzStephen, why are you still here?" The king asked as if the conversation with Walter Map had not taken place.

"As you wish, Sire." FitzStephen was in motion now, as if his life depended on it.

"And call my steward! How can a man run a castle without his steward to manage the servants? I will have food. Then I shall attend the court in the great hall. See that people are gathered. I want them to see me and hear me!"

And servants were sent flying by the king's men to do his will.

One hour later, Henry strode into the great hall of his castle at Argentan without announcement. The courtiers had been forewarned, however, and the hall was filled with Henry's men and even some of their ladies. All were agog to see the king after he had been laid low by the news of Becket's murder. He did not disappoint.

What they thought when their sovereign suddenly appeared, bathed, combed and nicely barbered after being closeted with his grief for three days was hidden. Indeed, they all straightened with alacrity, their faces arranged in practiced, noncommittal expressions. He deserved no less, thought de Lucy. Nothing their king did surprised them, not even in a crisis like this. They were accustomed to his peripatetic lifestyle, the sudden decisions to move his entire household on two hours' notice and the just-as-sudden reversal to delay. Even in a major crisis of state such as this event, he would not be predictable. The only thing they could count on was his bad temper if things did not go his way.

Henry, with his famous Angevin short cloak swirling about him and his "everyday" crown on his head, stalked through the hall, his voice booming out greetings. He mounted the two steps to the dais and cast himself into the open chair at the end of the large dining table. He shifted the chair so that it faced the expectant crowd and stretched out his legs in front of him.

Roger, Archbishop of York, stepped closer to the young man next to him, who happened to be Geoffrey Plantagenet, Henry's acknowledged eighteen-year-old natural son and, some thought, the man closest to him next to de Lucy. Roger was a short man and had to stretch some to reach the tall youth's ear.

"I take it by wearing the crown into the great hall the king is sending a signal?" he whispered.

Geoffrey the bastard, so-called to distinguish himself from Eleanor and Henry's son Geoffrey of Brittany, was good-looking, taller than his father but with the same Angevin tendency toward reddish hair and freckles. He glanced down at the man at his side. He also had already developed the same arch look as his father might have given to such a question. This archbishop was the man, perhaps more than any other, who was responsible for the current crisis of the realm—no, that was unfair,

Geoffrey thought quickly and amended his expression accordingly. "Yes," he whispered back, "the crown means business. The king is ready to act."

"What will he do?" Roger asked, unsettled and with good reason. After all, it was his trip across the channel with his brother bishops that had set in train the events that resulted in the murder of Thomas Becket.

"We'll have to wait and see," Geoffrey said.

"Whatever it is, you can count on his decisiveness now. He's back among the living." He paused, then leaned down again to Archbishop Roger. "Thank the heavens that de Lucy is here at court. Whatever action the king takes, he will listen first to him." Roger nodded his agreement. "And even William the Marshall has been summoned. The king will get good advice."

"Why are you whispering," the king had spotted his son and Roger, but his question had the ring of good humor. "Where is the steward?" the king called out, and someone immediately rang the large bell near the door. "Bring in the princes. I want to see my sons."

Suddenly the hall was abustle with servants and activity. Henry waved to William Marshall to join him, and the famed advisor to the king and the Prince Henry's new mentor motioned to Geoffrey and several other men to join him. The wine steward came with great cups and the servant with the bellows began to fan the flames in the fireplace to a roar.

The young princes came at a run and made for their father's place on the dais without pause. Henry, Richard and Geoffrey, each one blonder and more handsome than the last. The baby John, of course, was not present. Henry had enough sons to assure his dynasty, no matter what fate dealt him now. They piled up before him, accidentally jostling one another as they took their order according to birth and made their grave salutes. They did well, even Geoffrey who was only twelve and just beginning to ape his older brothers. Henry and Richard teased him unmercifully in private but encouraged his manners in front of the court. And especially in front of their father. Suddenly the hall, which had been quiet for the past two days, came alive. There was vigorous applause for the appearance of the young princes, and the king acknowledged all with a smile and a casual salute. De Lucy breathed a sigh of relief. The king was back.

The End Of The Affair

21 July 1174, Fathers and Sons
Canterbury Town, Kent, England

The king slouched back in his massive oak chair, resting his weary head on the high back and still grasping his goblet of mulled wine in his right hand. His hand was calloused from all the riding and reining he had done in the past three years, and his back ached like never before. If only he could settle the Scottish border wars and bring William the Lyon to his finish.

Not that I want William of Scotland dead. I still remember how I knighted him before Toulouse when he came so eagerly with forty knights to help me recover Eleanor's patrimony. His was a fresh and eager face. How can so much change in so few years . . . little more than a decade. Well, all right then, two. Time disappears, carrying with it our youth.

It feels good to be alone, to just think. Always the counsellors around, always the advice which may or may not be sound. Always I listen, but I must make the choices and take the consequences.

And where is the Prince Henry? He agreed to come when I summoned him but said he wanted to see me alone. Here I am, alone, and the hour has come. Or nearly so.

I should be thinking about tomorrow. It will not be pleasant. I cannot remember why I agreed to this. Leicester and de Lucy said I must, my obligation to submit once more to the scourge of those god-forsaken monks at Canterbury, to do penance for causing Becket's death. Not enough that I agreed to submit last year at Avranches. Oh, no, I must needs hustle back to the scene of the crime itself and abase myself on the cold floor, the very floor on which those idiot knights felled him three years ago.

Absolvo te nomine Dei. . . . I absolve you in the name of God. Why don't I just absolve myself. Even Thomas, wherever he is, must realize by this time I didn't want him dead.

Well, well, Thomas. Will this do it? Me, walking in sandals and bare feet through the rain and slush of the streets of Canterbury to your cathedral, me lying on the cold floor while those bastard monks whip me with their white corded belts, each one taking secret delight, probably in lust at the excitement. Will this be enough to put your ghost at rest?

Ah, Tom. Tom. I would give anything to have you back, to go once more hawking along the river with you at Northampton. I never intended things to go as far as they did. Eleanor was right. Revenge became an idée fixe, an obsession. Perhaps the war would never have ended until one of us was dead. But maybe if we had grown old, that might have ended our enmity. Your pride and my pride truly rode us for a time. And we've made a sorry mess of it all. And I'm left here alone.

Eleanor, gone too. My pride, my anger drove her away. I don't think she'll be back. She liked you, and she saw me clearly. But it was too late by the time I understood what she was telling me.

"Father?" The voice startled Henry, and he sat up suddenly, spilling some of the wine from the goblet onto his sleeve. "Sire," the young man amended.

The young king, as he was now called, the Lord Henry, the eldest son, the prince who held most of his father's dreams in his youthful hands, had entered the room unannounced. He walked toward the king now, a tall young man of nearly twenty years. He held his head high. The prince was slender of build, like his mother, but he had his father's broader shoulders, and there was strength in his arms. His stride was sure, his hand on his belt that held a small, jeweled dagger. A little too much pride, Henry thought, but a noble bearing and an intelligent face.

"Prince Henry," his father addressed him formally. The prince bowed before his father.

"I'm glad you came. I thought perhaps you would not, given our differences." The king struggled to rise from the depths of his chair, hampered by the deep cushions and the hold he had on the wine goblet. He finally handed the latter to his son and placed his hands on the carved arms of the chair, rising with difficulty.

"Will you take wine?" The king recovered his goblet and gestured toward the table that held a beaker of red burgundy, but the young king shook his head.

"You are coming to witness my penance tomorrow in the cathedral?" Henry's voice was uncertain, unusual for him.

"I was told by Leicester that you wanted me there." The prince made a small *moue* of distaste. "I would not wish it if it were left to me."

"Wish me to do penance at Canterbury or wish yourself to observe it?" the king asked, his fingers now playing with the stem of the recovered goblet. Then he put it down and began pacing a bit away.

"As for the penance, I think it a good thing, good for your soul. But I do not like to see my father and king humbled in this way." The prince spoke slowly, drawing out each word. His tone was haughty, and that hurt the king more than the words from his own son.

"And now, after these few years have elapsed, what do you think about your former tutor and master Thomas Becket?" The king threw this comment over his shoulder. He enjoyed being blunt. It saved time and often caught people off their guard so that their response was more honest.

But the young king was used to his father's ways. He looked at him for a long time. Henry stopped pacing and turned to face his son in the silence. The younger man's round face was framed by his short hair, straight cut across the front. Surely, he was too young to be the son of Henry and Eleanor, to see all he had seen.

Finally, the younger man spoke.

"I think he was a fine tutor, and he cared for me. I think it broke his heart when you had Roger of York crown me instead of the Archbishop of Canterbury." He fingered his dagger, but Henry took no notice.

"Fair enough. What else?" The father snapped.

"I think those four knights would never have left your court to murder the archbishop if they thought you did not want it."

"We can want many things, my boy. We can't have them all, nor do we intend that everything said in anger will be taken seriously." The king scanned his young son's face.

"My mother, the queen, said you wanted him ruined."

The king pursed his lips in thought. "Possibly those were my words at one point or another. I may have said something like that when I was frustrated and blocked, and, yes, my trust had been betrayed." Even as he spoke, Henry knew that he felt anger no longer. "But it was never my intention that it would come to pass. I always felt, deep in my heart, Tom and I, we could work things out."

"My queen mother says she will no longer keep Christmas with you. That we older children must choose where we will be."

Henry turned away from his son. "Yes, I suppose that is true. She has made known that she wants to stay in the south, in her own duchy. I have agreed."

"Is it because of Becket's death?" His son suddenly seemed very young, asking a child's question. A simple question that was impossible to answer.

Henry put his hand on the young king's shoulder. "It is because of many things, my son. The world is complicated, and nothing is more complicated than your parents' marriage." He could see his son was not satisfied, but what to ask next? And then the king was surprised by a brutal question.

"Did you want him dead?"

Henry stood still for once. Then he said: "Listen to me, boy, and remember. As king, you must think like a practical man, or you will fail utterly. But never forget respect for the mysteries of the human heart. The gospels knew this. 'Forgive them, Father, for they know not what they do.' As long as there is life, forgiveness is possible."

"But Father, how can someone forgive if he is gone?"

They stared at each other. Then the king turned away abruptly.

"I must prepare myself. These heavy downpours will continue as I walk through the rain of Canterbury town in sandals and pain. I will subject myself to the scourge of the monks. I will abase myself and suffer in body and spirit." The king spit out his words as he sat down and began to pull off his boots.

His son watched quietly.

"If you learn nothing from what I do here in Canterbury, from what a king must do for his people, you will be the poorer. Now, get out and trouble me no more this evening."

The king made no move of affection toward the young man, but he watched as the figure slowly melted away, fading into the woodwork until his form was no longer there. Perhaps it had never been present.

Sighing, Henry began to shed his clothes for the woolen hair shirt and thin cloak he was obliged to wear as a penitent. Outside, through the arrow holes, he could just glimpse the ropes of rain. He was going to have a wet journey of it to the Cathedral. Then he began to smile, inwardly at first, but then it spread to his face, and he wished he could share the humor of it all with someone who would truly understand.

"Well, well, Thomas. You would enjoy this." He paused in his dressing to sit back and said softly, "Oh, how I wish you were here."

Afterword

A Historical Footnote

King Henry awoke the morning following his scourging at the cathedral (five strokes from each of the bishops and abbots present, and three strokes from each of the eighty monks) and his all-night vigil of penitence at the tomb of Thomas, to find the bells of Canterbury ringing and Sir Ranulf de Glanville delivering the message that William the Lion of Scotland had finally been taken prisoner. That part of the war was ended. Henry could turn his attention to Ireland now.

Thomas Becket was canonized a saint by Pope Alexander III on February 21, 1173, three years after his death and the year before Henry did penance at Canterbury cathedral. Becket's church became his shrine, and people came from far and wide to ask for miracles. Many felt rewarded. The cult of Thomas Becket grew as stories of his brutal murder spread and his sanctity was magnified.

Young Henry could not have had that final conversation with his father as described in the last scene since by 1174, the young princes, encouraged by their mother, Queen Eleanor, had already revolted against their father. We are obliged to believe that the king had a need to imagine that entire conversation.

The final eighteen years of Henry's reign were as event-filled as the first eighteen years described in this work of fictional history, even though Becket was gone. Henry had his problems, but he was largely responsible for developing a system of justice that became known as English Common

Law (based on old Roman law) for ending determination of guilt by the old "trial by water," for setting up the jury system that still exists today and for generally hastening the modification and eventual ending of the feudal system as practiced in France in the twelfth century.

He eventually softened the stance he took on the Constitutions of Clarendon, agreeing with papal legates at the Compromise of Avranches in May 1172 to some modifications but, in his usual canny way, he negotiated some leeway so that the state still held the right to oppose the church when it felt its interests threatened.

Author's Note

This work I consider not historical fiction but fictional history. I have attempted to write history as it happened, staying close to dates, times and actual people involved. I used the imagination only to construct the conversations (although some are taken directly from the chronicles of the time, usually imparted to the chronicler by Becket himself) and to add some thoughts the king may or may not have had. Certain paragraphs contain whole speeches taken directly from historical chronicles.

Certainly, I've taken some minor liberties. Du Hommet was seneschal of Normandy, not chancellor of the exchequer. FitzStephen was actually attached to Canterbury as a monk, not the son of landed gentry. And there are other changes detailed below.

I created a much larger role for the queen, but not an altogether fictional one. She was, in fact, Henry's regent in England while he spent much of his time on the continent. It has always puzzled me that the chronicles do not write more about her in these years. I invented the reason why in the last chapters. It remains a puzzle as to why she was suddenly written out of the chronicles when she withdrew to the south. I have tied that to their bitter parting at Bures after the knights left, and there was a possibility that Becket would be harmed.

The research on primary resources I have left to my betters, the scholarly biographers upon whom I depended for detail. The most useful were the following: W. L. Warren's towering biography *Henry II*, part of the English Monarch series published by the University of California Press, and *Henry Plantagenet* by Richard Barber, reissued recently by Athenaeum Press Ltd in Great Britain. Also very useful is the classic biography by Amy Kelly: *Eleanor of Aquitaine and the Four Kings*, published by Harvard University Press. In addition, other useful biographies and histories were authored by Thomas Costain, Marion Meade, Alison Weir, John Harvey and Dan Jones. A complete listing of books I used can be found in the bibliography. Please understand that all of the scholars upon whom I depended did not agree with one another. Sometimes even dates were disputed among them. That gave me choices.

The reasons for the royal falling out remain somewhat of a mystery. Historians, or at least balladeers, like to opine that it was the famous Rosamund Clifford and Henry's alleged infatuation of her that drove Eleanor and Henry apart. But this hardly seems likely since adultery was as common in the twelfth century as it is today, and Henry and Eleanor were separated much of his peripatetic life. It's also been written that Henry did not allow Eleanor a share in the governance of his lands, but history belies that. She was regent in England when he was absent, and also in Anjou, as well as in her own duchy when she was there. Some imply the breach came about because Henry planned to unite all his kingdom under his oldest son, but that was clearly not the case, as he proclaimed to the feudal world publicly at Montmirail. Henry was to have England; Geoffrey Brittany and Richard, as Eleanor wished, her lands in the south.

So what could have caused the breach, which happened right at the time of Becket's murder? I have invented a fictional rationale where the mishandling of the Becket situation was the last straw for the queen, who may have grown tired of her role for many other reasons, and may, indeed, have grown tired of Henry.

One biographer asserts that Henry was mostly faithful, being a man busy with many worldly affairs not connected to women. This biographer cites the fact that Henry's two acknowledged bastards were born before his marriage to Eleanor and after their formal separation in 1170. It seems unlikely that Henry was always faithful but perhaps not quite the philanderer his enemies, including Gerald of Wales, make him out to be.

Of particular interest in this story is the medieval "kiss of peace." This was a sign that became part of the Mass and dates to the early Christian period. Instructions on it are seen in the sermons of St. Augustine (#227). Men gave it to men, and women to women and the kiss was given on the mouth. In the Middle Ages, it was seen as an inviolate promise of peace when given and gave another signal when withheld.

The reader will, I hope, allow certain liberties with history and place. For example, the current Westminster Abbey in London was not in existence at the time of the coronation of Henry and Eleanor or the young Prince Henry. Built by Edward the Confessor the translation or moving of the confessor's bones figures in the Becket-Henry story because their rift was at its height when the ceremony occurred in 1169, and Becket dared not avoid the ceremony even though he would have to meet the king. But that abbey gave way in 1245 to the new abbey built by Henry III, the great-grandson of our hero, Henry II. The present abbey was completed in 1272. The description in this book is based on the current abbey building since we do not have the complete plan of the original. But a writer must create a scene, and so I use the current abbey, still beautifully preserved and welcoming, as the detail for the coronation scene, aware that it is not entirely accurate. However, as a friend once said to me, "Truth bears no relation to accuracy."

One reason I have tried to stay close to actual historical events and timelines is that the story is all the more fascinating for actually having occurred. The twelfth century, as historian

Georges Duby has pointed out so well, was a time when everything was on the move, when massive social and cultural change was happening. And the characters who had or wielded the power—the kings and popes and dukes and bishops of the western world—were real people with actual personalities that shaped the events of their time.

The final reason I attempted to stay close to what we know happened in fashioning this account is simply this: history is often more dramatic than fiction. With regard to the story of the power struggle between the king and the archbishop, as they say, "you couldn't make this stuff up." (Nobody would believe it!)

Judith Koll Healey
2022

A Note:

Writers, biographers and historians don't agree on many factors. Some combine the Freteval and Amboise meetings of Becket and the king, but they happened separately and for dramatic effect they have been kept separate in this text.

Main Sources

Biographies

Barber, Richard. *Henry Plantagenet*. Ipswich, England: The Boydell Press, 1964.

Costain, Thomas. *The Conquering Family*. New York, NY: The Doubleday Company,1949.

Harvey, John, *The Plantagenets*. Great Britain: B. T. Batsford Limited, 1948.

Jones, Dan. *The Plantagenets*. New York: Viking Press, 2012.

Kelly, Amy. *Eleanor of Aquitaine and the Foud Kings*. Cambridge, MA, and London, England: Harvard University Press, 1950.

Meade, Marion, *Eleanor of Aquitaine: A Biography*. New York, London: Penguin Books, 1977.

Warren, W. L. *Henry II*. Berkely, California and Los Angeles, California: University of California Press, 1973.

Weir, Alison. *Eleanor of Aquitaine*. New York, NY: Ballantine Publishing Group, 1999.

Other Works (Selected) of General Interest

Butler, John. *The Quest for Becket's Bones*. New Haven and New York: Yale University Press, 1995.

Cantor, Norman F. *The Civilization of the Middle Ages*. New York, NY: Harper Collins,1963.

Lincoln, E. F. *The Story of Canterbury*. London: Staples Press Limited, 1955.

Mortimer, Ian. *The Time Traveler's Guide to Medieval England*. New York: Touchstone Press, 2008.

Southern, R. W. *The Making of the Middle Ages*. London: Hutchinson's University Library, 1953.

Trevor Rowley. *The Norman Heritage 1066–1200*. London, Boston, Melbourne and Henley: Routledge and Kegan Paul, 1983.

Peter King. *Western Monasticism*. Kalamazoo, MI: Cistercian Publications (The Institute of Cistercian Studies, Western Michigan University), 1999.

. . . And anything by Jacques le Goff.

About the Author

Judith Koll Healey is the author of several works of historical fiction, including *The Canterbury Papers* and *The Rebel Princess* (Harper Collins) and a biography of a nineteenth-century timber magnate, *Frederick Weyerhaeuser and the American West* (Minnesota Historical Society Press). She is also the author of *The Fire Thief* (Calumet Editions) ,a book of poems published recently.

Healey is the author of several books in her professional field published by the Council on Foundations, including *Family Foundation Retreats,* co-authored with Alice Buhl. She has authored chapters in numerous professional publications of the Council on Foundations and the National Center on Family Philanthropy (both located in Washington, DC). She has been a frequent contributor to the Op-Ed page of the *Star Tribune,* the daily newspaper in Minneapolis—her hometown.

In her professional work, Healey traveled to work with philanthropic clients all over the United States. Although she has always been a writer (she wrote her first short story at age twelve on a Rainbow Pad), much of her life for the past twenty-five years was spent on airplanes and in hotels, offering spaces of time for creative effort. Writing fiction became a regular part of her life.

Healey lives in Minneapolis, Minnesota. She has four sons who each eventually returned to the city of their youth along with their families. She spends part of each year in France and enjoys travel to many other places.

CPSIA information can be obtained
at www.ICGtesting.com
Printed in the USA
BVHW081658110123
656096BV00019B/293

9 781959 770466